McSWEENEY'S
MAMMOTH
TREASURY OF
THRILLING
TALES

McSWEENEY'S MAMMOTH TREASURY OF THRILLING TALES

EDITED BY MICHAEL CHABON

ILLUSTRATIONS BY HOWARD CHAYKIN

VINTAGE BOOKS

A DIVISION OF RANDOM HOUSE, INC.

NEW YORK

Library of Congress Cataloging-in-Publication Data
McSweeney's mammoth treasury of thrilling tales / edited by Michael Chabon.—
1st Vintage Books ed.
p.   cm.
Simultaneously published as McSweeney's, issue 10, winter 2002–3, no. 1.
ISBN 1-4000-3339-X (trade pbk.)
1. Short stories, American. I. Chabon, Michael. II. McSweeney's.
PS648.S5M39 2003
813'.0108—dc21   2002192265

www.vintagebooks.com

The Editor's Notebook

A Confidential Chat with the Editor

For the last year or so I have been boring my friends, and not a few strangers, with a semi-coherent, ill-reasoned, and doubtless mistaken rant on the subject of the American short story as it is currently written.

The rant goes something like this (actually this is the first time I have so formulated it): Imagine that, sometime about 1950, it had been decided, collectively, informally, a little at a time, but with finality, to proscribe every kind of novel from the canon of the future but the nurse romance. Not merely from the critical canon, but from the store racks and library shelves as well. Nobody could be paid, published, lionized, or cherished among the gods of literature for writing any kind of fiction other than nurse romances. Now, because of my faith and pride in the diverse and rigorous brilliance of American writers of the last half-century, I do believe that from this bizarre decision, in this theoretical America, a dozen or more authentic masterpieces would have emerged. Thomas Pynchon's *Blitz Nurse,* for example, and Cynthia Ozick's *Ruth Puttermesser, R.N.* One imagines, however, that this particular genre—that any genre, even one far less circumscribed in its elements and possibilities than the nurse romance—would have paled somewhat by the year 2002. Over the last year in that oddly diminished world, somebody, somewhere, would be laying down Michael Chabon's *Dr. Kavalier and Nurse Clay* with a weary sigh and crying out, "Surely, oh, surely there must be more to the novel than this!"

Instead of "the novel" and "the nurse romance," try this little *Gedankenexperiment* with "jazz" and "the bossa nova," or with "cinema" and "fish-out-of-water comedies." Now, go ahead and try it with "short fiction" and "the contemporary, quotidian, plotless, moment-of-truth revelatory story."

Suddenly you find yourself sitting right back in your very own universe.

Okay, I confess. I am that bored reader, in that circumscribed world, laying aside his book with a sigh; only the book is my own, and it is filled with my own short stories, plotless and sparkling with epiphanic dew. It was in large part a result of a crisis—a word much beloved of tedious ranteurs—in my own attitude toward my work in the short story form that sent me back into the stream of alternate time, back to the world as it was before we all made that fateful and perverse decision.

As late as about 1950, if I referred to "short fiction," I might have been talking about any one of the following kinds of stories: the ghost story; the horror story; the detective story; the story of suspense, terror, fantasy, or the macabre; the sea, adventure, spy, war, or historical story; the romance story. Stories, in other words, with plots. A glance at any dusty paperback anthology of classic tales proves the truth of this assertion, but more startling are the names of the authors of these ripping yarns: Poe, Balzac, Wharton, James, Conrad, Graves, Maugham, Faulkner, Twain, Cheever, Coppard. Heavyweights all, some considered among the giants of modernism, source of the moment-of-truth story that, like homo sapiens, appeared relatively late on the scene but has worked very quickly to wipe out all its rivals. Short fiction, in all its rich variety, was published not only by the pulps, which gave us Hammett, Chandler, and Lovecraft among a very few other writers now enshrined more or less safely in the canon, but also in the great slick magazines of the time: *The Saturday Evening Post, Collier's, Liberty,* and even *The New Yorker,* that proud bastion of the moment-of-truth story that has only recently, and not without controversy, made room in its august confines for the likes of the Last Master of the Plotted Short Story, Stephen King. Very often these stories contained enough plot and color to support an entire feature-length Hollywood adaptation. Adapted for film and radio, some of them, like "The Monkey's Paw," "Rain," "The Most Dangerous Game," and "An Occurrence at Owl Creek Bridge," have been imitated and parodied and have had their atoms scattered in the general stream of the national imagination and the public domain.

About six months ago, I was going on in this vein to Mr. Eggers, the publisher of this magazine, saying things like, "Actually, Dave, horror stories are all psychology," and "All short stories, in other words, are ghost stories, accounts of visitations and reckonings with the traces of the past." Emboldened by the fact that he had not completely succumbed to unconsciousness, I went on to say that it was my greatest dream in life (other than hearing Kansas's "Dust in the Wind" performed by a mariachi orchestra) someday to publish a magazine of my own, one that would revive the lost genres of short fiction, a tradition I saw as one of great writers writing great short stories. I would publish works both by "non-genre" writers who, like me, found themselves chafing under the strictures of the Ban, and by recognized masters of the genre novel who, fifty years ago, would have regularly worked and published in the short story form but who now have no wide or ready market for shorter work. And I would toss in a serialized novel, too, carrying the tradition all the way back to the days of *The Strand* and *Argosy.* I would—

"If I let you guest-edit an issue of *McSweeney's,*" said Mr. Eggers, "can we please stop talking about this?"

The *McSweeney's Mammoth Treasury of Thrilling Tales* is the result of this noble gesture. Whether the experiment has been a success, I leave to the reader to judge. I will say, however, that while they were working on their stories, a number of the writers found within these covers reported to me, via giddy e-mails, that they had forgotten how much fun writing a short story could be. I think that we have forgotten how much fun reading a short story can be, and I hope that if nothing else, this treasury goes some small distance toward reminding us of that lost but fundamental truth.

—*Michael Chabon*

McSWEENEY'S
MAMMOTH
TREASURY OF
THRILLING
TALES

McSweeney's MAMMOTH TREASURY of THRILLING TALES

Edited by MICHAEL CHABON

With Illustrations by Howard Chaykin

All Stories Original and Complete!

Tedford and the Megalodon

By JIM SHEPARD

He went in search of a relic of earth's past, and came face-to-face with the mortal specter of his own!

He'd brought some books with him on the way out, but had lost the lot of them on the transfer to the smaller boat. One of the lifting pallets had upset and spilled the crate down the side of the ship. His almanac had been saved, for which he was thankful.

Among the losses had been his Simpson and his Eldredge; his *Osteology and Relationships of Chondrichthyans*; his *Boys' Book of Songs,* Balfour's *Development of Elasmobranch Fishes,* and, thrown in from his childhood, his Beadle's Boy's Library, including *Wide Awake Ned: The Boy Wizard.*

Above his head, interstellar space was impossibly black. That night he wrote in his almanac, *Velvet set with piercing bits of light.* There seemed to be, spread above him, some kind of galactic cloud arrangement. Stars arced up over one horizon and down the other. The water nearest the ice seemed disturbingly calm. Little wavelets lapped the prow of the nearest kayak. The cold was like a wind from the stars.

Thirty-three-year-old Roy Henry Tedford and his little pile of provisions were braced on the lee side of a talus slope on a speck of an island at somewhere around degree of longitude 146 and degree of latitude 58, seven hundred miles from Adélie Land on the Antarctic Coast, and four hundred from the nearest landfall on any official map: the unprepossessing dot of Macquarie Island to the east. It was a fine midsummer night in 1923.

His island, one of three ice-covered rocks huddled together in a quarter-mile chain, existed only on the hand-drawn chart that had brought him here, far from those few shipping lanes and fishing waters this far south. The chart was entitled, in Heuvelmans's barbed-wire handwriting, alongside his approximation of the location, *The Islands of the Dead.* Under that Heuvelmans had printed in block letters the aboriginal word *Kadimakara,* or "Animals of the Dreamtime."

Tedford's provisions included twenty-one pounds of hardtack, two tins of biscuit flour, a sack of sweets, a bag of dried fruit, a camp-stove, an oilskin wrap for his almanac, two small reading-lanterns, four jerry cans of kerosene, a waterproofed one-man tent, a bedroll, a spare coat and gloves, a spare set of Wellington boots, a knife, a small tool set, waterproofed and double-wrapped packets of matches, a box camera in a specially made mahogany case in an oilskin pouch, a revolver, and a Bland's .577 Axite Express. He'd fired the Bland's twice, and both times been knocked onto his back by the recoil. The sportsman in Melbourne who'd sold it to him had assured him that it was the closest thing to field artillery that a man could put to his shoulder.

He was now four hundred miles from sharing a wish, or a word, or a memory. If all went well, it might be two months before he again saw a friendly face. Until she'd stopped writing, his mother had informed him regularly that it took a powerful perversity of spirit to send an otherwise intelligent young man voluntarily into such a life.

His plan looked excellent on paper. He'd already left another kayak, with an accompanying supply depot, on the third or western-most island, in the event bad weather or high seas prevented his return to this one.

He'd started as a student of J.H. Tate's in Adelaide. Tate had assured himself of volunteers for his fieldwork by making a keg of beer part of his collection kit, and had introduced Tedford to evolutionism and paleontology, enlivening the occasional dinner party by belting out, to the tune of "It's a Long Way to Tipperary":

> It's a long way from Amphioxus,
> It's a long way to us;
> It's a long way from Amphioxus
> To the meanest human cuss.
> Farewell, fins and gill slits,
> Welcome, teeth and hair—
> It's a long long way from Amphioxus,
> But we all came from there!

Tedford had been an eager acolyte for two years and then had watched his enthusiasm stall in the face of the remoteness of the sites, the lack of monetary support, and the meagerness of the finds. Three months for an old tooth, as old Tate used to put it. Tedford had taken a job as a clerk for the local land surveyor, and his duties had exposed him to a panoply of local tales, whispered stories, and bizarre sightings. He'd found himself investigating each, in his free time, in search of animals known to local populations but not to the world at large. His mode was analysis, logical dissection, and reassembly, when it came to the stories. His tools were perseverance, an appetite for observation, a tolerance for extended discomfort, and his aunt's trust fund. He'd spent a winter month looking for bunyips, which he'd been told inhabited the deep waterholes and roamed the billabongs at night. He'd found only a few fossilized bones of some enormous marsupials. He'd been fascinated by the paringmal, the "birds taller than the mountains," but had uncovered them only in rock paintings. He'd spent a summer baking on a blistering hardpan awaiting the appearance of the legendary cadimurka.

All that knocking about had become focused on the day that a fisherman had shown him a tooth he'd dredged up with a deep-sea net. The thing had revealed itself to be a huge whitish triangle, thick as a scone, the root rough, the blade enamel-polished and edged with twenty or so serrations per centimeter. The heft had been remarkable: that single tooth had weighed nearly a pound.

Tedford had come across teeth like it before, in Miocene limestone beds. They belonged, Tate had assured him, to a creature science had identified as *Carcharodon Megalodon,* or Great Tooth, a recent ancestor of the Great White Shark, but nearly three times as large: a monster shark, with jaws within which a tall man could stand without stooping, and a stout, oversized head. But the tooth that Tedford held in his hand was *white,* which meant it came from an animal either quite recently extinct, or not extinct at all.

He'd written up the find in the *Tasmanian Journal of Natural Science.* The editor had accepted the piece but refused its inflammatory title.

A year later nearly to the day, his eye had been caught by a newspaper account of the Warrnambool Sea Monster, christened for the home port of eleven fishermen and a boy, in three tuna boats, who had refused to go to sea for several days. They'd been at work at certain far-off fishing grounds that only they had discovered, which lay beside a shelf plunging down into very deep water, when an immense shark, of unbelievable proportions, had surfaced among them, taking nets, one of the boats, and a ship's dog back down with it. The boy in the boat that had capsized had called out, "Is that the fin of a great fish?" and then everything had gone topsy-turvy. Everyone had been saved from the vortex except the dog. They'd been unanimous that the beast had been something the like of which they'd never seen. In interviews conducted in the presence of both the local Fisheries Inspector and one B. Heuvelmans, dentist and naturalist, the men had been questioned very closely, and had all agreed upon the details, even down to the creature's length, which seemed absurd: at least sixty-five feet. They'd agreed that it was at least the length of the wharf shed back at their bay. The account made clear that these were men used to the sea and to all sorts of weather, and to all sorts of sharks, besides. They had seen whale sharks and basking sharks. They recounted the way the sea had boiled over from the thing's surfacing and its subsequent submersion. This was no whale, they'd insisted;

they'd seen its terrible head. They'd agreed on everything: the size of its dorsal, the creature's staggering width, its ghostly whitish color. What seemed most to their credit, in terms of their credibility, was their flat refusal to return to the sea for nearly a week, despite the loss of wages involved: a loss they could ill afford, as their wives, also present for the interviews, pointed out.

It had taken him a week to get away, and when he'd finally gotten to Warrnambool no one would speak to him. The fishermen had tired of being the local sport, and had told him only that they wished that anyone else had seen the thing rather than them.

He'd no sooner been back at his desk when other stories had appeared. For a week, there'd been a story every morning, the relevance of which only he apprehended. A small boat had been swamped south of Tasmania, in calm seas, its crew missing. A ninety-foot trawler had struck a reef in what was charted as deep water. A whale carcass, headless and bearing trenchlike gashes, had washed ashore near Hibbs Bay.

As soon as he could get away, he took the early coach back to Warrnambool and looked up B. Heuvelmans, the dentist, who turned out to be an untidy cockatoo of a man holed up in a sanctuary at the rear of his house, where he'd built himself a laboratory. As he explained impatiently to Tedford, in the afternoons he retired there, unavailable to his patients' pain and devoted to his entomological and zoological studies, many of which lined the walls. The room was oppressively dark and close. Dr. Heuvelmans was secretary to the local Scientific Society. Until recently he'd been studying a tiny but monstrous-looking insect found exclusively in a certain kind of dung, but since the fishermen's news, the Sea Monster story had entirely obsessed him. He sat in a rotating chair behind a broad table covered with books, maps, and diagrams, and suggested they do what they could to curtail Tedford's visit, which could hardly be agreeable to Tedford, and was inexpressibly irksome to his host. While he talked, he chewed on the end of what he assured Tedford was a dentifricial root. He sported tiny, horn-rimmed sunglasses and a severely pointed beard.

He wanted no help and he was perfectly content to be considered a lunatic. His colleagues only confirmed his suspicion that one of the marvels of Nature was the resistance that the average human brain offered to the introduction of knowledge. When it came to ideas, his associates stuck to their ruts until forcibly ejected from them. Very well. That ejection would come about soon enough.

Had he information beyond that reported in the newspapers? Tedford wanted to know.

That information alone would have sufficed for him, Heuvelmans retorted; his interviews at least had demonstrated to his satisfaction that if he believed in the beast's existence he did so in good company. But in fact, he *did* have more. At first he would proceed no further upon that point, refusing all direct inquiry. The insect he'd been studying was apparently not eaten by birds because of a spectacularly malodorous or distasteful secretion, which began to rise faintly from the man's clothing the longer Tedford sat in the stuffy little room.

But the longer Tedford did sit, mildly refusing to stir, the more information the excitable Belgian brought forth. He talked of a fellow tooth-puller who'd befriended some aborigines up near Coward Springs and Bopeechee and who'd reported that they spoke of hidden islands to the southeast infused with the spirit of the deep upwellings, something terrible, something malevolent, something to be avoided. He'd reported that they had a word for "shark that devours the sea." He displayed a piece of fisherman's slate—from a boat he said had gone entirely missing—on which was written "Please help us. Find us soon before we die."

Finally, when Tedford apparently seemed insufficiently impressed, he'd gone into a locked cabinet with a great flourish and had produced a tooth—white—identical to the tooth Tedford had been shown. The Warrnambool fishermen had pulled it from the tatters of their net-line, he said.

Moreover, the dentist said, working the dentifricial root around his back molars, he'd found the fishing grounds. And with them, the islands.

Tedford had been unsuccessful at concealing his shock and excitement.

The job had taken him a couple of weeks, Heuvelmans had gone on, but on the whole he was quite set up by his overall ingenuity and success. He was traveling there in a matter of days, to positively identify the thing, if not catch it. Could Tedford accompany him? Not by a long chalk.

What they were talking about, Heuvelmans mused, after they'd both had sufficient time to ponder the brutality of his refusal, would be second only to the Sperm Whale as the largest predator the planet had ever produced. He then lapsed into silence with the look of a man peering into deep space.

When Tedford finally asked what sort of weapons he intended to bring, the man quoted Job: "He esteemeth iron as straw, and brass as rotten wood." And when his guest responded, "Am I to understand that you're proceeding unarmed?" Heuvelmans said only merrily, "He maketh the deep to boil like a pot."

Tedford had taken his leave intending to return the next day, and the next, and the next, but had come back the following morning to discover Heuvelmans already gone, on, as his housekeeper put it, "a sea-voyage." He never returned.

Tedford finally asked the housekeeper to notify him if there was any news, and two weeks after that the good woman wrote to say that part of the stern of the ship her master had contracted, the *Tonny,* had floated ashore on the Tasmanian coast.

He'd prevailed upon the housekeeper to give him access to the sanctuary—in order that he might help solve the mystery of the poor man's disappearance—and there discovered, in the course of tearing the entire place apart, the man's notes, a copy of the precious map: everything. On one of the three islands there was said to be a secret opening, a hidden entry to a sort of lagoon otherwise completely encircled by rock and ice. He was to look for light blue ice along the water level, under a half-dome overhang, to paddle up to that place, and to push through what he found. That would be his private gate into the unknown.

It had reached the point at which his friends had noticed that the great majority of his expressions reflected discontent, and he'd started speaking openly about being crowded round by an oppressive world. Everything had been herded into a few narrow margins; everything had been boxed up and organized. What was zoology—or paleontology—but an obsessive reordering of the boxes? Finding what science insisted *wasn't* there—that was the real contribution.

He liked to believe that he was the sort of man who viewed the world with an unprejudiced eye and judged it in a reasonable way. In letters to those few undemanding correspondents who'd remained in touch, he described himself as suppliant before the mysteries of Nature.

He felt more frequently as though his only insight was his desire to be left alone. Passing mirrors, he noticed that his bearing was that of someone who'd seen his share of trouble and expected more on the way.

He didn't find himself to be particularly shy. When addressed he always responded. He had proposed to one woman, and she had visibly recoiled, and replied that their friendship had been so good and so pleasant that it would have been a pity to have spoiled it.

His first memory was of beating on the fireplace hob with a spoon. Asked by his father what he thought he was doing, he replied, "I'm playing pretty music."

His mother, whose family had made a fortune in shipbuilding, was prone to remarks like, "I have upgraded my emeralds, down through the years."

As a boy he'd felt his head to be full of pictures no one else could see. It was as if the air had been heavy-laden with strange thoughts and ideas. He'd grown up on an estate far outside of their little town, with his brother Freddy as his closest and only friend. Freddy had been two years older. They'd trapped bandicoots and potoroos in the understory of eucalyptus stands, and Freddy had taught him how to avoid getting nipped by jew lizards and scaly-foots. They'd ridden each other everywhere on the handlebars of their shared bicycle, and worked together on chores. They couldn't have been more different in their parents' eyes: tall and fair Freddy, who'd announced at the age of fourteen that he'd been called upon to minister to lost souls in the interior, once he came of age; and the diminutive Roy, with a mat of brown hair he'd never fully wrestled into order and a tendency to break jars of preserves or homemade wine just from restlessness. Freddy had helped out at the local hospital, while Roy had collected filthy old bones and left them lying around the house. Freddy's only failing, in fact, seemed to have been his inability to more fully transform his brother.

Until it all went smash, the day before Roy's fourteenth birthday, when Freddy, on an errand to the lumber mill, somehow had pitched into the circular saw and had been cut open from sternum to thigh. He'd lived for two days. His brother had visited him twice in the hospital, and each time Freddy had ignored him. Just before he had died, in Roy's presence, he had asked their mother if she could hear the angels singing. She had fallen to weeping again, and had told him she couldn't. "What a beautiful city," he had responded. And then he had died.

Tedford's father had never mentioned the accident again. His mother had talked about it only with her sister and a close cousin. They'd had one other daughter, Mina, who had caught a chill and died at the age of seven.

His father had become the kind of man who disappeared the moment attention was directed elsewhere. He seemed to leave just for the sensation of motion. He had developed a way of lingering on a word, kneading it for its sadness. His mother had evolved the belief that Providence put such people as Freddy on Earth to make everyone happy, and then to open everyone's eyes to certain virtues once they were gone.

Tedford had been found a month after the accident, asleep in the road with a mouthful of raw onion, and a paring knife in his hand.

No one had ever talked to him about his brother's refusal to see him. And until his brother had died, he would have said that his life story had been the story of a nuisance.

D awn came like a split along the horizon. The first night had gone well, he thought, peering out of his tent flap. He'd even slept. While he pulled on his over-clothes the walls of the tent bucked and filled in the wind. His arms and back ached from the previous day's paddling. Cold damp air filled his sleeves and the back of his shirt.

The night before it had occurred to him, the moment he'd extinguished his reading-lantern, that for the next two months he would be as far from human aid as he would be on the moon. If he ran into serious mishap, only his own qualities would save him.

Old Tate had used to remark, often after having noted some particularly odd behavior on Tedford's part, that there were as many different kinds of men in the world as there were mothers to bear them and experiences to shape them, and in the same wind, each gave out a different tune. Tedford had slowly discovered himself to be unfit for life in the land-surveyor's office as he had gradually come to understand his inability to express to anyone else the awful resiliency the image of *Carcharodon Megalodon* had taken on in his psyche.

The creature inhabited dreams that did not even feature marine settings. He'd once pronounced its name in church services. As far as *Carcharodon Megalodon* was concerned, he was still a caveman, squatting on his haunches and bewitched by the magic-conjuring representation he himself had drawn on the wall.

But if he was acting like a schoolboy, at least he'd resolved to address the problem, and see Life as it was, for its own sake, prepared to take the consequences. Lacing up his boots, he reasoned to himself that he wanted to see the animal itself, and not his fear and delight in it.

Fifteen million years ago, such monsters had been the lords of creation, the lords of time; then they'd remained nearly unchanged throughout the ages, carrying on until there were only a few stragglers hanging on the very edge of annihilation. Life had gone on around them, leaving them behind. The monsters science knew about, and the ones it didn't. The formation of the northern ice caps and the extension of the southern during the Pleistocene had resulted in the drastic lowering of the sea level, exposing the continental shelves around Australia and Antarctica and trapping all sorts of marine life in the deep pockets of isolated water. Tedford was convinced that in a few of those deep pockets—adjacent to the cold, nutrient-rich bottom current that seemed to originate along the edge of Antarctica, to flow north to all the other continents of the world—his quarry resided, surfacing every so often in the same remote feeding-zones.

What percentage of the sea's *surface* had been explored? (Never mind its abyssal depths.) And meanwhile, dunderheads who plowed back and forth across the same sea-lanes with their roaring engines announced with certainty that there was nothing unusual to see in the ocean. Outside of those narrow water-lanes, upon which everyone traveled, it was all darkness. He was in an unexplored area the size of Europe. He was in a region of astounding stories. And he had always lived for astounding stories.

His first day of searching came up a bust when a cresting wave swamped his kayak a few feet from camp. He spent the bulk of the afternoon shivering and beating his arms and having to disassemble and examine the camera for water damage. His second day was scotched when he slipped on an icy slope outside his tent and badly sprained an ankle. The third dawned gray and ominous and turned to an ice storm in the time it took him to outfit his kayak. The fourth dawned bright and clear and he lay in his tent, cold and wet, his ankle throbbing, unwilling to even believe that things were beginning to turn around.

He finally roused himself and hurried into his outer clothes and spent some time in the blinding sunlight chipping the glaze of ice off his kayak's control surfaces. He breakfasted on some dried fruit and tea. The sea was calm. He loaded the camera and rifle in their oilskin pouches into the storage basket on the kayak's prow, hung his compass around his neck, put his map-packet in his jacket pocket, settled into his seat, and shoved off from the ice with his paddle. His little tent seemed to be awaiting his return.

He traveled east along the lee side of the island. It was larger than he'd realized. He saw streaks of guano on some of the rocks but otherwise no sign of life. The paddling seemed to help the pain in his ankle, and the ice slipped by at a walking speed. Every so often he had to skirt what looked like submerged ice-reefs.

The easternmost island unveiled itself through a torus-shaped mist. From what he could see from his bobbing little boat, it looked to be the largest of the three. The seas around it displayed more chop, perhaps from the open ocean beyond. He spent the remainder of the day circling it twice, each time more slowly. He saw no light blue ice, no half-dome overhang, no hidden entry. Upon completion of the second full circuit, he despaired, and immediately upbraided himself for his lack of pluck.

The sun was getting low. To the south, in the far distance, ice-fields stretched from horizon to horizon, with peaks towering higher than mastheads.

He bobbed back and forth for a bit in the gathering swell, stymied, and then paddled a hundred yards or so offshore and began his circuit again, from a different perspective.

Halfway around on the northern side he spied a bit of yellow fifty feet up on an ice-shelf. He considered various approaches to it for some minutes, trying to calm his excitement, paddling this way and that, and finally puzzled out what looked like a workable route. He lost another half hour trying to find a secure tie-up. When he finally began climbing, he had only an hour or so of sunlight left.

Even with his ankle, it was an easier climb than he'd hoped. At the top he came upon a recent encampment sheltered in the lee of a convex wall of ice-covered rock. There were meat tins and an old bottle. It looked as if the contents of a small leather bag had been burned. Only two notebooks and a stylographic pencil were left. The notebooks were empty.

He assumed all of this was Heuvelmans's work. Perhaps he'd had the ship he'd contracted wait some distance away while he'd made the rest of the journey alone.

But what to make of it? He crouched among the tins, feeling himself maddeningly unable to concentrate. It was only when he stood, aware that the light was failing at such a rate that he had to leave without delay, that he saw the rock cairn, arranged in an arrow-shape, pointing to the west, and the island from which he'd come.

He spent the evening in his bedroll listening to his tent walls buffet madly in the wind, and trying to devise a method of measuring the salinity of his little bay. The morning revealed the interior canvas to be tapestried with thin sheets of ice crystals in fantastic designs.

Sunrise was a prismatic band in the east, violet near the water and shading to golden above. He found it difficult to conceive that along that violet line, steamers ran, and men talked about the small affairs of life.

He'd secured a packet from Hobart on the southeastern coast of Tasmania for the trip across the south Indian Ocean. In spite of the steamships and railways and motorcars, the whole place had felt close to the end of the earth, especially at night. Tedford had prowled around in his sleeplessness, and in the last hours before dawn, the hills around the docks had emanated with layers of unearthly noises. He'd spent a little time in some pubs but had found a general state of disinterest in science to be the case among the fishermen and dockhands. His ship had left in the predawn darkness of his third day in the town, and he remembered thinking as it pulled away from its moorings that he was now up to his neck in the tureen.

Three mackintoshed figures had been walking the quay alongside his ship in a thin, cold rain. He'd thought of calling out to them a last word, and had dismissed the notion. He'd seen big ships and little ships on his way out of the harbor, some with their deck-lights burning and some in darkness except for the riding lights upon their mainstays. He'd been able to make out the names of a few of them as his ship's light had passed over their overhanging sterns or bows. Lighters and small craft had been crowded into their darker shadows. Near a steamship's funnel, a great lamp had illuminated some coaling basins and the sides of a wharf.

Once the sun was up, he had passed the time imagining that every wave had its twin, and singling one out and searching for its mate. The islands had revealed themselves only a few miles west of Heuvelmans's coordinates, and he'd arranged his pickup date, descended the ship's ladder into his heaving kayaks, at that point lashed together, had given the ship's mate a cheery wave, and had set off from the hull. He'd looked back only once, and the ship had disappeared by that point.

He opened a tin and made sure of his breakfast. While he ate he observed how the snow around his campsite organized itself into little crescents, as though its lee sides had been scooped out with tablespoons.

How he'd liked life, he wanted to think—every bit of it, the colored and the plain, the highlights and the low! He wondered whether the mere feel of things—common things, all sorts of things—gave anyone else the intensities of contentment that they provided him.

He thought he would start with the windward side before the breeze picked up. When he set off, a petrel winged past overhead, in a leisurely manner: the first sign of life. A half an hour later he noted, out to sea, the steam-puff fountains blown into the air by the exhalations of whales.

Again he circled the entire island without finding anything. This time he repeated the circle even closer to the shore, however, his kayak often bumping and scraping on rocks. In a protected hollow, he found another arrow, this one hastily carved into the rock. It pointed the way into an unpromisingly narrow backwater, which, when he maneuvered it, opened a bit into an odd kind of anteroom. The water below him seemed to drop off into infinity. The wavelet sounds were excessively magnified in the enclosed space. Way below, he could make out thick schools of dull green fish, two to four feet long, which he assumed to be rock cod.

Before him was a wall of ice thirty feet high. He bumped and nudged his kayak back and forth. The wind played tricks down the natural chimney. He could see no opening, and he sat.

But in the late morning, when the sun cleared the opposite wall above him, it illuminated, through the ice, a ridge about ten feet high, in the middle of which a six-foot-wide fissure had opened. The ice in frozen cascade over the fissure turned a pearl blue.

He hacked at it and it came away in slabs which dunked themselves and swirled off in eddies. He kept low, poled his way in with his oar, and the mouth of a great blue cavern opened on his right hand.

When he passed clear of the cavern it was as though his vision was drowned in light. The sun rebounded everywhere off snow and ice. It took him minutes, shading his eyes, to get his bearings.

He was in an ice-walled bay, square in shape, perhaps four hundred yards across. The water seemed even deeper than it had before, and suffused with a strange cerulean light. There was no beach, no ledge. At their apex, the walls looked to be seventy feet high.

The atmosphere above them seemed to have achieved a state of perfect visibility. Away from the sun, in a deep purple sky, a single star was shining. The taste of the air was exhilarating.

He waited. He circled the bay. He felt a silent and growing desire for lunch. Schools of big fish roiled and turned, everywhere he looked in the depths.

He'd wait all day, if necessary. He'd wait all night. His kayak drifted to and fro, his paddle shipped and dripping from the blade, while he double-checked his rifle and his lantern. He removed his camera from its case.

The fish-schools continued to circle and chase themselves about, every so often breaking the surface. He waited. Halfway through the afternoon the detonations of an ice fall boomed off to the west. The sun started to dip. The shadows in the little bay seemed to grow cooler. He suppered on some hardtack and a sip of water.

There was a great upwelling that he rode, like a liquid dome; and then calm. He put a hand on his camera and then his rifle's stock as well. His pulse eventually steadied. A pale moon rose, not very high above the ice wall. While he watched, it acquired a halo. The temperature was dropping. His breath was pluming out before him.

He judged he'd been in the bay, floating, for six hours. His legs were stiff and his bum sore. When he rotated his foot, his ankle lanced and radiated with pain.

He'd been lucky with the weather, he knew. The South Pole was the Southern Hemisphere's brew vat of storms.

The darkness was now more complete. He switched on his lantern. As he swung it around, shadows became stones, or shards of ice. The water was as motionless as indigo glass, until he lifted his paddle and began to stroke with it, and every stroke sent more and more ripples across the shining surface.

As he paddled, he reiterated for himself what Tate had taught him regarding the cardinal features of Life: the will to live, the power to live, the intelligence to live, and the adaptiveness to overcome minor dangers. Life carried itself forward by its own momentum, while its mode was carved and shaped by its battle with its environment.

He sang a song his father had sung to him, while he paddled:

> Over his head were the maple buds
> And over the tree was the moon,
> And over the moon were the starry studs
> That dropped from the Angels' shoon.

He stopped and drifted once again, turning his bow so he could gaze at his wake. Freddy had always referred to him as Old Moony because of his daydreaming. Tedford carried in his almanac, back at his campsite, his membership card in the Melbourne Scientific Society and his only photograph of his brother: a murky rendering of a tall, sweet-looking boy with pale hair.

Above him the southern lights bloomed as green and pink curtains of a soap-bubble tenuousness. He could see the stars through them. The entire eastern sky was massed with auroral light. Draperies shimmered across it.

There in his bay, uplifted on the swell of the round earth, he could see how men had come to dream of Gardens of Eden and Ages of Gold. He wondered more things about *Carcharodon Megalodon* than he could have found out in a lifetime of observation; more than he had tools to measure. All that he could attend to now was a kind of dream noise, huge and muted, that the bay seemed to be generating, resonant on the very lowest frequencies. That, and a kind of emotional mirage of himself as the dying man taking his leave. He considered the picture as if from high on the ramparts of ice, and found it to be oddly affecting. The cold was insistent and he felt his every fiber absorbed in it, his consciousness taken up in some sort of ecstasy of endeavor. The air felt alive with its innumerable infinitesimal crystallizations. His ankle throbbed.

He fancied he heard submarine sounds. Then, more distinctly, the stroke of something on the surface. His lantern revealed only the after-turbulence.

He paddled over. In the moonlight, splashes made silvery rings. He would have said he was moving through a pool of quicksilver.

The moon disappeared and left him in darkness. He glided through it, close enough to whatever had surfaced to taste a mephitic odor upon the air.

For the first time he was frightened. He kept his lantern between his legs and shipped his paddle and pulled his Bland's to him by the stock. This thing was the very figure of the terrifying world around him, of the awfulness of nature.

The surface of the bay began to undulate. His little craft rocked and bobbed accordingly, in the darkness. He was very near the end but he had not, and would not, lose good cheer. Things had come out against him, but he had no cause for complaint.

Why had his brother refused to see him? Why had his brother refused to see him? Tears sprang to his eyes, making what little light there was sparkle.

The moonlight reemerged like a curtain raised upon the bay. Above it, the stars appeared to rise and fall on a canopy inflated by wind. But there was no wind, and everything was perfectly still. Everything was silent. His heart started beating in his ears.

The water alone dipped and swirled. Just below the surface, shoals of fish panicked, scattering like handfuls of thrown darts.

He caught sight of a faint illumination in the depths. As it rose, it took the shape of a fish. The illumination was like phosphorescence, and the glimmer gave it obscure, wavering outlines.

There was a turbulence where the moon's reflection was concentrated and then a rush of water like a breaking wave as the shark surged forward and up. The body towered over Tedford's head. He lost sight of the ice wall behind it in the spray.

It was as if the bottom itself had heaved surfaceward. The run-up of its splash as it dove sent his kayak six or seven feet up the opposite wall, and he was barely able to keep his seat. He lost both his rifle and his lantern.

The backwash carried him to the middle of the bay. He was soaked, and shaking. Seawater and ice slurried around his legs. He experienced electric spikes of panic. His camera bobbed and tipped nearby in its oilskin pouch, and then sank. A wake, a movement started circling him. The dorsal emerged, its little collar of foam at its base, and flexed and dripped, itself as tall as a man. The entire animal went by like a horrible parade. He estimated its length at fifty feet. Its thickness at twelve. It was a trolley car with fins.

It turned on its side, regarding him as well, its eye remarkable for its size and its blackness against the whiteness of the head, hobgoblin-like. It sank, dwindling away to darkness, and then, deep below, reemerged as a vast and gaping circle of teeth coming up out of the gloom.

Where would Tedford have taken his find, had he been able to bring it back? Who understood such a creature's importance? Who understood loss? Who understood separation? Who understood the terrors of inadequacy laid bare? The shark's jaws erupted on either side of Tedford's bow and stern, curtains of spray shattering outward, turning him topsy-turvy, spinning him to face the moon, leaving him with a flash of Jonah-thought, and arresting him an instant short of all for which he had hoped, and more.

Revenge is a sport best played by those whose memories are long—and that made her a dangerous foe, indeed.

The Tears of Squonk, and What Happened Thereafter

By GLEN DAVID GOLD

I n late March 1916, a week before the Nash Family Circus came to
Tennessee, their spotty poster advertisements clung to the sides of
buildings throughout the railroad town of Olson. Olson was best
described as sleepy, save for the constant rattle of the railroad yards;

it was not at all a place for murder. And the Nash Family and their hired performers seemed anything but evil.

The posters, stock images dated and fading already, promised tame acts. A horseback rider here, a clown there, a roaring lion, and finally a pair of juggling clowns pasted next to each other to lend some small company. Taken together, they looked as forlorn as the orphans who sometimes stood outside the tent and imagined far greater attractions than those that ever actually wheezed through their paces under the single, patched canvas big top.

The talents of the Nash family clowns were generally tepid. Some of the horses had been remarkable in their youth, true, but they were tired—granted, only half as tired as the acrobats, who mostly daydreamed of returning to Germany when the war was over. No, what the Nash Family Circus had to offer was the moral backbone of its patriarch, Ridley Nash.

Nash had been in the circus business since 1893, when the traveling carnival had been born. A cook in Chicago, and a splendid mimic of the world's cuisines, he had made the daily meals at the international pavilions at the Columbian Exposition. He had been so impressed by the clean family entertainment, he purchased his first wagon then and there, on credit, from a dealer in the dry goods pavilion.

By 1916, he was referred to as "Colonel" Nash, which dismayed him privately, as he had never served in the army, and he felt the term disrespected those who had. Still, it was the custom among traveling circuses to have a faux colonel at the helm, and so he bore it manfully.

Among the Nash Family Circus posters was a broadside of printed text which Nash had set himself. He insisted that every word be true, beginning with "A Moral Entertainment," and ending with "23 Years of Dealing Squarely with the American Public." In between were other promises, such as "8 funny clowns," and if the eighth clown was under the bottle that night, to keep the count honest, Colonel Nash donned the red nose and let himself be hit with the slapstick.

At the center of the broadsheet was a woodcut of an elephant, Mary, billed as the third-largest elephant in captivity. She was seen in a headdress and cape, with an indication by her side that she stood twelve feet at the shoulder.

The elephant was indeed the third-largest in captivity, and she stood exactly as high as the Colonel claimed, and one morning had been measured three inches taller, but the Colonel kept the smaller number, as he could count on it being verified.

The posters he'd designed to showcase the elephant were for many years treasured, not for their moral authority, but simply for how Mary was shown both head-on and from the side. Nash felt this presented her headdress and cape *squarely,* to use his preferred term, but more than one spectactor to her final performance commented— before spiriting away a copy of the broadsheet—how prescient the Colonel had been in showing her as if she were posed for a police blotter's mug book.

T he morning of Mary's last day, roustabouts swung sledgehammers along the stake line, and ring-makers were leveling the field exactly forty-two feet in all directions from the center pole, which was erected by a line of ten men chanting as they had since the days of Dan Rice, "easy, easy, easy, PULL."

The sky was iron gray with clouds, and the humidity brought an odd smell, something rusted and cruel, from the train yards, which surrounded and dwarfed the town. Tiny Olson sat in the shadow of Wildwood Hill, the top of which was a graveyard for freight cars. In the town, the parade band attempted in vain to tune their ratty instruments, and beyond and above them was the hulking, distant silhouette of Ol' 1400, the McKennon Railway's hundred-ton train derrick, which was used to snatch trains off the track and then drop them, helpless as baby turtles, onto the scrap heap.

The parade was a chance to show the town just a little for free, to build anticipation for that evening's show. At eleven AM, the brass band was fully engaged and marching: the scruffy and heartbroken Nash children, plus two pony boys and a mule skinner who had some legitimate use for the slide trombone. Next were the three acrobats who normally did handsprings in the street, but because of the mud, they rode on the back of a flatbed cart pulled by goats, and made a human pyramid at one end, tumbled down, then reassembled at the other end.

Next came the eight funny clowns, most of whom seemed, at eleven AM, not so much funny as wrestling with philosophical discontents.

The sole clown of merit was Squonk. When he and Mary had joined the Nash Family early in the season, the Colonel billed Squonk in the programs as "Joseph Bales, portraying Squonk the Clown," in the spirit of full disclosure, but Bales, a trained artist who had studied in Europe, was furious. "Nash," he said, folding his arms, "I'm a trained artist. And when I studied in Europe, we didn't give away our names, not for the world." Bales argued that pantomime, makeup, false nose, and floppy Bibleback shoes were all poetics, in the Aristotelian sense, intended to preserve mystery. Grudgingly, mostly to keep the temperamental Bales at ease, Nash—who wasn't quite sure about the Aristotelian reference, though it sounded impressive—billed him from then on, in entirety, as "Squonk."

That morning, Squonk—in his dunce's cap and bloated single-piece checked suit with three yellow pom-poms down the front—seemed to be everywhere at once, miming the trombonist's slide and puffed-out cheeks, then threatening to topple the human pyramid. In what warmed the crowd as a rib-tickling lampoon (though it lacked the same effect on his peers, who glared daggers at him), Squonk became stern with the other clowns, tutting their performances. He showed them the proper way to toss a child into the sky, lofting and catching a small girl and handing her a daisy all in one motion as smooth and delicate and transparent as glass.

But this was just the warm-up for the big finish. At the head of the parade, two front-door men began to wave their arms, standing as if to block the side streets. They cried out, "Hold your horses! Here comes the elephant!"

The crowd fell to a respectful hush, as there was something glorious and humbling about seeing, once a year at most, such an impossible beast. Some regarded the bizarre mix of parts—trunk, tusks, huge ears—as evidence of the existence of a bounteous and clever God. Nash, who was swayed by the God argument, also spent stray moments here and there staring Mary in the eye, sensing within her a wonderful intelligence. Squonk wrote out a quotation for him to use during his pitch: "Comte Georges Leclerc de Buffon, famed naturalist from France, tells us the elephant 'by his intelligence makes as near an approach to man, as matter can approach spirit.'"

Hence the warning about horses. Elephants would tolerate being chained to a freight car and stuck with a hooked pole, and forced to stand on their hind legs and trumpet. But they would not tolerate horses. The mere fact of horses drove them into an atavistic frenzy. The eye clouded over, almost as if *musth,* the elephant madness, had invaded the brain.

When the street was thought to be secure, Squonk loped forward, dropping all of his humorous antics. His years of European training rushed to the forefront. His rigid posture, his head tilted upward, arms flourishing gracefully, indicated that behind him stood a magnificent work of art known as an elephant. The crowd produced a kind of applause that was at once awed and hesitant.

Mary walked slowly, trunk held forth in a question mark that tilted left and right as she marched through the muck. She wore a sequined headdress, and a long cape with a Shakespearean ruff. There was a kind of knife-scarring on her ear, an M, made to indicate her name (elephant theft was rare, but costly). The more educated patrons of the circus, upon seeing the outfit, and the M, understood at once how fitting her name was. They would murmur, *Queen Mary,* as the ground trembled with each step.

Bales had trained Mary in a unique manner—she was never humiliated into squirting water at the crowd, or balancing a ball with her trunk. He was more demanding, more of a martinet than that. Mary performed ballet.

Thus the Nash broadside included mention of Mary's dynamic performances for the crowned heads of Europe (citing, as per Bales's résumé, Carlos II of Spain and Sophia of Greece, since Nash was aware that "crowned heads" was an unacceptably vague term that invited suspicion). The crowd at the parade was there to see ballet, and, had the show at Olson gone as had every other performance that season, Mary would have indulged them with one simple motion, a curtsy, that would have guaranteed a full house that night. It was such an indescribable gesture that most members of every previous crowd were driven to sputter to friends, "You have to see it—you just have to see it."

Alas, at 11:15, as the town clock was striking the quarter-hour, Mr. Timothy Phelps, senior director of the McKennon Railway, arrived at the parade via the narrow alley between the Second National Bank and Tannenbaum's hardware store. He appeared mounted, with exquisite form, on his English saddle-backed horse, Jasper.

What happened next was so terrible, so simple, so unbelievable, that townspeople's memories could never have been trusted to relay it accurately. In fact, the story would surely have been demoted to the realm of folklore were it not for a single motion picture camera.

The Pathé Prevost Camera, the camera of choice for professionals, had but one drawback: If the camera fell over and struck a hard object, the film stock tended to explode into flames. An amateur filmmaker named Alexander Victor was experimenting that morning with acetate "safety" film. He'd ridden the rails of the American South, tinkering with improvements in the optical range finder, and shooting endless locomotives in transit, train-crew razorbacks waving at the camera. Today, he had alighted on the circus parade, which was ideal to him for its interesting motion.

He hand-cranked his camera on the sidewalk, directly across from the alleyway. And so local memories, hazy in other details, are precise in this regard, all of them, no matter where they were that day, recalling it from the same vantage point. Their memories took on the scratched negative, the variable speed and mysterious lighting of amateur film. Mary broke from the parade route, trotting left with an almost magnetic attraction to Jasper and his rider, scattering to the four winds the townspeople between her and her quarry. Standing next to the brick wall of the bank, Phelps and his horse—rather a greyish smear in the frame-by-frame dissection of the scene—nervously paced back and forth, but couldn't make up their collective mind, and then Mary, headdress and cape buffeting with each step, was upon them. It was as if she needed to scratch an itch against the rough bricks, one quick flex of her shoulder, forward, then one slower, luxurious kind of return back, and horse and rider were no more.

This was horror enough. But next, camera still rolling, citizens of Olson sepia blurs crossing the foreground, Mary lowered one front foot to Phelps's back, as if holding the corpse steady, and then she wrapped her trunk around his neck. The next motion was fluid, like drawing a reluctant cork out of a champagne bottle.

There was pandemonium in the streets, people unsure of exactly which direction constituted proper fleeing, and Alexander Victor's film ends with a man in a bowler hat running his way, his vest and watch fob suddenly filling up the screen, and then, blackness.

Nash, rooted in the mud, hadn't seen exactly what happened, but tried to calm the situation, his clear showman's bellow ineffective. He saw the village blacksmith run forward and withdraw a pistol from his apron, which he proceded to empty at Mary's flank. The bullets made small pockmarks in Mary's hide, and she flapped her ears in concern, but she continued walking and there was no further outcome.

Squonk stood paralyzed, his jaw wavering, in the middle of the street. He removed his pointed, conical hat, and lowered his head. He put his palm over his eyes as Mary, his friend and companion, approached him and gingerly reached out her trunk for the apple she always received at the end of every parade.

The rumor that the show must go on was one started by patrons and furthered by newspapermen who liked how it sounded. Many a circus folds without a second thought, and Nash knew, at noon, and at one o'clock and at two o'clock, that there would be no performance that night. He had returned Mary to her freight car, and put most of his men around it to guard her. When a group of townspeople approached, excited as boys invited to their first dance, and armed with rifles, pistols, and sticks of dynamite, Nash stopped them himself. Nash had expected them, and had been girding himself all afternoon to tell a lie. It was the first lie he knowingly told the public.

"You can't kill an elephant that way," he announced.

His tone was so authoritative, so dismissive, he wondered where his voice was coming from. He sounded as if he were reciting Leviticus. "A gun, even a stick of dynamite, that will in no way pierce this beast's hide."

The men of Olson exchanged glances. There was a problem at hand, but some of them were known to be clever, and it was only a matter of time until someone yelled, "Electricity!"

Nash shook his head. "Edison himself attempted that once and failed. It just made the elephant angry." His second lie.

This caused murmurs, and Nash knew where this would go, a building kind of frustration and impatience. As soon as one man was telling the rest he could call his cousin in Frazer, who had a cannon from the War Between the States that might still work, Nash stopped them. He found himself saying, more of a circus man than he'd ever been, "We will settle it tonight, gentlemen. We will not leave this town without settling it, publicly, fully, and demonstrably." He wasn't sure why he added that last word, but it seemed to hold promise to the men, who, upon being assured that Mary would die somehow, turned, and walked away, holding their pistols or their rifles forlornly.

So the Colonel sat in his wagon, which was parked atop its brass brake shoes in a swampy depression nearest Mary's freight car. He was unsure of what to do. His elephant had killed someone—apparently done so with vigor, though he hadn't seen it, and continued to have his doubts. There was a very reasonable demand for vengeance. The idea of having a murderous animal in his charge made him feel ill. But what made him feel worse was the deeper source of his lie to the townspeople: if Mary were killed, he could never pay off his loan.

The finances of a circus were as arcane and toxic as the combinations of Ural Mountain herbs the property men used to jazz up the Sterno squeezings they swilled on long winter evenings. There were loan-outs, buybacks, reverse repurchase agreements for contracts based on projected earnings. In short, Nash only owned Squonk and Mary's contract because he had guaranteed a bank in Chicago $8000, payable in installments through the end of the summer season. He had paid off $1500 so far. There was no way he could now make up the balance, and for him, financial responsibility was the basis of modern civilization. He had never pitted that belief against his belief in animals' basic nobility, and when the two forces rubbed together like this, the friction upset him.

At three o'clock he called Joseph Bales into his wagon to see how best to proceed. Bales entered with his head hung low, and when Nash began to speak—he began with an overall statement of how he still believed in the intelligence of the elephant, and was about to discuss whether female elephants perhaps fell under the sway of *musth*—Bales interrupted him. "Hanging," he said.

"Pardon?"

It was a conversation Nash would recall, helplessly, without conscious effort, many times for the rest of his life. The specifics were worn away, but the general feeling of dread was quite solid.

"Mary committed a crime," Bales said. "She should pay. By hanging. It would be poetic."

Usually Bales spoke in sentences forged from many dependent clauses welded together by sarcasm. Tonight he sounded like a different person. Determined, a man who has made the right choice quickly, begging for no time to reconsider it. He leaned forward and pointed with one articulated, bony finger, out the window. And there, on the hilltop, was the hundred-ton railroad derrick, looming just like a gallows.

Nash shook his head, but said nothing. Bales stood, put his hand on the door handle, and as a way of departing, jammed his hat down upon his head. His back was shaking, shoulders quivering. Then, determined, he whispered, "And it would be more poetic, still, in the deepest sense—poetic justice—when we charge admission."

When the door closed, Nash stared after it, his own eyes welling up. A terrible taste came into his mouth, a vile copper flavor, exactly like that of a penny.

T hat night, the whole town of Olson turned out on Wildwood Hill. Also present were the whole towns of Softon, Burroughs,

Myers, and Carmel, over two thousand people, each of whom had paid the exorbitant sum of two dollars for the privilege of standing among the train wreckage to see an elephant hanged.

Nash himself elected not to attend. That an animal would be done such violence broke his heart. Just before dusk, he returned to Mary, who stood chained in her freight car, and looked her one last time in the eye. He saw within the same intelligence and kindness he had always seen. The longer he stood, the less he could forgive himself for taking the financially responsible way out of this. He retreated to his bed for the rest of the sleepless night.

Alexander Victor set up his camera, to no great effect. Even by the kerosene-fueled pan lights, with their reflectors and occasional flashes, there was not enough light, through the silt and smoke drifting over the excited crowd, to see anything more than vague shapes, suggestions of some tribal ritual.

Wildwood Hill was a gentle slope of about two hundred feet, with spiraling rails and a footpath, terminating in the antediluvian detritus of trains gone extinct. There were men and women and children walking gaily up the path, finding good vantage points surrounding the final length of railway track. The derrick's wheelhouse, belching diesel smoke, sat atop a power plant the size of a locomotive. And extending from the wheelhouse, at the midpoint of its iron belly, was a kind of mechanical trunk: a muscular crane with a superstructure of steel girders, and at the end of it, a dull steel hook.

At seven o'clock, the doors to Mary's freight car were thrown open and she was led by torchlight along the pathway to the hill. The crowd, upon seeing her at a great distance, cheered for a while, but as her stride was stiff and slow, and the circular pathway uphill quite long, they soon lost their appetite for cheers, and fell instead into muted conversations.

When she finally appeared, it looked at first as if Mary would pass toward the derrick without trouble, but when she came upon the crowd, she froze solid. Some swore that she seemed to eye the steel hook, but perhaps her psychology was more simple than that. She was usually led to perform at this time of night, and yes, she was wearing her headdress and cape, and yes, there was a cheering crowd.

But no tent. And the tenor of the crowd, for a creature that lived on emotion over reason, must have frightened her.

She shied away from the path, and it took several quick pokes of the elephant stick to keep her from retreating. Still, no power in the world could get her to go forward to her fate. Long minutes passed this way, with the crowd yelling out its disappointments, until resolution came from an unlikely source. A figure fought his way through the shoulder-to-shoulder overalls. It was Joseph Bales, out of his uniform. No makeup. Woolen jacket, beaten work trousers, a derby. From his occasional missteps and slurred speech, it was apparent he had ladled out applejack for himself from the canned heat wagon. If you looked closely, you could see a fine tapestry of broken capillaries around his eyes, which he wiped at with the back of his sleeve.

Mary immediately reached out her trunk for her friend, who patted her gently. "This way," he said, and walked several steps toward the derrick. She followed, but then stopped, and nothing, not all the pats and praise and reassurances in the world, could get her closer to the hook.

Bales tried to smile at her, but failed. Just as the crowd began again to grow unruly, he held out his hands to his sides, palms out, as if trying to stop a fight. He put his head down, and let out a sigh of awful resignation.

When he next raised his head—plainface or not—it was Squonk the Clown who looked up, light and limber as a dishrag. He did a mild leap, from foot to foot, and then back again, then once forward, once back, and then he pointed back at Mary. Understanding passed through her, and she, too, put her feet outward, then back. Then she stepped to the left, then the right, then turned around in a full circle. The audience let out a lusty cheer—Mary was doing her ballet!

The pas de deux was based on Plastikoff's La Chauvre-Souris Dorée, a rare work in that it celebrated not courtship, but daily love, the often-pale and unnoticed emotions that pass between a man and wife. When Squonk performed a *saut de l'ange,* Mary, who could not of course jump with all four feet in the air, nevertheless responded by extending one leg behind her, and her opposite forward leg straight ahead, in a perfect arabesque.

She did not notice that, far overhead, the crane was swinging into position.

Finally, Squonk performed a series of *assembles sur la point,* jumping with his legs together, turning in midair, going up on his toes, springing again, with a kind of grace that would seem unrepeatable until Mary followed him, shuffling in a circle like a trolley on a turntable. For her big finish, she did exactly what she'd done a thousand times before—rear legs slightly crossed, lowering herself until she was almost belly to the ground, and dropping her head as if in supplication: a perfect curtsy.

And that was when Squonk stepped forward and slipped the hook into the chain around her neck.

She startled backward, but it was too late. Gears far away, deep in the power plant, began to grind. Mary stood up herself, shaking her head like a dog shedding water. And then her forelegs were lifted off the dusty ground. She walked on her two legs, balancing, and the turbine whined awfully as something seemed to slip, and she started to return to the earth—briefly, though—as the crane applied inexorable force, she was pulled upward again, and her rear legs were removed from the earth, too.

All around, on the tops of dead scrap, of passenger cars stripped bare, of tankers gone to rust, the men and women and children lost their ability to cheer. An elephant is not meant to leave the ground, and the sight is sickening, a kind of rebuke to the natural order—fossils found in a churchyard, a rainfall of salt cod in the desert. There was a hush under the smoldering pan lights. Mary's stubby legs kicked in the air, and then, just once, after long moments, the eye startled wide in recognition of what was happening. The trunk sprang straight, a quick and disappointed half-strangling trumpet, and then she went limp.

No one knows for certain how long the elephant hung over Wildwood Hill. A man schooled in night photography offered to let people pose with the corpse, but there were no takers. There was a general call toward Squonk, and then confusion, then realization: He was gone. He had probably turned away the moment the crane began its work. He was never seen again.

* * *

A year passed. Then another. The Nash Family soldiered on, barely, sending in cash to cover a good portion of Mary and Squonk's contract, and then making small monthly payments. There was no longer a big finish to the Colonel's circus. Instead, Nash added a trained chimpanzee who, dressed in a toga, rode in a chariot pulled by two basset hounds. He also added a castaway from the Sparks circus, Captain Tiebor, who had a team of sea lions he claimed were college graduates. Nash dutifully wrote that into his new broadsides, and if that absurdity troubled him, he said nothing about it. He still claimed to offer a moral entertainment, though there was no longer a chronological measure of his dealing squarely with the American public.

In winter, 1918, the family went off the road for a season. Nash went alone to a rented ranch-style hacienda in an unincorporated valley not far from Los Angeles, California. His idea, expressed vaguely to the family he left behind, was to find new talent associated with the motion picture industry—perhaps some tumblers or wild animal acts were dissatisfied with the life behind the camera, and perhaps they truly wanted to see the world.

But the words seemed hollow to him, and in their letters, no one asked him how the quest was going. Since Mary's hanging, Nash had been directionless. He knew no one in Los Angeles or its environs, which he found lonely and strange—acres of olive groves and citrus trees somehow mysteriously kept alive in the desert climate. He half-heartedly visited Famous Players once, but was turned away at the secretarial pool when he couldn't remember the name of the man he was supposed to meet. He spent the rest of the afternoon riding the trolley cars home.

When he cared to think about it in culinary terms, a habit he retained from his previous career, Nash believed there were two types of circus attractions: the sweet and the sour. The sweet consisted of wholesome entertainments that were exactly as presented: the trapeze, the animals, the clowns. The sour were those that relied on fooling people. The India rubber pickled punks in jars, talked up as two-headed babies. The pink lemonade they sold that was actually water the clowns had washed their tights in. They had seemed too easy to keep apart, those worlds, but at some point Nash had crossed a line, and gone sour himself.

One February afternoon, Nash was interrupted in his morning ritual of shaving by a knock at his door. He peered out the keyhole, worried that it might be an associate come to take him back early to the circus; but no, the man on the other side of the door was no one he knew. Wiping away the foam, Nash let him in.

The stranger's face was broken and scorched, with patches of red skin among wrinkles, the expression a perpetual wince, as if he'd spent every moment of his life in hostile weather. His age was impossible to guess. He wore the familiar black cape and hat of a railway detective, which was the main reason Nash had so readily let him in.

Unaccustomed to company, Nash fumbled to offer him coffee, which the stranger accepted, announcing at the same time his name, "Leonard Pelkin." Pelkin had once been a railway detective, he continued, but he had retired and was now working privately.

They sat on either side of a galley that had been built into Nash's small kitchen, cramped but breezy, with a good view of the valley over Nash's shoulder. Pelkin took the opportunity to admire it while digging a portfolio out of his knapsack.

"Might I ask you some questions?"

"Certainly."

Pelkin carefully removed a stack of four-by-five photographs. As if dealing a hand of poker, he placed them facedown in a field of five. "It's about a murder," Pelkin said. He cleared his throat, as if he had more to say. Nash nodded, to indicate he was being helpful. Pelkin nodded back, and then took a sip of coffee. He gestured with the coffee cup, toward the photographs. "Suspects," he continued.

Then he turned over the photographs, each making a confident snap as they went faceup.

For a moment, Nash was silent.

"These are murder suspects?" he finally asked.

Pelkin nodded. "Do you recognize any of them?"

"They're elephants," Nash said.

"Look again."

Nash didn't need to look. He was upset, as he felt this was a problem that had been handled long ago, destroying a good part of himself in the bargain.

"I'm sure they're elephants. If you're here, talking to me, then you know why I'd know that."

Pelkin put up a finger. "One elephant," he said. "Just one."

The five photographs had been taken years apart, the earliest ones streaked and bubbling with emulsion. Each of them showed an elephant in the midst of carnivals or circuses—Nash recognized a wagon from the Sells organization, and a Ringling banner, and, finally, his own sagging big top, whose patches were as identifiable as surgical scars. It was like the sun breaking over a mountaintop.

"Mary," he said.

"Can you indicate where you see her?" Pelkin asked.

"Are you serious? She's the elephant standing before my tent."

"Is that her in the other photographs?"

It was hard to tell. In one, she wore a kind of tiara; in the rest, she was unadorned. "It could be."

"Did she have any identifying marks?"

"Well. Well. She was exactly twelve foot tall. Is that what you mean?"

Pelkin's eyes narrowed. "Twelve foot? Or twelve foot, three inches?"

"No, exactly twelve foot, as per the broadsides." He blew out his cheeks. "Of course, that one morning in Denver, she seemed to be twelve-foot-three."

Pelkin brought his hand down on the table hard enough to make the spoons jump.

"Yes!"

He leaned forward, and said, as if trying to be calm, "Is it possible she was, all those other times you measured her, slouching?"

"I don't understand."

Pelkin eased away. He looked over Nash's shoulder, at the elm trees beyond the window. "Any other marks you remember?" he asked, faintly.

"She had an M on her ear."

"Like this?" Pelkin thumbed through some photographs until he found what he was looking for, and snap, it went down on the table: It was a close-up of an elephant's ear.

Nash nodded. "Yes, except Mary had an M and this elephant has an N."

Weighing that statement with a frown, Pelkin brought out a fountain pen, shook it, then added a single downstroke. "An M like this, is what Mary had?"

"I'm sorry, how many elephants have letters on their ears? Perhaps all of them. I've only examined one up close."

And at once there came forth the bitterness Nash had been trying so hard not to taste. The glimpses he'd had into Mary's eye, the raw mind he'd seen there, how she had been betrayed.

"One elephant, I'm thinking," Pelkin said. "There was an elephant named Nommi, with Ringling, and four years ago she killed a man. I think they just hustled her out the back way in the middle of the night, changed her name, and sold her to you."

"That's impossible," Nash said, but as he did, he brought up the photographs one by one and stared at them. "These are Nommi?"

"One of them is. One is of a Sells elephant, name of Veronica. She was a killer too, six years ago. And the name, see, if you—" Pelkin awkwardly put up two fingers to make a V, and then joined with them a finger from the other hand, which made a backward N. He moved his fingers around, trying to get it right, and then gave up. "Before that, Ionia. That's the one with the tiara."

Nash wanted to tell Pelkin that he was insane, but could somehow not move his mouth to form the words. He had a sickly feeling, one tinged with guilt, as if he himself were being accused.

"The man Mary trampled in Olson, he was on a horse," he said, meaning by this to begin a conversation that would end with Mary being, if not blameless or excusable, than at least understandable: an animal pushed beyond her natural limit.

"Mary didn't exactly trample Phelps, did she?" Pelkin said.

"Well . . ."

Pelkin started packing up his photographs, and Nash hoped this meant it was over. But instead, there was a new photograph to study.

It was about eight inches tall, and of such length that it came in a roll, which Pelkin unwrapped. He smoothed it out, then weighted it down at either end with coffee cups.

It was a safari shot. Five men at the center, in white pith helmets, Springfields cracked open across their laps. Native bearers of a tribe Nash did not recognize were to the left and to the right. Some of them covered their faces before the camera, but left the rest of themselves exposed, including the women, a detail Nash dwelt on for a shameful amount of time before realizing what, exactly, he was being shown.

The five hunters were all posing with their trophies: one man atop them, two on either side, two kneeling before them—a half-dozen dead African elephants.

"Oh, my lord," Nash cried.

There were pencil marks around the men's faces, which were half-crinkled in the photograph, hardly recognizable to begin with. Pelkin tapped on the image of one man to the right, whose rifle was jauntily slung over his shoulder. "Timothy Phelps," he said, "when he was a much younger man. The Southern Crescent Railroad, in 1889, took its senior-most managers on safari to the dark continent. Five of them are now dead. Killed by elephants." He picked up his coffee cup; the photo rolled shut. "An elephant."

Nash smoothed out the photo, holding it open himself. He stared until full understanding settled in on him. He felt buoyed by it; he could make sense of this. Almost giddily, he whispered, "Mary's family, then?"

"What?"

"The elephants who were killed here on the hunt. They're Mary's family, aren't they? She's been having her revenge."

There was a rotten silence in the room as Pelkin sized him up, astonished. Not in a pleasant way. At once, the sourness of the circus returned to Nash. Pelkin's look was the kind reserved for the lowest hick, the kind who buys the Fiji Mermaid, the he/she dancer blow-off, the pickled punks and the lemonade, all of it, hook, line, and lead-heavy sinker.

"You think . . ." Pelkin grinned. "You think Mary, an elephant, is the mastermind, or something?"

"Well."

"Look." Pointing again into the group of hunters. Toward the left, isolated from his comrades, arms folded, wearing no gun himself, was Joseph Bales.

"Oh! How? How?" Nash paused, helplessly.

"You know him as Bales, right? That's not his name. His name is Bowles. The clever ones, when they change their names, make them similar enough they'll answer to them in their sleep. Bowles was supposed to be promoted, and he wasn't. I hear he was a terrible safari member, made a big fuss about everything, spent hours telling his fellow men around the campfire how uneducated they were. After the safari, he was fired. He went bitter, Nash. How bitter, no one knew. Some bitter guys, they scheme but they don't have any follow-through. They fade. Not Bowles. He went out and became a circus clown, the way some of the really bitter ones do. For the last dozen years, he has been luring these men to their deaths. The day before your circus arrived in Olson, Phelps received a telegram telling him to ride his horse to the parade, as a wonderful surprise was waiting." Pelkin shook his head. "Wasn't so wonderful, in my opinion."

For a great deal of time, Nash said nothing. He felt he should say something, but the specifics eluded him. Pieces of this macabre plot surfaced: Bowles scheming revenge, Bowles becoming a circus clown, alighting on the poetic justice of death-by-elephant. Finally, he said, "Aristotle."

"What?"

"He liked Aristotle," he said, blushing a bit.

Pelkin shrugged, and then wrote Aristotle on the back of one of the photographs. "Any ideas where Bowles might have gone?"

"Why did he kill her?"

"Pardon?"

With no difficulty, Nash was back in the circus wagon, with Bales opposite him, Bales holding back tears—or was he actually crying them?—and determined to have Mary hanged. "He said killing her would serve justice."

"Oh. Yeah, the justice expert. Sure. He was done, Nash. He'd managed to get her out of trouble four times before that. Slipped away in the dead of night four times, changing her name, changing his name. This time, he didn't need her anymore. He'd killed everyone he wanted to, and this way he wasn't going to leave any evidence behind."

"Hmmph." Nash nodded. "So he betrayed her."

"Sure," Pelkin said. Like most railway detectives, he was terse, but when revealing secrets he took a shameless delight in relaying the horrors behind them. "They were partners. She didn't know the game was rigged until the blow-off."

"I see."

He now wanted Pelkin to depart, as he was beginning to feel a strange and restless feeling, as if impatient for a loved one returning from a long trip. He wanted to throw open the door, look down the drive, and see, bags in hand, himself. He hardly listened as Pelkin snapped out another pair of photographs.

"These men, though, it seems Mary—or whatever her name was at first—she killed them in 1902. That was two years, as far as I can tell, before she met Bowles. It was a pretty fair partnership, I'd say. A good match."

"Yes, yes, I see," Nash said, impatiently. He was beginning to listen not to Pelkin but to a story unfolding in his brain. Mary, an animal, whose impulses were harnessed by a bad man. The tragedy of her life, coupled with the sheer evil of Bowles, made him hurry through the remainder of the interview with Pelkin. He was unsure of all things in the world, save one: He needed to be alone.

The conversation continued for less than five minutes. Pelkin had confirmed the trail was cold here. Abruptly, he shook Nash's hand, and he left.

When Nash was quite alone, he dug out a wax pencil and a sheet of butcher paper, and began to write down all he remembered about Mary, trying to balance the good (her intelligence and, generally speaking, kindness) with the bad—her having murdered people, for instance. He remembered then the salty tracks on Squonk's cheeks—if they had been there at all—and as he thought of them glistening, they enraged him. False, awful, sour, heedless crocodile tears, the worst kind of carny, the lowest of men, working Nash like a sucker.

He wrote long into the afternoon, had a snack, and then began to rewrite everything into a short and morally instructive playlet, which could be performed by a small circus. It was about a wicked clown and the elephant he tricked. When he was done, Nash realized he was about to shop for another elephant, and he made a note to send out wires to Sarasota, where the circus exchange kept track of such requests.

From 1919 to 1924, the Nash Family presented their circus as ever, sometimes lucky enough to adhere to a strict schedule when times were good, other times blowing the route and wildcatting it until business caught on again. The lynchpin of their show was Nash's playlet, a melodrama that featured the impish and terrible antics of Moxie, a clown, and Regina, a luckless and sad elephant suffering fits during which she accidentally murdered people. Finally, she was taken outside, and, as seen in a silhouette projected against the raw canvas tent, hanged until dead.

In his broadsides, and his talking before the performance, Nash explained that every word was the truth, including the hanging, though he had changed the names. It was said that the finale was done in shadow because of its graphic and disturbing nature, which was true, but actually secondary to its function as a special effect. Nash would never really harm the elephant, whom he loved: a second love, the cautious kind. This one was named Emily, and she had credentials so spotless her owner liked to say she could run for the Senate.

The crowds were entertained and disturbed by the spectacle, which was never quite the success Nash hoped. When the flaps to the tent opened after each performance, the crowds were hesitant to leave, and some audience members stayed behind to talk to Nash. There had been rumors, promulgated in whispers by other Nash Family performers, that Mary had killed even before she'd met Squonk. He was an awful man, to be sure, but wasn't Mary herself also guilty? Wasn't the execution, even if facilitated by Squonk, somewhat just? And Bales, did he escape, just like that? Did he kill again? Why wasn't he brought to justice in the end? And though Nash tried to answer the questions, he always grew flustered, as if the audience were missing the point, and he would retire to his wagon for the night.

There is no record of the last performance; it was never truly historical or important. It was unusual, a sort of passion play on a pachydermic scale, but though generous in spirit, it was too small a venue—melodrama—to incorporate a serious truth: Just as there are intelligent, wicked men, there are intelligent, wicked elephants. A thing of pure nature is not by necessity a good thing.

Just before the turn of the new century, the story of Mary was determined to be folklore, a confused truncation of the truth, something contradicted by old-time Olsonites, rerouted by oral historians: all a lie, it was now said. There were rumors of an amateur film (long-since disintegrated "safety" film that was no more stable than nitrate in the end)—exactly the kind of red herring "evidence" that indicated an urban legend at play. There had indeed been posters featuring an elephant named Mary, and several years later an odd play about hanging an elephant. But this was a play put on nowhere better than a circus, and it was apparent people had confused this with the truth. An elephant hanged? Papers were composed in the anthropology department of the University of Tennessee about the conflation of lynching narratives with that of an elephant. It was explained that the story evolved from a need to dehumanize the victims, or, in a contradictory interpretation, to enrage the very people who would never lift a finger to protect a fellow human being.

When facing the past, and attempting to do so squarely, it's difficult to understand what is marvelous, what is real, what is terrible, and what points overlap.

But there has been a recent development: Wildwood Hill, long ago surrounded by the blue fencing and tarpaulins of a Superfund site, has been purchased by the petrochemical combine that inherited the land in a deal with the vanished McKennon Railroad. There is a move to cap the area in advance of a toxic waste cleanup, and the first gesture is to dig wells into the hill's core, to test the soil for penetration of leeching chemicals.

Ten yards from the end of the tracks, under debris from six generations of abandoned railroad technology, is an excavation site twenty feet wide and twenty feet deep, scratched out of the clay almost a hundred years ago, and filled in again almost immediately. At the center, among the roots and weeds, the tiny stones and shards of broken glass and metal, lie elephant bones.

Caked with dirt, dark with dried tissues, they also gleam with a necklace of stainless-steel chain, and there is a shroud, once probably red, once likely ruffled and imperial, now as decayed and colorless as the dirt.

NOTE: This story could only have been written with the aid of *The Day They Hung the Elephant* by Charles Edwin Price.

The Bees

By DAN CHAON

*No hellhound hunts a man more implacably than
the memory of the son he once abandoned.*

Gene's son Frankie wakes up screaming. It has become frequent,
two or three times a week, at random times: midnight—three
AM—five in the morning. Here is a high, empty wail that severs
Gene from his unconsciousness like sharp teeth. It is the worst sound
that Gene can imagine, the sound of a young child dying violently—
falling from a building, or caught in some machinery that is tearing
an arm off, or being mauled by a predatory animal. No matter how

many times he hears it he jolts up with such images playing in his mind, and he always runs, thumping into the child's bedroom to find Frankie sitting up in bed, his eyes closed, his mouth open in an oval like a Christmas caroler. Frankie appears to be in a kind of peaceful trance, and if someone took a picture of him he would look like he was waiting to receive a spoonful of ice cream, rather than emitting that horrific sound.

"Frankie!" Gene will shout, and claps his hands hard in the child's face. The clapping works well. At this, the scream always stops abruptly, and Frankie opens his eyes, blinking at Gene with vague awareness before settling back down into his pillow, nuzzling a little before growing still. He is sound asleep; he is always sound asleep, though even after months Gene can't help leaning down and pressing his ear to the child's chest, to make sure he's still breathing, his heart is still going. It always is.

There is no explanation that they can find. In the morning, the child doesn't remember anything, and on the few occasions that they have managed to wake him in the midst of one of his screaming attacks, he is merely sleepy and irritable. Once, Gene's wife Karen shook him and shook him, until finally he opened his eyes, groggily. "Honey?" she said. "Honey? Did you have a bad dream?" But Frankie only moaned a little. "No," he said, puzzled and unhappy at being awakened, but nothing more.

They can find no pattern to it. It can happen any day of the week, any time of the night. It doesn't seem to be associated with diet, or with his activities during the day, and it doesn't stem, as far as they can tell, from any sort of psychological unease. During the day, he seems perfectly normal and happy.

They have taken him several times to the pediatrician, but the doctor seems to have little of use to say. There is nothing wrong with the child physically, Dr. Banerjee says. She advises that such things are not uncommon for children of Frankie's age group—he is five—and that more often than not, the disturbance simply passes away.

"He hasn't experienced any kind of emotional trauma, has he?" the doctor says. "Nothing out of the ordinary at home?"

"No, no," they both murmur, together. They shake their heads, and Dr. Banerjee shrugs.

"Parents," she says. "It's probably nothing to worry about." She gives them a brief smile. "As difficult as it is, I'd say that you may just have to weather this out."

But the doctor has never heard those screams. In the mornings after the "nightmares," as Karen calls them, Gene feels unnerved, edgy. He works as a driver for the United Parcel Service, and as he moves through the day after a screaming attack, there is a barely perceptible hum at the edge of his hearing, an intent, deliberate static sliding along behind him as he wanders through streets and streets in his van. He stops along the side of the road and listens. The shadows of summer leaves tremble murmurously against the windshield, and cars are accelerating on a nearby road. In the treetops, a cicada makes its trembly, pressure-cooker hiss.

Something bad has been looking for him for a long time, he thinks, and now, at last, it is growing near.

When he comes home at night everything is normal. They live in an old house in the suburbs of Cleveland, and sometimes after dinner they work together in the small patch of garden out in back of the house—tomatoes, zucchini, string beans, cucumbers—while Frankie plays with Legos in the dirt. Or they take walks around the neighborhood, Frankie riding his bike in front of them, his training wheels recently removed. They gather on the couch and watch cartoons together, or play board games, or draw pictures with crayons. After Frankie is asleep, Karen will sit at the kitchen table and study—she is in nursing school—and Gene will sit outside on the porch, flipping through a newsmagazine or a novel, smoking the cigarettes that he has promised Karen he will give up when he turns thirty-five. He is thirty-four now, and Karen is twenty-seven, and he is aware, more and more frequently, that this is not the life that he deserves. He has been incredibly lucky, he thinks. Blessed, as Gene's favorite cashier at the supermarket always says. "Have a blessed day," she says, when Gene pays the money and she hands him his receipt, and he feels as if she has sprinkled him with her ordinary, gentle beatitude. It reminds him of long ago, when an old nurse had held his hand in the hospital and said that she was praying for him.

Sitting out in his lawn chair, drawing smoke out of his cigarette, he thinks about that nurse, even though he doesn't want to. He thinks of the way she'd leaned over him and brushed his hair as he stared at her, imprisoned in a full body cast, sweating his way through withdrawal and DTs.

He had been a different person, back then. A drunk, a monster. At nineteen, he'd married the girl he'd gotten pregnant, and then had set about to slowly, steadily, ruining all their lives. When he'd abandoned them, his wife and son, back in Nebraska, he had been twenty-four, a danger to himself and others. He'd done them a favor by leaving, he thought, though he still felt guilty when he remembered it. Years later, when he was sober, he'd even tried to contact them. He wanted to own up to his behavior, to pay the back child-support, to apologize. But they were nowhere to be found. Mandy was no longer living in the small Nebraska town where they'd met and married, and there was no forwarding address. Her parents were dead. No one seemed to know where she'd gone.

Karen didn't know the full story. She had been, to his relief, uncurious about his previous life, though she knew he had some drinking days, some bad times. She knew that he'd been married before, too, though she didn't know the extent of it, didn't know that he had another son, for example, didn't know that he had left them one night, without even packing a bag, just driving off in the car, a flask tucked between his legs, driving east as far as he could go. She didn't know about the car crash, the wreck he should have died in. She didn't know what a bad person he'd been.

She was a nice lady, Karen. Maybe a little sheltered. And truth to tell, he was ashamed—and even scared—to imagine how she would react to the truth about his past. He didn't know if she would have ever really trusted him if she'd known the full story, and the longer they knew one another the less inclined he was to reveal it. He'd escaped his old self, he thought, and when Karen got pregnant, shortly before they were married, he told himself that now he had a chance to do things over, to do it better. They had purchased the house together, he and Karen, and now Frankie will be in kindergarten in the fall. He has come full circle, has come exactly to the point when his former life with Mandy and his son, DJ, had completely fallen apart. He looks up as Karen comes to the back door and speaks to him through the screen. "I think it's time for bed, sweetheart," she says softly, and he shudders off these thoughts, these memories. He smiles.

He's been in a strange frame of mind lately. The months of regular awakenings have been getting to him, and he has a hard time getting back to sleep after an episode with Frankie. When Karen wakes him in the morning, he often feels muffled, sluggish—as if he's hungover. He doesn't hear the alarm clock. When he stumbles out of bed, he finds he has a hard time keeping his moodiness in check. He can feel his temper coiling up inside him.

He isn't that type of person anymore, and hasn't been for a long while. Still, he can't help but worry. They say that there is a second stretch of craving, which sets in after several years of smooth sailing; five or seven years will pass, and then it will come back without warning. He has been thinking of going to A.A. meetings again, though he hasn't in some time—not since he met Karen.

It's not as if he gets trembly every time he passes a liquor store, or even as if he has a problem when he goes out with buddies and spends the evening drinking soda and nonalcoholic beer. No. The trouble comes at night, when he's asleep.

He has begun to dream of his first son. DJ. Perhaps it is related to his worries about Frankie, but for several nights in a row the image of DJ—aged about five—has appeared to him. In the dream, Gene is drunk, and playing hide-and-seek with DJ in the yard behind the Cleveland house where he is now living. There is the thick weeping willow out there, and Gene watches the child appear from behind it and run across the grass, happily, unafraid, the way Frankie would. DJ turns to look over his shoulder and laughs, and Gene stumbles after him, at least a six-pack's worth of good mood, a goofy, drunken dad. It's so real that when he wakes, he still feels intoxicated. It takes him a few minutes to shake it.

One morning after a particularly vivid version of this dream, Frankie wakes and complains of a funny feeling—"right here," he says—and points to his forehead. It isn't a headache, he says. "It's like bees!" he says. "Buzzing bees!" He rubs his hand against his brow. "Inside my head." He considers for a moment. "You know how the bees bump against the window when they get in the house and want to get out?" This description pleases him, and he taps his forehead lightly with his fingers, humming, "zzzzzzz," to demonstrate.

"Does it hurt?" Karen says.

"No," Frankie says. "It tickles."

Karen gives Gene a concerned look. She makes Frankie lie down on the couch, and tells him to close his eyes for a while. After a few minutes, he rises up, smiling, and says that the feeling has gone.

"Honey, are you sure?" Karen says. She pushes her hair back and slides her palm across his forehead. "He's not hot," she says, and Frankie sits up impatiently, suddenly more interested in finding a Matchbox car he dropped under a chair.

Karen gets out one of her nursing books, and Gene watches her face tighten with concern as she flips slowly through the pages. She is looking at Chapter Three: Neurological System, and Gene observes as she pauses here and there, skimming down a list of symptoms. "We should probably take him back to Dr. Banerjee again," she says. Gene nods, recalling what the doctor said about "emotional trauma."

"Are you scared of bees?" he asks Frankie. "Is that something that's bothering you?"

"No," Frankie says. "Not really."

When Frankie was three, a bee stung him above his left eyebrow. They had been out hiking together, and they hadn't yet learned that Frankie was "moderately allergic" to bee stings. Within minutes of the sting, Frankie's face had begun to distort, to puff up, his eye swelling shut. He looked deformed. Gene didn't know if he'd ever been more frightened in his entire life, running down the trail with Frankie's head pressed against his heart, trying to get to the car and drive him to the doctor, terrified that the child was dying. Frankie himself was calm.

Gene clears his throat. He knows the feeling that Frankie is talking about—he has felt it himself, that odd, feathery vibration inside his head. And in fact he feels it again, now. He presses the pads of his fingertips against his brow. Emotional trauma, his mind murmurs, but he is thinking of DJ, not Frankie.

"What are you scared of?" Gene asks Frankie, after a moment. "Anything?"

"You know what the scariest thing is?" Frankie says, and widens his eyes, miming a frightened look. "There's a lady with no head, and she went walking through the woods, looking for it. 'Give . . . me . . . back . . . my . . . head. . . .'"

"Where on earth did you hear a story like that!" Karen says.

"Daddy told me," Frankie says. "When we were camping."

Gene blushes, even before Karen gives him a sharp look. "Oh, great," she says. "Wonderful."

He doesn't meet her eyes. "We were just telling ghost stories," he says, softly. "I thought he would think the story was funny."

"My God, Gene," she says. "With him having nightmares like this? What were you thinking?"

It's a bad flashback, the kind of thing he's usually able to avoid. He thinks abruptly of Mandy, his former wife. He sees in Karen's face that look Mandy would give him when he screwed up. "What are you, some kind of idiot?" Mandy used to say. "Are you crazy?" Back then, Gene couldn't do anything right, it seemed, and when Mandy yelled at him it made his stomach clench with shame and inarticulate rage. I was trying, he would think, I was trying, damn it, and it was as if no matter what he did, it wouldn't turn out right. That feeling would sit heavily in his chest, and eventually, when things got worse, he hit her once. "Why do you want me to feel like shit," he had said through clenched teeth. "I'm not an asshole," he said, and when she rolled her eyes at him he slapped her hard enough to knock her out of her chair.

That was the time he'd taken DJ to the carnival. It was a Saturday, and he'd been drinking a little so Mandy didn't like it, but after all—he thought—DJ was his son, too, he had a right to spend some time with his own son, Mandy wasn't his boss even if she might think she was. She liked to make him hate himself.

What she was mad about was that he'd taken DJ on the Velocerator. It was a mistake, he'd realized afterward. But DJ himself had begged to go on. He was just recently four years old, and Gene had just turned twenty-three, which made him feel inexplicably old. He wanted to have a little fun.

Besides, nobody told him he couldn't take DJ on the thing. When he led DJ through the gate, the ticket-taker even smiled, as if to say, "Here is a young guy showing his kid a good time." Gene winked at DJ and grinned, taking a nip from a flask of peppermint schnapps. He felt like a good dad. He wished his own father had taken him on rides at the carnival!

The door to the Velocerator opened like a hatch in a big silver flying saucer. Disco music was blaring from the entrance and became louder as they went inside. It was a circular room with soft padded walls, and one of the workers had Gene and DJ stand with their backs to the wall, strapping them in side by side. Gene felt warm and expansive from the schnapps. He took DJ's hand, and he almost felt as if he were glowing with love. "Get ready, Kiddo," Gene whispered. "This is going to be wild."

The hatch door of the Velocerator sealed closed with a pressurized sigh. And then, slowly, the walls they were strapped to began to turn. Gene tightened on DJ's hand as they began to rotate, gathering speed. After a moment the wall pads they were strapped to slid up, and the force of velocity pushed them back, held to the surface of the spinning wall like iron to a magnet. Gene's cheeks and lips seemed to pull back, and the sensation of helplessness made him laugh.

At that moment, DJ began to scream. "No! No! Stop! Make it stop!" They were terrible shrieks, and Gene grabbed the child's hand tightly. "It's all right," he yelled jovially over the thump of the music. "It's okay! I'm right here!" But the child's wailing only got louder in response. The scream seemed to whip past Gene in a circle, tumbling around and around the circumference of the ride like a spirit, trailing echos as it flew. When the machine finally stopped, DJ was heaving with sobs, and the man at the control panel glared. Gene could feel the other passengers staring grimly and judgmentally at him.

Gene felt horrible. He had been so happy—thinking that they were finally having themselves a memorable father-and-son moment—and he could feel his heart plunging into darkness. DJ kept on weeping, even as they left the ride and walked along the midway, even as Gene tried to distract him with promises of cotton candy and stuffed animals. "I want to go home," DJ cried, and, "I want my mom! I want my mom!" And it had wounded Gene to hear that. He gritted his teeth.

"Fine!" he hissed. "Let's go home to your mommy, you little cry-baby. I swear to God, I'm never taking you with me anywhere again." And he gave DJ a little shake. "Jesus, what's wrong with you? Lookit, people are laughing at you. See? They're saying, 'Look at that big boy, bawling like a girl.'"

This memory comes to him out of the blue. He had forgotten all about it, but now it comes to him over and over. Those screams were not unlike the sounds Frankie makes in the middle of the night, and they pass repeatedly through the membrane of his thoughts, without warning. The next day, he finds himself recalling it again, the memory of the scream impressing his mind with such force that he actually has to pull his UPS truck off to the side of the road and put his face in his hands: Awful! Awful! He must have seemed like a monster to the child.

Sitting there in his van, he wishes he could find a way to contact them—Mandy and DJ. He wishes that he could tell them how sorry he is, and send them money. He puts his fingertips against his forehead, as cars drive past on the street, as an old man parts the curtains and peers out of the house Gene is parked in front of, hopeful that Gene might have a package for him.

Where are they? Gene wonders. He tries to picture a town, a house, but there is only a blank. Surely, Mandy being Mandy, she would have hunted him down by now to demand child support. She would have relished treating him like a deadbeat dad; she would have hired some company who would garnish his wages.

Now, sitting at the roadside, it occurs to him suddenly that they are dead. He recalls the car wreck that he was in, just outside Des Moines, and if he had been killed they would have never known. He recalls waking up in the hospital, and the elderly nurse who had said, "You're very lucky, young man. You should be dead."

Maybe they are dead, he thinks. Mandy and DJ. The idea strikes him a glancing blow, because of course it would make sense. The reason they'd never contacted him. Of course.

He doesn't know what to do with such premonitions. They are ridiculous, they are self-pitying, they are paranoid, but especially now, with their concerns about Frankie, he is at the mercy of his anxieties. He comes home from work and Karen stares at him heavily.

"What's the matter?" she says, and he shrugs. "You look terrible," she says.

"It's nothing," he says, but she continues to look at him skeptically. She shakes her head.

"I took Frankie to the doctor again today," she says, after a moment, and Gene sits down at the table with her, where she is spread out with her textbooks and notepaper.

"I suppose you'll think I'm being a neurotic mom," she says. "I think I'm too immersed in disease, that's the problem."

Gene shakes his head. "No, no," he says. His throat feels dry. "You're right. Better safe than sorry."

"Mmm," she says, thoughtfully. "I think Dr. Banerjee is starting to hate me."

"Naw," Gene says. "No one could hate you." With effort, he smiles gently. A good husband, he kisses her palm, her wrist. "Try not to worry," he says, though his own nerves are fluttering. He can hear Frankie in the backyard, shouting orders to someone.

"Who's he talking to?" Gene says, and Karen doesn't look up.

"Oh," she says. "It's probably just Bubba." Bubba is Frankie's imaginary playmate.

Gene nods. He goes to the window and looks out. Frankie is pretending to shoot at something, his thumb and forefinger cocked into a gun. "Get him! Get him!" Frankie shouts, and Gene stares out as Frankie dodges behind a tree. Frankie looks nothing like DJ, but when he pokes his head from behind the hanging foliage of the willow, Gene feels a little shudder—a flicker—something. He clenches his jaw.

"This class is really driving me crazy," Karen says. "Every time I read about a worst-case scenario, I start to worry. It's strange. The more you know, the less sure you are of anything."

"What did the doctor say this time?" Gene says. He shifts uncomfortably, still staring out at Frankie, and it seems as if dark specks circle and bob at the corner of the yard. "He seems okay?"

Karen shrugs. "As far as they can tell." She looks down at her textbook, shaking her head. "He seems healthy." He puts his hand gently on the back of her neck and she lolls her head back and forth against his fingers. "I've never believed that anything really terrible could happen to me," she had once told him, early in their marriage, and it had scared him. "Don't say that," he'd whispered, and she laughed.

"You're superstitious," she said. "That's cute."

He can't sleep. The strange presentiment that Mandy and DJ are dead has lodged heavily in his mind, and he rubs his feet together underneath the covers, trying to find a comfortable posture. He can hear the soft ticks of the old electric typewriter as Karen finishes her paper for school, words rattling out in bursts that remind him of some sort of insect language. He closes his eyes, pretending to be asleep when Karen finally comes to bed, but his mind is ticking with small, scuttling images: his former wife and son, flashes of the photographs he didn't own, hadn't kept. They're dead, a firm voice in his mind says, very distinctly. They were in a fire. And they burned up. It is not quite his own voice that speaks to him, and abruptly he can picture the burning house. It's a trailer, somewhere on the outskirts of a small town, and the black smoke is pouring out of the open door. The plastic window frames have warped and begun to melt, and the smoke billows from the trailer into the sky in a way that reminds him of an old locomotive. He can't see inside, except for crackling bursts of deep orange flames, but he's aware that they're inside. For a second he can see DJ's face, flickering, peering steadily from the window of the burning trailer, his mouth open in a unnatural circle, as if he's singing.

He opens his eyes. Karen's breathing has steadied, she's sound asleep, and he carefully gets out of bed, padding restlessly through the house in his pajamas. They're not dead, he tries to tell himself, and stands in front of the refrigerator, pouring milk from the carton into his mouth. It's an old comfort, from back in the days when he was drying out, when the thick taste of milk would slightly calm his craving for a drink. But it doesn't help him now. The dream, the vision, has frightened him badly, and he sits on the couch with an afghan over his shoulders, staring at some science program on television. On the program, a lady scientist is examining a mummy. A child. The thing is bald—almost a skull but not quite. A membrane of ancient skin is pulled taut over the eyesockets. The lips are stretched back, and there are small, chipped, rodent-like teeth. Looking at the thing, he can't help but think of DJ again, and he looks over his shoulder, quickly, the way he used to.

The last year that he was together with Mandy, there used to be times when DJ would actually give him the creeps—spook him. DJ had been an unusually skinny child, with a head like a baby bird and long, bony feet, with toes that seemed strangely extended, as if they were meant for gripping. He can remember the way the child would slip barefoot through rooms, slinking, sneaking, watching, Gene had thought, always watching him.

It is a memory that he has almost, for years, succeeded in forgetting, a memory he hates and mistrusts. He was drinking heavily at the time, and he knows now that alcohol had grotesquely distorted his perceptions. But now that it has been dislodged, that old feeling moves through him like a breath of smoke. Back then, it had seemed to him that Mandy had turned DJ against him, that DJ had in some strange way almost physically transformed into something that wasn't Gene's real son. Gene can remember how, sometimes, he would be sitting on the couch, watching TV, and he'd get a funny feeling. He'd turn his head and DJ would be at the edge of the room, with his bony spine hunched and his long neck craned, staring with those strangely oversized eyes. Other times, Gene and Mandy would be arguing and DJ would suddenly slide into the room, creeping up to Mandy and resting his head on her chest, right in the middle of some important talk. "I'm thirsty," he would say, in imitation baby-talk. Though he was five years old, he would playact this little tod-dler voice. "Mama," he would say. "I is firsty." And DJ's eyes would rest on Gene for a moment, cold and full of calculating hatred.

Of course, Gene knows now that this was not the reality of it. He knows: He was a drunk, and DJ was just a sad, scared little kid, try-ing to deal with a rotten situation. Later, when he was in detox, these memories of his son made him actually shudder with shame, and it was not something he could bring himself to talk about even when he was deep into his twelve steps. How could he say how repulsed he'd been by the child, how actually frightened he was. Jesus Christ, DJ was a poor wretched five-year-old kid! But in Gene's memory there was something malevolent about him, resting his head pettishly on his mother's chest, talking in that singsong, lisping voice, staring hard and unblinking at Gene with a little smile. Gene remembers catching DJ by the back of the neck. "If you're going to talk, talk normal," Gene had whispered through his teeth, and tightened his fingers on the child's neck. "You're not a baby. You're not fooling anybody." And DJ had actually bared his teeth, making a thin, hiss-ing whine.

He wakes and he can't breathe. There is a swimming, suffocating sensation of being stared at, being watched by something that hates him, and he gasps, choking for air. A lady is bending over him, and for a moment he expects her to say, "You're very lucky, young man. You should be dead."

But it's Karen. "What are you doing?" she says. It's morning, and he struggles to orient himself—he's on the living room floor, and the television is still going.

"Jesus," he says, and coughs. "Oh, Jesus." He is sweating, his face feels hot, but he tries to calm himself in the face of Karen's horrified stare. "A bad dream," he says, trying to control his panting breaths. "Jesus," he says, and shakes his head, trying to smile reassuringly for her. "I got up last night and I couldn't sleep. I must have passed out while I was watching TV."

But Karen just gazes at him, her expression frightened and uncertain, as if something about him is transforming. "Gene," she says. "Are you all right?"

"Sure," he says, hoarsely, and a shudder passes over him involuntarily. "Of course." And then he realizes that he is naked. He sits up, covering his crotch self-consciously with his hands, and glances around. He doesn't see his underwear or his pajama bottoms anywhere nearby. He doesn't even see the afghan, which he had draped over him on the couch while he was watching the mummies on TV. He starts to stand up, awkwardly, and he notices that Frankie is standing there in the archway between the kitchen and the living room, watching him, his arms at his sides like a cowboy who is ready to draw his holstered guns.

"Mom?" Frankie says. "I'm thirsty."

He drives through his deliveries in a daze. The bees, he thinks. He remembers what Frankie had said a few mornings before, about bees inside his head, buzzing and bumping against the inside of his forehead like a windowpane they were tapping against. That's the feeling he has now. All the things that he doesn't quite remember are circling and alighting, vibrating their cellophane wings insistently. He sees himself striking Mandy across the face with the flat of his hand, knocking her off her chair; he sees his grip tightening around the back of DJ's thin, five-year-old neck, shaking him as he grimaced and wept; and he is aware that there are other things, perhaps even worse, if he thought about it hard enough. All the things that he'd prayed that Karen would never know about him.

He was very drunk on the day that he left them, so drunk that he can barely remember. It was hard to believe that he'd made it all the way to Des Moines on the interstate before he went off the road, tumbling end over end, into darkness. He was laughing, he thought, as the car crumpled around him, and he has to pull his van over to the side of the road, out of fear, as the tickling in his head intensifies. There is an image of Mandy, sitting on the couch as he stormed out, with DJ cradled in her arms, one of DJ's eyes swollen shut and puffy. There is an image of him in the kitchen, throwing glasses and beer bottles onto the floor, listening to them shatter.

And whether they are dead or not, he knows that they don't wish him well. They would not want him to be happy—in love with his wife and child. His normal, undeserved life.

When he gets home that night, he feels exhausted. He doesn't want to think anymore, and for a moment, it seems that he will be allowed a small reprieve. Frankie is in the yard, playing contentedly. Karen is in the kitchen, making hamburgers and corn on the cob, and everything seems okay. But when he sits down to take off his boots, she gives him an angry look.

"Don't do that in the kitchen," she says, icily. "Please. I've asked you before."

He looks down at his feet: one shoe unlaced, half-off. "Oh," he says. "Sorry."

But when he retreats to the living room, to his recliner, she follows him. She leans against the door frame, her arms folded, watching as he releases his tired feet from the boots and rubs his hand over the bottom of his socks. She frowns heavily.

"What?" he says, and tries on an uncertain smile.

She sighs. "We need to talk about last night," she says. " I need to know what's going on."

"Nothing," he says, but the stern way she examines him activates his anxieties all over again. "I couldn't sleep, so I went out to the living room to watch TV. That's all."

She stares at him. "Gene," she says after a moment. "People don't usually wake up naked on their living room floor, and not know how they got there. That's just weird, don't you think?"

Oh, please, he thinks. He lifts his hands, shrugging—a posture of innocence and exasperation, though his insides are trembling. "I know," he says. "It was weird to me, too. I was having nightmares. I really don't know what happened."

She gazes at him for a long time, her eyes heavy. "I see," she says, and he can feel the emanation of her disappointment like waves of heat. "Gene," she says. "All I'm asking is for you to be honest with me. If you're having problems, if you're drinking again, or thinking about it. I want to help. We can work it out. But you have to be honest with me."

"I'm not drinking," Gene says, firmly. He holds her eyes, earnestly. "I'm not thinking about it. I told you when we met, I'm through with it. Really." But he is aware again of an observant, unfriendly presence, hidden, moving along the edge of the room. "I don't understand," he says. "What is it? Why would you think I'd lie to you?"

She shifts, still trying to read something in his face, still, he can tell, doubting him. "Listen," she says, at last, and he can tell she is trying not to cry. "Some guy called you today. A drunk guy. And he said to tell you that he had a good time hanging out with you last night, and that he was looking forward to seeing you again soon." She frowns hard, staring at him as if this last bit of damning information will show him for the liar he is. A tear slips out of the corner of her eye and along the bridge of her nose. Gene feels his chest tighten.

"That's crazy," he says. He tries to sound outraged, but he is in fact suddenly very frightened. "Who was it?"

She shakes her head, sorrowfully. "I don't know," she says. "Something with a 'B.' He was slurring so badly I could hardly understand him. B.B. or B.J. or . . ."

Gene can feel the small hairs on his back prickling. "Was it DJ?" he says, softly.

And Karen shrugs, lifting a now teary face to him. "I don't know!" she says, hoarsely. "I don't know. Maybe." And Gene puts his palms across his face. He is aware of that strange, buzzing, tickling feeling behind his forehead.

"Who is DJ?" Karen says. "Gene, you have to tell me what's going on."

But he can't. He can't tell her, even now. Especially now, he thinks, when to admit that he'd been lying to her ever since they met would confirm all the fears and suspicions she'd been nursing for—what?—days? weeks?

"He's someone I used to know a long time ago," Gene tells her. "Not a good person. He's the kind of guy who might . . . call up, and get a kick out of upsetting you."

They sit at the kitchen table, silently watching as Frankie eats his hamburger and corn on the cob. Gene can't quite get his mind around it. DJ, he thinks, as he presses his finger against his hamburger bun, but doesn't pick it up. DJ. He would be fifteen by now. Could he, perhaps, have found them? Maybe stalking them? Watching the house? Gene tries to fathom how DJ might have been causing Frankie's screaming episodes. How he might have caused what happened last night—snuck up on Gene while he was sitting there watching TV and drugged him or something. It seems far-fetched.

"Maybe it was just some random drunk," he says at last, to Karen. "Accidentally calling the house. He didn't ask for me by name, did he?"

"I don't remember," Karen says, softly. "Gene . . ."

And he can't stand the doubtfulness, the lack of trust in her expression. He strikes his fist hard against the table, and his plate clatters in a circling echo. "I did not go out with anybody last night!" he says. "I did not get drunk! You can either believe me, or you can . . ."

They are both staring at him. Frankie's eyes are wide, and he puts down the corncob he was about to bite into, as if he doesn't like it anymore. Karen's mouth is pinched.

"Or I can what?" she says.

"Nothing," Gene breathes.

There isn't a fight, but a chill spreads through the house, a silence. She knows that he isn't telling her the truth. She knows that there's more to it. But what can he say? He stands at the sink, gently washing the dishes as Karen bathes Frankie and puts him to bed. He waits, listening to the small sounds of the house at night. Outside, in the yard, there is the swing set, and the willow tree—silver-gray and stark in the security light that hangs above the garage. He waits for a while longer, watching, half-expecting to see DJ emerge from behind the tree as he'd done in Gene's dream, creeping along, his bony hunched back, the skin pulled tight against the skull of his oversized head. There is that smothering, airless feeling of being watched, and Gene's hands are trembling as he rinses a plate under the tap.

When he goes upstairs at last, Karen is already in her night-gown, in bed, reading a book.

"Karen," he says, and she flips a page, deliberately.

"I don't want to talk to you until you're ready to tell me the truth," she says. She doesn't look at him. "You can sleep on the couch, if you don't mind."

"Just tell me," Gene says. "Did he leave a number? To call him back?"

"No," Karen says. She doesn't look at him. "He just said he'd see you soon."

He thinks that he will stay up all night. He doesn't even wash up, or brush his teeth, or get into his bedtime clothes. He just sits there on the couch, in his uniform and stocking feet, watching television with the sound turned low, listening. Midnight. One AM.

He goes upstairs to check on Frankie, but everything is okay. Frankie is asleep with his mouth open, the covers thrown off. Gene stands in the doorway, alert for movement, but everything seems to be in place. Frankie's turtle sits motionless on its rock, the books are lined up in neat rows, the toys put away. Frankie's face tightens and untightens as he dreams.

Two AM. Back on the couch, Gene startles, half-asleep as an ambulance passes in the distance, and then there is only the sound of crickets and cicadas. Awake for a moment, he blinks heavily at a rerun of *Bewitched,* and flips through channels. Here is some jewelry for sale. Here is someone performing an autopsy.

In the dream, DJ is older. He looks to be nineteen or twenty, and he walks into a bar where Gene is hunched on a stool, sipping a glass of beer. Gene recognizes him right away—his posture, those thin shoulders, those large eyes. But now, DJ's arms are long and muscu-lar, tattooed. There is a hooded, unpleasant look on his face as he ambles up to the bar, pressing in next to Gene. DJ orders a shot of Jim Beam—Gene's old favorite.

"I've been thinking about you a lot, ever since I died," DJ mur-murs. He doesn't look at Gene as he says this, but Gene knows who he is talking to, and his hands are shaky as he takes a sip of beer.

"I've been looking for you for a long time," DJ says, softly, and the air is hot and thick. Gene puts a trembly cigarette to his mouth and breathes on it, choking on the taste. He wants to say, I'm sorry. Forgive me. But he can't breathe. DJ shows his small, crooked teeth, staring at Gene as he gulps for air.

"I know how to hurt you," DJ whispers.

Gene opens his eyes, and the room is full of smoke. He sits up, disoriented: For a second he is still in the bar with DJ before he realizes that he's in his own house.

There is a fire somewhere: he can hear it. People say that fire "crackles," but in fact it seems like the amplified sound of tiny creatures eating, little wet mandibles, thousands and thousands of them, and then a heavy, whispered whoof, as the fire finds another pocket of oxygen.

He can hear this, even as he chokes blindly in the smoky air. The living room has a filmy haze over it, as if it is atomizing, fading away, and when he tries to stand up it disappears completely. There is a thick membrane of smoke above him, and he drops again to his hands and knees, gagging and coughing, a thin line of vomit trickling onto the rug in front of the still chattering television.

He has the presence of mind to keep low, crawling on his knees and elbows underneath the thick, billowing fumes. "Karen!" he calls. "Frankie!" but his voice is swallowed into the white noise of diligently licking flame. "Ach," he chokes, meaning to utter their names.

When he reaches the edge of the stairs he sees only flames and darkness above him. He puts his hands and knees on the bottom steps, but the heat pushes him back. He feels one of Frankie's action figures underneath his palm, the melting plastic adhering to his skin, and he shakes it away as another bright burst of flame reaches out of Frankie's bedroom for a moment. At the top of the stairs, through the curling fog he can see the figure of a child watching him grimly, hunched there, its face lit and flickering. Gene cries out, lunging into the heat, crawling his way up the stairs, to where the bedrooms are. He tries to call to them again, but instead, he vomits.

There is another burst that covers the image that he thinks is a child. He can feel his hair and eyebrows shrinking and sizzling against his skin as the upstairs breathes out a concussion of sparks. He is aware that there are hot, floating bits of substance in the air, glowing orange and then winking out, turning to ash. The air is thick with angry buzzing, and that is all he can hear as he slips, turning end over end down the stairs, the humming and his own voice, a long vowel wheeling and echoing as the house spins into a blur.

And then he is lying on the grass. Red lights tick across his opened eyes in a steady, circling rhythm, and a woman, a paramedic, lifts her lips up from his. He draws in a long, desperate breath.

"Shhhhh," she says, softly, and passes her hand along his eyes. "Don't look," she says.

But he does. He sees, off to the side, the long black plastic sleeping bag, with a strand of Karen's blonde hair hanging out from the top. He sees the blackened, shriveled body of a child, curled into a fetal position. They place the corpse into the spread, zippered plastic opening of the body bag, and he can see the mouth, frozen, calcified, into an oval. A scream.

Catskin

By KELLY LINK

The witch had made her children what they were—literally. But when her blood cried out for revenge, only one had the wit and courage to undo her murderer.

Cats went in and out of the witch's house all day long. The windows stayed open, and the doors, and there were other doors, cat-sized and private, in the walls and up in the attic. The cats were large and sleek and silent. No one knew their names, or even if they had names, except for the witch.

Some of the cats were cream-colored and some were brindled. Some were black as beetles. They were about the witch's business.

Some came into the witch's bedroom with live things in their mouths. When they came out again, their mouths were empty.

The cats trotted and slunk and leapt and crouched. They were busy. Their movements were catlike, or perhaps clockwork. Their tails twitched like hairy pendulums. They paid no attention to the witch's children.

The witch had three living children at this time, although at one time she had had dozens, maybe more. No one, certainly not the witch, had ever bothered to tally them up. But at one time the house had bulged with cats and babies.

Now, since witches cannot have children in the usual way—their wombs are full of straw or bricks or stones, and when they give birth, they give birth to rabbits, kittens, tadpoles, houses, silk dresses, and yet even witches must have heirs, even witches wish to be mothers—the witch had acquired her children by other means: she had stolen or bought or made them.

She'd had a passion for children with a certain color of red hair. Twins she had never been able to abide (they were the wrong kind of magic) although she'd sometimes attempted to match up sets of children, as though she had been putting together a chess set, and not a family. If you were to say *a witch's chess set,* instead of *a witch's family,* there would be some truth in that. Perhaps this is true of other families as well.

One girl she had grown like a cyst, upon her thigh. Other children she had made out of things in her garden, or bits of trash that the cats brought her: aluminum foil with strings of chicken fat still crusted to it, broken television sets, cardboard boxes that the neighbors had thrown out. She had always been a thrifty witch.

Some of these children had run away and others had died. Some of them she had simply misplaced, or accidentally left behind on buses. It is to be hoped that these children were later adopted into good homes, or reunited with their natural parents. If you are looking for a happy ending in this story, then perhaps you should stop reading here and picture these children, these parents, their reunions.

*   *   *

Are you still reading? The witch, up in her bedroom, was dying. She had been poisoned by an enemy, a witch, a man named Lack. The child Finn, who had been her food taster, was dead already and so were three cats who'd licked her dish clean. The witch knew who had killed her and she snatched pieces of time, here and there, from the business of dying, to make her revenge. Once the question of this revenge had been settled to her satisfaction, the shape of it like a black ball of twine in her head, she began to divide up her estate between her three remaining children.

Flecks of vomit stuck to the corners of her mouth, and there was a basin beside the foot of the bed which was full of black liquid. The room smelled like cats' piss and wet matches. The witch panted as if she were giving birth to her own death.

"Flora shall have my automobile," she said, "and also my purse, which will never be empty, so long as you always leave a coin at the bottom, my darling, my spendthrift, my profligate, my drop of poison, my pretty, pretty Flora. And when I am dead, take the road outside the house and go west. There's one last piece of advice."

Flora, who was the oldest of the witch's living children, was redheaded and stylish. She had been waiting for the witch's death for a long time now, although she had been patient. She kissed the witch's cheek and said, "Thank you, Mother."

The witch looked up at her, panting. She could see Flora's life, already laid out, flat as a map. Perhaps all mothers can see as far.

"Jack, my love, my bird's nest, my bite, my scrap of porridge," the witch said, "you shall have my books. I won't have any need of books where I am going. And when you leave my house, strike out in an an easterly direction and you won't be any sorrier than you are now."

Jack, who had once been a little bundle of feathers and twigs and eggshell all tied up with a tatty piece of string, was a sturdy lad, almost full grown. If he knew how to read, only the cats knew it. But he nodded and kissed his mother, one kiss on each staring eye, and one on her gray lips.

"And what shall I leave to my boy Small?" the witch said, convulsing. She threw up again in the basin. Cats came running, leaning on the lip of the basin to inspect her vomitus. The witch's hand dug into Small's leg.

"Oh, it is hard, hard, so very hard, for a mother to leave her children (though I have done harder things). Children need a mother, even such a mother as I have been." She wiped at her eyes, and yet it is a fact that witches cannot cry.

Small, who still slept in the witch's bed, was the youngest of the witch's children. (Perhaps not as young as you think.) He sat upon the bed, and although he didn't cry, it was only because witches' children have no one to teach them the use of crying. His heart was breaking.

Small was ten years old and he could juggle and sing and every morning he brushed and plaited the witch's long, silky hair. Surely every mother must wish for a boy like Small, a curly-headed, sweet-breathed, tenderhearted boy like Small, who can cook a fine omelet, and who has a good strong singing voice as well as a gentle hand with a hairbrush.

"Mother," he said, "if you must die, then you must die. And if I can't come along with you, then I'll do my best to live and make you proud. Give me your hairbrush to remember you by, and I'll go make my own way in the world."

"You shall have my hairbrush, then," said the witch to Small, looking, and panting, panting. "And I love you best of all. You shall have my tinderbox and my matches, and also my revenge, and you will make me proud, or I don't know my own children."

"What shall we do with the house, Mother?" said Jack. He said it as if he didn't care.

"When I am dead," the witch said, "this house will be of no use to anyone. I gave birth to it—that was a very long time ago—and raised it from just a dollhouse. Oh, it was the most dear, most darling dollhouse ever. It had eight rooms and a tin roof, and a staircase that went nowhere at all. But I nursed it and rocked it to sleep in a cradle, and it grew up to be a real house, and see how it has taken care of me, its parent, how it knows a child's duty to its mother. And perhaps you can see how it is now, how it pines, how it grows sick to see me dying like this. Leave it to the cats. They'll know what to do with it."

*   *   *

All this time the cats have been running in and out of the room, bringing things and taking things away. It seems as if they will never slow down, never come to rest, never nap, never have the time to sleep, or to die, or even to mourn. They have a certain proprietary look about them, as if the house is already theirs.

The witch vomits up mud, fur, glass buttons, tin soldiers, trowels, hat pins, thumbtacks, love letters (mislabeled or sent without the appropriate amount of postage and never read), and a dozen regiments of red ants, each ant as long and wide as a kidney bean. The ants swim across the perilous stinking basin, clamber up the sides of the basin, and go marching across the floor in a shiny ribbon. They are carrying pieces of time in their mandibles. Time is heavy, even in such small pieces, but the ants have strong jaws, strong legs. Across the floor they go, and up the wall, and out the window. The cats watch, but don't interfere. The witch gasps and coughs and then lies still. Her hands beat against the bed once and then are still. Still the children wait, to make sure that she is dead, and that she has nothing else to say.

In the witch's house, the dead are sometimes quite talkative.

But the witch has nothing else to say at this time.

The house groans and all the cats begin to mew piteously, trotting in and out of the room as if they have dropped something and must go and hunt for it—they will never find it—and the children, at last, suddenly know how to cry, but the witch is perfectly still and quiet. There is a tiny smile on her face, as if everything has happened exactly to her satisfaction. Or maybe she is looking forward to the next part of the story.

The children buried the witch in one of her half-grown dollhouses. They crammed her into the downstairs parlor, and knocked out the inner walls so that her head rested on the kitchen table in the breakfast nook, and her ankles threaded through a bedroom door. Small brushed out her hair, and, because he wasn't sure what she should wear now that she was dead, he put all her dresses on her, one over the other over the other, until he could hardly see her white limbs at all, beneath the stack of petticoats and coats and dresses. It didn't matter: Once they'd nailed the dollhouse shut again, all they could see was the red crown of her head in the kitchen window, and the worn-down heels of her dancing shoes knocking against the shutters of the bedroom window.

Jack, who was handy, rigged a set of wheels for the dollhouse, and a harness so that it could be pulled. They put the harness on Small, and Small pulled and Flora pushed, and Jack talked and coaxed the house along, over the hill, down to the cemetery, and the cats ran along beside them.

T he cats are beginning to look a bit shabby, as if they are molting. Their mouths look very empty. The ants have marched away, through the woods, and down into town, and they have built a nest on your yard, out of the bits of time. And if you hold a magnifying glass over their nest, to see the ants dance and burn, Time will catch fire and you will be sorry.

O utside the cemetery gates, the cats had been digging a grave for the witch. The children tipped the dollhouse into the grave, kitchen window first. But then they saw that the grave wasn't deep enough, and the house sat there on its end, looking uncomfortable. Small began to cry (now that he'd learned how, it seemed he would spend all his time practicing), thinking how horrible it would be to spend one's death, all of eternity, upside down and not even properly buried, not even able to feel the rain when it beat down on the exposed shingles of the house, and seeped down into the house and filled your mouth and drowned you, so that you had to die all over again, every time it rained.

The dollhouse chimney had broken off and fallen on the ground. One of the cats picked it up and carried it away, like a souvenir. That cat carried the chimney into the woods and ate it, a mouthful at a time, and passed out of this story and into another one. It's no concern of ours.

The other cats began to carry up mouthfuls of dirt, dropping it and mounding it around the house with their paws. The children helped, and when they'd finished, they'd managed to bury the witch properly, so that only the bedroom window was visible, a little pane of glass like an eye at the top of a small dirt hill.

On the way home, Flora began to flirt with Jack. Perhaps she liked the way he looked in his funeral black. They talked about what they planned to be, now that they were grown-up. Flora wanted to find her parents. She was a pretty girl; someone would want to look after her. Jack said he would like to marry someone rich. They began to make plans.

Small walked a little behind, slippery cats twining around his ankles. He had the witch's hairbrush in his pocket, and his fingers slipped around the figured horn handle for comfort.

The house, when they reached it, had a dangerous, grief-stricken look to it, as if it was beginning to pull away from itself. Flora and Jack wouldn't go back inside. They squeezed Small lovingly, and asked if he wouldn't want to come along with them. He would have liked to, but who would have looked after the witch's cats, the witch's revenge? So he watched as they drove off together. They went north. What child has ever heeded a mother's advice?

J ack hasn't even bothered to bring along the witch's library: He says there isn't space in the trunk for everything. He'll rely on Flora and her magic purse.

S mall sat in the garden, and ate stalks of grass when he was hungry, and pretended that the grass was bread and milk and chocolate cake. He drank out of the garden hose. When it began to grow dark, he was lonelier than he had ever been in his life. The witch's cats were not good company. He said nothing to them and they had nothing to tell him, about the house, or the future, or the witch's revenge, or about where he was supposed to sleep. He had never slept anywhere except in the witch's bed, so at last he went back over the hill and down to the cemetery.

Some of the cats were still going up and down the grave, covering the base of the mound with leaves and grass, birds' feathers and their own loose fur. This looked strange, but it was a soft sort of nest to lie down on, Small discovered. The cats were still busy when he fell asleep—cats are always busy—cheek pressed against the cool glass of the bedroom window, hand curled in his pocket around the hairbrush, but in the middle of the night, when he woke up, he was swaddled, head to foot, in warm, grass-scented cat bodies.

A tail is curled around his chin like a scarf, and all the bodies are soughing breath in and out, whiskers and paws twitching, silky bellies rising and falling. All the cats are sleeping a frantic, exhausted, busy sleep, except for one, a white cat who sits near his head, looking down at him. Small has never seen this cat before, and yet he knows her, the way that you know the people who visit you in dreams: She's white everywhere, except for reddish tufts and frills at her ears and tail and paws, as if someone has embroidered her with fire around the edges.

"What's your name?" Small says. He's never talked to the witch's cats before.

The cat lifts a leg and licks herself in a private place. Then she looks at him. "You may call me Mother," she says.

But Small shakes his head. He can't call the cat that. Down under the blanket of cats, under the pane of window glass, the witch's Spanish heel is drinking in moonlight.

"Very well then, you may call me The Witch's Revenge," the cat says. Her mouth doesn't move, but he hears her speak inside his head. Her voice is furry and sharp, like a blanket made out of needles. "And you may comb my fur."

Small sits up, displacing sleepy cats, and lifts the brush out of his pocket. The bristles have left rows of little holes indented in the pink palm of his hand, like some sort of code. If he could read the code, it would say: Comb my fur.

Small combs the fur of The Witch's Revenge. There's grave dirt in the cat's fur, and one or two red ants, who drop and scurry away.

The Witch's Revenge bends her head down to the ground, snaps them up in her jaws. The heap of cats around them is yawning and stretching. There are things to do.

"You must burn her house down," The Witch's Revenge says. "That's the first thing."

Small's comb catches a knot, and The Witch's Revenge turns and nips him on the wrist. Then she licks him in the tender place between his thumb and his first finger. "That's enough," she says. "There's work to do."

So they all go back to the house, Small stumbling in the dark, moving farther and farther away from the witch's grave, the cats trotting along, their eyes lit like torches, twigs and branches in their mouths, as if they plan to build a nest, a canoe, a fence to keep the world out. The house, when they reach it, is full of lights, and more cats, and piles of tinder. The house is making a noise, like an instrument that someone is breathing into. Small realizes that all the cats are mewing, endlessly, as they run in and out the doors, looking for more kindling. The Witch's Revenge says, "First we must latch all the doors."

So Small shuts all the doors and windows on the first floor, and The Witch's Revenge shuts the catches on the secret doors, the cat doors, the doors in the attic, and up on the roof, and the cellar doors. Not a single secret door is left open. Now all the noise is on the inside, and Small and The Witch's Revenge are on the outside.

All the cats have slipped into the house through the kitchen door. There isn't a single cat in the garden. Small can see the witch's cats through the windows, arranging their piles of twigs. The Witch's Revenge sits beside him, watching. "Now light a match and throw it in," says The Witch's Revenge.

Small lights a match. He throws it in. What boy doesn't love to start a fire?

"Now shut the kitchen door," says The Witch's Revenge, but Small can't do that. All the cats are inside. The Witch's Revenge stands on her hind paws and pushes the kitchen door shut. Inside, the lit match catches something on fire. Fire runs along the floor and up the kitchen walls. Cats catch fire, and run into the other rooms of the house. Small can see all this through the windows. He stands with his face against the glass, which is cold, and then warm, and then hot.

Burning cats with burning twigs in their mouths press up against the kitchen door, and the other doors of the house, but all the doors are locked. Small and The Witch's Revenge stand in the garden and watch the witch's house and the witch's books and the witch's sofas and the witch's cooking pots and the witch's cats, her cats, too, all her cats burn.

You should never burn down a house. You should never set a cat on fire. You should never watch and do nothing while a house is burning. You should never listen to a cat who says to do any of these things. You should listen to your mother when she tells you to come away from watching, to go to bed, to go to sleep. You should listen to your mother's revenge.

You should never poison a witch.

In the morning, Small woke up in the garden. Soot covered him in a greasy blanket. The Witch's Revenge, white and red and clean-smelling, was curled up asleep on his chest. The witch's house was still standing, but the windows had melted and run down the front of the house.

The Witch's Revenge, waking, licked Small clean with her small sharkskin tongue. She demanded to be combed. Then she went into the house and came out, carrying a little bundle. It dangled, boneless, from her mouth, like a kitten.

It is a catskin, Small sees, only there is no longer a cat inside it.

He picked it up and something shiny fell out of the loose light skin. It was a piece of gold, sloppy, slippery with fat. The

Witch's Revenge brought out dozens and dozens of catskins, and there was a gold piece in every skin. While Small counted his fortune, The Witch's Revenge bit off one of her own claws, and pulled one long witch hair out of the witch's comb. She sat up, like a tailor, cross-legged in the grass, and began to stitch up a bag, out of the many catskins.

Small shivered. There was nothing to eat for breakfast but grass, and the grass was black and cooked.

"Are you cold?" said The Witch's Revenge. She put the bag aside, and picked up another catskin, a fine black one. She slit a sharp claw down the middle. "We'll make you a warm suit."

She used the coat of a black cat, and the coat of a calico cat, and she put a trim around the paws, of gray and white striped fur.

While she did this, she said to Small, "Did you know that there was once a battle, fought on this very patch of ground?"

Small shook his head no.

"Wherever there's a garden," The Witch's Revenge said, scratching with one paw at the ground, "I promise you there are people buried down under it. Look here." She plucked up a little brown clot, put it in her mouth, and cleaned it with her tongue.

When she spat the little circle out again, Small saw it was an ivory regimental button. The Witch's Revenge dug more buttons out of the ground—as if buttons of ivory grew in the ground—and sewed them onto the catskin. She fashioned a hood with two eyeholes and a set of fine whiskers, and sewed four fine cat tails to the back of the suit, as if the one that grew there wasn't good enough for Small. She threaded a bell on each one. "Put this on," she said to Small.

H e does and the bells chime and The Witch's Revenge laughs. "You make a fine-looking cat," she says. "Any mother would be proud."

The inside of the catsuit is soft and a little sticky against Small's skin. When he puts the hood over his head, the world disappears. He can only see the vivid corners of it through the eyeholes—grass, gold, the cat who sits cross-legged, stitching up her sack of skins—and air seeps in, down at the loosely sewn seam, where the skin droops and sags over his chest and around the gaping buttons. Small holds his tails in his clumsy fingerless paw, like a handful of eels, and swings them back and forth to hear them ring. The sound of the bells and the sooty, cooked smell of the air, the warm stickiness of the suit, the feel of his new fur against the ground: He falls asleep and dreams that hundreds of ants come and lift him and gently carry him off to bed.

When Small tipped his hood back again, he saw that The Witch's Revenge had finished with her needle and thread. Small helped her fill the bag with the gold pieces. The Witch's Revenge stood up on her hind legs, took the bag between her paws, and swung it over her shoulders. The gold coins went sliding against each other, mewling and hissing. The bag dragged along the grass, picking up ash, leaving a green trail behind it. The Witch's Revenge strode along as if she were carrying a sack of air.

Small put the hood on again, and he got down on his hands and knees. And then he trotted after The Witch's Revenge. They left the garden gate wide open, and went into the forest, toward the house where the witch Lack lives.

The forest is smaller than it used to be. Small is growing, but the forest is shrinking. Trees have been cut down. Houses have been built. Lawns rolled, roads laid. The Witch's Revenge and Small walked alongside one of the roads. A school bus rolled by: The children inside looked out their windows and laughed when they saw The Witch's Revenge striding along, and at her heels, Small, in his catsuit. Small lifted his head and peered out of his eyeholes after the school bus.

"Who lives in these houses?" he asked The Witch's Revenge.

"That's the wrong question, Small," said The Witch's Revenge, looking down at him and striding along.

Miaow, the catskin bag says. Clink.

"What's the right question then?" Small said.

"Ask me who lives under the houses," The Witch's Revenge said.

Obediently, Small said, "Who lives under the houses?"

"What a good question!" said The Witch's Revenge. "You see, not everyone can give birth to their own house. Most people give birth to children instead. And when you have children, you need houses to put them in. So children and houses: most people give birth to the first and have to build the second. The houses, that is. A long time ago, when men and women were going to build a house, they would dig a hole first. And they'd make a little room—a little, wooden, one-room house—in the hole. And they'd steal, or buy, a boy or a girl to put in the house in the hole, to live there. And then they built their house over that first little house."

"Did they make a door in the lid of the little house?" Small said.

"They did not make a door," said The Witch's Revenge.

"But then how did the girl or the boy climb out?" Small said.

"The boy or the girl stayed in that little house," said The Witch's Revenge. "They lived there all their life, and they are living in those houses still, under the other houses where the people live, and the people who live in the houses above may come and go as they please, and they don't ever think about how there are little houses with children sitting in little rooms, under their feet."

"But what about the mothers and fathers?" Small asked. "Didn't they ever go looking for their boys and girls?"

"Ah," said The Witch's Revenge. "Sometimes they did and sometimes they didn't. And after all, who was living under *their* houses? But that was a long time ago. Now people mostly bury a cat when they build their house, instead of a child. That's why we call cats *house cats*. Which is why we must walk along smartly. As you can see, there are houses under construction here."

And so there are. They walk by clearings where men are digging little holes. First Small puts his hood back and walks on two legs, and then he puts on his hood again, and goes on all fours: He makes himself as small and slinky as possible, just like a cat. But the bells on his tails jounce and the coins in the bag that The Witch's Revenge carries go clink, miaow, and the men stop their work and watch them go by.

How many witches are there in the world? Have you ever seen one? Would you know a witch if you saw one? And what would you do if you saw one? For that matter, do you know a cat when you see one? Are you sure?

Small followed The Witch's Revenge. Small grew calluses on his knees and the pads of his fingers. He would have liked to carry the bag sometimes, but it was too heavy. How heavy? You would not have been able to carry it, either.

They drank out of streams. At night they opened the catskin bag and climbed inside to sleep, and when they were hungry they licked the coins, which seemed to sweat golden fat, and always more fat. As they went, The Witch's Revenge sang a song:

> I had no mother
> and my mother had no mother
> and her mother had no mother
> and her mother had no mother
> and her mother had no mother
> and you have no mother
> to sing you
> this song

The coins in the bag sang along, miaow, miaow, and the bells on Small's tails kept the rhythm.

Every night Small combs The Witch's Revenge's fur. And every morning The Witch's Revenge licks him all over, not neglecting the places behind his ears, and at the backs of his knees. And then he puts the catsuit back on, and she grooms him all over again.

Sometimes they were in the forest, and sometimes the forest became a town, and then The Witch's Revenge would tell Small stories about the people who lived in the houses, and the children who lived in the houses under the houses. Once, in the forest, The Witch's Revenge showed Small where there had once been a house.

Now there was only the stones of the foundation, covered in soft green moss, and the chimney stack, propped up with fat ropes and coils of ivy.

The Witch's Revenge rapped on the grassy ground, moving clockwise around the foundation, until both she and Small could hear a hollow sound.

The Witch's Revenge dropped to all fours and clawed at the ground, tearing it up with her paws and biting at it, until they could see a little wooden roof. The Witch's Revenge knocked on the roof, and Small lashed his tails nervously.

"Well," said The Witch's Revenge, "shall we take off the roof and let the poor child go?"

Small crept up close to the sunken roof. He put his ear against it and listened, but he heard nothing at all. "There's no one in there," he said.

"Maybe they're shy," said The Witch's Revenge. "Shall we let them out, or shall we leave them be?"

"Let them out!" said Small, but what he meant to say was, "Leave them alone!" Or maybe he said "Leave them be!" although he meant the opposite. The Witch's Revenge looked at him, and Small thought he heard something then—beneath him where he crouched, frozen—very faint: a scrabbling at the dirty, moldering roof.

Small sprang away. The Witch's Revenge picked up a stone and brought it down hard, caving the roof in. When they peered inside, there was nothing except blackness and a faint, dry smell. They waited, sitting on the ground, to see what might come out, but nothing came out, and after a while, The Witch's Revenge picked up her catskin bag, and they set off again.

For several nights after that, Small dreamed that someone, something, small and thin and cold and dirty, was following them. One night it crept away again, and Small never knew where it went. But if you come to that part of the forest, where they sat and waited by the stone foundation, perhaps you will meet the thing that they set free.

No one knew the reason for the quarrel between the witch Small's mother and the witch Lack, although the witch Small's mother had died for it. The witch Lack was a handsome man and he loved his children dearly. He had stolen them out of the cribs and beds of palaces and manors and harems. He dressed his children in silk, as befitted their station, and they wore gold crowns and ate off gold plates. They drank from cups of gold. Lack's children, it was said, lacked nothing.

Perhaps the witch Lack had made some remark about the way the witch Small's mother was raising her children, or perhaps the witch Small's mother had boasted of her children's red hair. But it might have been something else. Witches are proud and they like to quarrel.

When Small and The Witch's Revenge came at last to the house of the witch Lack, The Witch's Revenge said to Small, "Look at this monstrosity! I've produced finer turds and buried them under leaves. And the smell, like an open sewer! How can his neighbors stand the stink?"

Male witches have no wombs, and must come by their houses in other ways, or else buy them from female witches. But Small thought it was a very fine house. There was a prince or a princess at each window staring down at him, as he sat on his haunches in the driveway, beside The Witch's Revenge. He said nothing, but he missed his brothers and sisters.

"Come along," said The Witch's Revenge. "We'll go a little ways off and wait for the witch Lack to come home."

Small followed The Witch's Revenge back into the forest, but in a little while, two of the witch Lack's children came out of the house, carrying baskets made of gold. They went into the forest as well and began to pick blackberries.

The Witch's Revenge and Small sat in the briar and watched.

Small was thinking of his brothers and sisters. He thought of the taste of blackberries, the feel of them in his mouth, which was not at all like the taste of fat. Deep in the briar, the hood of his catsuit thrown back, he pressed his face against the briar, a berry plumped against his lips. The wind went through the briar and ruffled his fur and raised gooseflesh on his skin beneath the fur.

The Witch's Revenge nestled against the small of Small's back. She was licking down a lump of knotted fur at the base of his spine. The princesses were singing.

Small decided that he would live in the briar with The Witch's

Revenge. They would live on berries and spy on the children who came to pick them, and The Witch's Revenge would change her name. The name Mother was in his mouth, along with the sweet taste of the blackberries.

"Now you must go out," said The Witch's Revenge, "and be kittenish. Be playful. Chase your tail. Be shy, but don't be too shy. Don't talk to them. Let them pet you. Don't bite."

She pushed at Small's rump, and Small tumbled out of the briar, and sprawled at the feet of the witch Lack's children.

The Princess Georgia said, "Look! It's a dear little cat!"

Her sister Margaret said doubtfully, "But it has five tails. I've never seen a cat that needed so many tails. And its skin is done up with buttons and it's almost as large as you are."

Small, however, began to caper and prance. He swung his tails back and forth so that the bells rang out and then he pretended to be alarmed by this. First he ran away from his tails and then he chased his tails. The two princesses put down their baskets, half-full of blackberries, and spoke to him, calling him a silly puss.

At first he wouldn't go near them. But slowly he pretended to be won over. He allowed himself to be petted and fed blackberries. He chased a hair ribbon and he stretched out to let them admire the buttons up and down his belly. Princess Margaret's fingers tugged at his skin, then she slid one hand in between the loose catskin and Small's boy skin. He batted her hand away with a paw, and Margaret's sister Georgia said knowingly that cats didn't like to be petted on their bellies.

They were all good friends by the time The Witch's Revenge came out of the briar, standing on her hind legs and singing:

> *I have no children*
> *and my children*
> *have no children*
> *and their children*
> *have no children*
> *and their children*
> *have no whiskers*
> *and no tails*

At this sight, the Princesses Margaret and Georgia began to laugh and point. They had never heard a cat sing, or seen a cat walk on its hind legs. Small lashed his five tails furiously, and all the fur of the catskin stood up on his arched back, and they laughed at that too.

When they came back from the forest, with their baskets piled with berries, Small was stalking close at their heels, and The Witch's Revenge came walking just behind. But she left the bag of gold hidden in the briar.

That night, when the witch Lack came home, his hands were full of gifts for his children. One of his sons ran to meet him at the door and said, "Come and see what followed Margaret and Georgia home from the forest! Can we keep them?"

And the table had not been set for dinner, and the children of the witch Lack had not sat down to do their homework, and in the witch Lack's throne room, there was a cat with five tails, spinning in circles, while a second cat sat impudently upon his throne, and sang:

> *Yes!*
> *your father's house*
> *is the shiniest*
> *brownest largest*
> *the most expensive*
> *the sweetest-smelling*
> *house*
> *that has ever*
> *come out of*
> *anyone's*
> *ass*

The witch Lack's children began to laugh at this, until they saw the witch, their father, standing there. Then they fell silent. Small stopped spinning.

"You!" said the witch Lack.

"Me!" said The Witch's Revenge, and sprang from the throne. Before anyone knew what she was about, her jaws were fastened about the witch Lack's neck, and then she ripped out his throat. Lack opened his mouth to speak and his blood fell out, making The Witch's Revenge's fur more red, now, than white. The witch Lack fell down dead, and red ants went marching out of the hole in his neck and the hole of his mouth, and they held pieces of time in their jaws as tightly as The Witch's Revenge had held Lack's throat in hers. But she let Lack go and left him lying in his blood on the floor, and she snatched up the ants and ate them, quickly, as if she had been hungry for a very long time.

While this was happening, the witch Lack's children stood and watched and did nothing. Small sat on the floor, his tails curled about his paws. Children, all of them, they did nothing. They were too surprised. The Witch's Revenge, her belly full of ants and time, her mouth stained with blood, stood up and surveyed them.

"Go and fetch me my catskin bag," she said to Small.

Small found that he could move. Around him, the princes and princesses stayed absolutely still. The Witch's Revenge was holding them in her gaze.

"I'll need help," Small said. "The bag is too heavy for me to carry."

The Witch's Revenge yawned. She licked a paw and began to pat at her mouth. Small stood still.

"Very well," she said. "Take those big strong girls, the Princesses Margaret and Georgia, with you. They know the way."

The Princesses Margaret and Georgia, finding that they could move again, began to tremble. They gathered their courage and they went with Small, the two girls holding each other's hands, out of the throne room, not looking down at the body of their father, the witch Lack, and back into the forest.

Georgia began to weep, but the Princess Margaret said to Small: "Let us go!"

"Where will you go?" said Small. "The world is a dangerous place. There are people in it who mean you no good." He threw back his hood, and the Princess Georgia began to weep harder.

"Let us go," said the Princess Margaret. "My parents are the king and queen of a country not three days' walk from here. They will be glad to see us again."

Small said nothing. They came to the briar, and he sent the Princess Georgia in, to hunt for the catskin bag. She came out scratched and bleeding, the bag in her hand. It had caught on the briars and the end had ripped. Gold coins dripped out, like glossy drops of fat, falling on the ground.

"Your father killed my mother," said Small.

"And that cat, your mother's devil, will kill us, or worse," said Princess Margaret. "Let us go!"

Small lifted the catskin bag. There were no coins in it now. The Princess Georgia was on her hands and knees, scooping up coins and putting them into her pockets.

"Was he a good father?" Small asked.

"He thought he was," Princess Margaret said. "But I'm not sorry he's dead. When I grow up, I will be queen. I'll make a law to put all the witches in the kingdom to death, and all their cats, as well."

At this, Small became afraid. He took up the catskin bag and ran back to the house of the witch Lack, leaving the two princesses in the forest. And whether they made their way home to the Princess Margaret's parents, or whether they fell into the hands of thieves, or whether they lived in the briar, or whether the Princess Margaret grew up and kept her promise and rid her kingdom of witches and cats, Small never knew, and neither do I, and neither shall you.

When he came back into the witch Lack's house, The Witch's Revenge saw at once what had happened. "Never mind," she said.

There were no children, no princes and princesses, in the throne room. The witch Lack's body still lay on the floor, but The Witch's Revenge had skinned it like a coney, and sewn up the skin into a bag. The bag wriggled and jerked, the sides heaving as if the witch Lack were still alive somewhere inside. The Witch's Revenge held the witchskin bag in one hand, and with the other, she was stuffing a cat into the neck of the skin. The cat wailed as it went into the bag. The bag was full of wailing. But the discarded flesh of the witch Lack lolled, slack.

There was a little pile of gold crowns on the floor beside the flayed corpse, and transparent, papery things which blew about the room, on a current of air, surprised looks on the thin, shed faces.

Cats were hiding in the corners of the room, and under the

throne. "Go catch them," said The Witch's Revenge. "But leave the three prettiest alone."

"Where are the witch Lack's children?" Small said.

The Witch's Revenge nodded around the room. "As you see," she said, "I've slipped off their skins, and they were all cats underneath. They're as you see now, but if we were to wait a year or two, they would shed these skins as well and become something new. Children are always growing."

Small chased the cats around the room. They were fast, but he was faster. They were nimble, but he was nimbler. He had worn a catsuit for longer. He drove the cats down the length of the room, and The Witch's Revenge caught them and dropped them into her bag. At the end, there were only three cats left in the throne room, and they were as pretty a trio of cats as anyone could ask for. All the other cats were inside the bag.

"Well done, and quickly done, too," said The Witch's Revenge, and she took her needle and stitched shut the neck of the bag. The skin of the witch Lack smiled up at Small, and a cat put its head through his slack, stained mouth, wailing. But The Witch's Revenge sewed Lack's mouth shut too, and the hole on the other end, where a house had come out. She left only his earholes and his eyeholes and his nostrils, which were full of fur, rolled open so that the cats could breathe.

The Witch's Revenge slung the skin full of cats over her shoulder and stood up.

"Where are you going?" Small said.

"These cats have mothers and fathers," The Witch's Revenge said. "They have mothers and fathers who miss them very much."

She gazed at Small. He decided not to ask again. So he waited in the house, with the two princesses and the prince in their new catsuits, while The Witch's Revenge went down to the river. Or perhaps she took them down to the market and sold them. Or maybe she took each cat home, to its own mother and father, back to the kingdom where it had been born. Maybe she wasn't so careful to make sure that each child was returned to the right mother and father. After all, she was in a hurry, and cats look very much alike at night.

No one saw where she went: but the market is closer than the palaces of the kings and queens whose children had been stolen by the witch Lack, and the river is closer still.

When The Witch's Revenge came back to Lack's house, she looked around her. The house was beginning to stink very badly. Even Small could smell it now.

"I suppose the Princess Margaret let you fuck her," said The Witch's Revenge, as if she had been thinking about this while she ran her errands. "And that is why you let them go. I don't mind. She was a pretty puss. I might have let her go myself."

She looked at Small's face and saw that he was confused. "Never mind," she said.

She had a length of string in her paw, and a cork, which she greased with a piece of fat she had cut from the witch Lack. She threaded the cork on the string, calling it a good, quick little mouse, and greased the string as well, and she fed the wriggling cork to the tabby who had been curled up in Small's lap. And in a little while, when she had the cork again, she greased it again, and fed it to the little black cat, and then she fed it to the cat with two white forepaws, so that she had all three cats upon her string.

She sewed up the rip in the catskin bag, and Small put the gold crowns in the bag, and it was nearly as heavy as it had been before. The Witch's Revenge carried the bag, and Small took the greased string, holding it in his teeth, so the three cats were forced to run along behind him, as they left the house of the witch Lack.

Small strikes a match, and he lights the house of the dead witch, Lack, on fire, as they leave. But shit burns slowly, if at all, and that house might be burning still, if someone hasn't gone and put it out. And maybe, someday, someone will go fishing in the river near that house, and hook their line on a bag full of princes and princesses, wet and sorry and wriggling in their catsuit skins—that's one way to catch a husband or a wife.

Small and The Witch's Revenge walked without stopping and the three cats came behind them. They walked until they reached a little village very near where the witch Small's mother had lived and there they settled down in a room The Witch's Revenge rented from a butcher. They cut the greased string, and bought a cage and hung it from a hook in the kitchen. They kept the three cats in it, but Small bought collars and leashes, and sometimes he put one of the cats on a leash and took it for a walk around the town.

Sometimes he wore his own catsuit, and went out prowling, but The Witch's Revenge used to scold him if she caught him dressed like that. There are country manners and there are town manners, and Small was a boy about town now.

The Witch's Revenge kept house. She cleaned and she cooked and she made Small's bed in the morning. Like all of the witch's cats, she was always busy. She melted down the gold crowns in a stewpot, and minted them into coins. She opened an account in a bank, and she enrolled Small in a private academy.

The Witch's Revenge wore a silk dress and gloves and a heavy veil, and ran her errands in a fine carriage, Small at her side. She bought a piece of land to build a house on, and she sent Small off to school every morning, no matter how he cried. But at night she took off her clothes and slept on his pillow and he combed her red and white fur.

Sometimes at night, she twitched and moaned, and when he asked her what she was dreaming, she said, "There are ants! Can't you comb them out? Be quick and catch them if you love me."

But there were never any ants.

One day when Small came home, the little cat with the white front paws was gone. When he asked The Witch's Revenge, she said that the little cat had fallen out of the cage and through the open window and into the garden and before The Witch's Revenge could think what to do, a crow had swooped down and carried the little cat off. They moved into their new house a few months later, and Small was always very careful when he went in and out the doorway, imagining the little cat, down there in the dark, under the doorstep, under his foot.

S mall got bigger. He didn't make any friends in the village, or at his school, but when you're big enough, you don't need friends.

One day while he and The Witch's Revenge were eating their dinner, there was a knock at the door. When he opened the door, there stood Flora and Jack, looking very shabby and thin. Jack looked more than ever like a bundle of sticks.

"Small!" said Flora. "How tall you've become!" She burst into tears, and wrung her beautiful hands. Jack said, looking at The Witch's Revenge, "And who are you?"

The Witch's Revenge said to Jack, "Who am I? I'm your mother's cat, and you're a handful of dry sticks in a suit two sizes too large. But I won't tell anyone if you won't tell, either."

Jack snorted at this, and Flora stopped crying. She began to look around the house, which was sunny and large and well appointed.

"There's room enough for both of you," said The Witch's Revenge, "if Small doesn't mind."

Small thought his heart would burst with happiness to have his family back again. He showed Flora to one bedroom and Jack to another. And then they went downstairs and had a second dinner, and Small and The Witch's Revenge listened, and the cats in their hanging cage listened, while Flora and Jack recounted their adventures.

A pickpocket had taken Flora's purse, and they'd sold the witch's automobile, and lost the money in a game of cards. Flora had found her parents, but they were a pair of old scoundrels who had no use for her. (She was too old to sell again. She would have realized what they were up to.) She'd gone to work in a department store, and Jack had sold tickets in a movie theater. They'd quarreled and made up, and then fallen in love with other people, and had many disappointments. At last they had decided to go home to the witch's house and see if it would do for a squat, or if there was anything left to carry away and sell.

But the house, of course, had burned down. As they argued about what to do next, Jack had smelled Small, his brother, down in the village. So here they were.

"You'll live here, with us," Small said.

Jack and Flora said they could not do that. They had ambitions, they said. They had plans. They would stay for a week, or two weeks, and then they would be off again. The Witch's Revenge nodded and said that this was sensible.

Every day Small came home from school and went out again, with Flora, on a bicycle built for two. Or he stayed home and Jack taught him how to hold a coin between two fingers, and how to follow the egg as it moved from cup to cup. The Witch's Revenge taught them to play bridge, although Flora and Jack couldn't be partners. They quarreled with each other as if they were husband and wife.

"What do you want?" Small asked Flora one day. He was leaning against her, wishing he were still a cat, and could sit in her lap. She smelled of secrets. "Why do you have to go away again?"

Flora patted Small on the head. She said, "What do I want? To never have to worry about money. I want to marry a man and know that he'll never cheat on me, or leave me." She looked at Jack as she said this.

Jack said, "I want a rich wife who won't talk back, who doesn't lie in bed all day, with the covers pulled up over her head, weeping and calling me a bundle of twigs." And he looked at Flora when he said this.

The Witch's Revenge put down the sweater that she was knitting for Small. She looked at Flora and she looked at Jack and then she looked at Small.

Small went into the kitchen and opened the door of the hanging cage. He lifted out the two cats and brought them to Flora and Jack. "Here," he said. "A husband for you, Flora, and a wife for Jack. A prince and a princess, and both of them beautiful, and well brought up, and wealthy, no doubt."

Flora picked up the little tomcat and said, "Don't tease at me, Small! Whoever heard of marrying a cat!"

The Witch's Revenge said, "The trick is to keep their catskins in a safe hiding place. And if they sulk, or treat you badly, sew them back into their catskin and put them into a bag and throw them in the river."

Then she took her claw and slit the skin of the tabby-colored cat-suit, and Flora was holding a naked man. Flora shrieked and dropped him on the ground. He was a handsome man, well made, and he had a princely manner. He was not a man whom anyone would ever mistake for a cat. He stood up and made a bow, very elegant, for all that he was naked. Flora blushed, but she looked pleased.

"Go fetch some clothes for the prince and the princess," The Witch's Revenge said to Small. When he got back, there was a naked princess hiding behind the sofa, and Jack was leering at her.

A few weeks after that, there were two weddings, and then Flora left with her new husband, and Jack went off with his new wife. Perhaps they lived happily ever after.

The Witch's Revenge said to Small, that night at dinner, "We have no wife for you."

Small shrugged. "I'm still too young," he said.

But try as hard as he can, Small is getting older now. The catskin barely fits across his shoulders. The buttons strain when he fastens them. His grown-up fur—his people fur—is coming in. At night he has dreams.

The witch his mother's Spanish heel beats against the pane of glass. The princess hangs in the briar. She's holding up her dress, so he can see the cat fur down there. Now she's under the house. She wants to marry him, but the house will fall down if he kisses her. He and Flora are children again, in the witch's house. Flora lifts up her skirt and says, See my pussy? There's a cat down there, peeking out at him, but it doesn't look like any cat he's ever seen. He says to Flora, I have a pussy too. But his isn't the same.

At last he knows what happened to the little, starving, naked thing in the forest, where it went. It crawled into his catskin, while he was asleep, and then burrowed into his own skin, and now it is nestled in his chest, still cold and lonely and hungry. It is eating him from the inside, and getting bigger, and one day there will be no Small left at all, only that nameless, hungry child, wearing a Small skin.

Small moans in his sleep.

There are ants in The Witch's Revenge's skin, leaking out of her seams, and they march down into the sheets and pinch at him, down in his private places, down where his fur is growing in, and it hurts, it aches and aches. He dreams that The Witch's Revenge wakes now, and comes and licks him all over, until the pain melts, the pane of glass melts, and the ants march away again, on their long, greased thread.

"What do you want?" says The Witch's Revenge.

Small is no longer dreaming. He says, "I want my mother!"

Light from the moon comes down through the window over their bed. The Witch's Revenge is very beautiful—she looks like a queen, like a knife, like a burning house, a cat—in the moonlight. Her fur shines. Her whiskers stand out like pulled stitches, wax, and thread. The Witch's Revenge says, "Your mother is dead."

"Take off your skin," Small says. He's crying and The Witch's Revenge licks his tears away. Small's skin pricks all over, and down under the house, something small wails and wails. "Give me back my mother," he says.

"What if I'm not as beautiful as you remember?" says his mother, the witch, The Witch's Revenge. "I'm full of ants. Take off my skin, and all the ants will spill out, and there will be nothing left of me."

Small says, "Why have you left me all alone?"

His mother the witch says, "I've never left you alone, not even for a minute. I sewed up my death in a catskin so I could stay with you."

"Take it off! Let me see you!" Small says.

The Witch's Revenge shakes her head and says, "Tomorrow night. Ask me again, tomorrow night. How can you ask me for such a thing, and how can I say no to you? Do you know what you're asking me for?"

All night long, Small combs his mother's fur. His fingers are looking for the seams in her catskin. When The Witch's Revenge yawns, he peers inside her mouth, hoping to catch a glimpse of his mother's face. He can feel himself becoming smaller and smaller. In the morning he will be so small that when he tries to put his catskin on, he can barely do up the buttons. He'll be so small, so sharp, you might mistake him for an ant, and when The Witch's Revenge yawns, and opens her mouth, he'll creep inside, he'll go down into her belly, he'll go find his mother. If he can, he will help his mother cut her catskin open so that she can get out again, and if she won't come out, then he won't either. He thinks he'll live there, the way that sailors sometimes live inside the belly of fish who have eaten them, and keep house for his mother inside the house of her skin.

This is the end of the story. The Princess Margaret grows up to kill witches and cats. If she doesn't, then someone else will have to do it. There is no such thing as witches, and there is no such thing as cats, either, only people dressed up in catskin suits. They have their reasons, and who is to say that they might not live that way, happily ever after, until the ants have carried away all of the time that there is, to build something new and better out of it?

How Carlos Webster Changed His Name to Carl and Became a Famous Oklahoma Lawman

By ELMORE LEONARD

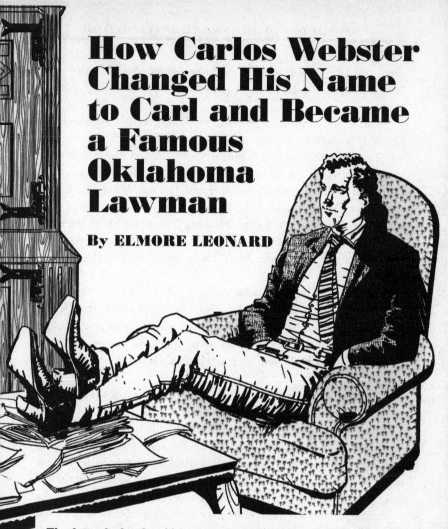

The fate of a bank-robbing murderer resided in two scoops of peach ice cream on top of a sugar cone.

Carlos Webster was fifteen years old the time he witnessed the robbery and murder at Deering's drugstore. It was in the summer of 1921. He told Bud Maddox, the Okmulgee chief of police, he had driven a load of cows up to the yard at Tulsa and by the time he got back it was dark. He said he left the stock trailer across the street from Deering's and went inside to get an ice-cream cone. When he identified one of the robbers as Frank Miller, Bud Maddox said, "Son, Frank Miller robs banks, he don't bother with drugstores no more."

Carlos had been raised on hard work and respect for his elders. He said, "I could be wrong," knowing he wasn't.

They brought him over to police headquarters in the courthouse to look at photos. He pointed to Frank Miller staring at him from a $500 wanted bulletin and picked the other one, Jim Ray Monks, from mug shots. Bud Maddox said, "You're positive, huh?" and asked Carlos which one was it shot the Indian. Meaning Junior Harjo with the tribal police, who'd walked in not knowing the store was being robbed.

"Was Frank Miller shot him," Carlos said, "with a .45 Colt."

"You sure it was a Colt?"

"Navy issue, like my dad's."

"I'm teasing," Bud Maddox said. He and Carlos's dad, Virgil Webster, were buddies, both having fought in the Spanish-American War, and for a number of years were the local heroes; but now doughboys were back from France telling about the Great War over there.

"If you like to know what I think happened," Carlos said, "Frank Miller only came in for a pack of smokes."

Bud Maddox stopped him. "Tell it from the time you got there."

Okay, well, the reason was to get an ice-cream cone. "Mr. Deering was in back doing prescriptions—he looked out of that little window and told me to help myself. So I went over to the soda fountain and scooped up a double dip of peach on a sugar cone and went up to the cigar counter and left a nickel by the cash register. That's where I was when I see these two men come in wearing suits and hats I thought at first were salesmen. Mr. Deering calls to me to wait on them as I know the store pretty well. Frank Miller comes up to the counter—"

"You knew right away who he was?"

"Once he was close, yes sir, from pictures of him in the paper. He said to give him a deck of Luckies. I did and he picks up the nickel I'd left by the register. Hands it to me and says, 'This ought to cover it.'"

"You tell him it was yours?"

"No, sir."

"Or a pack of Luckies was fifteen cents?"

"I didn't argue with him. But see, I think that's when he got the idea of robbing the store, the cash register sitting there, nobody around but me holding my ice-cream cone. Mr. Deering never came out from the back. The other one, Jim Ray Monks? He wanted a tube of Unguentine, he said, for a heat rash was bothering him, under his arms. I got it for him and he didn't pay either. Then Frank Miller says, 'Let's see what you have in the register.' I told him I didn't know how to open it as I didn't work there. He leans over the counter and points to a key—a man who knows his cash registers—and says, 'That one right there. Hit it and she'll open for you.' I press the key—Mr. Deering must've heard it ring open, he calls from the back of the store, 'Carlos, you able to help them out?' Frank Miller raised his voice, saying, 'Carlos is doing fine,' using my name. He told me then to take out the scrip but leave the change."

"How much did he get?"

"No more'n fifty dollars," Carlos said. He took his time thinking about what happened right after, starting with Frank Miller looking at his ice-cream cone. Carlos saw it as personal, something between him and Frank Miller, so he skipped over it, telling Bud Maddox:

"I put the money on the counter for him, mostly singles. I look up—"

"Junior Harjo walks in," Bud Maddox said, "a robbery in progress."

"Yes sir, but Junior doesn't know it. Frank Miller's at the counter with his back to him. Jim Ray Monks is over at the soda fountain getting into the ice cream. Neither of them had their guns out, so I doubt Junior saw it as a robbery. But Mr. Deering sees Junior and calls out he's got his mother's medicine. Then says for all of us to hear, 'She tells me they got you raiding stills, looking for moonshine.' He said something about setting a jar aside for him and that's all I heard. Now the guns are coming out, Frank Miller's Colt from inside his suit . . . I guess all he had to see was Junior's badge and his sidearm, that was enough, Frank Miller shot him. He'd know with that Colt one round would do the job, but he stepped up and shot Junior again, lying on the floor."

There was a silence.

"I'm trying to recall," Bud Maddox said, "how many Frank Miller's killed. I believe six, half of 'em police officers."

"Seven," Carlos said, "you count the bank hostage had to stand on his running board. Fell off and broke her neck?"

"I just read the report on that one," Bud Maddox said. "Was a Dodge Touring, same as Black Jack Pershing's staff car over in France."

"They drove away from the drugstore in a LaSalle," Carlos said, and gave Bud Maddox the license number.

Here was the part Carlos saw as personal and had skipped over, beginning with Frank Miller looking at his ice-cream cone.

Then asking, "What is that, peach?" Carlos said it was and Frank Miller reached out his hand, saying, "Lemme have a bite there," and took the cone to hold it away from him as it was starting to drip. He bent over to lick it a couple of times before putting his mouth around a big bite he took from the top dip. He said, "Mmmmm, that's good," with a trace of peach ice cream along the edge of his mustache. Frank Miller stared at Carlos then like he was studying his features and began licking the cone again. He said, "Carlos, huh?" cocking his head to one side. "You got the dark hair, but you don't look like any Carlos to me. What's your other name?"

"Carlos Huntington Webster, that's all of 'em."

"It's a lot of name for a boy," Frank Miller said. "So you're part greaser on your mama's side, huh? What's she, Mex?"

Carlos hesitated before saying, "Cuban. I was named for her dad."

"Cuban's the same as Mex," Frank Miller said. "You got greaser blood in you, boy, even if it don't show much. You come off lucky there." He licked the cone again, holding it with the tips of his fingers, the little finger sticking out in a dainty kind of way.

Carlos, fifteen years old but as tall as this man with the ice cream on his mustache, wanted to call him a dirty name and hit him in the mouth as hard as he could, then go over the counter and bulldog him to the floor the way he'd put a bull calf down to brand and cut off its balls. Fifteen years old but he wasn't stupid. He held on while his heart beat against his chest. He felt the need to stand up to this man, saying finally, "My dad was on the battleship *Maine* when she was blown up in Havana Harbor, February 15, 1898. He survived and fought the dons with Huntington's Marines in that war in Cuba and met my mother, Graciaplena. When the war was over he went back and brought her to Oklahoma when it was still Indian territory. She died having me, so I never knew her. I never met my dad's mother, either. She's part Northern Cheyenne, lives on a reservation out at Lame Deer, Montana," saying it in a voice that was slow and calm compared to what he felt inside. Saying, "What I want to ask you— if having Indian blood *too,* makes me something else besides a greaser." Saying it in Frank Miller's face, causing this man with ice cream on his mustache to squint at him.

"For one thing," Frank Miller said, "the Indian blood makes you and your daddy breeds, him more'n you." He kept staring at Carlos as he raised the cone, his little finger sticking out, Carlos thinking to lick it again, but what he did was toss the cone over his shoulder, not looking or caring where it would land.

It hit the floor in front of Junior Harjo just then walking in, badge on his tan shirt, revolver on his hip, and Carlos saw the situation turning around. He felt the excitement of these moments but with some relief, too. It picked him up and gave him the nerve to say to Frank Miller, "Now you're gonna have to clean up your mess." Except Junior wasn't pulling his .38; he was looking at the ice cream on the linoleum and Mr. Deering was calling to him about his mother's medicine and about raiding stills and Frank Miller was turning from the counter with the Colt in his hand, firing, shooting Junior Harjo and stepping closer to shoot him again.

There was no sign of Mr. Deering. Jim Ray Monks came over to have a look at Junior. Frank Miller laid his Colt on the glass counter, picked up the cash in both hands, and shoved the bills into his coat pockets before looking at Carlos again.

"You said something to me. Geronimo come in and you said something sounded smart-aleck."

Carlos said, "What'd you kill him for?" still looking at Junior on the floor.

"I want to know what you said to me."

Frank Miller waited.

Carlos looked up, rubbing the back of his hand across his mouth. "I said, 'Now you'll have to clean up your mess.' The ice cream on the floor."

"That's all?"

"It's what I said."

Frank Miller kept looking at him. "You had a gun you'd of shot me, huh? Calling you a greaser. Hell, it's a law of nature, you got any of that blood in you you're a greaser. I can't help it, it's how it is. Being a breed on top of it—I don't know if that's called anything or not. But you could pass if you want, you look enough white. Hell, call yourself Carl, I won't tell on you."

C arlos and his dad lived in a big new house Virgil said was a California bungalow, off the road and into the pecan trees, a house that was all porch across the front and windows in the steep slant of the roof, a house built last year with oil money—those derricks pumping away on a back section of the property. The rest of it was graze and over a thousand acres of pecan trees, Virgil's pride, land gathered over twenty years since coming home from Cuba. He could let the trees go and live high off his oil checks, never work again as long as he lived. Nothing doing—harvesttime Virgil was out with his crew shaking pecan trees. He had Carlos seeing to the cows, a hundred or so head of cross-Brahmas at a time feeding till the day they were shipped to market.

When Carlos got back from a haul Virgil would be sitting on the porch with a bottle of Mexican beer. Prohibition was no bother; Virgil had a steady supply of beer, tequila, and mescal brought up through Texas by the oil people, part of the deal.

The night he witnessed the robbery and murder Carlos sat with his old dad and told him the whole story, including what he'd left out of his account to Bud Maddox, even telling about the ice cream on Frank Miller's mustache. Carlos was anxious to know if his dad thought he might've caused Junior Harjo to get shot. "I don't see how," Virgil said, "from what you told me. I don't know why you'd even think of it, other than you were right there and what you're wondering is if you could've prevented him from getting shot."

Virgil Webster was forty-six years old, a widower since Graci-aplena died in aught-six giving him Carlos and requiring Virgil to look for a woman to nurse the child. He found Narcissa Raincrow, sixteen, a pretty little Creek girl, daughter of Johnson Raincrow, deceased, an outlaw so threatening peace officers shot him while he was asleep. Narcissa had lost her own child giving birth, wasn't married, and Virgil hired her on as a wet nurse. By the time little Carlos had lost interest in her breasts, Virgil had acquired an appreciation. It wasn't long after Narcissa became their housekeeper she was sleeping in Virgil's bed. She cooked good, put on some weight but was still pretty, listened to Virgil's stories and laughed when she was supposed to. Carlos loved her, had fun talking to her about Indian ways, and her murderous dad, but never called her anything but Narcissa. Carlos liked the idea of being part Cuban; he saw himself wearing a panama hat when he was older.

He said to his dad that night on the dark porch, "Are you thinking I should've done something?"

"Like what?"

"Yell at Junior it's a robbery? No, I had to say something smart to Frank Miller. I was mad and wanted to get back at him somehow."

"For taking your ice-cream cone?"

"For what he said."

"What part was it provoked you?"

"What *part*? What he said about being a greaser."

"You or your mama?"

"Both. And calling me and you breeds."

Virgil said, "You let that bozo get to you? Probably can't read nor write, the reason he has to rob banks. Jesus Christ, get some sense." He swigged his Mexican beer and said, "I know what you mean though, how you felt."

"What would you have done?"

"Same as you, nothing," Virgil said. "But if you're talking about in my time, when I was still a marine? I'd of shoved the ice-cream cone up his goddamn nose."

*   *   *

Three days later sheriff's deputies spotted the LaSalle in the back-yard of a farmhouse near Checotah, the house belonging to a woman by the name of Faye Harris. Her former husband, Olin "Skeet" Harris, deceased, shot dead in a gun battle with U.S. marshals, had at one time been a member of the Frank Miller Gang. The deputies waited for marshals to arrive, as apprehending armed fugitives was their specialty. The marshals slipped into the house at first light, fed the dog, tiptoed into Faye's bedroom, and got the drop on Frank Miller before he could dig his Colt from under the pillow. Jim Ray Monks went out a window, started across the barn lot, and caught a load of double-aught that put him down. The two were brought to Okmulgee and locked up to await trial.

Carlos said to his dad, "Boy, those marshals know their stuff, don't they? Armed killer—they shove a gun in his ear and yank him out of bed."

He was certain he'd be called to testify and was anxious, couldn't wait. He told his dad he intended to look directly at Frank Miller as he described the cold-blooded killing. Virgil advised him not to say any more than he had to. Carlos said he wondered if he should mention the ice cream on Frank Miller's mustache.

"Why would you want to?" Virgil said.

"Show I didn't miss anything."

"You know how many times the other night you told me about the ice cream on his mustache?" Virgil said. "I'm thinking three or four times."

"You had to see it. Here's this Frank Miller everybody's scared of, doesn't know enough to wipe his mouth."

"I'd forget that," Virgil said. "He shot a lawman in cold blood. That's all you need to remember about him."

A month passed and then another, Carlos becoming fidgety. Virgil found out why it was taking so long, came home to Narcissa putting supper on the table, Carlos sitting there, and told them the delay was caused by other counties wanting to get their hands on Frank Miller. So the matter was given to a district court judge to rule on, each county laying out its case, sounding like they'd make a show out of trying him. "His Honor got our prosecutor to offer Frank Miller a deal. Plead guilty to murder in the second degree, the motive self-defense as the victim was armed, and give him ten to fifty years. That would be the end of it, no trial needed. In other words," Virgil said, "your Frank Miller will get sent to McAlester and be out in five years."

"There was nothing self-defense about it," Carlos said. "Junior wasn't even looking at him when he got shot." Carlos sounding like he was in pain.

"You don't know the system," Virgil said. "The deal worked 'cause Junior's Creek, or else Cherokee. He was a white man Frank Miller'd be doing twenty-five to life."

Another event of note took place that same year, 1921, toward the end of October and late in the afternoon, dusk settling in the orchards. Carlos shot and killed a cattle thief by the name of Wally Tarwater.

Virgil's first thought: It was on account of Frank Miller. The boy was ready this time and from now on would always be ready.

He phoned the undertaker, who came with sheriff's people, and pretty soon two deputy U.S. marshals arrived, Virgil knowing them as serious lawmen in their dark suits and the way they cocked their soft felt hats down on their eyes. The marshals took over, the one who turned out to be the talker saying this Wally Tarwater—now lying in the hearse—was wanted on federal charges of running off livestock and crossing state lines to sell to meat packers. He said to Carlos to go on and tell in his own words what happened.

Virgil saw Carlos start to grin just a little, about to make some remark like, "You want it in my own words?" and cut him off quick with, "Don't tell no more'n you have to. These people want to get home to their families."

Well, it began with Narcissa saying she felt like a rabbit stew, or squirrel if that's all was out there. "I thought it was too late in the day," Carlos said, "but took a twenty-gauge and went out in the orchard. The pecans had been harvested, most of 'em, so you could see through the trees good."

"Get to it," Virgil said. "You see this fella out in the pasture driving off your cows."

"On a cutting horse," Carlos said. "You could tell this cowboy knew how to work beef. I got closer and watched him, admiring the way he bunched the animals without wearing himself out. I went back to the house and exchanged the twenty-gauge for a Winchester, then went to the barn and saddled up. She's right over there, the claybank? The sorrel's his."

The marshal, the one who talked, said, "You went back to get a rifle but don't know yet who he is?"

"I knew it wasn't a friend stealing my cows. He's driving them down towards the Deep Fork bottom where a road comes in there. I nudge Suzie out among the cows still grazing, got close enough to call to him, 'Can I help you?'" Carlos started to smile. "He says, 'Thanks for offering but I'm done here.' I told him he sure was and to get down from his horse. He started to ride away and I fired one in the air to bring him around. I move closer but kept my distance, not knowing what he had under his slicker. By now he sees I'm young, he says, 'I'm picking up cows I bought off your daddy.' I tell him I'm the cattle outfit here, my dad grows pecans. All he says is, 'Jesus, quit chasing me, boy, and go on home.' Now he opens his slicker to let me see the six-shooter on his leg. And now way off past him a good four hundred yards, I notice the stock trailer, a man standing there by the load ramp."

"You can make him out," the marshal who did the talking said, "from that distance?"

"If he says it," Virgil told the marshal, "then he did."

Carlos waited for the marshals to look at him before saying, "The cowboy starts to ride off and I call to him to wait a second. He reins and looks back. I said, 'But you try to ride off with my stock I'll shoot you.'"

"You spoke to him like that?" the talker said. "How old are you?"

"Going on sixteen. The same age as my dad when he joined the marines."

The quiet marshal spoke for the first time. He said, "So this fella rode off on you . . . ?"

"Yes, sir. Once I see he isn't gonna turn my cows, and he's

approaching the stock trailer by now, I shot him." Carlos dropped his tone, saying, "I meant to wing him, put one in the edge of that yellow slicker . . . I should've stepped down 'stead of firing from the saddle. I sure didn't mean to hit him square. I see the other fella jump in the truck, doesn't care his partner's on the ground. He goes to drive off and tears the ramp from the trailer. It was empty, no cows aboard. What I did was fire at the hood of the truck to stop it and the fella jumped out and ran for the trees."

The talkative marshal spoke up. "You're doing all this shooting from four hundred yards?" He glanced toward the Winchester leaning against a pecan tree. "No scope on your rifle?"

"You seem to have trouble with the range," Virgil said to him. "Step out there about a hundred yards and hold up a live snake by its tail. My boy'll shoot its head off for you."

"I believe it," the quiet marshal said.

He brought a card from his vest pocket and handed it between the tips of his fingers to Virgil. He said, "Mr. Webster, I'd be interested to know what your boy sees himself doing in five or six years."

Virgil looked at the card and then handed it to Carlos, meeting his eyes for a second. "You want you can ask him," Virgil said, watching Carlos reading the card that bore the deputy's name, R.C. "Bob" Cardell, and a marshal's star in gold you could feel. "I tell him join the marines and see foreign lands, or get to love pecans if you want to stay home." He could see Carlos moving his thumb over the embossed star on the card. "Tell you the truth, I don't think he knows yet what he wants to be when he grows up," Virgil said to the marshal, and to Carlos, "Isn't that right?"

Carlos raised his head.

"Sir, were you speaking to me?"

Later on Virgil was in the living room reading the paper. He heard Carlos come down from upstairs and said, "Will Rogers is appearing at the Hippodrome next week, with the Follies. You want to go see him?"

Carlos had his hand on his stomach. "I don't feel so good. I upchucked my supper."

Virgil lowered the newspaper to look at his boy. He said, "You took a man's life today," and watched Carlos nod his head thinking about it. "You never said, but did you look at him laying there?"

"I got down to close his eyes."

"Made you think, huh?"

"It did. I wondered why he didn't believe I'd shoot."

"He saw you as a kid on a horse."

"He knew stealing cows could get him shot or sent to prison. I mean anytime, but it's what he chose to do."

"That's what you thought looking at him? You didn't feel any sympathy for the man?"

"I did; I felt if he'd listened to me he wouldn't be lying there dead."

The room was silent, and now Virgil asked, "How come you didn't shoot the other one?"

"There weren't any cows on the trailer," Carlos said, "else I might've."

It was his son's quiet tone that got to Virgil and made him realize, My Lord, but this boy has a hard bark on him.

II

June 13, 1927, Carlos Huntington Webster, now a six-footer, was in Oklahoma City wearing a new light-gray suit of clothes and a panama with the brim curved on his eyes just right, staying at a hotel, riding a streetcar for the first time, and being sworn in as a Deputy United States Marshal; while Lindbergh was being honored in New York City, tons of ticker tape dumped on the Lone Eagle for flying across the ocean; and Frank Miller, released from McAlester in bib overalls, was back in Checotah with Faye Harris, his suit hanging in the closet these six years since the marshals hauled him off in his drawers. The first thing Frank Miller did, once he got off of Faye, was make phone calls to get his gang back together.

Carlos was given a leave to go home after his training and spent it with his old dad, telling him things:

What the room was like at the Huskin Hotel.

What he had to eat at the Plaza Grill.

How he saw a band called Walter Page's Blue Devils that was all colored guys.

How when firing a pistol you put your weight forward, one foot ahead of the other, so if you get hit you can keep firing as you fall.

And one other thing.

Everybody called him Carl instead of Carlos. At first he wouldn't answer to it and got in arguments, a couple of times almost fistfights.

"You remember Bob Cardell?"

"R.C. 'Bob' Cardell," Virgil said, "the quiet one."

"My boss now. He says, 'I know you're named for your grandaddy to honor him, but you're using it like a chip on your shoulder instead of a name.'"

Virgil was nodding his head. "Ever since that moron Frank Miller called you a greaser. I know what Bob means. Like, 'I'm Carlos Webster, what're you gonna do about it?' You were little I'd call you Carl sometimes. You liked it okay."

"Bob Cardell says, 'What's wrong with Carl? All it is, it's a nickname for Carlos.'"

"There you are," Virgil said. "Try it on."

"I've been wearing it the past month or so. 'Hi, I'm Deputy U.S. Marshal Carl Webster.'"

"You feel any different?"

"I do, but I can't explain it."

A call from Bob Cardell cut short Carl's leave. The Frank Miller Gang was back robbing banks.

What the marshals tried to do over the next few months was anticipate the gang's moves. They robbed banks in Shawnee, Seminole, and Bowlegs on a line south. Maybe Ada would be next. No, it turned out to be Coalgate.

An eyewitness said he was in the barbershop as Frank Miller was getting a shave—except the witness didn't know who it was till later, after the bank was robbed. "Him and the barber are talking, this one who's Frank Miller mentions he's planning on getting married pretty soon. The barber happens to be a minister of the Church of Christ and offers to perform the ceremony. Frank Miller says he might take him up on it and gives the reverend a five-dollar bill for the shave. Then him and his boys robbed the bank."

Coalgate was on that line south, but then they veered way over west to Kingfisher, took six thousand from the First National but lost a man: Jim Ray Monks, slow coming out of the bank on his bum legs, was shot down in the street. Before Monks knew he was dying he told them, "Frank's sore you never put more'n five hundred on his head. He's out to show he's worth a whole lot more."

The bank after Kingfisher was American National in Baxter Springs, way up on the Kansas line. The gang appeared to specialize in robbing banks in dinky towns, rush in with gunfire to get people's attention, and ride out with a hostage or two on the running board as a shield. Hit three or four banks in a row and then disappear for a time. There were reports of gang members spotted during these periods of lying low, but Frank Miller was never one of them.

"I bet anything," Carl said, standing before the wall map in Bob Cardell's office, "he hides out in Checotah, at Faye Harris's place."

"Where we nabbed him," Bob Cardell said, nodding, remembering. "Faye was just a girl then, wasn't she?"

"I heard Frank was already seeing her," Carl said, "while she's married to Skeet, only Skeet didn't have the nerve to call him on it."

"You heard, huh?"

"Sir, twice I drove down to McAlester on my day off, see what I could find out about Frank Miller."

"The convicts talk to you?"

"One did, a Creek use to be in his gang. He said it wasn't a marshal shot Skeet Harris in the gun battle that time. It was Frank Miller himself to get Skeeter out of the way so he could have his wife."

"You learned this on your own?"

"Yes, sir. It was after that witness in Coalgate said he spoke of getting married. I thought it must be to Faye—don't you think? I mean if he's so sweet on her he killed her husband? That's what tells me he hides out there."

Bob Cardell said, "Well, we been talking to people, watching every place he's known to frequent. Look it up, I'm sure Faye Harris is on the list."

"I did," Carl said. "She's checked off as having been questioned and deputies are keeping an eye on her place. But I doubt they do more than drive past, see if Frank Miller's drawers are hanging on the line."

"You're a marshal four months," Bob Cardell said, "and you know everything."

Carl didn't speak, Bob Cardell staring at him.

Bob Cardell saying after a few moments, "I recall the time you shot that cattle thief off his horse at four hundred yards." Bob Cardell saying after another silence but still holding Carl with his stare, "You have some kind of scheme you want to try."

"I've poked around and learned a few things about Faye Harris," Carl said, "where she used to live and all. I believe I can get her to talk to me."

Bob Cardell said, "How'd you get so sure of yourself?"

M arshals dropped Carl off a quarter mile from the house, turned the car around, and drove back to Checotah; they'd be at the Shady Grove Café. Carl was wearing work clothes and boots, his .38 Special holstered beneath a limp old suitcoat of Virgil's, a black one, his star in a pocket.

Walking the quarter mile his gaze held on this worn-out homestead, the whole dismal hundred and sixty looking deserted, the dusty Ford coupe in the backyard abandoned. Carl expected Faye Harris to be in no better shape than her property, living here like an outcast. The house did take on life as he mounted the porch, the voice of Uncle Dave Macon coming from a radio somewhere inside; and now Faye Harris was facing him through the screen, a girl in a silky nightgown that barely came to her knees, barefoot, but with rouge giving her face color and her blonde hair marcelled like a movie star's. . . .

You dumbbell, of *course* she hadn't let herself go, she was waiting for a man to come and marry her. Carl smiled, meaning it.

"Miz Harris, I'm Carl Webster." He kept looking at her face so she wouldn't think he was trying to see through her nightgown, which he could, easy. "I believe your mom's name is Atha Trudell? She worked at the Georgian Hotel in Henryetta doing rooms at one time and belonged to Eastern Star?"

It nudged her enough to say, "Yeah . . . ?"

"So'd my mom, Narcissa Webster?"

Faye shook her head.

"Your daddy was a coal miner up at Spelter, pit boss on the Little Gem. He lost his life that time she blew in '16. My dad was down in the hole laying track." Carl paused. "I was ten years old."

Faye said, "I just turned fifteen," her hand on the screen door to open it, but then hesitated. "Why you looking for me?"

"Lemme tell you what happened," Carl said. "I'm at the Shady Grove having a cup of coffee, the lady next to me at the counter says she works at a café serves way better coffee 'n here. Purity's, up at Henryetta."

Faye said, "What's her name?"

"She never told me."

"I use to work at Purity."

"I know, but wait," Carl said. "The way you came up in the conversation, the lady says her husband's a miner up at Spelter. I tell her my dad was killed there in '16. She says a girl at Purity lost her daddy in that same accident. She mentions knowing the girl's mom from Eastern Star, I tell her mine belonged too. The waitress behind the counter's pretending not to listen, but now she turns to us and says, 'The girl you're talking about lives right up the road there.'"

"I bet I know which one it was," Faye said. "She have kind of a Betty Boop hairstyle?"

"I believe so."

"What else she say?"

"You're a widow, lost your husband."

"She tell you marshals gunned him down?"

"Nothing about that."

"It's what everybody thinks. She mention any other names?"

What everybody thinks. Carl put that away and said, "No, she got busy serving customers."

"You live in Checotah?"

He told her Henryetta, he was visiting his old grandma about to pass. She asked him, "What's your name again?" He told her and she said, "Well, come on in, Carl, and have a glass of ice tea." Sounding now like she wouldn't mind company.

There wasn't much to the living room besides a rag rug on the floor and stiff black furniture, chairs and a sofa, their cane seats giving way from years of being sat on. The radio was playing in the kitchen. Faye went out there and pretty soon Carl could hear her chipping ice. He stepped over to a table laid out with magazines, *True Confession, Photoplay, Liberty, Dime Western,* one called *Spicy.* . . .

Her voice reached him, asking, "You like Gid Tanner?"

Carl recognized the radio music. He said, "Yeah, I do," as he looked at pictures in *Spicy* of girls doing housework in their underwear, one girl up on a ladder in teddies with a feather duster.

"Gid Tanner and his Skillet Lickers," Faye's voice said. "You know who I kinda like? That Al Jolson, he sure sounds like a nigger on that mammy song. But you want to know who my very favorite is?"

Carl said, "Jimmie Rodgers?" looking at pictures of Joan Crawford and Elissa Landi now in *Photoplay.*

"I like Jimmie o*kay.* . . . How many sugars?"

"Three'll do 'er. How about Uncle Dave Macon? He was on just a minute ago."

"'Take Me Back to My Old Carolina Home.' I don't care for the way he half-sings and half-talks a song. If you're a singer you oughta sing. No, my favorite's Maybelle Carter and the Carter Family. The pure loneliness she gets in her voice just tears me up."

"Must be how you feel," Carl said, "living out here."

She said, "Don't give it another thought."

"Sit here by yourself reading magazines . . ."

"Honey," Faye said, "you're not as cute as you think you are. Drink your ice tea and beat it."

"I'm sympathizing with you," Carl said. "The only reason I came, I wondered if you and I might even've known each other from funerals, and our moms being in the same club. . . . That's all." He smiled just a little, saying, "I wanted to see what you look like."

Faye said, "All right, you *are* cute, but don't get nosy."

She left him with his iced tea and went in the bedroom. Now what? Carl took *Photoplay* across the room to sit in a chair facing the table of magazines and the bedroom door, left open. He turned pages in the magazine. It wasn't a minute later she stuck her head out.

"You've been to Purity, haven't you?"

"Lot of times."

She stepped into plain sight now wearing a pair of sheer, peach-colored teddies, the crotch sagging beneath her white thighs. Faye said, "You hear about the time Pretty Boy Floyd came in?"

Carl could see London, he could see France. . . . "While you were working there?"

"Since then, not too long ago. The word got around Pretty Boy Floyd was at Purity and it practically shut down the whole town. Nobody'd come out of their house." She stood with hands on her hips in kind of a slouch. "I did meet him one time. Was at a speak in Oklahoma City."

"You talk to him?"

"Yeah, we talked about . . . you know, different things." She looked like she might be trying to think of what they did talk about, but said then, "Who's the most famous person you ever met?"

He wasn't expecting the question. Still, he thought about it for no more than a few seconds before telling her, "I guess it would have to be Frank Miller."

Faye said, "Oh . . . ?" like the name didn't mean much to her. Carl could tell, though, she was being careful, on her guard.

"Was in a drugstore when I was a kid," Carl said, "and Frank Miller came in for a pack of Luckies. I'd stopped there for a peach ice-cream cone, my favorite. You know what Frank Miller did? Asked could he have a bite—this famous bank robber."

"You give him one?"

"I did, and you know what? He kept it, wouldn't give me back my cone."

"He ate it?"

"Licked it a few times and threw it away." Carl didn't mention the trace of ice cream on Frank Miller's mustache; he kept that for himself. "Yeah, he took my ice-cream cone, robbed the store, and shot a policeman. You believe it?"

She seemed to nod, thoughtful now, and Carl decided it was time to come out in the open.

"You said people think it was marshals gunned down your husband, Skeet. But you know better, don't you?"

He had her full attention, staring at him now like she was hypnotized.

"And I'll bet it was Frank himself told you. Who else'd have the nerve? I'll bet he said you ever leave him he'll hunt you down and kill you. On account of he's so crazy about you. I can't think of another reason you'd stay here these years. You have anything to say to that?"

Faye began to show herself, saying, "You're not from a newspaper . . ."

"Is that what you thought?"

"They come around. Once they're in the house they can't wait to leave. No, you're not at all like them."

Carl said, "Faye, I'm a Deputy United States Marshal. I'm here to put Frank Miller under arrest or in the ground, one."

III

He worried she might've acquired an affection for the man, but it wasn't so. Once Carl showed her his star Faye sat down and breathed with relief. Pretty soon her nerves did take hold and she became talkative. Frank had phoned this morning and was coming. Now what was she supposed to do? Carl asked what time she expected him. She said going on dark. A car would drive past and honk twice; if the front door was open when it drove past again Frank would jump out and the car would keep going. Carl said he'd be sitting here reading about Joan Crawford. He said introduce him as a friend of the family happened to stop by, but try not to talk too much. He asked if Frank brought the magazines. She said they were supposed to be her treat. He asked out of curiosity if Frank could read. Faye said she wasn't sure, but believed he only looked at the pictures. What was it Virgil called him that time, years ago? A bozo.

He said to Faye, "What you want to do is pay close attention. Then later on you can tell what happened here as the star witness and get your name in the paper. I bet even your picture."

"I hadn't thought of that," Faye said. "You really think so?"

They heard the car beep twice as it passed the house.

Ready?

Carl was, in the chair facing the magazine table where the only lamp in the room was lit. Faye stood smoking a cigarette, smoking three or four since drinking the orange-juice glass of gin to settle her down. Light from the kitchen, behind her, showed her figure in the kimono she was wearing. Faye looked fine to Carl.

But not to Frank Miller. Not the way he came in with magazines under his arm and barely paused before saying to her, "What's wrong?"

"Nothing," Faye said. "Frank, I want you to meet Carl, from home." Frank staring at him now as Faye said he was a busboy at Purity the same time she was working there. "And our moms are both Eastern Star."

"You're Frank," Carl said, sounding like a salesman. "Glad to know you, Frank." Carl looking at a face from six years ago, the same dead-eyed stare beneath the hat brim. He watched Frank Miller carry his magazines to the table, drop them on top of the ones there and glance over at Faye; watched him plant both hands on the table now, hunched over, taking time to what, rest? Unh-unh, decide how to get rid of this busboy so he could take Faye to bed, Carl imagining Frank doing it to her with his hat still on . . . and remembered his dad saying, "You know why I caught the Mauser round that time, the Spanish sniper picking me off? I was thinking instead of paying attention, doing my job."

Carl asked himself what he was waiting for. He said, "Frank, bring out your pistol and lay it there on the table."

Faye Harris knew how to tell it. She had recited her story enough times to marshals and various law enforcement people. This afternoon she was describing the scene to newspaper reporters—and the one from the *Oklahoman,* the Oklahoma City paper, kept interrupting, asking questions that were a lot different than ones the marshals asked.

She referred to Deputy Marshal Webster as "Carl" and the one from the *Oklahoman* said, "Oh, you two are on intimate terms now? You don't mind he's just a kid? Has he visited you here at the hotel?" Faye was staying a few days at the Georgian in Henryetta. The other reporters in the room would tell the *Oklahoman* to keep quiet for Christ sake, anxious for Faye to get to the gunplay.

"As I told you," Faye said, "I was in the doorway to the kitchen.

Frank's over here to my left, and Carl's opposite him but sitting down, his legs stretched out in his cowboy boots. I couldn't believe how calm he was."

"What'd you have on, Faye?"

The *Oklahoman* interrupting again, some of the other reporters groaning.

"I had on a pink and red kimono Frank got me at Kerr's in Oklahoma City. I had to wear it whenever he came."

"You have anything on under it?"

Faye said, "None of your beeswax."

The *Oklahoman* said his readers had a right to know such details of how a gun moll dressed. This time the other reporters were quiet, like they wouldn't mind hearing such details themselves, until Faye said, "If this big mouth opens his trap one more time I'm through and y'all can leave." She said, "Now where was I?"

"Frank was leaning on the table."

"That was it. He looked over at me like he was gonna say something, and right then Carl said, 'Frank?' He said, 'Draw your pistol and lay it there on the table.'"

The reporters wrote it down in their notebooks and then waited as Faye took a sip of iced tea.

"I told you Frank had his back to Carl? Now I see him turn his face to his shoulder and say to him, 'Do I know you from someplace?' Maybe thinking of McAlester, Carl an ex-convict looking to earn the reward money. Frank asks him, 'Have we met or not?' And Carl says, 'If I told you, I doubt you'd remember.' Then—this is where Carl says, 'Frank, I'm a Deputy United States Marshal. I'll tell you one more time to lay your pistol on the table.'"

A reporter said, "Faye, I know they did meet. I'm from the *Okmulgee Daily Times* and I wrote the story about it. Was six years ago to the month."

"What you're doing," Faye said, "is holding up my getting to the good part." Messing up her train of thought, too.

"But the circumstances of how they met," the reporter said, "could have something to do with this story."

"Would you *please*," Faye said, "wait till I'm done?"

It gave her time to tell the next part: how Frank had no choice but to draw his gun, this big pearl-handled automatic, from inside his coat and lay it on the edge of the table, right next to him. "Now as he turns around," Faye said, starting to grin, "this surprised look came over his face. He sees Carl sitting there, not with a gun in his hand but *Photoplay* magazine. Frank can't believe his eyes. He says, 'Jesus Christ, you don't have a gun?' Carl pats the side of his chest where his gun's holstered under his coat and says, 'Right here.' Then he says, 'Frank, I want to be clear about this so you understand. If I pull my weapon I'll shoot to kill.'" Faye said to the reporters, "In other words, the only time Carl Webster draws his gun it's to shoot somebody dead."

It had the reporters scribbling in their notebooks and making remarks to each other, the one from the *Daily Times* saying now, "Listen, will you? Six years ago Frank Miller held up Deering's drugstore in Okmulgee and Carl Webster was there. Only he was known as Carlos then, he was still a kid. He stood by and watched Frank Miller shoot and kill an Indian from the tribal police happened to come in the store, a man Carl Webster must've known." The reporter looked at Faye and said, "I'm sorry to interrupt, but I think the drugstore shooting could've been on Carl Webster's mind."

Faye said, "I can tell you something else about that."

But now voices were chiming in, commenting and asking questions about the Okmulgee reporter's views:

"Carl carried it with him all these years?"

"Did he remind Frank Miller of it?"

"You're saying the tribal cop was a friend of his?"

"Both from Okmulgee, Carl thinking of becoming a lawman?"

"Carl ever say he was out to get Frank Miller?"

"This story's bigger'n it looks."

Faye said, "You want to hear something else happened?

"How Carl was eating an ice-cream cone that time and what Frank did?"

They sat on the porch sipping tequila at the end of the day, insects out there singing in the dark. A lantern hung above Virgil's head so he could see to read the newspapers on his lap.

"Most of it seems to be what this little girl told."

"They made up some of it."

"Jesus, I hope so. You haven't been going out with her, have you?"

"I drove down, took her to Purity a couple times."

"She's a pretty little thing. Has a saucy look about her in the pictures, wearing that kimona."

"She smelled nice, too," Carl said.

Virgil turned his head to him. "I wouldn't tell Bob Cardell that. One of his marshals sniffing around a gun moll." He waited, but Carl let that one go. Virgil looked at the newspaper he was holding. "I don't recall you were ever a buddy of Junior Harjo's."

"I'd see him and say hi is all."

"The *Daily Times* has you two practically blood brothers. What you did was avenge his death. They wonder if it might even be the reason you joined the marshals."

"Yeah, I read that," Carl said.

Virgil put the *Daily Times* down and slipped the *Oklahoman* out from under it. "But now the Oklahoma City paper says you shot Frank Miller 'cause he took your ice-cream cone that time in the drugstore. They trying to be funny?"

"I guess," Carl said.

"They could make up a name for you, as smart-aleck newspapers do, start calling you Carl Webster, the Ice Cream Kid?"

"What if they do?"

"I'm getting the idea you like this attention."

Virgil saying it with some concern and Carl giving him a shrug. Virgil picked up another paper from the pile. "Here they quote the little girl saying Frank Miller went for his gun and you shot him through the heart."

"I thought they have her saying, 'straight through the heart,'" Carl said. He turned to see his old dad staring at him with a solemn expression. "I'm kidding with you. What Frank did, he tried to bluff me. He looked toward Faye and called her name thinking I'd look over. But I kept my eyes on him, knowing he'd pick up his Colt. He came around with it and I shot him."

"As you told him you would," Virgil said. "Every one of the newspapers played it up, your saying, 'If I draw my weapon I shoot to kill.' You tell 'em that?"

"The only one I told was Frank Miller," Carl said. "It had to've been Faye told the papers."

"Well, that little girl sure tooted your horn for you."

"She only told what happened."

"All she had to. It's the telling that did it, made you a famous lawman overnight. You think you can carry a load like that?"

"I was born to," Carl said, starting to show himself.

It didn't surprise his old dad. Virgil picked up his glass of tequila and raised it to his boy, saying, "God help us showoffs."

The General

By CAROL EMSHWILLER

*They had conquered his people, then raised him
as one of their own. How far would they be willing
to go to destroy their own creation?*

One of the enemy has escaped into the mountains. An important
general. He knows our language, he knows our ways, but we
don't know his nor where his men are, nor even if there are any
of his men left at all. We were holding him in our maximum-security
facilities and we had thought to torture him until he told us what he
knew of his own army. We had called in others to torture him because
we don't believe in torture, but he escaped before they arrived.

There's a large reward for his capture. For a sum like this, even his own men would turn him in. He can't count on anybody. There's no way that he can survive very long anyway. It's too cold and everybody is on our side around here. Most likely they'll fight among themselves over the reward. There'll be a few more of us dead.

We had dressed him in orange. He'll have to steal some clothes. We hope he won't kill any of us to get them. He must be very stupid to try to escape in a place like this and at this season. The weather can only get worse. But perhaps death is better than our (deliberately) rat-infested, latrineless cells. He has been trained by us in our own schools to laugh at death. Most likely his body is already out there somewhere. We've sent local children to search the rocks and bushes. They know the area better even than our experts. We'll give them pennies and salt for any clues they pick up. We warned them if they find him and he's not dead, they should run, as he is extremely dangerous and has probably obtained or made a weapon.

I'm on a trail now. At first I just headed out, not following any road or path, but there's no way to cross these mountain passes and not be on one. Every now and then there's a hut. This time of year they're all empty. I don't dare spend the night in any. I stole clothes from one, long underwear, and a worn-out sheepskin jacket. I found a knit cap. They shaved my head so I needed a good hat. Everything I took was worn out and smelled bad, but I wear them anyway. I stole food and a blanket. I was wearing leg irons. At the hut I found tools to break them off. I'll be able to go a little faster now. I stole a sickle but dropped it later. I don't want to be tempted to lash out at anyone, especially not with a sickle.

I sleep several yards from the trail in any handy sheltered spot. Or if there are scattered boulders I cover myself with the blanket and lie along them as if I were just another stone. I haven't met a single person up here, but I don't dare relax.

I sleep the sleep of exhaustion. I'll think to myself: This is a good spot, and that's all I know until I wake up.

I'm aware that I'm walking through great beauty but if I sit down to appreciate it for a minute I fall asleep. Sometimes the moon has risen and I lie back and think to look at the sky and take some time to realize I'm in a wondrous place and this is a luminous moment, but no sooner do I have that thought than I'm asleep.

Notices have been put up on every corner:

WANTED REWARD. Wild and dangerous man. Medium height, shaved head, dark eyes. He'd as soon kill you as look at you. By now he may have weapons. If you harbor him or give him food, you'll be considered as guilty as he is. There's a microchip imbedded in his shoulder where he can neither see it or reach it. Anyone who has removed it will be considered as traitorous as he is. The sentence for helping him is death.

The irony is, we brought him up ourselves in our own military schools. We thought contact with us would civilize him, but he's no more civilized than he was at the age of nine when we took him in. At that time he said he'd kill us all and, in spite of all these years in our care, that's what he still wants to do.

We thought he would soon see that life with us was preferable to the primitive ways of his own people. We had thought he would realize our superiority. Anybody with any sense, we thought, even a child with any sense at all, could see we had the science, the money, the schools, the workforce, the wealth. . . . And we were ready to share our wealth with him. He was, after all, at the top of his graduating class. The top! We were surprised that a savage child had beaten out our own. We took it as a sign we could mold the wild ones to our civilized ways if we caught them in time. We were glad to have him on our side. Until he defected, we suspected nothing.

I wake with a child looking down on me—so bundled up I wonder how she can move at all. A dirty child but I'm dirtier. At first I think a boy, but then I think, girl. I see her skirt and coarse hand-knit wooly petticoat hanging below it. I'm not a good judge of the ages of children, but I'd guess about nine or ten years old. Beside her there's a bundle of sticks she's been gathering.

I distrust everybody. I wake up in a rage as usual, ready to strike out. I think, Here's one of them, but then she smiles and I smile back.

I can't help groaning as I try to sit up. I'm always so stiff, waking after a day of climbing. (When I was younger I never had this problem. I suppose it'll only get worse.) I ask her, "What are you doing way up here this time of year?" and she asks, "What are you?"

Her name is Loo. I tell her I'm Sang. Not too much of a lie, especially if you take it to mean blood and pronounce it "sans," and now I am sans everything. (For a long time I was called rubbish.)

It's been three days and we still haven't captured him, therefore sweeping changes from the top on down. Higher-ups have been brought in. Those in charge are no longer in charge. How can one half-starved man, possibly wearing orange, and with a microchip, have escaped us all? We have the know-how and the wherewithal.

Loo won't go home without more sticks. I help her. She's all smiles when she sees how much I get. I shoulder a dead log, too. I think to chop it up when we get . . . wherever. First we climb on the main trail and then turn off on a smaller path, so small you have to know it's there to follow it.

We come to a hut of stone and weathered wood. It looks like part of the mountain. It's a hut as if out of a painting of a troll's house in a book of fairy tales. The roof slopes almost to the ground. I remember fairy tales from before I was taken, otherwise I'd not know about them.

Loo's grandma greets us at the door. I look past her and see it's like a troll's hut inside, too. Heavy handmade furniture, a worn-down board floor, a squat black stove, a squat black kettle steaming . . .

Loo and her grandma must have gotten marooned up here someway. I don't ask how. The grandma has a hard time walking from the stove to the doorway. Perhaps she could no longer climb down. Yet to leave her here alone with just a child for help . . . I don't see how they get by. They don't look in good shape.

I don't go in. I stand in the doorway. I say, "I am your enemy. I'm a fugitive. You risk your life if you take me in. I have a chip imbedded in my shoulder." I tell the grandma about the reward though I don't say how much. I hardly dare. It's a sum hard to resist. It would make anyone rich for life.

For answer the old woman motions me in, motions me to sit down, motions me to take off my jacket and mittens, and then hands me a cup of strong strange tea. It tastes of pine needles. They have two rooms. Two nanny goats stay in with them.

I say, "You don't realize."

The grandma says, "I realize." Her voice is a breathy growl.

She shows me men's clothes hanging behind the door, but she won't talk about them. In fact she'll hardly talk at all. Just gives me stew full of tiny bones. Then she gets out a paring knife and motions me to lean over the table. I do. It'll give her a chance to cut my throat if she feels like it.

(I had covered my shoulder first thing with pieces of foil from the dump on the outskirts of town so they couldn't home in on me.)

Afterward she makes me a different sort of tea for the pain. The way I'm slurping down every odd-tasting thing she hands me, she could poison me in a minute, and I'll bet she has whatever it takes to do it.

She wraps the chip back in my foil and puts it by the door. She says, "Take this out on the trail tomorrow. Throw it over the cliff."

They make me a bed under the table I just bled on. I think to thank them but, warm and full of hot food, I fall asleep before I can get the words out.

We've sent out six units. We've commandeered the first huts along several trails as base camps. One unit has discovered a place where someone spent the night. No one is on the mountain at this time of year so who but the general could have slept there? We moved all our units to this one mountain trail.

An early snow falls all night and is still going on in the morning. I go out in it. I'll not do as the grandma said. I'll get rid of that chip at the top of one of the peaks. I'll unwrap it so as to give them a false clue. Useless and foolish, I know, but I want to do it anyway. Perhaps if it's so hard to get to they'll not bother. They'll think I'm already dead up there and let me be. They'll say it's just like me to die at the top of something. I wish I'd saved my orange suit to use as a flag.

I say I may not be back tonight, but I'll be back soon. I'm thinking it'll take all day to climb a mountain even if I'm more than half-way up right here.

The grandma bundles me in hand-knit scarves. She winds them around me under my stolen jacket. I don't know if I can climb in all this. She wants to give me dried acorn cakes but I don't let her. I don't believe they have much food any more than they have much firewood. Soon as I get back I'll chop up more.

The grandma lends me her staffs. She uses two. I'll need two also. "Bring them back," she says.

We've found the chip, brown from his blood. One unit climbed to the top of the mountain thinking what the General can do, they can do. Thinking he would be there laughing down at them. Or dead, but with a smile at having forced them to climb there. He was no doubt laughing, but he wasn't there. One member of the unit fell on the rocks near the top and broke his ankle. One got altitude sickness. They have been flown out. We appointed new squad leaders.

There's fish. I caught some myself on the way up when the trail dipped down beside a creek. I ate them raw. Now I catch more on the way back to the cabin.

When I get there, Loo says she saw a group of men in white suits filing up the trail. They're two days' climb away. Loo takes me yet farther up into a cave, well off the path. Rattlesnakes sleep there. If I make a fire they'll wake up.

There's already a bed of old rotten hay. Loo gives me a bundle of food. She insists. I say I'll eat rattlesnake. She says, "Yes, but this, too." Then she chops off the heads of several big ones to take back to the grandma. They're so cold they don't come to. "In the morning I'll bring some back fried," she says. She leaves me the ax and goes.

There's a little sort of porch in front of the cave. I watch her till she's out of sight, lumpy little figure, accepting everything that comes along—though what else can children ever do?

I sit down on a rock and look out at the mountains—for once without falling asleep. A long time ago these peaks used to be the border—a no-man's-land several miles long between my country and theirs. But no need for any borders now. It's all theirs. The beauty is still as it was and will be no matter who owns it. Does it matter? Grandma and Loo? Why do I even wonder what side they're on?

The search parties below have already camped for the night. I see their smoke.

I start to chant to myself as I did when I was a child locked in solitary. I rock back and forth. I remember the cell, too small for a man, but big enough for me. I remember my classmates called me Rubbish all the time and I called myself that to myself. If I slipped I'd look at my feet and call them Rubbish. If I dropped something I'd call my hands Rubbish. Rubbish, I said about myself.

My parents were murdered before my eyes and I, taken to an enemy school to be educated as one of them. I didn't even know their language. Even when I began to understand, I refused to speak it. I didn't know their food. I finally got hungry enough to eat it. I profited by that education. I got to know them as I used to know my own. Better in fact. I almost forgot my own language. I almost forgot our ways. I was told my people were a lower order of civilization, but I couldn't see much difference.

In the beginning of military school I ran away a lot. Escaping wasn't hard; it was not being found afterward that I never managed. The enemy was everywhere. After four or five times it seemed useless. The punishment was solitary confinement. (They don't believe in hitting children. Besides, we were not to be marked in any way.) I burned my uniform three times, but there were plenty more. After a while I obeyed. It seemed a waste to go to all that trouble of running away for nothing.

I tested myself every chance I got. Heat, cold, fire, hunger, thirst . . . On our matches, I stood out in storms and let icy rain trickle down the back of my neck while the others took shelter in a shed. I wondered how high a ledge I could jump from. (I found out by breaking my ankle.) I tested myself in the cold until I almost lost my toes. After that I realized I might go too far, cripple myself and defeat my own purposes.

Being in solitary . . . that was a test, too, and I passed it to my own satisfaction. How I managed was through chants and songs. I chanted myself up into the trees I used to climb. I chanted to make myself into a cat. I practiced stalking the mice in my cell. When I finally caught one I made it into a pet. First I named it Sang, and then I named it Sans.

I never cried. Crying was a waste of valuable energy that I needed to fulfill my promises. My father would have told me that.

But then I realized there was a better way than all this escaping. (My father would have said that, too.) I did as I was told. I spoke their language when called upon, I excelled at everything, and became, at the age of twenty-eight, their youngest general ever. Years later, I fled and became one of ours.

They trapped us in our caves. Killed us except for me. I was saved for worse things than mere death.

We had learned to laugh at death. (They taught us that.) Death holds no terror, but we didn't learn to laugh at the torture of our loved ones, therefore I have no loved ones, neither wife nor children. After they killed my parents, my aunts, and my grandmother, I made sure there was nobody else, ever, to take from me.

In those early days I fell in love so often I thought to change my plans and be their general after all. I would marry and live on the hills above the towns, but I stayed true to the vows I made when I was nine.

At our graduation from military school, a eulogy full of kindness and humor so that we not only laughed at death, but laughed along with the dead. Their dead were to be my dead, and yet I thought only of my own. Even though I could hardly remember them alive, I thought only of their deaths.

It was hard keeping to my resolutions when I got to know the enemy. I began to care for them—those who treated me well, though many didn't, but I had knelt by my parents, covered with their blood, and swore . . . not to any God, but to myself—to the man I would become. I said, "You! You, as a man. You will remember this right here and now. No other thing will ever be as clear as this." And that has turned out to be true. I've remembered nothing more clearly than the blood, and the gurgling and coughing and the jerking back and forth of dying.

I ran, and thought to hide in a closet full of my father's uniforms as if they might save me, but they guessed where I was. I bit them, so then they put me in a dusty bag that smelled bad. I remember the taste of their sweaty, salty wrists.

Loo and Grandma? I wonder if they even know which side they're on. This side of the mountain . . . no one was sure who it belonged to, but the other side used to belong to the scattered armies of my child-hood. My home was over there somewhere. I wonder if I would rec-ognize it? I wonder if it still stands?

Ever since I was taken away, I haven't had much to do with any but military people. Even my women were soldiers. I don't know what civilians are like. And I've never had anything to do with chil-dren, though I guess we all remember how it was to be one. Except I doubt if my memories pertain to many other children. I hope they don't. Loo is ten, the age I was when I first escaped and was recap-tured and put in solitary as punishment.

I look out from the porch of my cave. I can hear the stream rushing down. I can see it sparkling below if I lean over the cliff. The sound will soothe me as I sleep. I begin to chant. I chant, You, and Loo, and owl. *Owl* meant *ouch* in my childhood language, and *row, row, row,* meant *remember, remember.* I chant You, you, you, as I used to chant it to my grown-up self. But I also chant, But, but, but. . . .

But . . . There were no buts in my chant language back then. But . . . I've seen plenty of blood on both sides. But . . . Isn't it best to look forward? See to it that children, and this one child, Loo, never see such things as I did? But . . . She already has. Those men's clothes behind the door. Next time she comes up I'll ask her about herself. I wonder if she'd like a doll. I have a kitchen knife. I look around for some wood.

* * *

She comes the next morning, bringing fried rattlesnake and dried crawdads. She sneaks in. I had my eyes shut, my face to the rising sun. I was chanting, Jolly, jolly, joll, joll. My secret words for my aunt June Harvest. When I open my eyes, there's Loo, watching. She's not surprised. Not wondering that I'm sitting cross-legged, nodding, muttering to myself.

I show her the doll. She receives it as though she's never known about dolls before. Perhaps she hasn't. She doesn't say a word, but I see her pleasure on her face. How nice to give something and have it so well received.

I sit on my porch stone. There's room for two. "Come, sit with me. Eat some yourself."

"I've had."

She examines the doll as I eat.

I had made it a dress out of pieces of the clothes I'd stolen. I hooked the arms and legs on with threads. "When I get some fishing line I'll put the arms and legs on in a stronger way. I'll find better cloth for a nice dress." (Too bad I hadn't saved a little piece of my orange suit.)

"I like this cloth," she says, even though it's a piece from the leg of my long underwear.

We sit quietly for a while; she turns the doll this way and that. I did a good job carving the face. It has a nice smiling look. I was always good at such things.

And then I ask what I've been waiting to ask. "Your father? Are those his clothes hanging behind the door? Is he all right?"

She starts to cry but turns away and stops herself.

I say, "I know. I know." And I do know. I wonder if, as I did, she had to watch it as it happened. I wonder if I dare reach out to her. I'm not used to touching people. My awkwardness would show all the more clearly to a child.

But she comes to me of her own accord, leans against me, still not crying. We hold each other. All I can think to say is, "I know, I know, I know," though I wonder, What good does that do? It's like another of my chants. So I chant, I know, and rock her.

I can feel there's not much to her. Skin and bones. Take off all these clothes and she'd look like a wet cat inside there. Grandma is probably about the same under her wooly petticoats and shawls. I could easily see to it that they got enough to eat. If I'd be let, I could live up here for the rest of my life. Wood gatherer, gatherer of acorns and pine nuts, trap setter, fisherman . . . I could make a bigger, better doll. I'd look out at mountains. I never knew . . . or never let myself know how much I'd like a quiet life.

Then I see the search and capture squads on the path below, three groups of three. They've passed the cottage. I'm afraid for Grandma. I don't think they would hurt an old woman, but Grandma might have said something, or there may have been some sign that I'd been there. Even a larger woodpile might be suspicious. She'd be in as much trouble as I am.

Loo feels my fear. I must have suddenly held her tighter without knowing it. She turns around and looks, too. Then looks back at me as if I'd know what to do. "Loo, is there a back way?"

But she should stay up here, safe. She wouldn't. She should lead me. "I'll go down with you, but first I have something that needs doing."

At least they'll have a harder time coming beyond this point. Why didn't I think of this before?

We had brought him up as one of our own. Spared no expense. And now look. He has worn us out. Fooled us. Played tricks. As if climbing a mountain peak were a game and he won. They say, Once a savage, always a savage. And now yet another game. He has rolled boulders down and started a landslide. Our second team had to rescue our first team out from under gravel and dust. It could have been worse; they only received a few bruises. But that slide shut off the upper part of the trail. That will be proof he's gone on higher. We'll drop our squads off above the slide area.

There's no trail as Loo leads me down a back way, so it's hard. We scramble over rocks. Loo tears her skirt and unravels her knit petticoats. She's upset by it. She says Grandma can't see well enough to sew or knit anymore. I say I'll repair them for her. She says, "Men don't sew," and I say, "Many's the time I've repaired my clothes myself. I'd have made the doll clothes better if I'd had a needle."

When we get almost to the hut it's beginning to be twilight. We curve around to the side and see a guard. He's across from the door partly hidden by a currant bush. Had we come straight in by the path he might have shot us.

Loo wants to run right out but I hold her back. I clamp my hand over her mouth just in time to stop her yell. "Wait. One of us should stay a secret. I'll find out if Grandma's all right. You stay here." I find her a good spot farther back. "We may need you later. You may have to rescue both of us."

I take off my cap so the guard will know it's me. I give it to Loo. I was thinking she needed something to take care of, but all this time she's been holding the doll, tight in her mitten. I had forgotten about it, but she hadn't. I say, "Find it a name." But she's a child like I was a child so not a child at all, yet she hung on to the doll through all this scrabbling over rocks. Makes me think of my pet mouse. This last time in solitary I had not made a pet of any of the rats. I had not chanted and still I had escaped. Is that proof of the uselessness of chanting?

I walk straight in from the path with no hat. By now it's starting to get dark. The guard recognizes me with delight. He points the automatic straight at me.

I say, "Hold it. Not as much of a reward for me dead. Where's Grandma?"

I don't think any of his men are nearby. Why would they need more than one man to guard Grandma? Earlier we heard their copters dropping men off above my landslide. "You know all your teams are busy elsewhere."

He looks uncertain. He's very young.

Then we see rockets lighting up the sky far below us. I think: But there are no more armies. And then I think: Loo! Will she be frightened? By now it's almost dark.

The guard and I turn to look out at the sky, but I turn back before he does. I grab the automatic and use it to knock him down. I hold the butt against his throat. He chokes. I let up some. He gags.

"Grandma!"

When he tries to talk his voice is hoarse. I leaned too hard. Another little bit and his Adam's apple would have pierced his esophagus.

We are celebrating Victory Day with the usual cannon volleys, fireworks, and flag waving. Even though a most important enemy is still at large, no need not to celebrate. We are unlikely to be harmed by this single escaped general. We have taken down the WANTED notices. To us he is no more than a gnat, though vexatious. Some are laughing, enjoying the fact that one man has eluded us all this time. They are traitors. We are putting up new notices that say: NO LONGER WANTED.

Winter is coming. The weather will worsen. We've postponed our search, perhaps until spring, perhaps forever.

I had forgotten about Victory Day . . . Victory over us day. Not forgotten about it, but I'd lost track of time. I've had to celebrate it ever since military school. At least now I'm not forced to cheer and dance or wave a hated flag. I can yell my rage if I want to. I do. The soldier looks up at me terrified. I yell louder. I've not let myself do that ever before. I yell and then here's Grandma hobbling out. I fall on the young man, the automatic hard between us. He doesn't dare move. Then here's Loo, holding my head. Still I yell. I roll away from the soldier and the gun. I have to stop yelling because I can't breathe.

Grandma has picked up the automatic. It's clear she knows how to use it. She's going to shoot. I'd try to stop her but I'm breathless. My first thought is: I'll take the blame. I'm already blamed for many more things than I've done, anyway. One more won't make a difference. I'm considered a killer though I've never even pointed a gun at anyone. When I was on their side I shot to miss and when I was on our side I was a general and didn't have to shoot.

The gun seems too heavy for her. Her aim wavers. It makes her look all the more dangerous. "Go home," she says. Her old-crow voice is scary. "Home. I mean it."

It's dark now but he goes—stumbling, tripping.

I'm still panting—groaning at every breath as though I were in pain. Something has been let loose inside me.

I never chanted except secretly to myself. I believe Loo is the only person who ever heard me. I've always wondered if chanting had anything to do with anything. As a child I thought it did. Escape always seemed so easy. I thought I'd done it with my songs. And sometimes after a good chant I thought, Any minute, people will come to rescue me. Even Aunt June Harvest would come, and she was dead with the rest. She's the one started my chanting. I remember standing in her doorway listening. We were a family that didn't believe in any of the old superstitions, but Aunt June Harvest believed things the rest of us didn't or weren't supposed to.

As a child in solitary, I usually chanted up my father. I thought of him opening the door, letting in sunlight—Pada, in full dress uniform, bringing our kind of food. I shouted, "Pada!" Often, after chanting I knew all that I'd seen with my own eyes was false; there had been no deaths and my father was come to rescue me.

I can't breathe. Loo sits beside me, says, "Sang, Sang." At first I think she must mean my pet mouse and then I remember I am Sang. She puts the doll in my hand, giving it back. I take it. I turn over onto my hands and knees, then hunker down. Even though I easily escaped this last time, I no longer think chanting has any effect on anything except for my own need to chant, yet I do it now. Though breathless, I chant. How, how, and, And. And, Row, Row. And *Row* begins to mean *row* indeed, instead of *remember, remember,* and I'm as if in our old flat-bottom boat on our pond with my little sister. My sister leans to pull at a water lily. Oarlocks creak. A red-winged blackbird clings to a reed. I hear the bird's song. At first so sweet and then loud and then much too loud. And then I must have passed out. That's never happened before.

I come to with Grandma rubbing snow on my face. Then she helps me turn over, raises my head, and holds tea to my lips. Loo and

Grandma help me into my sleeping spot under the table. I shiver. They pile quilts on me. Loo puts the doll beside my pillow. I try to give it back but she won't let me. I say, "I made it for you." But then I let her. I sleep a sick sleep. Whenever I wake myself up with my yelling, they are there, Grandma in the rocking chair and Loo and the goats on the floor beside me.

The celebration of Victory Day was a success. We had temporarily removed all the WANTED! DANGEROUS MAN AT LARGE posters. The mood was as it should be. We have made them forget that the General still eludes us. We shot into the air, but, as far as we know, all the bullets came down safely. We are pleased. We have toasted ourselves. "Long live and forever," we said to each other, and "Victory Day throughout eternity."

Next I know good smells wake me. Grandma is baking an elder-berry pie. I don't wake up angry as I usually do even though at first I think Grandma is celebrating Victory Day, but she says it's not to cele-brate any victories; it's for me. She says they haven't had pie in a long time.

"Which side?" I say, thinking to find out at last what side they're on.

"Just us," she says, and then, "No sides. Lupine, snakeweed, fire-weed people. Asters and rock fringe people."

The General is to be presumed dead. We'll not waste any more resources hunting him. He's no longer of any meaning. What army could he be the general of anymore? We'll celebrate his death with another night of cannon volleys. The reward set aside for his capture is withdrawn and will revert back to the army, though, just in case, we'll not publicize that it no longer exists. All the better if people think it's still on.

I make a little outdoor oven so I can smoke fish for them. I chop more wood. There's already dried kinnikinnick here. In the evenings I carve myself a pipe to smoke it. Loo and I together repair her wooly petticoats. I start to make her a bigger better doll but she says she just wants the old small one with my underwear for a dress, so I strengthen the arms and legs with fishing line. I carve a little goat. I make Loo guess what it's going to be as I go along. I wear the men's clothes that were hanging behind the door. I sit by the stove of an evening smoking or sewing more dresses for the doll. I still sleep under the table. I keep the fire burning all night. The stovepipe curls through to the other room so they stay warm. All my life since I was nine, I have awakened every morning in a rage, renewing my promises. All my life I have distrusted people, but not now.

Loo is teaching me how to be a child. Or perhaps we're teaching each other. I make the doll dance, and then she does it. Suppertimes, I wave a tidbit . . . a dried crawdad or some such, in front of her and let her snap at it. I throw a walnut up and catch it in my mouth. She tries but she can't do it. I make pancakes and flip them almost to the ceiling when I turn them. I remember the peasant dances my men used to do and, though I've never tried to do one, I try now. I take Loo's hand and make her dance with me. I growl out a song. We even make Grandma smile. We even make her sing.

They're both getting fatter. I'll leave in the spring. In the spring Loo can gather all sorts of sprouts, fiddlehead ferns, mushrooms. . . . She's gotten good at fishing. I'll cross the pass and go home—if I can find it—if anything remains. I haven't thought of home for a long time. I hadn't thought I had one, nor did I want one. Perhaps I should look for the remains of my army. Though . . . I'd like to be finished with that sort of life. Perhaps I'll live the rest of my life home, if it still exists. Or here.

A group of our people hoping for the reward found him on the trail. (They thought the reward was still operative. All the better then, if people do.) Or perhaps he found them. It might have been him, but could he grow that much hair and that much beard in this length of time? There might be other fugitives on the mountain. However that may be, this man jumped them at the perfect spot and pushed them over, all three. None died but all slid down and were found at the bottom, scratched and bruised. Harassing us is just the sort of thing he would do. We had thought he was much higher up by now. Perhaps even over on the other side. But then again, we aren't sure this man was him. Perhaps it wasn't the General at all but some other man with something else against us. How many wild men roam the mountains looking for their chances at us? The mountains could be full of them. We'll not waste any more time on him—or them.

B ut then Loo wakes me in the middle of the night. Grandma is trying to talk but can't. The whole right side of her face is lopsided. I recognize right away she's had a stroke. I'll need to get help. No, they'll arrest me before I have a chance to bring up a doctor. I'll have to get her down to town. It will be the quickest anyway. I've already made a skid for hauling logs. I wrap Grandma in all our quilts and blankets and tie her to it. There's still quite a bit of snow here on the upper slopes; that'll make the first part easier. I feed Loo cold smoked fish and goat's milk, grab whatever food is handy to bring along, wrap Loo up in scarves, and start out. I see to it she doesn't forget her doll and she sees to it I don't forget my pipe. (At the last minute I throw in Grandma's scissors and Loo's father's razor.) Though it's still hardly dawn, I grab the rope and we start out. I won't be careful this time; I'll just be fast.

The farther down we get the warmer it'll be. We'll hit true spring in a day.

We spend the first night in an empty cabin. We burn their wood, not worried who sees the smoke. We use their barley to make gruel. There's a small mirror. I shave my beard and I have Loo help me shave my head. I don't tell her why and she doesn't ask. (Afterward she says she liked me better hairy.) Until the time comes, I'll keep my cap on.

Farther down there are no more snowy patches so it's harder. At one point the skid gets going down a scree slope. I get a bump on my head trying to stop it. That fits with my plans.

After we leave Grandma at the clinic, I tell Loo, "Tie me up and lead me to the prison. There's a big reward for my capture. Turn me in and request it. Make them set up the money in a bank account for Grandma, to dole out little by little. It's a lot of money." (I still don't dare tell her how much even though I'm sure she'd not be able to understand it anyway.)

But even as I speak I realize they won't do it for a child. Perhaps I should turn myself in for my own reward. Have an account in my own and Grandma's name. Will they let me do that? What if Grandma dies or never recovers her senses? Loo's name then. They won't, but they might. It would change their life. I may as well try.

I show Loo how to tie me up.

"The bruise on my head . . . tell them you did that."

She starts to cry. "I won't."

"You'll see. You'll be a hero. Everything will be better this way."

"It won't be."

"I'll be fine. I have my chants and I can think about you."

She tries to give me her doll.

"They'll not let me keep anything. You keep the pipe, too. I can only take unreal things like remembering."

But we're too late. There's been no reward since winter. I can't believe it. I'm no longer of any importance. At first I feel a great relief. My stomach lurches. I almost throw up. It's over. This is better than any reward no matter how large. Loo and I can walk away.

But they grab me anyway. I struggle though I know it's useless. In half a minute I'm shackled again. I yell at Loo to go to the clinic, but when I look back, they've got her, too. I can't think why. I suppose she's guilty of helping me. I never should have let them help. I wonder what they'll do to Grandma. They know I have loved ones now. I wonder if Loo has the sense to chant.

We put up new posters: THE GENERAL IS IN OUR CUSTODY. Finding him and capturing him was difficult but we prevailed. Congratulations to all our Search and Capture teams. They will be rewarded. Prepare your flags and trumpets; tomorrow there will be another day of celebrating.

Closing Time

By NEIL GAIMAN

It was in the nature of boys to get into trouble.
But sometimes you had to knock.

There are still clubs in London. Old ones, and mock-old, with elderly sofas and crackling fireplaces, newspapers, and traditions of speech or of silence, and new clubs, the Groucho and its many knockoffs, where actors and journalists go to be seen, to drink, to enjoy their glowering solitude, or even to talk. I have friends in both kinds of club, but am not myself a member of any club in London, not anymore.

Years ago, half a lifetime, when I was a young journalist, I joined a club. It existed solely to take advantage of the licensing laws of the day, which forced all pubs to stop serving drinks at eleven PM, closing time. This club, the Diogenes, was a one-room affair located above a record shop in a narrow alley just off the Tottenham Court Road. It was owned by a cheerful, chubby, alcohol-fueled woman called Nora, who would tell anyone who asked and even if they didn't that she'd called the club the Diogenes, darling, because she was still looking for an honest man. Up a narrow flight of steps, and, at Nora's whim, the door to the club would be open, or not. It kept irregular hours.

It was a place to go once the pubs closed, that was all it ever was, and despite Nora's doomed attempts to serve food or even to send out a cheery monthly newsletter to all her club's members reminding them that the club now served food, that was all it would ever be. I was saddened several years ago when I heard that Nora had died; and I was struck, to my surprise, with a real sense of desolation last month when, on a visit to England, walking down that alley, I tried to figure out where the Diogenes Club had been, and looked first in the wrong place, then saw the faded green cloth awnings shading the windows of a tapas restaurant above a mobile phone shop, and, painted on them, a stylized man in a barrel. It seemed almost indecent, and it set me remembering.

There were no fireplaces in the Diogenes Club, and no armchairs either, but still, stories were told there.

Most of the people drinking there were men, although women passed through from time to time, and Nora had recently acquired a glamorous permanent fixture in the shape of a deputy, a blonde Polish émigré who called everybody "darlink" and who helped herself to drinks whenever she got behind the bar. When she got drunk, she would tell us that she was by rights a countess, back in Poland, and swear us all to secrecy.

There were actors and writers, of course. Film editors, broadcasters, police inspectors, and drunks. People who did not keep fixed hours. People who stayed out too late, or who did not want to go home. Some nights there might be a dozen people there, or more. Other nights I'd wander in and I'd be the only person there—on those occasions I'd buy myself a single drink, drink it down, and then leave.

That night, it was raining, and there were four of us in the club after midnight.

Nora and her deputy were sitting up at the bar, working on their sitcom. It was about a chubby-but-cheerful woman who owned a drinking club, and her scatty deputy, an aristocratic foreign blonde who made amusing English mistakes. It would be like *Cheers,* Nora used to tell people. She named the comical Jewish landlord after me. Sometimes they would ask me to read a script.

The rest of us were sitting over by the window: an actor named Paul (commonly known as Paul-the-actor, to stop people confusing him with Paul-the-police-inspector or Paul-the-struck-off-plastic-surgeon, who were also regulars), a computer gaming magazine editor named Martyn, and me. We knew each other vaguely, and the three of us sat at a table by the window and watched the rain come down, misting and blurring the lights of the alley.

There was another man there, older by far than any of the three of us. He was cadaverous, and gray-haired and painfully thin, and he sat alone in the corner and nursed a single whiskey. The elbows of his tweed jacket were patched with brown leather, I remember that quite vividly. He did not talk to us, or read, or do anything. He just sat, looking out at the rain and the alley beneath, and, sometimes, he sipped his whisky without any visible pleasure.

It was almost midnight, and Paul and Martyn and I had started telling ghost stories. I had just finished telling them a sworn-true ghostly account from my school days: the tale of the Green Hand. It had been an article of faith at my prep school that there was a disembodied, luminous hand that was seen, from time to time, by unfortunate schoolboys. If you saw the Green Hand you would die soon after. Fortunately, none of us were ever unlucky enough to encounter it, but there were sad tales of boys there before our time, boys who saw the Green Hand and whose thirteen-year-old hair had turned white overnight. According to school legend they were taken to the sanatorium, where they would expire after a week or so without ever being able to utter another word.

"Hang on," said Paul-the-actor. "If they never uttered another word, how did anyone know they'd seen the Green Hand? I mean, they could have seen anything."

As a boy, being told the stories, I had not thought to ask this, and now that it was pointed out to me it did seem somewhat problematic.

"Perhaps they wrote something down," I suggested, a bit lamely.

We batted it about for a while, and agreed that the Green Hand was a most unsatisfactory sort of ghost. Then Paul told us a true story about a friend of his who had picked up a hitchhiker, and dropped her off at a place she said was her house, and when he went back the next morning, it turned out to be a cemetery. I mentioned that exactly the same thing had happened to a friend of mine as well. Martyn said that it had not only happened to a friend of his, but, because the hitchhiking girl looked so cold, the friend had lent her his coat, and the next morning, in the cemetery, he found his coat all neatly folded on her grave.

Martyn went and got another round of drinks, and we wondered why all these ghost-women were zooming around the country all night and hitchhiking home, and Martyn said that probably living hitchhikers these days were the exception, not the rule.

And then one of us said, "I'll tell you a true story, if you like. It's a story I've never told a living soul. It's true—it happened to me, not to a friend of mine—but I don't know if it's a ghost story. It probably isn't."

This was over twenty years ago. I have forgotten so many things, but I have not forgotten that night, nor how it ended.

This is the story that was told that night, in the Diogenes Club.

I was nine years old, or thereabouts, in the late 1960s, and I was attending a small private school not far from my home. I was only at that school less than a year—long enough to take a dislike to the school's owner, who had bought the school in order to close it, and to sell the prime land on which it stood to property developers, which, shortly after I left, she did.

For a long time—a year or more—after the school closed the building stood empty before it was finally demolished and replaced by offices. Being a boy, I was also a burglar of sorts, and one day before it was knocked down, curious, I went back there. I wriggled through a half-opened window and walked through empty classrooms that still smelled of chalk dust. I took only one thing from my visit, a painting I had done in Art of a little house with a red door-knocker like a devil or an imp. It had my name on it, and it was up on a wall. I took it home.

When the school was still open I walked home each day, through the town, then down a dark road cut through sandstone hills and all grown over with trees, and past an abandoned gatehouse. Then there would be light, and the road would go past fields, and finally I would be home.

Back then there were so many old houses and estates, Victorian relics that stood in an empty half-life awaiting the bulldozers that would transform them and their ramshackle grounds into blandly identical landscapes of desirable modern residences, every house neatly arranged side by side around roads that went nowhere.

The other children I encountered on my way home were, in my memory, always boys. We did not know each other, but, like guerrillas in occupied territory, we would exchange information. We were scared of adults, not each other. We did not have to know each other to run in twos or threes or in packs.

The day that I'm thinking of, I was walking home from school, and I met three boys in the road where it was at its darkest. They were looking for something in the ditches and the hedges and the weed-choked place in front of the abandoned gatehouse. They were older than me.

"What are you looking for?"

The tallest of them, a beanpole of a boy, with dark hair and a sharp face, said, "Look!" He held up several ripped-in-half pages from what must have been a very, very old pornographic magazine. The girls were all in black and white, and their hairstyles looked like the ones my great-aunts had in old photographs. The magazine had been ripped up, and fragments of it had blown all over the road and into the abandoned gatehouse front garden.

I joined in the paper chase. Together, the three of us retrieved almost a whole copy of *The Gentleman's Relish* from that dark place. Then we climbed over a wall, into a deserted apple orchard, and looked at it. Naked women from a long time ago. There is a smell, of fresh apples, and of rotten apples moldering down into cider, which even today brings back the idea of the forbidden to me.

The smaller boys, who were still bigger than I was, were called Simon and Douglas, and the tall one, who might have been as old as fifteen, was called Jamie. I wondered if they were brothers. I did not ask.

When we had all looked at the magazine, they said, "We're going to hide this in our special place. Do you want to come along? You mustn't tell, if you do. You mustn't tell anyone."

They made me spit on my palm, and they spat on theirs, and we pressed our hands together.

Their special place was an abandoned metal water tower, in a field by the entrance to the lane near to where I lived. We climbed a high ladder. The tower was painted a dull green on the outside, and inside it was orange with rust that covered the floor and the walls. There was a wallet on the floor with no money in it, only some cigarette cards. Jamie showed them to me: each card held a painting of a cricketer from a long time ago. They put the pages of the magazine down on the floor of the water tower, and the wallet on top of it.

Then Douglas said, "I say we go back to the Swallows next."

My house was not far from the Swallows, a sprawling manor house set back from the road. It had been owned, my father had told me once, by the Earl of Tenterden, but when he had died his son, the new earl, had simply closed the place up. I had wandered to the edges of the grounds, but had not gone farther in. It did not feel abandoned. The gardens were too well cared for, and where there were gardens there were gardeners. Somewhere there had to be an adult.

I told them this.

Jamie said, "Bet there's not. Probably just someone who comes in and cuts the grass once a month or something. You're not scared, are you? We've been there hundreds of times. Thousands."

Of course I was scared, and of course I said that I was not. We went up the main drive, until we reached the main gates. They were closed, and we squeezed beneath the bars to get in.

Rhododendron bushes lined the drive. Before we got to the house there was what I took to be a groundskeeper's cottage, and beside it on the grass were some rusting metal cages, big enough to hold a hunting dog, or a boy. We walked past them, up to a horseshoe-shaped drive and right up to the front door of the Swallows. We peered inside, looking in the windows, but seeing nothing. It was too dark inside.

We slipped around the house, into a rhododendron thicket and out again, into some kind of fairyland. It was a magical grotto, all rocks and delicate ferns and odd, exotic plants I'd never seen before: plants with purple leaves, and leaves like fronds, and small half-hidden flowers like jewels. A tiny stream wound through it, a rill of water running from rock to rock.

Douglas said, "I'm going to wee-wee in it." It was very matter-of-fact. He walked over to it, pulled down his shorts, and urinated in the stream, splashing on the rocks. The other boys did it too, both of them pulling out their penises and standing beside him to piss into the stream.

I was shocked. I remember that. I suppose I was shocked by the joy they took in this, or just by the way they were doing something like that in such a special place, spoiling the clear water and the magic of the place, making it into a toilet. It seemed wrong.

When they were done, they did not put their penises away. They shook them. They pointed them at me. Jamie had hair growing at the base of his.

"We're cavaliers," said Jamie. "Do you know what that means?"

I knew about the English Civil War, Cavaliers (wrong but romantic) versus Roundheads (right but repulsive), but I didn't think that was what he was talking about. I shook my head.

"It means our willies aren't circumcised," he explained. "Are you a cavalier or a roundhead?"

I knew what they meant now. I muttered, "I'm a roundhead."

"Show us. Go on. Get it out."

"No. It's none of your business."

For a moment, I thought things were going to get nasty, but then Jamie laughed, and put his penis away, and the others did the same. They told dirty jokes to each other then, jokes I really didn't understand at all, for all that I was a bright child, but I heard them and remembered them, and several weeks later was almost expelled from school for telling one of them to a boy who went home and told it to his parents.

The joke had the word fuck in it. That was the first time I ever heard the word, in a dirty joke in a fairy grotto.

The principal called my parents into the school, after I got in trouble, and said that I'd said something so bad they could not repeat it, not even to tell my parents what I'd done.

My mother asked me, when they got home that night.

"Fuck," I said.

"You must never, ever say that word," said my mother. She said this very firmly, and quietly, and for my own good. "That is the worst word anyone can say." I promised her that I wouldn't.

But after, amazed at the power a single word could have, I would whisper it to myself, when I was alone.

In the grotto, that autumn afternoon after school, the three big boys told jokes and they laughed and they laughed, and I laughed too, although I did not understand any of what they were laughing about.

We moved on from the grotto. Out into the formal gardens, and over a small bridge that crossed a pond; we crossed it nervously, because it was out in the open, but we could see huge goldfish in the blackness of the pond below, which made it worthwhile. Then Jamie led Douglas and Simon and me down a gravel path into some woodland.

Unlike the gardens, the woods were abandoned and unkempt. They felt like there was no one around. The path was grown over. It led between trees, and then, after a while, into a clearing.

In the clearing was a little house.

It was a playhouse, built perhaps forty years earlier for a child, or for children. The windows were Tudor-style, leaded and crisscrossed into diamonds. The roof was mock-Tudor. A stone path led straight from where we were to the front door.

Together, we walked up the path to the door.

Hanging from the door was a metal knocker. It was painted crimson, and had been cast in the shape of some kind of imp, some kind of grinning pixie or demon, cross-legged, hanging by its hands from a hinge. Let me see . . . how can I describe this best: it wasn't a good thing. The expression on its face, for starters. I found myself wondering what kind of a person would hang something like that on a playroom door.

It frightened me, there in that clearing, with the dusk gathering under the trees. I walked away from the house, back to a safe distance, and the others followed me.

"I think I have to go home now," I said.

It was the wrong thing to say. The three of them turned and laughed and jeered at me, called me pathetic, called me a baby. They weren't scared of the house, they said.

"I dare you!" said Jamie. "I dare you to knock on the door."

I shook my head.

"If you don't knock on the door," said Douglas, "you're too much of a baby ever to play with us again."

I had no desire ever to play with them again. They seemed like occupants of a land I was not yet ready to enter. But still, I did not want them to think me a baby.

"Go on. We're not scared," said Simon.

I try to remember the tone of voice he used. Was he frightened too, and covering it with bravado? Or was he amused? It's been so long. I wish I knew.

I walked slowly back up the flagstone path to the house. I reached up, grabbed the grinning imp in my right hand, and banged it hard against the door.

Or rather, I tried to bang it hard, just to show the other three that I was not afraid at all. That I was not afraid of anything. But something happened, something I had not expected, and the knocker hit the door with a muffled sort of a thump.

"Now you have to go inside!" shouted Jamie. He was excited. I could hear it. I found myself wondering if they had known about this place already, before we came. If I was the first person they had brought there.

But I did not move.

"You go in," I said. "I knocked on the door. I did it like you said. Now you have to go inside. I dare you. I dare all of you."

I wasn't going in. I was perfectly certain of that. Not then. Not ever. I'd felt something move; I'd felt the knocker twist under my hand as I'd banged that grinning imp down on the door. I was not so old that I would deny my own senses.

They said nothing. They did not move.

Then, slowly, the door fell open. Perhaps they thought that I, standing by the door, had pushed it open. Perhaps they thought that I'd jarred it when I knocked. But I hadn't. I was certain of it. It opened because it was ready.

I should have run, then. My heart was pounding in my chest. But the devil was in me, and instead of running I looked at the three big boys at the bottom of the path, and I simply said, "Or are you scared?"

They walked up the path toward the little house.

"It's getting dark," said Douglas.

Then the three boys walked past me, and one by one, reluctantly perhaps, they entered the playhouse. A white face turned to look at me as they went into that room, to ask why I wasn't following them in, I'll bet. But as Simon, who was the last of them, walked in, the door banged shut behind them, and I swear to God I did not touch it.

The imp grinned down at me from the wooden door, a vivid splash of crimson in the gray gloaming.

I walked around to the side of the playhouse and peered in through all the windows, one by one, into the dark and empty room. Nothing moved in there. I wondered if the other three were inside hiding from me, pressed against the wall, trying their damnedest to stifle their giggles. I wondered if it was a big-boy game.

I didn't know. I couldn't tell.

I stood there in the courtyard of the playhouse, while the sky got darker, just waiting. The moon rose after a while, a big autumn moon the color of honey.

And then, after a while, the door opened, and nothing came out.

Now I was alone in the glade, as alone as if there had never been anyone else there at all. An owl hooted, and I realized that I was free to go. I turned and walked away, following a different path out of the glade, always keeping my distance from the main house. I climbed a fence in the moonlight, ripping the seat of my school shorts, and I walked—not ran, I didn't need to run—across a field of barley stubble, and over a stile, and into a flinty lane that would take me, if I followed it far enough, all the way to my house.

And soon enough, I was home.

My parents had not been worried, although they were irritated by the orange rust-dust on my clothes, by the rip in my shorts. "Where were you, anyway?" my mother asked.

"I went for a walk," I said. "I lost track of time."

And that was where we left it.

I t was almost two in the morning. The Polish countess had already gone. Now Nora began, noisily, to collect up the glasses and ashtrays, and to wipe down the bar. "This place is haunted," she said, cheerfully. "Not that it's ever bothered me. I like a bit of company, darlings. If I didn't, I wouldn't have opened the club. Now, don't you have homes to go to?"

We said our good nights to Nora and she made each of us kiss her on her cheek, and she closed the door of the Diogenes Club behind us. We walked down the narrow steps past the record shop, down into the alley and back into civilization.

The underground had stopped running hours ago, but there were always night buses, and cabs still out there for those who could afford them. (I couldn't. Not in those days.)

The Diogenes Club itself closed several years later, finished off by Nora's cancer, and, I suppose, by the easy availability of late-night alcohol once the English licensing laws were changed. But I rarely went back after that night.

"Was there ever," asked Paul-the-actor, as we hit the street, "any news of those three boys? Did you see them again? Or were they reported as missing?"

"Neither," said the storyteller. "I mean, I never saw them again. And there was no local manhunt for three missing boys. Or if there was, I never heard about it."

"Is the playhouse still there?" asked Martyn.

"I don't know," admitted the storyteller.

"Well," said Martyn, as we reached the Tottenham Court Road, and headed for the night bus stop, "I for one do not believe a word of it."

There were four of us, not three, out on the street long after closing time. I should have mentioned that before. There was still one of us who had not spoken, the elderly man with the leather elbow-patches, who had left the club when the three of us had left. And now he spoke for the first time.

"I believe it," he said, mildly. His voice was frail, almost apologetic. "I cannot explain it, but I believe it. Jamie died, you know, not long after Father did. It was Douglas who wouldn't go back, who sold the old place. He wanted them to tear it all down. But they kept the house itself, the Swallows. They weren't going to knock that down. I imagine that everything else must be gone by now."

It was a cold night, and the rain still spat occasional drizzle. I shivered, but only because I was cold.

"Those cages you mentioned," he said. "By the driveway. I haven't thought of them in fifty years. When we were bad he'd lock us up in them. We must have been bad a great deal, eh? Very naughty, naughty boys."

He was looking up and down the Tottenham Court Road, as if he were looking for something. Then he said, "Douglas killed himself, of course. Ten years ago. When I was still in the bin. So my memory's not as good. Not as good as it was. But that was Jamie all right, to the life. He'd never let us forget that he was the oldest. And you know, we weren't ever allowed in the playhouse. Father didn't build it for us." His voice quavered, and for a moment I could imagine this pale old man as a boy again. "Father had his own games."

And then he waved his arm and called "Taxi!" and a taxi pulled over to the curb. "Brown's Hotel," said the man, and he got in. He did not say good night to any of us. He pulled shut the door of the cab.

And in the closing of the cab door I could hear too many other doors closing. Doors in the past, which are gone now, and cannot be reopened.

Otherwise Pandemonium

By NICK HORNBY

It was just a lousy secondhand VCR—but it brought him to the very brink of love and desolation!

Mom always sings this crappy old song when I'm in a bad mood. She does it to make me laugh, but I never do laugh, because I'm in a bad mood. (Sometimes I sort of smile later, when I'm in a better mood, and I think about her singing and dancing and making the dorky black-and-white-movie face—eyes wide, all her teeth showing—she always makes when she sings the song. But I never tell her she makes me smile. It would only encourage her to sing more often.) This song is called "Ac-cent-chu-ate the Positive," and I have to listen to it whenever she tells me we're going to Dayton to see Grandma, or when she won't give me the money for something I need, like CDs or even clothes, for Christ's sake. Anyway, today I'm going to do what the song says. I'm going to accentuate the positive, and eliminate the negative. Otherwise, according to the song and to my mom, pandemonium's liable to walk upon the scene.

O K. Well, here is the accentuated positive: I got to have sex. That's the upside of it. I know that's probably a strange way of looking at things, considering the circumstances, but it's definitely the major event of the week so far. It won't be the major event of the year, I know that—Jesus, do I know that—but it's still a headline news item: I just turned fifteen, and I'm no longer a virgin. How cool is that? The target I'd set for myself was sixteen, which means I'm a whole year ahead of schedule. Nearly two years, in fact, because I'll still be sixteen in twenty-two months' time. So let's say this is the story of how I ended up getting laid—a story with a beginning, and a weird middle, and a happy ending. Otherwise I'd have to tell you a Stephen King–type story, with a beginning and a weird middle and a really fucking scary ending, and I don't want to do that. It wouldn't help me right now.

S o. You probably think you need to know who I am, and what kind of car my brother drives, and all that Holden Caulfield kind of crap, but you really don't, and not just because I haven't got a brother, or even a cute little sister. It's not one of those stories. Insights into my personality and all that stuff aren't going to help you or me one bit, because this shit is real. I don't want you to get to the end of this and start thinking about whether I'd have acted different if my parents had stayed together, or whether I'm a typical product of our times, or what I tell you about being fifteen, or any of those other questions we have to discuss when we read a story in school. It's not the point. All you need to know is where I got the video recorder from, and maybe, I suppose, why I got it, so I'll tell you.

I found it a couple blocks from my house, in this store that sells used electronic stuff. It cost fifty bucks, which seemed pretty good to me, although now it doesn't seem like such a great bargain, but that's another story. Or rather, it's this story, but a different part of it. And I bought it because . . . OK, so maybe I will have to give you a little background, but I won't make it into a big drama. I'll just give you the facts. My mom and I moved from L.A. to Berkeley about three months ago. We moved because Mom finally walked out on my asshole of a father, who writes movies for a living—although as none of them ever got made, it would be more accurate to say that he writes scripts for a living. Mom is an art teacher, and she paints her own stuff, too, and she says there are millions of people in Berkeley with an artistic bent or whatever, so she thought we'd feel right at home here. (I like it that she says "we." I haven't got an artistic bone in my whole body, and she knows that, but for some reason she thinks I take after her. It was pretty much always me and her against him, so that became me and her against L.A., and because I was against L.A., that somehow made me able to paint. I don't mind. Painting's pretty cool, some of it.)

B erkeley's nice, I guess, but I didn't have any friends here, so Mom made me join this dumb jazz orchestra thing. I'd just started to take trumpet lessons in L.A., and I didn't suck too bad; a couple months after we moved, she saw an ad in a local bookstore for something called the Little Berkeley Big Band, which is like for people under the age of seventeen, and she signed me up. She had to sing the Ac-cent-chu-ate song a lot in the car the first evening I went to a rehearsal, because I'd be the first to admit that I wasn't feeling very positive. But it was OK, not that I'd ever admit that to her. You can make a pretty fucking great noise when you're part of a horn section. I can't say I'm going to make any friends, though. The kind of people who want to play in the Little Berkeley Big Band . . . well, let's just say that they're not my kind of people. Apart from Martha, but I'll tell you about her later. (And now you'll probably have guessed some of the ending, but I don't care, because you only know her name, and not how we ended up having sex. How we ended up having sex is the interesting part.) All you need to know about Martha: a) She's hot; b) but hot in a not-slutty way. In other words, if you saw her, you would never guess in a million years that I'd persuade her to sleep with me. (Hopefully that has made you very curious—"Man, how the fuck did he get to sleep with her?"—which means you'll be more interested in the happy ending, rather than the weird middle, which means I don't have to take the Stephen King route.)

B ut my argument for the video recorder was this: not only was I not making friends at the band rehearsals, but the rehearsals were actually stopping me from making friends. Here's how it works: I go to rehearsals. We don't have a VCR. (We left ours in L.A. with Dad, and for some insane reason Mom didn't want to buy a replacement right away, I guess because we were supposed to read books and paint and play trumpets every night, like we were living in the Little House on the Prairie or something.) I can't tape the NBA play-offs. I can't talk about the games next day. Everyone thinks I'm a dweeb. Obvious, right? Not to her. I had to threaten to go back and live with Dad before she gave in, and even then she more or less told me I had to find the cheapest, crappiest machine in the Bay Area.

A nyway, it's pretty great, this place. It sells old TVs—like really old, *Back to the Future* old—and guitars, and amps, and stereos and radios. And VCRs. I just asked the old hippie guy who runs the place for the cheapest one he had that actually worked, and he pointed me over to this pile right in the corner of the store.

"That one on the top works," he said. "Or at least, it was working a few days ago. Used to be mine."

"So why aren't you using it anymore?" I asked him. I was trying to be sharp, but that doesn't often work for me. Give me an hour or two and I'm sharp as a box cutter, but sometimes in the moment, things don't work out as good as I'd want.

"I got a better one," he said. I couldn't really argue with that. He could probably have made one that was better. Shit, I could probably have made one that was better.

"But it records?"

He just looked at me.

"Records and plays?"

"No, kid. It does everything else, just doesn't record or play."

"So if it doesn't record or play, what's the point . . ." Then I realized he was being sarcastic, so of course I felt pretty dumb.

"And you never had any trouble with it?"

"Depends what you mean by trouble."

"Like . . . with recording? Or playing?" I couldn't think of another way of putting it.

"No."

"So what sort of trouble did you have?"

"If this conversation lasts any longer, I'll have to put the price up. Otherwise it's not worth my time."

"Does it come with a remote?"

"I can find you one."

So I just dug in my pocket for the fifty bucks, handed it to him, and went and got the thing off the top of the pile. He found a remote and put it in my jacket pocket. And then, as I was walking out, he said this weird thing.

"Just . . . forget it."

"What?"

"I did."

"What?"

This guy was old-school Berkeley, if you know what I mean. Gray beard, gray ponytail, dirty old vest.

"Cos it can't know anything, right? It's just a fucking VCR. What can it know? Nothing."

"No, man," I said. Because I thought I had a handle on him then, you know? He was nuts, plain and simple. Weed had destroyed his mind. "No, it can't know anything. Like you say, what could it know?"

He smiled then, like he was really relieved, and it was only when he smiled that I could tell how sad he looked before.

"I really needed to hear that," he said.

"Happy to oblige."

"I'm forty-nine years old, and I got a lot to do. I got a novel to write."

"You'd better hurry."

"Really?" He looked worried again. I didn't know what the fuck I'd said.

"Well. You know. Hurry in your own time." Because I didn't care when he wrote his stupid novel. Why should I?

"Right. Right. Hey, thanks."

"No problem."

And that was it. I thought about what he'd said for maybe another minute and a half, and then forgot about him. For a while, anyway.

So I was all set. I had a band rehearsal that night, so I wired the VCR up to the TV in my room, and then I did a little test on it. I recorded some news show for a couple minutes, and then I played it back—A-OK. I checked out the remote—fine. I even put my tape of *The Matrix* in the machine, to see what kind of picture quality I was getting. (The kind of picture quality you get on a fifty-buck VCR was what I was getting.) Then I worked out the timer, and set it for the last part of that night's Lakers game. Everything was cool. Or rather, everything would have been cool, if my mom hadn't decided to interfere, although as it turned out, it was a good sort of interference.

What happened was, I got a lift home from Martha's dad. With Martha in the car. I mean, of course Martha was in the car, because that was why her dad had turned up at the community center, but, you know. Martha was in the car. Which meant . . . well, not too much, if you really want to analyze it that closely. I didn't talk a whole lot. Like I said, give me a few hours to think about it and I'm William fucking Shakespeare; I'm just not so good in real time. I guess it's my dad's genes coming through. He can write OK dialogue if he has enough time to think about it—like a year. But ask him the simplest question, like "What's going on with you and Mom?" and he's, you know, "Duh, yeah, well, blah." Thanks, Dad. That's made things real clear.

Anyway, we got in the car, and . . . Oh—first of all, I should tell you that it's turning into a regular thing, which is how come I wasn't too disgusted by my performance that night. And maybe I should confess that I nearly blew it, too. This is where Mom's good/bad interference comes in. What happened was, she dropped into this little gallery in the neighborhood, to see if they'd be interested in exhibiting her stuff, and she got talking to the owner, who turns out to be Martha's dad. And somehow they got onto the subject of the Little Berkeley Big Band, and like two seconds later they've divided up the rides. I'll be honest here: I completely freaked out when she told me. No amount of singing her song would have calmed me down. She explained that she met this guy who lives real near and his daughter was in the band and so he was going to drop us off and pick us up this week and it was her turn next week and . . .

"Stop right there."

"What?"

"Do you realize what a bunch of pathetic losers they are in that band? You really expect me to sit in a car with one of them every week?"

"I'm not asking you to date her. I'm asking you to sit in a car with her for ten minutes once a week."

"No way."

"Too late."

"Fine. I'm quitting the band. As from this second."

"You don't think that's an overreaction?"

"No. Goodbye."

And I went up to my bedroom. I meant it. I was going to quit. I didn't care. Even if I was giving up a future career as a superstar jazz trumpeter, it was worth it if it meant not sitting in a car with Eloise and her bad breath. Or Zoe and her quote unquote gland problem (in other words her intense fatness problem). Anyway, Mom came up five minutes later and said that she'd called the guy and canceled the ride, told him I had a doctor's appointment first so I wouldn't be leaving from home.

"A doctor's appointment? Great, so now everyone thinks I've got some gross disease. Thanks a lot."

"Jesus." She shook her head.

"And anyway, how am I going to get out of coming back with them?" I will admit, I was being pretty difficult.

She shook her head again. If I hadn't been so mad, I might have felt sorry for her. "I'll think of something."

"Like what?"

"I don't know. Just get in the car. We'll be late."

"No. Now it's too embarrassing. I'm still quitting."

"Paul will be disappointed. I got the impression that he had high hopes for you and Martha. He thought you sounded like . . ."

"Whoa. Martha?"

"Do you know her?"

"Maybe."

"Do you like her?"

I tried to be cool about it. "She's OK. I'll just go and find my trumpet."

Respect where it's due to Mom: she didn't say anything. Didn't even smile in a way that would have made me freak out all over again. Just waited for me downstairs. She was still in the wrong, though. OK, it turned out well, but there was like a 99.9% chance (or rather, because there are maybe fifteen girls in the band, a ninety-four-point-something percent chance) that it could have been a total disaster. She didn't know it was Martha, or even who Martha is, so she was just plain lucky.

Before we get back to me in the car with Martha, which sounds way more exciting than it actually was, there's one more bit of the story that's important, but I'm not too sure where to put it. It should either go here—which was roughly where it happened—or later, when I get back from rehearsal, which is where I actually discovered it, and where it has a bit more dramatic effect. But the thing is, if I put it later, you might not believe it. You might think it's just like a story trick, or something I just made up on the spur of the moment to explain something, and it would really piss me off if you thought that. And anyway, I don't need any dramatic effects, man. This story I need to calm down, not pump up. So I'll tell you here: I messed up the VCR recording of the Lakers game. I was so mad that I watched five minutes of *The Matrix*, which meant removing the blank tape. I remembered to take out *The Matrix* tape, but I forgot to put another one back in. (I forgot because once Mom mentioned Martha, I was in kind of a hurry.) But I didn't know I'd messed up then. See what I mean? If I'd left that part until later, it might have had a little kick to it—"Oh, no, he didn't tape the game. So how come . . ." But if that little kick means you believe me any less, it's not worth it.

Anyway, again. We got in the car after the rehearsal, me, Martha, and her dad, and . . . You know what? None of this part matters. Shit, maybe I should have left the tape thing until later, because now I've brought it up, I kind of want to get back to it. I can't just keep it back for suspense purposes. And if you think about it, that's how you know most stories aren't true. I mean, I read a lot of horror writers, and those guys are always delaying the action to build it up a little. As in, I don't know, "She ran down the path and slammed the front door with a sigh of relief. Little did she know that the Vampire Zombie was in her bathroom.

"MEANWHILE, two thousand miles away, Frank Miller of the NYPD was frowning. There was something about this case that was troubling him . . ."

See, if that shit with the Vampire Zombie was real—REAL AND HAPPENING TO YOU—you wouldn't care whether Frank Miller was frowning or not. You've got a zombie in your apartment with a fucking chain saw or a blowtorch or something, so what does it matter what a cop does with his eyebrows on the other side of the country? Therefore, if you'll permit me to point something out that may ruin your reading pleasure forever, you know that the story has been made up.

But you know this story, the one I'm telling you, hasn't been made up. You know it a) because I told you that thing about the tape straightaway, when it happened, rather than trying to get a little zinger going later, and b) because I'm not going to go into who said what to who on a car ride, just to bump up the page numbers, or to make you forget about the tape thing. You just need to hear this much: Martha and I didn't say an awful lot, but we did some smiling and whatever, so at the end of the ride we maybe both knew we liked each other. And then I got out of the car, said "Hi" to Mom, and went upstairs to watch the game.

Well, you know now that there wasn't a tape in the machine, but I didn't. I sat down on the bed and turned on the TV. Letterman was just starting. He was doing one of those dumb list things that everyone pretends is funny but which really no one understands. I pressed the rewind on the remote: nothing. Not surprising, right? And then I pressed the fast-forward button, I guess because I thought the timer recording hadn't worked, and I wanted to check that there was a tape in there.

This is what happened: I started fast-forwarding through Letterman. I was pretty confused. How could I do that? The show wasn't even finished, so how could I have taped it? I pressed the eject, and finally I found out what you've known for a while: that there was no cassette in there. With no cassette, I can't be fast-forwarding. But my TV doesn't seem to know that, because meanwhile, Letterman's waving his hands in the air really really fast, and then we're racing through the ads, and then it's the closing credits, and then it's the *Late Late Show,* and then more ads. . . . And that's when I realize what's going on: I'm fast-forwarding through network fucking television.

I mean, obviously I checked this theory out. I checked it out by keeping my finger on the remote until I got to the next morning's breakfast news, which took maybe an hour. But I got there in the end: they showed the next day's weather, and the best plays from what they said was last night's Lakers game—even though it wasn't last night to me—and, a little later, a big pileup on the freeway near Candlestick Park that had happened in the early morning fog. I could have stopped it, if I'd known any of the drivers. I got bored after a while, and put the remote down; but it took me a long time to get to sleep.

I woke up late, and I had to rush the next morning, so I didn't get to move any further through the day's TV schedule. On my way to school, I tried to think about it all—what I could do with it, whether I'd show it to anyone, whatever. Like I said, I'm not as quick as I'd like to be. Mentally speaking, I'm not Maurice Greene. I'm more like one of those Kenyan long-distance runners. I get there in the end, but it takes like two hours and an awful lot of sweat. And to tell you the absolute truth, when I went to school that morning, I didn't see it was such a big deal. I was, like, I saw this morning's weather forecast last night; well, so what? Everyone knew what the weather was now. Same with the pileup. And I'd seen a few of the best plays from the Lakers game, but everyone who didn't rehearse in a stupid jazz band had seen the whole game anyway. Like, I was supposed to boast to people that I'd seen stuff they saw before I did?

Imaginary conversation:

"I saw the best plays from the Lakers game."

"So did we. We watched the game."

"Yeah, but I saw them on the breakfast news show."

"So did we."

"Yeah, but I saw them on the breakfast news show last night."

"You're a jerk. You need to have your ass kicked." What's fun about that? Watching breakfast news seven hours early didn't seem like such a big deal to me.

It took me a while longer than it should have done to get the whole picture: If I just kept fast-forwarding, I could see all kinds of stuff. The rest of the play-offs. The next episodes of *Buffy,* or *Friends.* The next season of *Buffy* or *Friends.* Next month's weather, whatever that's worth. Some news stuff, like, maybe, a psycho with a gun coming into our school one day next year, so I could warn the people I liked. (In other words not Brian O'Hagan. Or Mrs. Fleming.) It took me longer than it should have, but I began to see that fast-forwarding through network TV could be awesome.

And for the next two days, that's all I did: I sat in my bedroom with the remote, watching the TV of the future. I watched the Lakers destroy the Pacers in the NBA finals. I watched the A's get smashed by the Yankees. I watched "The One Where Phoebe and Joey Get Married." I fast-forwarded until I got blisters. I watched TV until even my dreams got played out on a 14" screen. I was in my bedroom so often that Mom thought I had just discovered jerking off, and wanted me to call my father and talk. (Like, hello, Mom? I'm fifteen?) I could rewind, too; I could watch reruns of the TV of the future if I wanted.

And none of it was any use to me. Who wants to know stuff before it happens? People might think they do, but believe me, they don't, because if you know stuff before it happens, there's nothing to talk about. A lot of school conversation is about TV and sports; and what people like to talk about is what just happened (which I now can't remember, because it was three games back, or the episode before last) or what might happen. And when people talk about what might happen, they like to argue, or make dumb jokes; they don't want someone coming in and squashing it all flat. It's all, "No, man, Shaq's not looking so young anymore, I think the Pacers can take them." "No way! The Pacers have no defense. Shaq's going to destroy them." Now, what do you say if you know the score? You tell them? Of course not. It sounds too weird, and there's nothing to bounce off anyway. So all I ever did was agree with the guy whose prediction was closest to the truth, to what I knew, and it was like I hadn't seen anything, because the knowledge I had was no fucking good to anyone. One thing I learned: School life is all about anticipation. We're fifteen, and nothing's happened to us yet, so we spend an awful lot of time imagining what things will be like. No one's interested in some jerk who says he knows. That's not what it's about.

But of course I kept going with the remote. I couldn't stop myself. I'd come back from school and watch, I'd wake up in the morning and watch, I'd come back from rehearsals and watch. I was a month, maybe five weeks, into the future—time enough to know that Frazier gets engaged to some writer, that there's a dumb new sitcom starting soon about a rock star who accidentally becomes three inches tall, and that half the Midwest gets flooded in a freak storm.

And then. . . . Well, OK, maybe I should say that I had noticed something: The news programs were becoming really fucking long. It took a whole lot of fast-forwarding to get through them. And then one night I came back from school and picked up the remote, and all I could find was news. As far as I could tell, in about six weeks' time, all of network TV—every channel—is just like one long fucking news show. No *Buffy,* no sports, no nothing; just guys in suits with maps, and people in weird countries you've never heard of talking into those crappy video things which make them go all jerky and fuzzy. It was like that for a couple days after 9/11, if you remember that long ago, but sooner or later everything went back to normal; I was trying to find that part, but I couldn't get there.

Now and again I stopped to watch the people talking, but I didn't really understand it; there was stuff about India and Pakistan, and Russia, and China, and Iraq and Iran, and Israel and Palestine. There were maps, and pictures of people packing up all their shit in all these places and getting the hell out. The usual stuff, but worse, I guess.

And then, a few days' TV-time later, I found the president. I watched some of that—it was on every channel at the same time. She was sitting in the Oval Office, talking to the American people, with this really intense expression on her face. She was so serious it was scary. And she was telling us that these were the darkest days in our history, and that we were all to face them with courage and determination. She said that freedom came at a price, but that price had to be worth paying, otherwise we had no identity or value as a nation. And then she asked God to bless us all. Straight after the show they cut to live pictures of more people getting the hell out of their homes, carrying bundles of their possessions under one arm and small children under another. These people were walking down the steps of a subway station, trying to get underground. The pictures weren't fuzzy or jerky, though. These people lived in New York City.

I didn't want to watch it anymore, so I picked up the remote; never in my life have I wanted to see the opening credits of *Sabrina* so bad. But after a couple of hours of news stuff there was nothing. The TV just stops. Network TV canceled. I've spent most of my time since then trying to see if I can get beyond the static, but I'm not there yet.

Now, all this time, I haven't spoken to anyone about any of this shit. Not to Mom, not to anyone at school, not to Martha. That's one thing they get right in stories, even though I didn't use to think so: You don't want to talk about spooky stuff. In the stories, there's always some reason for it, like, I don't know, the words don't come out when they try to speak, or the magic thing only works for the guy who's telling the story, something like that, but the real reason is, it just sounds dumb. When it finally clicked that I could watch NBA games before they happened, then obviously I thought I was going to ask a bunch of guys to come over to watch. But how do you say it? How do you say, I've got a video recorder that lets me fast-forward through the whole of TV? You don't, is the answer, unless you're a complete jerk. Can you imagine? The only quicker way to get a pounding would be to wear a STA-COOL T-shirt to school. (I just thought of something: If you're reading this, you might not know about STA-COOL. Because if you're reading this, it's way off in the future, after the static, and you might have forgotten about STA-COOL, where you are. Maybe it's a better world where people only listen to good music, not stupid pussy boy-band shit, because the world understands that life is too short for boy bands. Well, good. I'm glad. We did not die in vain.) And I was going to tell Mom, but not yet, and then when I got to the static . . . People should be allowed to enjoy their lives, is my view. Sometimes when she gives me a hard time about my clothes or playing my music loud, I want to say something. Like, "Don't stress out, Mom, because in a month or so someone's going to drop the big one." But most of the time I just want her to enjoy her painting, and living in Berkeley. She's happy here.

When I remembered the guy I bought the machine from, though, I wanted to speak to him. He'd seen the static too; that's what that conversation in his shop had been all about, except I didn't know it. He realized why I'd come as soon as I walked in. I didn't even say anything. He just saw it in my face.

"Oh, man," he said after a little while. "Oh, man. I never even started my novel." Which I couldn't believe. I mean, Jesus. What else did this guy need to help him understand that time is running out? He'd seen the end of the fucking world on live TV, and he still hadn't gotten off his stoned ass. Although maybe he'd figured he wasn't going to find a publisher in time. And he certainly wasn't going to get too many readers.

"Maybe we're both crazy," I said. "Maybe we're getting it all wrong."

"You think network TV would stop for any other reason? Like, to encourage us to get more exercise or something?"

"Maybe the thing just stopped working."

"Yeah, and all those people were going into the subway with their kids because they couldn't find any child care. No, we're fucked, man. I never voted for that bitch, and now she's killed me. Shit."

At least you've had a life, I wanted to say. I haven't done anything yet. And that was when I decided to ask Martha out.

(OK. That was the weird middle. Now I'm going to give you the happy ending: the story of how I got to sleep with the hottest girl in the Little Berkeley Big Band, even though I'm only fifteen, and even though she doesn't look like the sort of girl who gives it up for anybody.)

One thing about knowing the world is going to end: It makes you a lot less nervous about the whole dating thing. So that's a plus. And she made it easy, anyway. We were talking in her dad's car about movies we'd seen, and movies we wanted to see, and it turned out we both wanted to see this Vin Diesel movie about a guy who can turn himself into like a bacteria anytime he feels like it and hang out in people and kill them if necessary. (Although to tell you the truth, I used to want to see it more than I do now. There are a lot of things I used to want to do more than I do now. Like, I don't know, buying stuff. It sounds kind of dumb, I guess, but if you see a cool T-shirt, you're thinking about the future, aren't you? You're thinking, Hey, I could wear that to Sarah Steiner's party. There are so many things connected to the future—school, eating vegetables, cleaning your teeth. . . . In my position, it'd be pretty easy to let things slide.) So it seemed like the logical next step to say, Hey, why don't we go together?

The movie was OK. And afterward we went to get a pizza, and we talked about what it would be like to be a bacteria, and about the band, and about her school and my school. And then she told me that one of the reasons she liked me was that I seemed sad.

"Really?"

"Yeah. Does that sound dumb?"

"No." Because a) nothing she says sounds dumb; b) even if it did, it would be dumb to tell her; c) I'm sad. With good reason. So I'm not surprised I look it.

"Most guys our age don't look sad. They're always laughing about nothing."

I laughed—a little—because what she said was so true, and I hadn't even noticed it before.

"So are you really sad? Or is that just the way your face is?"

"I guess . . . I don't know. I guess I'm sad sometimes."

"Me too."

"Yeah? Why?"

"You first."

Oh, man. I've seen enough movies and soaps to know that the sad guy is supposed to be the quiet, sensitive, poetic one, and I'm not sure that's me. I wasn't sad before I knew there was going to be a terrible catastrophe and we're all in trouble; suddenly, I went from like NBA fan to tortured genius-style dude. I think she's got the wrong impression. If PJ Rogers, who's this really really stupid trombonist kid in the orchestra, the kind of jerk whose wittiest joke is a loud fart, had seen what I'd seen, he'd be a tortured genius too.

"There's some stuff I'm worried about. That's all. It's not like I'm this really deep thinker."

"Lots of kids don't worry even when there's something to worry about. They're too insensitive."

"How about you?" I wanted to change the subject. I was getting way too much credit.

"I don't know why I'm sad half the time. I just am."

I wanted to say to her, Now, see, that's the real deal. That's being sensitive and screwed up . . . the classic *Breakfast Club* stuff. I'm an amateur compared to you. But I didn't. I just nodded, like I knew what she was talking about.

"Do you want to tell me about the things you're worried about? Would it help?"

"It'd help me. I think it would fuck you up."

"I can take it."

"I'm not sure."

"Try me."

And I was so sick of being on my own that I took her up on the offer. It's probably the most selfish thing I've ever done in my whole life.

I asked her over to my house for lunch, after a Saturday morning rehearsal. Mom took us back and fixed us sandwiches, and when we'd eaten we went up to my room to listen to music—or that's what she thought we were going to do. When we got upstairs, though, I explained everything, right from the beginning. I'd prepared this; I'd rewound to the point where the news started taking over the networks, and I'd found a section where they were talking about what happened when, and all the dates they mentioned were in the future. That was my evidence, and Martha believed it. It took a couple more hours to get back to the New York City subway scenes, but she wanted to see them, so we just sat there waiting. And then she watched, and then she started to cry.

Listen: There's something that's bothering me. Before, when I said that I asked Martha out on a date because I haven't done anything in my life yet . . . I'm not so much of an asshole that this was the first thing I thought of. It wasn't. It was one of the first, sure, but, you know—six weeks! There are lots of other things I wanted to achieve in my life, but I'm not going to get them done in six weeks. I'm not going to go to film school, and I'm not going to have a kid, and I'm not going to drive across the U.S.; at least sex is something achievable. And it's not like I was just looking for the first available piece of ass, either. I really like Martha a lot. In fact, if . . . but let's not go there. This is the happy ending, right?

Anyway. The next part came naturally. She stopped crying, and we talked, and we tried to understand what had happened. Martha knows more about that shit than I do; she said things were already pretty bad, now, in the present, but because things are happening in other countries a long ways away, I hadn't noticed. I've been watching the basketball, not the news. And then we had this real sad conversation about the stuff I'd already been thinking—about what we'd miss, and what we'd never do. . . .

The truth is, she suggested it, not me. I swear. I mean, I wasn't going to say no, but it was her idea. She said that she wanted us to get good at it, which meant starting like straightaway. (She said this before, by the way. She didn't say it in response to anything, if that's what you're thinking.) So I made sure Mom was still out, and then we kissed, and then we got undressed and made love in my bed. We didn't use anything. Neither of us can have any sexual disease, and if she gets pregnant, well, that's fine by us. We'd love to have a kid, for obvious reasons.

W ell, that's it. That brings you up-to-date, whoever you are. Martha and I see each other all the time, and this weekend we're going to go away together; I'm going to tell Mom that I want to see Dad, and she's going to give her parents some other excuse, and we'll take off somewhere, somehow. And that'll be something else we've checked on the list—we'll have spent a whole night together. I know it's maybe not the happy ending you were hoping for, but you probably weren't hoping for a happy ending anyway, because you already know about the Time of the Static. Unless you're reading this in the next six weeks, and I'm sure as hell not going to show anybody. How is it where you are? Have people learned their lesson? How was that show about the three-inch rock star? Maybe they canceled it.

The Tale of Gray Dick

By STEPHEN KING

They had looked everywhere for protection from their most devastating foe—except to the murderous know-how of their old wives' tales.

When evening came, Roland Deschain returned on horseback from the Manni village to Eisenhart's Lazy B. He'd spent the afternoon in a long palaver with Henchick, the dinh of the Manni. Only here in Calla Bryn Sturgis, the head of clan was called the heart-stone. In the case of Henchick, Roland thought the term fit very well. Yet the man understood that trouble was on the way. Stony-hearted he might be; stupid he was not.

Roland sat behind the ranch house, listening to the boys shout and the dog bark. Back in Gilead (where the gunslinger had come from a thousand years before), this sort of porch, facing the barns, stock-well, and fields, would have been called the work-stoop.

"Boys!" Eisenhart bawled. "What in the name of the Man Jesus am I going to tell yer mothers if you kill yer sad selfs jumpin out of that barn?"

"We're okay!" Benny Slightman called. He was the son of Eisenhart's foreman. Dressed in bib overalls and barefooted, he was standing in the open bay of the barn, just above the carved letters which said LAZY B. "Unless . . . do you really want us to stop, sai?"

Eisenhart glanced toward Roland, who saw his own boy, Jake, standing just behind Benny, impatiently waiting his chance to risk his bones. Jake was also dressed in bib overalls—a pair of his new friend's, no doubt—and the look of them made Roland smile. Jake wasn't the sort of boy you imagined in such clothes.

"It's nil to me, one way or the other, if that's what you want to know," Roland said.

"Garn, then!" the rancher called. Then he turned his attention to the bits and pieces of hardware spread out on the boards. "What do'ee think? Will any of 'em shoot?"

Eisenhart had produced all three of his guns for Roland's inspection. The best was the rifle. The other two were pistols of the sort Roland and his friends had called "barrel-shooters" as children, because of the oversized cylinders which had to be revolved with the side of the hand after each shot. Roland had disassembled Eisenhart's shooting irons with no initial comment. Once again he had set out gun oil, this time in a bowl instead of a saucer.

"I said—"

"I heard you, sai," Roland said. "Your rifle is as good as I've seen this side of Lud, the great city. The barrel-shooters . . ." He shook his head. "That one with the nickel plating might fire. The other you might as well stick in the ground. Maybe it'll grow something better."

"Hate to hear you speak so," Eisenhart said. "These were from my da' and his da' before him and on back at least this many." He raised four fingers and both thumbs. "They was always kept together and passed to the likeliest son by dead-letter. When I got 'em instead of my elder brother, I was some pleased."

"I'm sorry."

"Say thankya."

The sun was going down red in the west, turning the yard the color of blood. There was a line of rockers on the porch. Eisenhart was settled in one of them. Roland sat cross-legged on the boards, housekeeping Eisenhart's inheritance. That the pistols would probably never fire meant nothing to the gunslinger's hands, which had been trained to this work long ago and still found it soothing.

Now, with a speed that made the rancher blink, Roland put the weapons back together in a rapid series of clicks and clacks. He set them aside on a square of sheepskin, wiped his fingers on a rag, and sat in the rocker next to Eisenhart's. He guessed that on more ordinary evenings, Eisenhart and his wife sat out here side by side, watching the sun abandon the day.

The wife had been part of his palaver that afternoon, more important because of what was not said than because of what was.

Roland rummaged through his purse for his tobacco pouch, found it, and built himself a cigarette with the priest's fresh, sweet tobacco. The Pere's housekeeper, Rosalita, had added her own present, a little stack of delicate papers she called "rice-pulls." Roland thought they wrapped as good as any cigarette paper, and he paused a moment to admire the finished product before tipping the end into the match Eisenhart had popped alight with one horny thumbnail. The gunslinger dragged deep and exhaled a long plume that rose but slowly in the evening air, which was still and surprisingly muggy for summer's end. "Good," he said, and nodded.

"Aye? May it do ya fine. I never got the taste for it myself."

The barn was far bigger than the ranch house, at least fifty yards long and fifty feet high. The front was festooned with reap-charms in honor of the season; stuffy-guys with huge sharproot heads stood guard. From above the open bay over the main doors, the butt of the headbeam jutted. A rope had been fastened around this. Below, in the yard, the boys had built a good-sized stack of hay. Oy stood on one side of it. The dog was looking up as Benny Slightman grabbed the rope, gave it a tug, then retreated back into the loft and out of sight. Oy began to bark in anticipation. A moment later Benny came pelting forward with the rope wrapped in his fists and his hair flying out behind him.

The boy let go, flew into the haystack, disappeared, then came up laughing. Oy ran around him, barking.

Roland watched Jake reel in the rope. Benny lay on the ground, playing dead, until Oy licked his face. Then he sat up, giggling.

To one side of the barn was a remuda of workhorses, perhaps twenty in all. A trio of cowpokes in chaps and battered shor' boots were leading the last half-dozen mounts toward it. On the other side of the yard was a slaughter-pen filled with steers. In the following weeks they would be butchered and sent downriver on the trading boats.

Jake retreated into the loft, then came pelting forward and launched himself into space along the arc of the rope. The two men watched him disappear, laughing, into the pile of hay.

"We bide, gunslinger," Eisenhart said. "Even in the face of the outlaws, we bide. They come . . . but then they go. Do'ee ken?"

"Ken very well, say thankya."

Eisenhart nodded. "If we stand against 'em, all that may change. To you and yours, it might not mean s'much as a fart in a high wind either way. If ye survive, you'll move along, win or lose. We have nowhere to go."

"But—"

Eisenhart raised his hand. "Hear me, I beg. Would'ee hear me?"

Roland nodded. Beyond them, the boys were running back into the barn for another leap. Soon the coming dark would put an end to their game.

"Suppose they send fifty or sixty, as they have before, and we wipe them out? And then, suppose that a week or a month later, after you're gone, they send five *hundred* against us?"

Roland considered this. As he was doing so, Margaret Eisenhart—Margaret Henchick that was—joined them. She was slim, fortyish, small-breasted, dressed in jeans and a shirt of gray silk. She was a pretty woman. She was also a problematic woman, stuffed with unspoken rage. After meeting her father—he that was called the heart-stone, he with the uncut, ungroomed beard which signified that he was childless—Roland thought he understood that rage a little better. As far as Henchick was concerned, this woman was bound for hell simply for the ankle she showed the world below the cuff of her jeans. And her husband? The children they'd made together? Better not to ask Henchick's opinion of them, and Roland hadn't. Sai Eisenhart's hair, pulled into a bun against her neck, was black threaded with white. One hand hid beneath her apron.

"How many harriers might come against us is a fair question," she said, "but this might not be a fair time to ask it."

Eisenhart gave his sai a look that was half humorous and half irritated. "Do I tell you how to run your kitchen, woman? When to cook and when to wash?"

"Only four times a week," said she. Then, seeing Roland rise from the rocker next to her husband's: "Nay, sit still, I beg you. I've been in a chair this last hour, peeling sharproot with Edna, yon's mother." She nodded in Benny's direction. "It's good to be on my feet." She watched, smiling, as the boys swung out into the pile of hay and landed, laughing, while Oy danced and barked. "Vaughn and I have never had to face the full horror of it, Roland. We had six, all twins, but all grown in the times between raids. So we may not have all the understanding needed to make such a decision as you ask."

"Being lucky doesn't make a man stupid," Eisenhart said. "Quite the contrary, is what I think. Cool eyes see clear."

"Perhaps," she said, watching the boys run back into the barn. They were bumping shoulders and laughing, each trying to get to the ladder first. "Perhaps, aye. But the heart must call for its rights, too, and a man or woman who doesn't listen is a fool. Sometimes 'tis best to swing on the rope, even if it's too dark to see if the hay's there or not."

Roland reached out and touched her hand.

She gave him a small, distracted smile. It was only a moment before she returned her attention to the boys, but it was long enough for Roland to see that she was frightened. Terrified, in fact. Knowing your gold or your crops were at risk was one thing. Knowing it was your children, that was another.

"Ben, Jake!" she called. "Enough! Time to wash and then come in! There's pie for those can eat it, and cream to go on top!"

Benny came to the open bay. "My da' says we can sleep in my tent over on the bluff, sai, if it's all right with you."

Margaret Eisenhart looked at her husband. Eisenhart nodded. "All right," she said, "tent it is and give you joy of it, but come in now if you'd have pie. Last warning! And wash first, mind'ee! Hands *and* faces!"

"Aye, say thankya," Benny said. "Can Oy have pie?"

Margaret Eisenhart thudded the pad of her left hand against her brow, as if she had a headache. The right, Roland was interested to note, stayed beneath her apron. "Aye," she said, "pie for the bumbler-dog too, as I'm sure he's Arthur Eld in disguise and will reward me with jewels and gold and the healing touch."

"Thankee, sai," Jake called. "Could we have one more swing first? It's the quickest way down."

"Well," Eisenhart said, "the broken leg usually hides in the last caper, but have on, if'ee must."

They had on, and there were no broken legs. Both boys hit the haypile squarely, popped up laughing and looking at each other, then footraced for the kitchen with Oy running behind them appearing to herd them.

"It's wonderful how quickly children can become friends," Margaret Eisenhart said, but she didn't look like one contemplating something wonderful. She looked sad.

"Yes," Roland said. "Wonderful it is." He laid his purse across his lap, seemed on the verge of pulling the knot that anchored the laces, then didn't. "Which are your men good with?" he asked Eisenhart. "Bow or bah? For I know it's surely not the rifle or revolver."

"We favor the bah," Eisenhart said. "Fit the bolt, wind it, aim it, fire it, 'tis done."

Roland nodded. It was as he had expected. Not good, because the bah was rarely accurate at a distance greater than twenty-five yards, and that only on a still day. On one when a strong breeze was kicking up . . . or, gods help us, a gale . . .

But Eisenhart was looking at his wife. Looking at her with a kind of reluctant admiration. She stood with her eyebrows raised, looking back at her man. Looking him back a question. What was this? It surely had to do with the hand under the apron.

"Garn, tell 'im," Eisenhart said. Then he pointed an almost-angry finger at Roland, like the barrel of a pistol. "It changes nothing, though. Nothing! Say thankya!" This last with the lips drawn back in a kind of savage grin. Roland was more puzzled than ever, but he felt a faint stirring of hope. It might be false hope, probably would be, but anything was better than the worries and confusions—and the aches—that had beset him lately.

"Nay," Margaret said with maddening modesty. "'Tis not my place to tell. To show, perhaps, but not to tell."

Eisenhart sighed, considered, then turned to Roland. "Ye know Lady Oriza."

Roland nodded. The Lady of the Rice, in some places considered a goddess, in others a heroine, in some, both.

"And ye know how she did away with Gray Dick, who killed her father?"

Roland nodded again.

According to the story—a good one that he must remember to tell Jake, when once more there was time for storytelling—Lady Oriza invited Gray Dick, a famous outlaw prince, to a vast dinner party in Waydon, her castle by the River Send. She wanted to forgive him for the murder of her father, she said, for she had accepted the Man Jesus into her heart and such was according to His teachings.

Ye'll get me there and kill me, be I stupid enough to come, said Gray Dick.

Nay, nay, said the Lady Oriza, never think it. All weapons will be left outside the castle. And when we sit in the banqueting hall below, there will be only me, at one end of the table, and thee, at the other.

You'll conceal a dagger in your sleeve or a *bola* beneath your dress, said Gray Dick. And if you don't, I will.

Nay, nay, said the Lady Oriza, never think it, for we shall both be naked.

At this Gray Dick was overcome with lust, for Lady Oriza was fair. It excited him to think of his prick getting hard at the sight of her bare breasts and bush, and no breeches on him to conceal his excitement from her maiden's eye. And he thought he understood why she would make such a proposal. "His haughty heart will undo him," Lady Oriza told her maid (whose name was Marian and who went on to have many fanciful adventures of her own).

The lady was right. *I've killed Lord Grenfall, wiliest lord in all the river baronies,* Gray Dick told himself. *And who is left to avenge him but one weak daughter?* (Oh, but she was fair.) *So she sues for peace. And maybe even for marriage, if she has audacity and imagination as well as beauty.*

So he accepted her offer. His men searched the banquet hall downstairs before he arrived and found no weapons—not on the table, not under the table, not behind the tapestries. What none of them could know was that for weeks before the banquet, Lady Oriza had practiced throwing a specially weighted dinner plate. She did this for hours a day. She was athletically inclined to begin with, and her eyes were keen. Also, she hated Gray Dick with all her heart and had determined to make him pay no matter what the cost.

The dinner plate wasn't just weighted; its rim had been sharpened. Dick's men overlooked this, as she and Marian had been sure they would. And so they banqueted, and what a strange banquet that must have been, with the laughing, handsome outlaw naked at one end of the table and the demurely smiling but exquisitely beautiful maiden thirty feet from him at the other end, equally naked. They toasted each other with Lord Grenfall's finest rough red. It infuriated the lady to the point of madness to watch him guzzle that exquisite country wine down as though it were water, scarlet drops rolling off his chin and splashing to his hairy chest, but she gave no sign; simply smiled coquettishly and sipped from her own glass. She could feel the weight of his eyes on her breasts. It was like having unpleasant bugs lumbering on her skin.

How long did this charade go on? Some tale-tellers had her putting an end to Gray Dick after the second toast. (His: *May your beauty ever increase.* Hers: *May your first day in hell last ten thousand years, and may it be the shortest.*) Others—the sort of spinners who enjoyed drawing out the suspense—recounted a meal of a dozen courses before Lady Oriza gripped the special plate, looking Gray Dick in the eyes and smiling at him while she turned it, feeling for the dull place on the rim where it would be safe to grip.

No matter how long the tale, it always ended the same way, with Lady Oriza flinging the plate. Little fluted channels had been carved on its underside, beneath the sharpened rim, to help it fly true. And it *did* fly true, humming weirdly as it went, casting its fleeting shadow on the roast pork and turkey, the heaping bowls of vegetables, the fresh fruit piled on crystal serving dishes.

A moment after she flung the plate on its slightly rising course—her arm still outstretched, her first finger and cocked thumb pointing at her father's assassin—Gray Dick's head flew out through the open door and into the foyer behind him. For a moment longer Gray Dick's body stood. For a moment longer Gray Dick's penis pointed at her like an accusing finger. But a dick can't stand stiff for long when the neck of its Dick is spouting blood in a geyser. It shriveled with shocking suddenness. For a moment longer the body stood where it was, and then Gray Dick crashed forward onto a huge roast of beef and a mountain of herbed rice.

Lady Oriza, whom Roland would hear referred to as the Lady of the Plate in some of his wanderings, raised her glass of wine and toasted the body. She said . . .

"**M**ay your first day in hell last ten thousand years," Roland murmured.

Margaret nodded. "Aye, and let that one be the shortest. A terrible toast, but one I'd gladly give each of the outlaws who dare to take our babies. Each and every one!" Her visible hand clenched. In the fading red light she looked feverish and ill. And, Roland thought, she looked like her father. "We had six, do ya. An even half-dozen. Has my husband told you why none of them are here, to help with the reaptide slaughtering and penning? Has he told you that, gunslinger?"

"Margaret, there's no need," Eisenhart said. He shifted uncomfortably in his rocker.

"Ah, but mayhap there is. It goes back to what we were saying before. Mayhap ye pay a price for leaping, but sometimes ye pay an even higher one for looking. Our children grew up free and clear, with no child-thieves to worry about. I gave birth to my first two, Tom and Tessa, less than a month before the Wolves came last time.

The others followed along, neat as peas out of a pod. The youngest be only fifteen, do ya see. And I'd never turn my back on 'em, or my face from 'em, as some would to their get, simply because they have the audacity to wriggle out from beneath a hard fist. Some ye may have visited even this day, gunslinger, or am I wrong?"

"Margaret—" her husband began.

She ignored him. "But ours'd not be s'lucky with their own children, and they knew it. And so they're gone. Some north along the Arc, some south. Looking for a place where the Wolves don't come."

She turned to Eisenhart, and although she spoke to Roland, it was her husband she looked at as she had her final word.

"One of every two; that's the outlaw bounty. That's what they take every twenty-some years. Except for us. They took *all* of our children, although they never laid their hands on a single one."

Silence fell on the back porch. The condemned steers in the slaughter-pen mooed moronically. From the kitchen came the sound of boy-laughter.

Eisenhart had dropped his head. Roland could see nothing but the extravagant bush of his mustache, but he didn't need to see the man's face to know that he was either weeping or struggling very hard not to.

"I'd not make'ee feel bad for all the rice of the Arc," she said, and stroked her husband's shoulder with infinite tenderness. "And they come back betimes, aye, which is more than the dead do, except in our dreams. They're not so old that they don't miss their mother, or have how-do-ye-do-it questions for their da'. But they're gone, nevertheless. And that's the price of safety." She looked down at Eisenhart for a moment, one hand on his shoulder and the other still beneath her apron. "Now tell how angry with me you are," she said, "for I'd know."

Eisenhart shook his head. "Not angry," he said in a muffled voice.

"And have'ee changed your mind?"

Eisenhart shook his head again.

"Stubborn old thing," she said, but she spoke with good-humored affection. "Stubborn as a stick, aye, and we all say thankya."

"I'm thinking about it," he said, still not looking up. "Still thinking, which is more than I expected at this late date—usually I make up my mind and there's the end of it.

"Roland, I understand young Jake showed Overholser and the rest of 'em some shooting out in the woods. Might be we could show you something right here that'd raise your eyebrows. Maggie, go in and get your Oriza."

"No need," she said, at last taking her hand from beneath her apron, "for I brought it out with me, and here 'tis."

It was a blue plate with a delicate webbed pattern. A for-special plate. After a moment Roland recognized the webbing for what it was: young oriza, the seedling rice plant. When sai Eisenhart tapped her knuckles on the plate, it gave out a peculiar high ringing. It looked like china, but wasn't. Glass, then? Some sort of glass?

He held his hand out for it with the solemn, respectful mien of one who knows and respects weapons. She hesitated, biting the corner of her lip. Roland reached into his holster, which he'd strapped back on before leaving this woman's father, and pulled his revolver. He held it out to her, butt first.

"Nay," she said, letting the word out on a long breath of sigh. "No need to offer me a hostage, Roland. I reckon I c'n trust you with my Oriza. But mind how you touch, or you'll lose another finger, and I think you could ill afford that, for I see you're already two shy on your right hand."

A single look at the blue plate—the sai's Oriza—made it clear how wise that warning was. At the same time, Roland felt a bright spark of excitement and appreciation. It had been long years since he'd seen a new weapon of worth, and never one like this.

The plate was metal, not glass—some light, strong alloy. It was the size of an ordinary dinner plate, a foot in diameter. Three-quarters of the edge (or perhaps a bit more) had been sharpened to suicidal keenness.

"There's never a question of where to grip, even if ye're in a hurry," Margaret said. "For, do'ee see—"

"Yes," Roland said in a tone of deepest admiration. Two of the rice-stalks crossed in what could have been the great letter "Hn," which by itself means both *here* and *now*. At the point where these stalks crossed (only a sharp eye would pick them out of the bigger pattern to begin with), the rim of the plate was not only dull but slightly thicker. Good to grip.

Roland turned the plate over. Beneath, in the center, was a small metal pod. To Jake, it might have looked like the plastic pencil-sharpener he'd taken to school in his pocket as a first-grader. To Roland, who had never seen a pencil-sharpener, it looked a little like the abandoned egg case of some insect.

"That makes the whistling noise when the plate flies, do ya ken," she said. She had seen Roland's honest admiration and was reacting to it, her color high and her eyes bright. She looked thus more like her father than ever.

"It has no other purpose?"

"None," she said. "But it must whistle, for it's part of the story, isn't it?"

Roland nodded. Of course it was.

The Sisters of Oriza, Margaret Eisenhart said, was a group of women who liked to help others—

"And gossip amongst theirselves," Eisenhart growled, but he sounded good-humored.

"Aye, that too," she allowed.

They cooked for funerals and festivals. They sometimes held sewing circles and quilting bees after a family had lost its belongings to fire or when one of the river-floods came every six or eight years and drowned the smallholders closest to the Whye. It was the Sisters who kept the Pavilion well tended and the Town Gathering Hall well swept on the inside and well kept on the outside. They put on dances for the young people, and chaperoned them. They were sometimes hired by the richer folk to cater wedding celebrations, and such affairs were always fine, the talk of the Calla for months afterward, sure. Among themselves they *did* gossip, aye, she'd not deny it; they also played cards, and Points, and Castles. (How Henchick's brow would have furrowed at the thought of gossip, Roland thought. How his eye, cold to begin with, would have chilled at the mention of cards!)

"And you throw the plate," Roland said.

"Aye," said she, "but ye must understand we only do it for the fun of the thing. Hunting's men's work, and they do fine with the bah." She was stroking her husband's shoulder again, this time a bit nervously, Roland thought. He also thought that if the men really did do fine with the bah, she never would have come out with that pretty, deadly thing held under her apron. Nor would Eisenhart have encouraged her.

Roland opened his tobacco pouch, took out one of Rosalita's rice-pulls, and drifted it toward the plate's sharp edge. The square of thin paper fluttered to the porch a moment later, cut neatly in two. *Only for the fun of the thing,* Roland thought, and almost smiled.

"What metal?" he asked. "Does thee know?"

She raised her eyebrows slightly at this Manni form of address but didn't comment on it. "Titanium is what Andy calls it. It comes from a great old factory building, far north, in Calla Sen Chre. There are many ruins there. I've never been, but I've heard the tales. It sounds spooky."

Roland nodded. "And the plates—how are they made?"

"It's the ladies of Calla Sen Chre who make them, and send them to the Callas all round about. Although Calla Divine is as far south as that sort of trading reaches, I think."

"The ladies make these," Roland mused. "The *ladies.*"

"Somewhere there's a machine that still makes 'em, that's all it is," Eisenhart said. Roland was amused at his tone of gruff defensiveness. "Comes down to no more than pushing a button, I 'magine."

Margaret, looking at him with a woman's smile, said nothing to this, either for or against. Perhaps she didn't know about the manufacture of the plates, but she certainly knew the politics that keep a marriage sweet.

"So there are Sisters north and south of here along the Arc," Roland said. "And all of them throw the plate."

"Aye—from Sen Chre to Divine south of us. Further south or north, I don't know. We like to help and we like to talk. We throw our plates once a month, in memory of how Lady Oriza did for Gray Dick, but few of us are any good at it."

"Are *you* good at it, sai?"

She was silent, biting at the corner of her lip again.

"Show him," Eisenhart growled. "Show him and be done."

They walked down the steps, the rancher's wife leading the way, Eisenhart behind her, Roland third. Behind them the kitchen door opened and banged shut.

"Gods-a-glory, missus Eisenhart's gonna throw the dish!" Benny Slightman cried gleefully. "Jake! You won't believe it!"

"Send 'em back in, Vaughn," she said. "They don't need to see this."

"Nar, let 'em look," Eisenhart said. "Don't hurt a boy to see a woman do well."

"Send them back, Roland, aye?" She looked at him, flushed and flustered and very pretty. To Roland she looked ten years younger than when she'd come out on the porch, but he wondered how she'd fling in such a state. It was something he much wanted to see, because ambushing was brutal work, quick and emotional.

"I agree with your husband," he said. "I'd let them stay."

"Have it as you like," she said. Roland saw she was actually pleased, that she *wanted* an audience, and his hope increased. He thought it increasingly likely that this pretty middle-aged wife, this exile from the Manni with her small breasts and salt-and-pepper hair, had a hunter's heart. Not a gunslinger's heart, but at this point he would settle for a few hunters—a few killers—male *or* female.

She marched toward the barn, and when they were fifty yards from the stuffy-guys flanking its door, he touched her shoulder and made her stop.

"Nay," she said, "'tis too far."

"I've seen you fling as far and half again," her husband said, and stood firm in the face of her angry look. "I have."

"Not with a gunslinger from the Line of Eld standing by my right elbow, you haven't," she said, but she stayed where she was.

Roland went to the barn door and took the grinning sharproot head from the stuffy on the left side. He went into the barn. Here was a stall filled with freshly picked potatoes. He took one of the potatoes and set it atop the stuffy-guy's shoulders, where the sharproot had been. It was a good-sized spud, but the contrast was still comic; the stuffy-guy now looked like Mr. Tinyhead in a carnival show or street fair.

"Oh, Roland, no!" she cried, sounding genuinely shocked. "I could never!"

"I don't believe you," he said, and stood aside. "Throw."

For a moment he thought she wouldn't. She looked around for

her husband. If Eisenhart had still been standing beside her, Roland thought she would have thrust the plate into his hands and run for the house and never mind if he cut himself on it, either. But Vaughn Eisenhart had withdrawn to the foot of the steps. The boys stood above him, Benny Slightman watching with mere interest, Jake with closer attention, his brows drawn together and the smile suddenly gone from his face.

"Roland, I—"

"None of it, missus, I beg. Your talk of leaping was all very fine, and certainly you leaped when you left your father and his *folken,* but that was years ago and I'd see if you're still limber. *Throw.*"

She recoiled a little at the mention of her father, eyes widening as if she had been slapped. Then she turned to face the barn door and drew her right hand above her left shoulder. The plate glimmered in the late light, which was now more pink than red. Her lips had thinned to a white line. For a moment all the world held still.

"*Riza!*" she cried in a shrill, furious voice, and cast her arm forward. Her hand opened, the index finger pointing precisely along the path the plate would take. Of all of them in the yard (the cowpokes had also stopped to watch), only Roland's eyes were sharp enough to follow the flight of the dish.

True! he exulted. *True as ever was!*

The plate gave a kind of moaning howl as it bolted above the dirt yard. Less than two seconds after it had left her hand, the potato lay in two pieces, one by the stuffy-guy's gloved right hand and the other by its left. The plate itself stuck in the side of the barn door, quivering.

The boys raised a cheer. Benny hoisted his hand as his new friend had taught him, and Jake slapped him a high five.

"Great going, sai Eisenhart!" Jake called.

"Good hit! Say thankya!" Benny added.

Roland observed the way the woman's lips drew back from her teeth at this hapless, well-meant praise—she looked like a horse that has seen a snake. "Boys," he said, "I'd go inside now, were I you."

Benny was bewildered. Jake, however, took another look at Margaret Eisenhart and understood. You did what you had to . . . and then the reaction set in. "Come on, Ben," he said.

"But—"

"Come *on*." Jake took his new friend by the shirt and tugged him back toward the kitchen door.

Roland let the woman stay where she was for a moment, head down, trembling with reaction. Strong color still blazed in her cheeks, but everywhere else her skin had gone as pale as milk. He thought she was struggling not to vomit.

He went to the barn door, grasped the plate at the grasping-place, and pulled. He was astounded at how much effort it took before the plate first wiggled and then came loose. He brought it back to her, held it out. "Thy tool."

For a moment she didn't take it, only looked at him with a species of bright hate. "Why do you mock me with speech, Roland? What did my father tell thee?"

In the face of her rage he only shook his head. "I do not mock thee."

Margaret Eisenhart abruptly seized Roland by the neck. Her grip was dry and so hot her skin felt feverish. She pulled his ear to her uneasy, twitching mouth. He thought he could smell every bad dream she must have had since deciding to leave her people for Calla Bryn Sturgis's big rancher.

"I know thee spoke with Henchick today," she said. "Will'ee speak to him more? Ye will, won't you?"

Roland nodded, transfixed by her grip. The strength of it. The little puffs of air against his ear. Did a lunatic hide deep down inside everyone, even such a woman as this?

"Good. Say thankya. Tell him Margaret of the Redpath Clan does fine with her heathen man, aye, fine still." Her grip tightened. "Tell him she regrets *nothing*! Will'ee do that for me?"

"Aye, lady, if you like."

She snatched the plate from him, fearless of its lethal edge. "What would ye visit on us, ye gunstruck man?"

Eisenhart joined them. He looked uncertainly at his wife, who had endured exile from her people and the hardening of her father's heart for his sake. For a moment she looked at him as though she didn't know him.

"I only do as ka wills," Roland said.

"Ka!" she cried, and her lip lifted. A sneer transformed her good looks to an ugliness that was almost startling. It would have frightened the boys. "Every troublemaker's excuse! Put it up your bum with the rest of the dirt!"

"I do as ka wills and so will you," Roland said.

She looked at him, seeming not to comprehend. Roland took the hot hand that had gripped him and squeezed it, not quite to the point of pain.

"And so will you."

She met his gaze for a moment, then dropped her eyes. "Aye," she muttered. "Oh, aye, so do we all."

She left him for the house.

Blood Doesn't Come Out

By MICHAEL CRICHTON

*A man can only be pushed so far—especially
when his mother is the one pushing.*

It wasn't my day. When I hit him in the mouth, I cut my hand and
the blood dripped onto my new mauve Lauren tie. And blood
doesn't come out. It made me mad so I kicked him a couple of
times while he rolled on the ground in the alley, swearing in Spanish.
Nobody saw us. The alleys of Beverly Hills are pretty deserted at
eight in the morning. The stores don't open until ten.

I got back in my new Mustang and tossed the digital camera on
the passenger seat. I stuck a Kleenex on my knuckles and started the

ignition. The guy was on his feet by then, shaking his fist at me as I drove away, but he had only himself to blame. He shouldn't have been stealing all those nice leather jackets from the store. The client wanted pictures and now I had them. A dozen digital hi-res snaps showing the guy taking stuff out of the truck in the early morning sun and putting it into his car. I figured I'd earned my money. Wrongful termination suits are expensive and I'd nipped this one in the bud.

I called the client on my cell phone and left a message on his answering machine. By now it was time for breakfast. I would have gone around the corner to Nate 'n Al's except I had blood on my tie. So I went home.

I had one of those small houses in the flats south of Pico. Beverly-wood, they call it. It's a good neighborhood, real people with real jobs live there. I've had the same house for forty years, now. It was reasonable when my mother bought it in the sixties. Now it's north of half a million for eighteen hundred square feet, two baths, and a backyard the size of a walk-in closet. You've got to wonder. My mother lived in it with me until I came back from college. But she's been in a home for years now. I hardly ever see her. Sometimes I feel guilty, but not often.

The client called back right as I pulled into the driveway. He was screaming. He said I'd got the wrong guy, and what the fuck was I doing beating up poor Fernando? I told him I had the pictures to prove it, but he wasn't listening. I could see my fee slipping away. The client never wants to hear that his lover is a thief. Not while he's in love, anyway. Afterward, of course, he wants to kill. But I could tell this guy was still in love.

All his yelling at me was making me feel bad. Losing the fee was making me feel worse. I was already behind on my car payments. I pretended my connection was going bad, and hung up. Clearly, it wasn't my day. I stripped off my tie and went in the house. I noticed I had a couple of blood spots on my shirt, so I started unbuttoning it as I went into the bedroom. I felt like a drink, but it was a little too early.

There was a suitcase lying open on the bed. Janis's clothes were folded in neat piles around the room. The closet door was open and some of her clothes were already gone. I looked in the bathroom but she wasn't there so I went into the kitchen. It was time for that drink after all.

Through the windows I saw Janis in the backyard, pacing back and forth with the portable phone to her ear. She was wearing a halter top and sweatpants. The perpetual exerciser. Janis picked up an acting job about three days a year, just enough to keep her health insurance. The rest of the time she exercised. She was in good shape for thirty-five. We'd been together two years, off and on.

She hadn't seen me standing there yet. I went to the wall phone by the refrigerator and punched the speaker button.

"—just can't stand it," she was saying. "I can't take it anymore."

A man's voice said, "Did you tell him?"

"I can't talk to him."

"Don't you think you should?" the man said. He had a deep, confidential voice. He sounded like an older guy. But then, I was an older guy too. I was fifteen years older than she was. My next big one was five-oh.

Janis was still pacing. "I've tried to talk to him, Armand. You know I've tried."

I thought, Armand? Who the fuck is Armand? I started to sweat. I took off my sports coat so I wouldn't crease it. Sometimes when I sweat I get creases at the elbow and the shoulder. Then I have to get it pressed. I slipped the jacket over the back of the kitchen chair.

"I'm tired of faking it," she was saying.

"Faking what?"

"Faking everything. Faking conversations, faking smiles, faking orgasms. Faking everything."

Armand chuckled. "Everything?"

"He likes it when I scream," Janis said. "So I scream. What the fuck."

I was sweating more. I wiped my forehead. I felt dizzy. I hated him for that knowing chuckle. They were still talking but I couldn't hear them for a while. I got the bottle of scotch down from above the refrigerator. I noticed I had only three bottles left. I twisted off the cap. I took a slug and felt it burn all the way down.

"He's such an old lady," Janis was saying. "I mean it's his house, he's been here forever, but he won't let me change anything, or move anything. Everything has to be just so."

"I thought he chased around. I heard he was a big ladies' man."

"Yeah, well, maybe back when. All I know is, nobody can move Mom's picture on the piano. I can tell you that."

I was looking at the piano in the living room. I hadn't remembered the picture was even there. Why didn't she tell me if she didn't like it? Hell, I didn't care. My mother was in a home, for Christ's sake. She didn't care either.

I took another slug, and didn't feel it. So I took another to keep it company. My stomach was warm and I coughed. She heard it and looked over.

"I got to go," she said quickly, and there was a dial tone. I clicked the speakerphone off as she came in. "Very nice, Ray," she said. "Very fucking classy. What're you, investigating *me* now?"

I said, "You want to move the picture, go ahead and move it. I don't give a shit."

"I'm leaving," she said, sweeping into the bedroom. "So why don't you just give me an hour alone? Be civilized about it."

"I don't feel civilized."

"Then have another belt."

"Fuck you."

"What're you going to do now, tough guy, beat me up?"

"No," I said, "I'm not going to beat you up."

"That's good, Ray."

"I'm not even going to touch you."

"That's good," she said, "because if you do, Ray, I'll have your ass in jail so fucking fast you won't know what hit you."

"I said I won't touch you."

"And I heard you. We've communicated. Now just go away, will you?" she said. She slammed the bedroom door behind her.

I said, "Who the fuck is Armand?"

She didn't answer. I was standing there in the kitchen with my half-unbuttoned shirt and my tie streaked with blood. I took another slug, buttoned my shirt, and left.

I didn't have anywhere to go, so I just drove around the neighborhood. The scotch sat hard in my stomach, turning sour. I stopped at a 7-Eleven and bought a pack of Marlboros. I stood outside on the pavement and watched the guys going in to buy Lotto tickets. I smoked a couple of cigarettes, and got a newspaper from the sidewalk dispenser. I sat in the car and flipped through the sections, not really reading. I checked my watch. I'd given her twenty minutes. I figured that was enough.

I wanted to go back and argue with Janis some more; I was feeling like an argument. I turned the key in the ignition, drove a block, then pulled over and parked again. The more I thought about her, the more I decided I didn't give a damn. I'd always known those screams were fake. That's what you get with an actress. A lot of rich, fake emotion. And a thirty-five-year-old broad in good shape. I was better off without her. I wouldn't have to listen to her talk about her fucking diets.

It was hot, sitting in the car. I got out and walked back to the 7-Eleven. I bought a pint of Red Label and took some to settle my stomach. I went back to my car. I waited until forty minutes had passed, and then decided to go back.

When I got there she was gone. Her clothes were gone from the closet. I pulled out the dresser drawers. Her underwear was gone. The bathroom, all her cosmetics were gone. The lacy bras that hung over the shower rod, the thong panties dangling from the tub spout, they were gone too. Hell, it was the first time in two years she'd cleaned up after herself.

I didn't look for a note.

I knew she wouldn't bother.

The mail came. I heard it rattle through the slot. I went out to get it. It was mostly bills. I sat on the couch in the living room and shuffled through it. The sun was coming in through the front windows. It was glaring and bright where I sat. I moved over to the piano bench, which was still in shade.

I finished with the mail. There were a couple of pieces for her. I tossed them aside. I looked down at the piano bench, noticing how scratched up it was, how old. I didn't know why I'd kept it all these years. For that matter, I didn't know why I'd kept the piano. My mother used to play it, occasionally, when she lived here.

And when I was a kid, she sat on the bench beside me and made me do my lessons. Every day, she sat beside me and corrected me, getting angrier and angrier because I wasn't paying attention, and then she'd start smacking me on the shoulder every time I made a mistake.

She thought it would make me pay attention. But for me it was just a daily challenge, to see if I could take what she dished out, and not cry. I refused to cry after about the age of eight. Of course she wanted to make me to cry so she hit me harder, and harder. My arm would get red, and sometimes it was bruised. But I wouldn't cry.

We played that little game every day for about four years, until I had football after school, and could stay away until dinner. Once I was a teenager, I avoided her as much as I could. By then she was drinking hard, anyway. She'd snarl at me that I was a fuckup like my father, that I'd never amount to anything. My father had left her before I was born. Made sense to me.

In later years, she was usually drunk asleep when I got home. I was grateful she was passed out, because I wouldn't have to listen to her abuse. I'd fix dinner for myself, do my homework. It was all right. Then I went back east to college, so I didn't see her much after that.

The sun was moving. It had almost crossed the living room to find me at the piano bench. I wondered how long I had been sitting there, remembering old times. The sun reflected off the black polished surface of the piano and glinted on the silver frame that had my mother's picture. The picture was faded, the colors washed out. It showed my mother smiling. She always smiled for a camera, and then dropped it as soon as the shutter clicked.

I don't know where the picture was taken. It was on the piano when I got back from college. By that time my mother was unable to care for herself. She had bleeding ulcers and trouble with her balance, and she walked with that shuffling gait that marks the real drunks. You know the way they never pick their feet off the floor, because they can't feel anything anymore.

R ight out of college I had a job as an insurance claims investigator. My hours were long and erratic. Left alone in the house, she kept falling down and hurting herself. Broke her arm one time, cut her forehead open another time. Finally I put her in a home. I got her to sign the papers one night when she was really drunk. She was furious when I took her to the home and dropped her off. She called me every name she could think of. And she told me I'd never amount to anything. Screaming at me as I walked out the door.

For the first year or so, I didn't go near her. Then she had a stroke, and they called me up, so I went over to see her. I needn't have worried. After the stroke, she seemed to be calmer. And they had her sedated, too. I don't know what. Anyway, she was better. Not so abusive.

I flipped the picture on the piano down so I didn't have to look at it. I was careful when I put it down, so I wouldn't scratch the polished surface. Then I thought, What the fuck. I took the picture and held it on edge, and gouged a big scratch into the piano. It dug through the polished black surface, leaving a white scratch. I gouged another, and another. Made the piano look like hell.

I began to wonder why I had never done this before. I hated this fucking piano. I didn't know why I had left it here all these years. I told myself I didn't know what to put in its place. It took up a lot of space in the living room and I would have to redecorate if it was gone.

Well, I'd have to redecorate now.

I thought maybe Mother would like to see her piano. I went out to the car to get the digital camera, but her eyesight isn't good anymore, and I thought maybe she couldn't see the little screen at the back. So I opened the glove compartment for the Polaroid, and it fell out along with the gun. The damn glove compartments just aren't large enough in newer cars. I don't know what the manufacturers are thinking. Saving money, cutting corners, screwing the consumer. The usual shit.

I picked the gun off the floor and put it on the seat, and took the Polaroid back inside. I took several pictures of the scratches from different angles, but none really showed them off to advantage. I wasn't sure Mother would really notice. But I owed her a visit anyway.

I went back to the kitchen, had another belt, and smoked a satisfying cigarette. Janis never let me smoke in the house, but those days were over. I stubbed the butt out in the sink, relishing the black crust against the porcelain. Like gunpowder against pale skin.

Then it was time to see Mother.

*   *   *

S he was in a very nice home on Third Street, opposite a church. The building was from the fifties, single story, ranch-style, designed not to look institutional. The sign was made from cutout white letters and said "SeaSide Convalescent." It was at least five miles from the ocean, but it had a pleasant ring.

I parked down the block, and scooped up the Polaroids. The gun was still on the passenger seat and I couldn't leave it there so I stuck it in my pocket, pulled on my jacket, and went inside.

The SeaSide lobby was small with a cheery ocean motif, sea fans and starfish painted on the walls. You didn't mind the bedpan smell. The room was crowded with three elderly women in wheelchairs, waiting to be taken somewhere. One of the women was reading a book, one was asleep, and the other was just staring at nothing.

The receptionist was a harried, frowning fat lady who was talking on the phone. I heard her say, "They've been waiting an *hour,* George," and then she listened a moment. "It's too early for your lunch break, George, get your ass over here." With the phone to her ear, she glanced up at me, still frowning.

I said, "I'm here to see Mrs. Chambers."

"And you are?"

"Her son."

She held out her hands, snapped her fingers. "Identification?" Into the phone she said, "George, did you hear anything I said?"

I gave her my driver's license. She hardly looked at it.

"George, damn it, you better get over here now. Someone might decide to call the INS, you know what I mean?" She cupped her hand over the phone. To me: "You know where she is?"

I said I did.

"Go ahead."

I slipped past the wheelchairs, and went down a long hallway. The doors to individual rooms were open on either side. Cheerful sunlight poured in. But people in the rooms looked insubstantial as ghosts against the white bed linen, and the hallway smelled faintly of beef stew. Or something like that.

Mother was in a room near the back. It looked out onto a small enclosed garden with potted trees. You could see a row of garbage cans off to one side. She was sitting in a wheelchair, watching a soap opera.

I said, "Hello, Mother."

She looked over at me and said nothing. For a moment I had a flash of panic, thinking she didn't recognize me. Then she gave that evil little smile of hers. "Well. It's about time."

"Miss me?"

"You're a joke." She turned away from me to the television.

I said, "I wanted you to see some pictures I took today."

"Still peeping in bedrooms for a living?"

"Only yours." I took the Polaroids and spread them out on her lap, one after another, like cards.

She frowned. "What's this?"

"Your piano."

"It's all messed up."

"That's right, Mother."

"You can't take care of anything, can you?"

"No," I said. "I did this myself."

She didn't understand. She shrugged and looked back at the television. I heard a voice say, "Margo, you'll never get away with this, you know that, don't you?"

"Mother," I said. "I did this to your piano."

She sighed. "Why don't you grow up, Ray? How old are you now, anyway?"

"And you know what I'm going to do next? I'm going to have someone come in with an axe, and smash it up, and burn it for firewood."

"You smell like liquor."

"Are you listening, Mother?"

She turned to me, suddenly interested. "Got any with you?"

"As a matter of fact, I do. But you can't have it."

"It's in your pocket. I can see it."

She was seeing the gun. "No," I said. "It's not liquor. And you can't have it."

"I don't care, Ray. Why do you bother to come here? I don't care if I never see you again."

"I thought you'd want to see the piano."

She swept her hand across her lap, sending the pictures flying. "You worthless piece of shit."

"Now, Mother."

She paused. She squinted at me. "What happened, did she leave you?"

"Who?"

"She did, didn't she?"

"I don't know what you're talking about."

"That's why you're here. Stinking of scotch at eleven in the morning." She sat back in the wheelchair. "You want to make it my fault. Your worthless life is my fault. Your good-for-nothing life is my fault. Christ. What a disappointment you are. You pussy. Give me the fucking bottle in your pocket."

"It's not a bottle," I said. I brought out the gun to show her. "It's this."

"I'm so impressed. Put your little penis away, dear."

I just stood there. It was always the same with her. I had some idea when I came to visit her, some plan for how things would go, but it never turned out right. She could always change things around. I continued to hold the gun in my hand because I didn't want her telling me what to do. But I felt foolish.

"Put it away, Ray. You might scare the nurses." She sighed, and rolled her eyes upward. "And to think that once I had hopes for you."

I bent over in front of her wheelchair, and began to pick up the pictures of the scratched piano. She smacked me on the head. "Get away from me, you little turd."

I don't know exactly what happened but when I looked up the gun went off, firing past her ear. It shattered the window behind her. The noise was loud. There was smoke in the room. I said, "Mother, I'm sorry, I didn't mean it—"

"You can't do *anything* right, can you? Look at the mess you made. They're going to charge you for it."

Because I wanted to scare her, because I wanted her to take that back, because I was angry, I stood up and shoved the gun against her forehead, the barrel right above her eyes. I said, "Mother, this is it."

"This is *nothing*," she hissed.

So I shot her and her brains spattered all over the back of the room, like sticky red-and-white cottage cheese. Now the room was really a mess, I thought. People were yelling somewhere down the hall. I saw a nurse poke her head in and then run off, screaming, "He has a gun!" My mother's head was tilted way back on her neck, at an extreme angle. So I could only see her chin and her nostrils. Blood was dripping onto the floor from the back of her head. Maybe it wasn't my day, I thought. But it wasn't hers, either. From out in the hallway, a guy yelled for me to put the gun down, so I put it down. I felt better then.

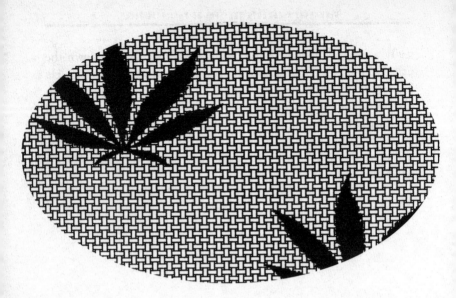

Weaving the Dark

By LAURIE KING

*As the darkness gathered around her,
she embarked upon the greatest adventure
of her life—in her own backyard.*

We're all blind to something—the mind's eye can't hold everything at once. And we're all dying—just some more rapidly than others.

But platitudes were only so much whistling in the dark, mantras to reassure the senses, soothe the terrors, distract the rat-mind gnawing at the vitals. The truth of the matter was, Janna was dying and Suze Blackstock was more the type to blast the dark with a bonfire than whistle into it. Suze did not want to be soothed, not even when she woke, as she did now, to an unrelieved blackness. *Ah shit*, she thought. *It's gone, I'm blind.*

And it had happened while she slept, not even a last flicker to grab on to, or to wish goodbye.

Then rationality elbowed its way to the fore: Maybe it actually was still dark. This was, after all, a place without streetlights, so it could be—

But no. She didn't just wake; she'd been awakened by . . . yes, by the sound of digging, a shovel blade biting into soil. That meant Andy was here. And builders did not work in the dark of night, not even eccentric, senior-citizen odd-job-men builders like Andy.

So, that was it, then. Her optic nerves had given up the fight, closed down in the night, died. Once, she'd been left in a desert without water; another time she spent a week trapped by a blizzard, but she'd never been abandoned so completely, never left with two vestigial lumps on her face that would do nothing more than dribble weak tears, as they did now onto the pillow. She lay back, prodding the soft, useless skin and the wet, cowardly lashes, then pressed down in a sudden spasm of anger that she hadn't even been there to see her sight off. And the night flared in reaction.

She froze, then flipped over and stretched for the big flashlight under the edge of the bed, kept there for times like this when she needed to know that the world of light was still there for her. She fumbled after the handle, knocked it away, lunged for it and thumbed the switch and—light! The brilliance of it assaulted her retinas, blinding her with glory, making her head spin with relief. She laughed, even, and patted her eyelids in apology, loving the wetness of the lashes, the slight ache from where she had pressed down hard.

A full five minutes went by before she remembered the sound of shovel blades digging into soil. Obviously it hadn't been the builders; Andy was a conscientious old coot, but surely he wouldn't come out here in the middle of the night. Besides, hadn't he finished with the retaining wall?

She switched off the beam and sat, listening, but the noise did not come again. After a while, she stowed the light in its place under the edge of the bed and got back under the covers, wondering, as she'd wondered for the past five weeks, just what the hell she was going to do.

Suze Blackstock had always been a woman who met her fears head-on. From the day she took her first steps she'd been called a tomboy, a reckless kid, a daredevil. The pattern of her adult life had been set when a high school boyfriend turned first possessive, then violent, and in a desperate bid for self-respect, she'd signed up for a karate class. Lesson learned: When life spit on you, pull back and let fly. She'd set out for Europe at nineteen with $104 in her pocket, spent the next six years walking and hitching across five continents, and come home with eleven dollars and change. She started skydiving at the age of thirty-one during a nasty, threat-filled divorce, the mind-blowing rush of each near-suicide stripping the mess of her life down to essentials. Rock climbing followed at thirty-seven, when her mother died in April and a close friend four weeks later. And she swallowed her claustrophobia and went caving a few years after that, when her world was crumbling in six directions at once. In each case, death looking over her shoulder steadied her; flirting with it and then walking away left her strong and cleansed. Will the parachute open this time? Will that tiny jut of rock hold me? Will the huge weight of the earth above me choose now to sigh and settle down? It was as if, when life spiraled out of control, seizing Death and staring him down was the only way to bleed off the intolerable pressures. In the face of death, she felt most alive.

But she'd never met a pressure like the one now, measurably tiny, insidious, deadly, and taking over her life. An infinitesimal buildup of the aqueous humor inside her eyeballs, a slight malfunction in the drainage that led to an increase in pressure, and a degeneration in the sensitive nerves. Glaucoma. A pressure she'd been forced to meet, not with fury, but with patience and humility.

Suze was forty-eight years old, a woman who'd lived with desert nomads and jungle rebels, who'd fought free of robbers in three countries, who'd lost a toe to Everest; a woman now sitting in a cabin in the woods, waiting for a half-known lover to die or to recover. Suze was really bad at patience and humility.

She lay in the bed that had been hers for ten short weeks, remembering the power-moments in her life: the time the chute lines had tangled and she'd felt the Arizona desert rushing up at her; the sensation of looking down the barrel of an Ethiopian rebel's gun; the incredible high when her right foot found a ledge, stopping her free fall two hundred feet from the Scottish soil below. The line between terror and exultation was so thin as to be nonexistent. And the tiny pressure in her eyes was pulling her back from that line, so far away she didn't think she'd find it again.

Toward dawn, Suze dozed, and when she woke, the sun shining into the room made the moment of panic brief. Still, it was there, and she hated it.

Suze was coming to hate Courtney, too, although she took care not to show it. Courtney was Suze's sixteen-and-a-half-year-old neighbor, housekeeper, and errand-runner—or more precisely, Janna's neighbor, passed on to Suze in this peculiarly uncertain period. Janna had not lived here for five weeks, might (nearly time to face this) never live here again. But still Courtney came, and now that it was summer she was here four mornings a week to help Suze. She organized the bills, did the shopping, drove Suze to appointments in town, performed those daily functions that required the service of eyes that could do more than distinguish white from black. She was, Suze had to admit, sensible for a girl her age, though oddly conservative, and possessed a priceless knack for putting everything back precisely as she had found it, so that when Suze was prowling up and down the unlit house at night she didn't trip over a stray lamp cord or bark her shins on a misplaced chair. Suze was glad for the girl's compulsiveness, overlooked her complete lack of humor, and tried her best not to snap at the child too often.

Today was Tuesday, so they went through the week's mail. Bills came first.

"The mortgage is here, and Andy's account, and the insurance," Courtney told her.

"House or car?"

"House."

"Then send it all down to the bank." If it had been the car insurance, Suze would have paid it herself, since Courtney was driving Janna's car for Suze's benefit.

"And the electricity. Boy, that's sure gone down a lot," she said, as if the savings were the result of her own work. "When I told Mom what the bill was for March, she said we ought to have the meter checked."

Great, Suze thought; *now the girl's whole family knows how much Janna spends on her utilities.* "I'll pay that, and the phone bill." She'd also pay for the propane, when it came—those costs she considered her responsibility. Not that she'd had any chance to talk the arrangement over with Janna: One minute they'd been sitting in Janna's living room planning a trip to Tahoe; the next, Janna was slumped on the wood floor making terrifying noises while Suze scrambled to locate the dark telephone on the dark table. And five weeks after the stroke, Janna was still only half-conscious of the world around her. Tuesdays, Suze dictated a letter which the nurses assured her they read to their patient. Sundays and Thursdays, Courtney drove her thirty miles to visit the nursing home. It was an impossible situation, and not becoming any easier. She and Janna had only been together a few months; if Janna didn't regain her senses pretty soon, her family would take over her affairs, and Janna would become a what-if in Suze's life, a brief fling.

But loyalty and the beginnings of love kept her here, in Janna's cabin in the woods, edgy and frustrated and in limbo. As soon as the constrained letter to Janna was in its envelope and the checks made out (Courtney repeating her satisfaction that the winter's enormous electrical bills had settled down) she let the girl get to the mop and the shopping, and with a sigh of relief moved over to the loom.

As she slid onto the weaver's bench, Suze reflected, as she had a thousand times before, how odd it was that she felt so comfortable there. This middle-aged daredevil, this adrenaline junkie who dangled from precipices, walked across continents, and flung her body out of planes into thin air, returned home to make her living as a weaver—just about the least impetuous, most encumbered, most tightly controlled art form there was. In weaving, one set of threads was strung onto five hundred pounds of loom, the other attached to a shuttle: right to left then back again, the threads locking into a pattern predetermined before the warp threads were on the loom. In weaving, there was little scope for wild improvisation even on the big hangings; in weaving, focused intensity counterbalanced the boisterous disorder of her wanderings.

Oddly enough, before her sight had begun to fail, she had already been turning from the intense colors she had worked in for so many years—colors she had learned along with the techniques, in Guatemala and Rajasthan—to stark black and white. Almost as if her mind had known that the world of sight was about to draw in on her. Last year, she had produced a series of all-black or all-white pieces, with subtle patterns emerging from the tactile qualities of the thread. An astute gallery owner had dubbed the pieces *Weaving Darkness,* a couple of important critics had commented on the interesting things Suze Blackstock had to say concerning texture and about color-in-colorlessness; to her considerable surprise, Suze was on her way to becoming famous in the weaving world. She "saw" the growing piece with her fingers as she was weaving it; fully sighted people saw it in a slightly different manner when it was hanging on the wall. A gallery in New York wanted her pieces for a one-woman show in the fall, there was talk about an article in *Time,* the Smithsonian had written about acquiring a hanging.

Suze was not unaware of the irony of her success.

Today she was working on a white piece, a glowing expanse on her vision where the sun poured through the south window onto it. She could as easily have worked at night, and occasionally did with the black pieces, but the sensation of brightness seemed to emphasize the sensations in her fingertips, and make the piece more of a whole. She barely noticed when Courtney left for town; was surprised, when the girl returned, to find she'd been at it for an hour and a half.

When Courtney asked her from the kitchen if she wanted tuna fish or turkey, she told the girl to choose, and went to wash her hands. She and the girl usually ate lunch together; she thought it made Courtney feel noble to think she was providing company to the lonely old lesbian instead of just cleaning her floors and buying her groceries. And in fact, although she didn't care much for being the object of Christian charity, Suze didn't mind eating with the girl, even though the conversation was sometimes hard going.

Courtney had chosen tuna, and set it out, as always, four-square, with the glass a precise two inches from the plate's one o'clock mark. The glass held iced tea, as usual. When Suze had suggested a beer one warm day, the girl had gone silent. Courtney was willing to overlook the irregularity of her neighbors' relationship, would dutifully run her dust rag over the bottles of gin and scotch on the sideboard (replenished periodically by odd-job Andy), washed up without complaint the glasses smelling of Suze's nighttime sins, but even if she'd been old enough to buy the stuff, Suze knew that she wouldn't ask her. Drugs, too, even when they were by prescription, could fall under Courtney's disapproving gaze: Twice, the girl had failed to bring Suze's bottle of sleeping pills back from the drugstore. Her parents were probably alcoholics.

She was, Suze had to say, scrupulous about bringing the drops and pills that kept down the intraocular pressure. It had, of course, occurred to Suze that cannabis was a specific for her type of eye degeneration, but she had instantly dismissed the possibility of asking the girl for the phone number of one of the high-school potheads. Sooner or later, the ophthalmologist would decide the standard medications weren't keeping her IOP low enough, and they'd start the rounds of medicinal pot. In the meantime, she'd just have to wait— with the way her luck had been going lately, the first person she asked about buying grass would turn out to be a narc.

Courtney might look askance on a lesbian relationship, but she was dutiful at her Christian goodwill, and as she sat down to eat, she asked, "Any news on Janna last night?"

"Much the same. That new nurse suggested I bring some music when we go on Sunday."

"You want me to help pick some out?"

"I'll do it," Suze said. Then, hearing the shortness in her answer, she added, "If I have any problems, I'll ask for help."

"We prayed for her in youth group last night. I hope you don't mind."

Suze did, but what could she do? Tell the girl to stop? "Of course not."

"My friend Lin's grandmother had a stroke last year; she's a lot better now, just a small limp and she slurs certain words."

"Good for her."

"I only meant—"

"I know, Courtney. I'm just finding it tough to be upbeat." Five weeks of limbo; at what point should she think about getting on with her own life? And maybe she should let the girl choose the music; Courtney probably knew more about Janna's taste than Janna's whirlwind lover did.

When Courtney drove away, as always, Suze felt a great relief. With, as always, a sense that the cabin was terribly remote.

Some evenings, after her ritual call to Janna's nursing home, Suze turned up every light in the cabin, setting the small world to blazing, giving form to the uncertainty in which she lived. Other nights she settled into the darkness as she would have stepped into a woodland pool, slowly, half apprehensive of encountering some slippery creature underfoot, but intimately aware of the rich sensations to be gained by allowing the cool water to rise around her, submerge her, transform her into one of its own.

Tonight was a night for darkness. For one thing, she was nearly finished with the piece on the loom, and tomorrow or the next day she would cut it off, put it aside for finishing, and prepare the warp for the next one. The next piece would be black, and she needed to think about it for a while, in the darkness.

The night was cool. She poured a glass of whiskey and picked up the thick alpaca-and-silk blanket she had made for Janna, her first piece off the new loom, finished just days before the stroke. She curled into the deck chair on the porch, wrapped in warmth, sipping the drink, shaping the weaving in her inner eye. It would be a big one, as wide as this sixteen-harness loom would take. And for once, she would incorporate color—although even the sighted would only be aware of it peripherally, as a texture in the darkness. She had once, several years ago, worked with a glossy, seemingly black thread that in fact had a few, a very few infinitesimal threads of intense color spun into it, turquoise and coral and emerald, invisible from more than a few inches but adding an emotional richness to the final black. She'd already had the spinner do the yarn for her, knew it would be precisely as her memory held it, knew that if she blended it on the loom with the same unrelieved flat ebony linen as the warp threads, it would give her a strong contrast while appearing monochromatic. The mind, she reflected, often saw things the eyes did not perceive.

The glass emptied, the night felt its way through the soft wool, and Suze was about to throw the wrap off and go inside when all her senses rose as one: a digging sound. She'd forgotten all about it, thought it was a dream, but here it was again. What kind of animal made a sound like a shovel in the soil? A burrowing creature, raccoon or opossum, maybe? Not a skunk—she'd surely smell it.

But this was not the scurry of claws in the earth; the *chink* of metal against stone, the purposeful rhythm, the size of the thing in the night were those of a shovel. Suze's first outlandish reaction was to wish she'd brought her cell phone out with her, followed instantly by anger, good and clean and scouring away the timidity.

The noise persisted for ten minutes or so. By the time it stopped, she had eased herself down from the porch and crept softly down the gravel drive, far enough to get a rough idea of the source of the digging, two hundred yards away, past the first curve. She knew the drive intimately, an easy stroll when she didn't feel like risking her ankle on an unseen hole or her skin on a stand of poison oak; by now her feet knew the road's hazards as well as they knew the cabin floor. But her mind could not make an image of what was happening out there.

When the digging sounds ceased, she stayed where she was, head down and concentrating. She couldn't quite tell, but she didn't think the sounds had stopped completely: nothing distinct, but the audial impression of footsteps, the sensation of clicks and taps, once a sawing noise that lasted for perhaps twenty seconds. This went on for a quarter of an hour; then the digging noise started up again, although the pace was quicker and it did not go on as long.

Then silence. This time the night settled into a more profound quiet, like a lake of darkness after the ripples passed, placid and undisturbed. A cricket buzzed; a horned owl called; Suze was alone again. She made her way back to the cabin, where she reluctantly—resentfully—checked to be sure all the doors and windows were locked before going to bed.

The next day was Wednesday, not one of Courtney's days, but already Andy, Janna's ninety-year-old odd job man (actually only seventy-three, but his complaints were those of a geriatric) was due in the afternoon. She ate her breakfast, listened to the morning news, dismantled the white warp threads from the loom, and began measuring the black linen on her warping mill, all the while waiting for the sun to brighten and reach the proper angle for illuminating the drive.

Finally, she could wait no longer. She went back to the lean-to where Janna kept her gardening tools, locating a trowel more by memory than by sight. She stuck its handle into the back pocket of her jeans, and set off up the drive.

Janna's road was dirt, graded and graveled when the ruts became too deep, with concrete only on one brief steep stretch near the main road. As Suze approached the first curve, she found that she was deliberately scuffing her boots through the loose rock as if to warn intruders. She made herself stop, and pulled the trowel from her pocket, holding it in her hand like a weapon. Not that she expected to find anyone there—whoever had come by dead of night would hardly hang around to see what came along in broad daylight. Still, she wanted to get some idea of what had happened here before Andy the builder came—he was elderly, but he was a male, and his immediate instinct would be to take control. And although Suze might have got herself bogged down in a morass of cowardice and indecision, she did not wish to be taken control of, thank you very much.

At the curve, she stopped, letting her eyes give her what fuzzy information they could, which wasn't much. So she closed them and went on, allowing her other senses to come into play. The soft patch of ground underfoot here was as usual, the odor of the oak trees, the faint underlay of wild mint, and the single eucalyptus someone had planted decades ago, fading as she walked on. Soft earth gave way to gravel again where the bulldozer's blade had cut into the slope to the right last year. Fragrance rose from underfoot at the bay tree where Janna used to pause, pulling off a fragrant twig—Suze caught herself: where Janna would soon again pause, to strip the leaves and breathe in their clean, acrid smell. Gravel now, then the crunch of deeper gravel, and the moist air rising from the streambed, carrying with it odors of redwood and ferns and the sound of water—a muscular rush when she'd first come here, now reduced to a trickle. And in a few more paces, her feet would hit the hollowness of the old culvert that contained the stream. But before that, a change: Where normally the gravel thinned under her boots, today she felt the stiffness of fallen leaves.

Puzzled, Suze squatted to let her fingertips play along the ground. Yes, as she'd thought, the roadway was littered with the distinctively prickly leaves of the live-oak tree. But the next one of those was around the bend, and it hadn't been at all windy; how then had they gotten here?

Standing, she peered at the vague patches of light and dark. She was too early; the sun was still caught in the branches of the redwoods that rose from the streambed. She stuck the trowel back into her pocket and went to sit on the railing over the culvert, counseling patience as she listened to the murmurs of the stream.

A squirrel spotted her, and coughed irritably for a long time in the branches overhead. A distant plane vibrated the sky, vague bird-shapes ducked across her vision, and the brightness slowly crept toward the relevant patch of ground. Suze got up, brushed off the back of her pants, and walked forward.

Darkness and light, textures rather than objects. She had a pair of glasses thicker than cut-glass tumblers, glasses so heavy they made her whole face ache, but all that weight only brought objects into greater contrast, not clarity. So—typically—she'd gone to the other extreme and begun doing without them, allowing the sides of her vision to interpret shapes, seeing with her mind, not her retinas. As now she saw a swath of pale texture against the darker background of undisturbed leaves.

The path stretched down from the road at the same angle as the stream. There was, Suze knew, a rough deer track along the bank, clear of the poison oak and blackberry tangles that demanded greater sunlight. It had been one of Janna's favorite moonlight walks. She remembered the dampness against her face, the tickle of the ferns against her calf. Remembered, too, Janna, pressed between Suze and the padded bark of a massive redwood; Janna's mouth.

It would happen again, Suze told herself fiercely, and knelt down with the trowel in her hand.

Her fingers found disturbed soil underneath the scattered leaves, soil her trowel dug into with ease. She mounded it on the gravel road, excavating one, then two lengths of the trowel blade. Her fingers probed the soft, dry earth, seeking for she knew not what. Buried treasure? In these mountains, more likely a buried body part.

At this thought, her fingertips cringed back from their seeking. Jesus; what would it be like, to encounter dead flesh with her own warm hands? Would she ever be able to scrub the sensation away? Gingerly, she lowered her hand again, delicately fingering the soil where she had been pushing. But it was the trowel blade that found what she was seeking, when it hit something and slid to one side.

She followed the metal blade down with her left hand, encountering a shape that was unnaturally smooth and hard. Almost like a tree root, but as she rubbed at the soil, she knew that no tree could have produced a thing as smooth and unblemished as this. It was a pipe—plastic, by the feel, and when she'd dug a bit more, the sun confirmed it: white PVC pipe. She scraped the soil away, working in the direction of the road until she encountered another pipe, larger and at right angles to the first. This larger one would be the cabin's main water supply, winding along the edge of the drive from the well and storage tank near the main road a mile away. The smaller pipe joined the main line smoothly; the faint odor of fresh plastic cement rose from her trench.

Someone had recently tapped into the cabin's water supply.

Suze stared at the patterns in front of her, shades of brown with flashes of white running through it, and thought about leaving the hole for Andy to find when he came along the road in two or three hours. But without knowing quite why, she found herself scraping the dirt back over the pipe, slowly at first, then more rapidly, as if she had heard the old man's truck chugging up from the road. She scraped and tamped and scraped some more, getting up to walk the fresh mound flat with her boots. She kicked some of the leaves back over the trampled earth, and then went across the drive to the inside curve where the gravel accumulated and scooped up one trowel-load after another, flinging the gravel over the offending patch until it had obscured in her vision.

When she was finished, she was satisfied to note that a legally blind woman could do a better job of concealment than her thieving neighbor had at night. She scrubbed at her caked hands, then climbed cautiously down the confusing darkness of the stream bank to where the water played, and washed the dirt from her hands and the trowel blade, humming under her breath.

When Andy drove up later that afternoon, she had coffee for him, money for the two bottles he brought her, and questions. She made it seem like a friendly chat, sitting him down on the porch to talk over the projects he was near to finishing up, suggesting one or two more things that Janna might have had in mind (the roof, for one—Andy didn't think the flat area had been done right, and was going to leak come a heavy storm.)

Then she casually asked, "Do you have a lot of illegal building around here?"

"What, like people neglecting to call the building inspectors when they're adding a room? Sure."

"I was thinking more along the lines of building from scratch."

"That'd be tough to do," he said after a moment's judicious thought. "Hard to hide the access road, for one thing. The neighbors might not report them, but the inspectors are up and down these hills all the time; they'd spot it eventually."

"What if you didn't build an access road?"

"Then how'd you get in and out? It's a fair walk to town. And how'd you take delivery of building materials? Unless you're talking about a teepee, or a cave with a bush dragged over the mouth, you'd need wood, cement, window glass. There's only so far you can carry a sheet of plywood through the bushes. Why do you ask?"

"I was just wondering how hard it would be to live completely off the land in these hills."

"Pretty tough. Oh, there's probably a few here and there, but I'd doubt they stay for long. One winter'd do it for any Thoreau fantasies. You haven't been bothered by any strangers, have you?" the old man said, suddenly catching on to the gist of the conversation.

"Oh, no. Just something Courtney and I were talking about the other day, got me to wondering. Now, about that roof . . ."

The next night, Suze was not disturbed by the sound of digging. Nor the next, and although she knew that she should report her mysterious, water-usurping neighbor, it seemed to her that if all he wanted was a little clean water, she couldn't really begrudge him. After all, she was living here off the goodwill of a woman she barely knew; why not this Thoreau in the woods?

And then came the call from the nursing home, the long-awaited, nearly despaired-of call to say that Janna seemed to be waking up and alert, and maybe Suze would like to come and talk to her? In the flurry of the days that followed, in the exhilaration of feeling that limp hand finally squeeze back, in the first slurred words from the long-empty mouth, the digging noises were forgotten. The weaving was neglected for long hours at the nursing home, and Courtney's housekeeping and shopping skills were supplanted by those of driving Suze and pushing Janna's chair through the grounds.

Two weeks later, on a spectacular summer's Sunday afternoon, Janna's doctor asked Suze to stop by his office for a talk. She had to ask a nurse for the correct door, and then had to allow the doctor to lead her to a chair. His news was good and bad.

"I think Janna's going to be ready to go home before too long," he said, but before Suze's heart could begin to sing, added, "We need to think about her care. She tells me you have glaucoma."

"It's under control," she said quickly, not a complete lie.

"Who's your doctor?" Suze told him, and his form shifted in a way she knew meant a nod. "A good man. But you can't drive. And caring for Janna is going to require a lot of effort in the early days. Can you ask that girl to move in full-time, maybe for the first month?"

Suze very nearly stood up and walked out. She'd stuck by Janna all these weeks, stretching the bonds between them far beyond the flimsy beginnings. She wanted to tell this man, "Look, I barely know Janna—I only met her in January, moved here on a whim. Really, it's time I moved on." Nearly told him, "If I have to live with that hymn-spouting child, I'll go nuts." Almost decided that she'd done her part as a faithful friend, and that now she'd seen Janna back on her feet, it was best to clear the way to putting two lives back on track.

But she did not. She'd seen the beginnings of something real with Janna, felt the rare touch of a person who understood the forces that drove her. Janna had never once told Suze that she shouldn't do something because of her sight, had even egged her on; who was Suze to tell Janna goodbye?

"Her insurance won't cover a full-time nurse?" Suze asked, not expecting much. She was answered by the rustle and shift of a shaking head.

"Afraid not."

"Then I guess we'll have to try Courtney."

The child was overjoyed. They had ten days before Janna would be released, and Courtney spent it in a whirlwind of busybody virtue, overseeing Andy's building of a wheelchair ramp (which Suze insisted be made temporary), rearranging furniture (each shift accompanied by multiple reminders to Suze to take care not to trip over the sofa, the table, the rug), fretting about throw rugs and wheelchair access and the cabin's apparently inadequate water supply (which had been fine until the child had decided to launder every bit of bedding in the house on Monday morning). Spare furniture was stored in the shed, a bed was brought in for the girl, and Suze's loom shoved as far into the corner as it would go. Suze knew damn well that they'd be hard put to get rid of Courtney when school started up next month, even if Janna was up and dancing.

Janna was set to come home on the twenty-fourth of July, a Wednesday. With two days to go, the water tank again ran dry, and Courtney spilled over in shrill cries of distress and disaster. The rest of the day was taken up with Andy. He looked at the small tank behind the house, then at the big one near the road, and scratched under his baseball cap in puzzlement.

"This here pressure pump's working fine now," he told Suze, who had driven down with him, more to escape the flurry of last-minute housecleaning than because she thought she could do any good.

"Some kind of intermittent fault?"

"Can't see any. Sometime you get bugs on the contacts, breaks the flow of electricity. I've cleaned 'em off, gave 'em a shot of Raid—we'll see if that does it. If it doesn't, you'll probably want to get the water people in, pull the well pump itself and see if it's packing up."

"How many gallons did you say this tank holds?"

"You got a five thousand–gallon tank here, five hundred near the house. That's a hundred loads of laundry, or a couple days of leaving the hose running. Shouldn't happen."

Suze looked at the green plastic monolith of the tank, her mind's

eye clearly seeing that length of PVC pipe cutting into the main supply line. She teetered on the edge of telling the old builder about it,
of ratting out on her Thoreau. But Courtney would have a thousand
fits, and Andy would take manly command, and Suze's preferences
would be trampled underfoot. So she'd think about it, before she said
anything to Andy.

Tuesday, Courtney arrived with Janna's car crammed to the brim
with boxes and bulging trash bags filled with clothes and essential
teenage equipment. She spent the day settling in, having made no
such proposal to Suze. At three that afternoon, she came out of the
guest room, clearly intending to start dinner. Suze had other ideas.

"Well, I guess we'll see you tomorrow," she said cheerily.

"What do you mean?"

"When you come and get me in the morning, so we can go get
Janna."

"But I thought I might stay here tonight."

"Oh, Courtney, I couldn't ask you to do that. Your parents will
be missing you so much in the next three weeks, before school starts,
I really think you should let them have a last night with you." She
was at the loom, and kept her face down, her voice without guile.

"I have most of my stuff here, now."

"That was foresighted of you. But I'm sure you could find a
toothbrush and pajamas. I'll see you in the morning," she said, and
continued working.

Hurt, and making sure Suze knew it, Courtney flounced into the
car and drove off.

When she had gone, Suze poured herself a stiff drink and went
out onto the porch, wanting to scream. She wanted to walk away
down the road, never to look back. Wanted to get roaring drunk, take
off for the Amazon in a canoe, leap out of a plane without checking
to see if she had her chute on. Tomorrow the earth would sigh and
settle onto her the combined weight of an invalid lover she barely
knew, a good Christian girl with head-nurse fantasies, and a pair of
dying eyes.

Pressures all, and as her only release, the knowledge of digging in
the night, ten thousand gallons of missing water, and a remembered
conversation concerning the exorbitant seasonal cost of electricity.

She swallowed the last of her drink, feeling the pounding of anticipation in her veins, thinking, *Tomorrow the weight comes, but by God, I still have tonight.*

That night, Suze went for a walk in the woods.

In her early days and weeks here, Janna had taken Suze on countless "blind walks," as if those remnants of the touchy-feely days would make an actual blind woman feel better. The odd thing was, they did. The first few were terrifying: It was one thing to jump out of a plane able to see the ground below, quite another to step onto a moon-dappled path surrounded by vague shapes and incomprehensible motion. But somehow Janna had known that although she had to bully Suze out the door for their first five-minute outing along the drive, by the end of the week Suze would relish the challenge of setting off into the night with only three senses to guide her. The feel of the ground underfoot, the smell of the air, the sounds of creatures and the trees themselves guided her into an intoxicating foreign country. By the end of the second week, she was leading Janna.

She didn't know how far she'd go tonight, but following the stream, how lost could she get?

She armed herself with the big flashlight; as she was headed out the door, she paused and went back, tucking one of the tall spools of black warp thread into the waist pack with the light. If she had to leave the stream, she could always lay an Ariadne's thread through the trees. At the door, she picked up the thin, flexible stripped branch she sometimes used as a cane, and stepped off the porch to the ground.

The full moon created a pale smear in her vision and a sense of texture to the night, as if she were entering one of her black-on-black hangings. It was distracting; she closed her eyes to concentrate on memory, and after a minute, found the drive in her mind. She set confidently off, her feet locating the defining patches of gravel here and soil there, her nostrils finding the tang of eucalyptus and the approach of the stream, until she was through the curve and standing on the misplaced oak leaves over the intruder's pipe. Apprehension bubbled in her chest, and she waited: The old Suze Blackstock wouldn't have panicked; would the new one? But the apprehension warmed her, like buckling on her helmet as the wind battered her body, like looking upward for her first sight of virgin rock wall; the welcome quickening of her heart was more excitement than fear.

Suze smiled, and stepped off the road.

The deer track ran along the hill above the stream, a faint flat trail cut by generations of delicate hooves. At first, Suze inched her way along, tapping trees with the stick-cane, not entirely trusting her feet, pushing back the fear that jabbered at her mind, *You can't do this, you're nearly blind, you have to be sensible. . . .*

But she went on, and it became easier. Then suddenly, a mile along, the shrubs ahead of her exploded in a thunder and rush of movement, and she nearly leapt into the creek in terror before the noise resolved itself into the identifiable repeated *thump-swish* of a pair of fleeing deer. She leaned against a tree, weak with reaction, and tried to laugh.

Another half mile, and she was beginning to wonder if she'd imagined the whole scenario, the electricity and water—

And then she stopped. Between one step and the next, a peculiar tang brushed the air: not trees, not the odors of damp and stone from the creek. It was such an unexpected addition to the night, it took her a while to identify it.

Chilies. Someone in the area had recently cooked a meal of chilies and cumin and tomato. Mexican food, and now the savor of coffee. It was incongruous, and brought in its wake a note of the ominous that kept her where she stood, undecided. What the hell did she expect, that the men illegally camping here would offer her a plate of rice, a cup of coffee, take her on a tour of their patch?

Because she could smell that now, too, an acrid odor of exotic vegetation. The breeze that brought the odor also stirred up the rich susurration of plants, tall and full, rising up before her. Suze had smelled cannabis growing before, in hilltop patches in Mexico and South America. It smelled much the same here.

It had taken her some time to put together all the threads. Courtney's exclamations over the winter's high electrical bills, when power stolen from Janna's lines had warmed and illuminated someone's well-concealed greenhouses. Digging in the night, but only when the cabin was dark. Ten thousand gallons drained from the tank, watering the crop when it had been transplanted into open ground, flowing into the roots once a week, on Mondays.

And the other threads, those that stretched into the future, the unknown: How the local drug squad's helicopters would be gearing up for its annual sky searches, while the stand, nearly ready for harvest, stood vulnerable to potential thieves. How paranoia would be at its height. How the boss man would not trust his year's income to hired hands; he would be out here, keeping guard.

How he would be armed.

Suze's recent, timorous self quailed at the thought of what she was about to do. *Go back to the cabin,* it urged; *You can get a prescription, for Christ's sake. Be sensible!* But sensible was not what Suze Blackstock was all about. Suze Blackstock was a woman who wove darkness and walked into the unknown, a woman who used adrenaline to bleed off unbearable pressures. Who used near-suicide to keep her from the real thing.

She straightened her shoulders and stepped into the luxurious growth, heading toward a dancing glow as if toward a lover's eyes. When the stand was at an end, she held her hands up as if seizing the straps of a parachute, and took a last step out in the open. Her blood thudded through her veins as she prepared to weave herself, one way or another, into this place: On the one hand, the joy of Janna coming home; on the other, the terror that she, Suze Blackstock, was about to be shot dead; the two extremes acted as counterbalances, with her in the middle, standing firm.

But the shot did not come, not with her first appearance from the plants. When the flurry of movement near the fire had ceased, she cleared her throat and sent some words out toward the indistinct figure that remained, wondering which way the words would tip the balance.

"You guys are using kind of a lot of our water and power," she said. "I wonder if you might be interested in a trade, once your harvest is in?"

—*With thanks to Susan Orrett and Zoe King*

Chuck's Bucket

By CHRIS OFFUTT

*Sometimes a man makes such a hash of his life that his only
recourse is to bend the temporal fabric of reality itself!*

I pumped air into my bicycle tire and rode slowly across town, stopping twice to adjust my glasses. The cheap tape on the arms was giving out. To make matters worse, I could not see through the left lens, which naturally was my better eye. Such diminished capacity a year ago would have embarrassed me, but I am now undergoing what appears to be a midlife crisis of severe parameters. I recently broke all contact with my family except being cc'ed by e-mail betwixt my siblings. Next I left my wife but only managed to move a few blocks away. To top things off, my new place has a ghost that has begun to haunt me nightly.

At the University of Iowa campus, I leaned my bike beside the Van Allen building, named for the physics professor who'd discovered the Van Allen belt in the night sky, and also inventor of the roccoon—half rocket, half balloon. Several years ago, a Chinese grad student went on a rampage and murdered several physics professors here. Now the security is tight, but I'd recently taught fiction writing as an adjunct professor at UI and still had a faculty ID to show the guard. I waited half an hour for Professor Charles Andrews to emerge from his lab.

I'd met Chuck in a local low-stakes poker game that had gone on for many years in Iowa City. He was the fish, the absolute worst player at the table, but charming and affable because he truly didn't care about winning. He was there to study chance itself. He'd played cards with John Cage, Jasper Johns, and Richard Feynman. Chuck was impressed that I knew the work of all three men. Since the game, we met periodically for lunch and talked about my writing and his research.

Last night the ghost had woken me several times, and at dawn I stepped on my glasses, which had fallen from the nightstand. Then my car wouldn't start. I could get by on a single-speed bicycle and duct-taped spectacles, but the lens kept popping free of the twisted frame. I tried to glue the lens in place and only managed to smear the glass until it was translucent. I sat at my computer to work on a short story. It was about a guy who got himself cloned but the clone died and started haunting him every night. For two weeks I'd been unable to get past the opening.

After half an hour of self-torture, I called Chuck, seeking information about clones.

"Clones suck," he had said on the phone. "The ultimate goal of clone research is to produce an army of Swoffies."

"What's that?"

"They cloned the most elite military specimen—a marine scout-sniper named Swofford—and now they just crank out Swoffies like a Xerox machine."

"Well, maybe I can use them in my story."

"I wouldn't," he said. "It's classified information just to know the term 'Swoffie.' You do and they'll come after you."

"Well, it's really a ghost story anyhow."

His diffident tone changed to sharp interest.

"Why ghosts, Chris?"

"It's kind of complicated."

"So's quantum physics, but I manage to stay afloat."

"It's personal," I said.

"Try me."

"I think my place is haunted."

"Was it always?"

"No, since about a month."

"Come to my lab as soon as you can."

I agreed and hung up the phone, surprised by Chuck's curiosity about something as absurd as a ghost. Any excuse not to write was sadly welcome, and I rode my bike to his office.

He came striding down the hall, his white lab coat billowing like an old-time cloak. He vouched for me at the first guard booth, then guided me through a series of security points to what was obviously his working office, an unbelievably cluttered mess reminiscent of Francis Bacon's studio. A narrow aisle led through the knee-high debris of paper, books, drawings, empty pop cans, and candy bar wrappers. The walls held chalkboards filled with equations. There was no tech equipment in sight, no machines, not even a computer. Chuck became visibly relaxed in the disarray, and upended a garbage can for me to sit on.

"The ghost," he said. "I want the whole story."

I laid it all out and the longer I yakked, the more preposterous it sounded. For the past four weeks I'd slept quite poorly, despite changing my mattress and the position for sleep. I tried hot baths, warm milk, deep breathing, valerian, melatonin, and shiatsu. I tucked pillows beneath my neck, between my legs, and under my hips until I lay in a cradle of shims. Nothing worked. The ghost still woke me every night. When I snapped awake, it was there, lurking just beyond my sight.

Chuck demanded details of time, frequency, clarity, sound,

smell, and temperature of the room. For the first time in our friendship, I had his full focus, like being scrutinized by a Cyclops. He inquired after my diet, alcohol and substance use, vitamin intake, family history of mental illness. When I finished, Chuck sat motionless, his eyes shrouded as if turning his gaze inward.

"First of all," he said, "there's absolutely no such thing as ghosts."

"I know."

"Death means awareness ends and tissue decays. It is such a terrifying concept that we imagine an afterlife. Some form of immortality is the one common denominator of all religions and many superstitions. Nevertheless, I believe you."

"Maybe I'm nuts."

"Could be," he said. "Are there any extenuating circumstances in your life?"

"I got divorced six months ago."

"I mean in the past month."

I nodded, humiliated by the truth.

"I haven't been able to finish a story," I said.

He sat patient as a lighthouse keeper while I explained myself. A month ago, Michael Chabon invited me to write a story for an all-genre issue he's guest editing of *McSweeney's,* a San Francisco magazine. I refused because my father was a genre writer who'd published more than 150 books under various pseudonyms. I've long been terrified of copying him further than I already do.

Michael urged me to participate and I agreed. That night the ghost woke me and I lay in the dark for a few hours, realizing that I didn't want to write anything anymore. I never really wanted to be a writer, and had only pursued the occupation in the hope that my father would like me.

I sent Michael an e-mail trying to beg off, saying genre writing was too connected to my father's work. Michael e-mailed back saying that he'd read my father's books when he was young and wasn't it cool that my dad was my dad. He also told me another contributor was Harlan Ellison, a science fiction author with whom my father had a public and long-running feud that began nearly thirty years ago at WorldCon.

Then I broke my glasses, and my car shit the bed, and I had returned to the story out of financial desperation.

"So," Chuck said, when I finished telling him all this, "you have writer's block."

"No, I don't believe in that. Other artists don't suffer that way. You never hear of ballerina's block. I just can't finish this story. It's never happened before and I think it's the ghost's fault."

"It all fits together perfectly to me."

"What are you talking about?"

"Time travel, Chris."

"Yeah, sure. Maybe we should go back to the clones."

"Think about e-mail. You send a note to someone, but they don't check their e-mail for a week. Did your message arrive from the past, or did it enter their future?"

"I guess it's the same."

"Exactly! Anything in motion leaves a trail, even through time. What we call a ghost is really the footprint of a time traveler."

"Great!" I said. "All you need is to invent a time machine."

"I did. A month ago. I've been using chimps."

Chuck was incapable of lying; to do so would violate his concept of science. I'd never seen him with such a grave expression, yet the skin of his face twitched with enthusiasm. After the poker game, Chuck had entrusted me with his biggest secret: "I don't sleep with women," he'd said, "because I'm gay. And I don't sleep with men because all men are pigs. I love my lab and that's enough." Chuck's an odd guy with odd quirks such as endlessly readjusting the ball cap he perpetually wore. No one would suspect him of being Iowa City's resident genius, the intellectual darling of the academic community. If the quirky bastard said he invented a time machine, he had.

"Well," I said. "Let's have a look at it."

He strode in a tight circle, gesticulating like a demented rap singer as he spoke.

"First of all, the math is outrageous. I mean it is completely out of hand, but wicked elegant."

"Skip the math, Chuck. I'll trust you on that."

"Space-time bends, which means there can be shortcuts between specific points."

"Oh, sure," I said, as if this were common knowledge. "You're talking about wormholes. I saw it in a movie."

Chuck gave me a look like I was a pup that had crapped on the porch. His voice was patient, yet clearly annoyed.

"I prefer to call them ERBs. It's an acronym for Einstein-Rosen Bridge, since they came up with it in the thirties."

"How do you get inside one?"

"Here's the simple way of thinking about it. I make a photocopy of DNA and convert the image to digital information. I attach each binary numeral to a p-brane, and send it into an ERB, using a particle beam. And voilà!"

"Nothing to it. Like making rice that won't stick."

"Two drawbacks," he said. "Time travel is one-way."

"You mean you get stuck?"

"No, that's impossible. Writers make that stuff up. Think of e-mail. You send a message, but unless your friend is wired, he can't receive it. Right now, time travel is one-way until we build a machine to reconstitute the information. It's possible, but the math will take quantum computing."

"What's that?"

"It's a computer that uses the spinning nuclei of atoms to represent binary code. Ike Chuan out at MIT has one up and running, but the field is still young."

"You said two drawbacks."

"Controlling destination," he said.

"What's to control? I mean if you're going to Des Moines, it's always there. Des Moines never changes."

"You have to adjust your thinking to a model. Imagine time as a wet mop in a bucket with the strings all tangled together. An ERB is your route into the bucket. You just don't know which string you'll land on."

"Like getting on a bus to Des Moines and winding up in Cedar Rapids."

"I know you're being facetious, Chris. But you're actually close. It's more like going to a depot and getting on the first bus you see, knowing it's leaving soon, but not knowing where it's headed."

"None of that explains my ghost."

"It's not a ghost, Chris. You are perceiving digital information encased in a cluster of mobile and sentient p-branes. This ghost suddenly manifested, right?"

"About a month ago."

"The same time when I completed my machine. According to my hypothesis, you are being visited by yourself. The fact that you came here today is proof. There's no choice but to send you into the bucket. We have to fulfill our end of time's bargain. Your ghost compels it."

"You're out of your mind, Chuck."

"No, I'm afraid that you quite literally were out of your mind when you haunted yourself last night."

"You can't shove me through an ERB down a mop handle to a bucket in Des Moines."

"What'll it take to try?"

"New glasses," I said, "and a car."

"You can have my car, Chris. I abhor the combustion engine. Such little innovation in all these years. And I can arrange for new glasses through my insurance."

I sighed, wishing I'd asked for cash since he'd acquiesced so easily.

"Chris," he said. "What have you got to lose?"

The fact was, I had nothing to lose except my life and I didn't like my current circumstances anyway. Twenty years ago I'd set out to be a Great American Writer. I wanted to live in New York with literary buddies but instead I was divorced and unemployed with few friends in a small Midwestern town surrounded by corn, soy, and white people. Everything I owned was secondhand. I didn't even have insurance. I was lonely and my work was going nowhere. It occurred to me that if Chuck could send me into the future, I could read my story, then return and write the ending.

"Okay," I said, "I'll give it a whirl."

"Good." He nodded, his eyes delirious with suppressed happiness. "I need to take a blood sample, and make a full digitization of your DNA."

He led me through a door into a small space equipped as a physician's examining room. I stripped to my socks and he ran me through a rapid battery of medical tests. Chuck fed my blood into a machine that separated the DNA and began converting it to binary code. He left the room to make further preparations.

I wondered if other people went to such extremes for a story. Normal S.F. writers probably snapped off time travel ideas like downing coffee. This made me chuckle as I recalled my father telling me that Edgar Rice Burroughs's first publication was under the name "Normal Bean" because he was afraid readers would consider him unbalanced. At one time I'd thought of using a pseudonym. My father's only S.F. novel, *The Castle Keeps,* was about a writer in Kentucky, and the name I considered was the son of the protagonist. I decided against the idea because it granted my father too much influence over my writing. Besides, he used over a dozen pseudonyms and I didn't want to be like him.

Dad was essentially a fantasy writer of sword-and-sorcery, soft- and hard-core porn. But when I was a kid, he and Harlan Ellison were the new young Turks in the science fiction field. After their falling-out, Dad used to impersonate Ellison at the supper table—talking fast in a high voice, cursing a lot, and calling himself "Arlen Hellraiser." I was at the stage where I copied my father, and thus refused to read Ellison. A few years later, after realizing that Dad disliked me, I read all of Ellison's work, particularly enjoying his short stories.

Chuck entered the room and asked if I was ready.

"You bet," I said.

"Listen, Chris," he said. "The chimps come back different— healthy, but different. I sedate them first, and maybe that's the reason."

"Different how?"

"It's intangible, as if they return more alert."

"Okay," I said. "But no sedation. I have to finish my story."

He led me to a large chamber that contained a transparent metal table with a giant Lucite lid. An entwined network of cables was attached to the underside of the table, then ran along the floor to a surprisingly small console of computer equipment. The room was otherwise quite austere, silent, and oddly calm. Chuck explained that everything would be recorded on digital video. I lay on the gel-foam table, which re-formed itself to my body. Chuck began easing the lid shut.

"What's that for?" I said. "Makes me think of a coffin."

"Maintenance of adequate oxygen supply. It's got tiny sensors embedded in it that monitor your vitals. I can also administer a CAT scan, X ray, MRI. Only three of these machines exist. They are often used for—"

"Okay, okay, okay."

"How do you feel?"

"Like a moron, mainly."

"You are a pioneer, Chris. First human in the bucket."

"What's going to happen?"

"I have no idea."

"Well, fuck it then."

He latched the lid. It occurred to me that I was quite possibly trusting a madman.

I felt rather than heard a distant hum, like cicadas thrumming against my skin. At varying times in my life I have attempted meditation that placed me in an odd state of non-waking, non-sleep, similar to a hypnotic trance, which I have entered at least three times—once by a traveling hypnotist who came to my high school and induced me to sing like Elvis, again by a Kevin Bacon movie in which I was hypnotized when Kevin was, and once when I was very young and my father put me into a trance on the couch and I only recall waking in the darkness with him scared and kneeling beside me, something I've long been curious about and even considered being rehypnotized in order to learn what happened then, and now in Chuck's lab I entered a trance-like state for an indeterminate time until I was abruptly aware of the greatest liberty I'd ever known.

Gravity ceased to exert a hold on me. I was buoyant with no water, hovering with no atmosphere. I had become mobile perception, yet unable to see, hear, feel, smell, or taste in the conventional way. I was grok. I was all. I felt each distinct beat of a hummingbird's wing, saw the infinitesimal difference in every snowflake. I could follow the path of the merest speck of water falling to earth as rain and rising as steam to drop again. I had an understanding of how existence fit together from a sunflower to a quark, the Bermuda Triangle to an amoeba. I experienced the sheer joy of awareness. There was no me. For the first time in my life, I liked myself—precisely because I did not exist.

I slowly understood that I was in my bedroom watching myself sleep. The clock face was a red blur. I could direct my consciousness about the room like aiming a stream of light one photon at a time. I was an unseen packet of cognizant information capable of motion in any direction. I aimed my awareness to the hall beyond the closed door, which I passed through easily, not even sensing molecular friction, and I understood that the door existed no more or less than I did. This was a world without borders. I reentered my room and watched my corporeal self stir on the bed. A brassiere lay on the floor and I suddenly knew that I had a girlfriend, but I was also still married.

I moved my synapses to my writing desk, where the manuscript of my ghost story sat neatly stacked. I became aware of changes within the manuscript. The story was not yet complete but was longer, with greater detail and a different opening than the one I'd been working on for a month. In a sudden rush of intuition, I knew everything I had already written. Then I realized that I already knew that. My cognition expanded in every direction as if peering into an infinite number of mirrors that reflected each other endlessly.

My bedroom grew indistinct at the edges, losing its sense of reality, the walls simultaneously expanding and contracting. As I felt my awareness begin to fade, I directed perception to the figure on the bed and for the briefest possible moment my own eyes opened but I was gone.

Chuck's face was magnified by the glass lid, distorted into a caricature of itself. He pressed tiny keys on a handheld computer to open the lid. Warm air hissed across my body as the lid lifted.

"What's my name?" he said. "Who are you? Where are you?"

"Chuck, Chris, the lab. I need paper and pencil."

He hurried away and I sat, dangling my legs off the table. I could feel the memory of future knowledge moving away from me like concentric circles spreading from a rock thrown into a pond. Chuck gave me a lab book and I quickly wrote all the changes in the story that my mind had gleaned in the bucket.

"What is this?" Chuck said. "Your handwriting is worse than Gell-Mann's."

"It's a revision of my story."

"How could you read it?"

"I didn't. I just knew what I'd written."

"A form of telepathy?"

"No, I was aware of my physical self sleeping at the time. It's hard to explain. Just being there made me know what my life was like."

"Were you in the future?"

"I don't know. I had a girlfriend. But I was still married. That couldn't be my future since I'm divorced now."

"That proves you entered the bucket. Each strand of the mop is a reality that is occurring simultaneously. You moved laterally in time rather than forward or backward."

"You mean every mop string is different?"

"Perhaps. They might be interwoven. Maybe each point where a string touches another makes for a commonality in both realities."

"What about now, Chuck? You and me talking?"

"Just another mop string."

"I want to go back."

"It might not be safe."

"I'm going in, Chuck. It was nirvana. Glory, rapture, paradise. Pure bliss. I don't have that in my life. Maybe I never did."

"All right, Chris."

"Besides, I have to finish my story."

For the next twelve hours, Chuck dunked me into time's bucket, where I followed a different strand of reality. Each journey slid my mind into the same zone of unfettered awareness as before. It was as if I'd lived for years in a house with utter and intimate knowledge of its architecture, wiring, ductwork, floor creaks and window squeaks, then suddenly discovered an extra room previously unknown to me, bathed in gorgeous light. I now wanted to spend all my time in that room. It was serene freedom without the friction of motion. My consciousness glided like a dolphin. I entered each reality in my bedroom and began to notice differences—some subtle, others shockingly drastic—but in every string I was always a writer.

Between visits to my multiple realities, Chuck yanked me back to the lab on his techno-leash and recorded my body temperature, blood pressure, and pulse rate. He made a DNA scraping for later analysis. He withdrew blood, checked my hearing, vision, reflexes, and alertness. Everything tested normal. We agreed that I could remain in the bucket for longer periods, as long as there were no physical changes.

While Chuck ran his medical tests, I revised the story based on what I'd learned. Each reality offered a different beginning, but the rewriting was so total that I could never quite complete the story. After several excursions into the bucket, it became clear that none of the parallel realities included finishing the story. It was perpetually snared in the process of revision.

Chuck speculated that I had entered a Möbius time loop that brought me full circle no matter what my embarking point, like the intercoastal waterways that always led small craft to the sea. Finally I gave up on the story and concentrated on comprehending the full scope of my life in each reality string. With practice, I learned to remember more. I directed my consciousness closer and closer to my sleeping form in the apartment, finally summoning the ability to enter my own head and instantly know every facet of my life, both past and future.

Chuck was supremely interested in this, theorizing that I had learned to straddle time. Upon each return I rapidly transcribed a synopsis of that specific reality into a lab book. They are as follows:

Owing to chronic joint pain as a result of time travel, I visit a Reiki master, which leads to a macrobiotic diet, yoga classes, meditation, and a pilgrimage to Tibet, where I write a travel book that gets banned in China.

My father and Harlan Ellison coedit an anthology of short stories called More Dangerous Visions *and ask me to write the preface detailing their feud and subsequent peace, a task I am unable to complete.*

I remarry and father twin daughters who die in a car wreck, prompting me to change my name, move to Las Vegas, and work as a blackjack dealer, marry a former prostitute, and open a used bookstore in Lake Tahoe.

I publish an article about my experiences traveling in time, become the laughingstock of both science and literature, and drink myself into a halfway house, where I am stabbed three times by a schizophrenic woman.

My wife and I reconcile and move to the East Coast for a tenure-track job with a high salary at a prestigious university that offers the children of its professors free tuition at a variety of top-notch colleges.

I publish a short story about time travel, expand the story to a novel that is made into a successful film, which leads to marrying Jodie Foster, with whom I only speak French around the house, and hobnobbing with Bob Dylan, Jim Jarmusch, and Julian Schnabel.

I commit suicide in despair over my failed marriage, the rejection of my latest book, and an inability to find a teaching job.

I write a memoir of my childhood that details the bizarre and sad family dynamics, and though it is critically panned as being needlessly narcissistic, the book goes on to become a best-seller.

I receive the Pulitzer prize for a novel about model railroads and offer support to my fellow writer Michael Chabon, who is highly frustrated by the progress of his novel dealing loosely with comic books.

I return to school for a doctorate in physics and claim all Professor Charles Andrews's findings as my own, which leads to an endowed chair at Harvard for me.

I remain in Iowa for the next thirty years, working as an adjunct teacher, publish a third collection of stories, a third memoir, and several novels, get short-listed for major prizes, and enter my dotage with a certain bitterness which I conceal behind a series of young girlfriends.

Chuck invents a device to reconstitute a time traveler into physical form and I go back in time and kill my father, which instantly changes me into the illegitimate son of Harlan Ellison, and I am adopted by a very nice couple named Mr. and Mrs. Chabon in California.

I emigrate to France and cowrite futuristic screenplays with Norman Spinrad, who moved there a decade before, then return to Iowa and marry a dairy heiress, and live out my days peacefully on her family farm.

I fly home to my father's deathbed, where we forgive each other for all our cruelties, and I hold his hand as he dies, knowing that he truly did like me but was unable to express it due to the trauma of his own childhood.

The United States military incarcerates me under the charge of treason for exposing the Swofford Project, which produces an outraged though futile outcry from the ACLU, protesting the abandonment of civil rights under the Home-land Security Act.

Barb Bersche, the publisher of McSweeney's, *refuses to publish my story as is, and we enter into a prolonged literary feud, until Professor Charles Andrews makes his findings known in a leading scientific journal, and I am vindicated when Bersche invites me to guest-edit an issue of her magazine.*

I develop profound emotional problems due to the time travel, am treated with medication that makes a dent in them, but I remain off-kilter the rest of my life, during which I don't write and don't mind.

I pseudonymously write a series of crime novels that make a fortune, move to Jamestown, Rhode Island, and live with a painter, grow my prematurely gray hair very long, and become an utter recluse.

After publishing this story I am sued by Harlan Ellison, my father, Michael Chabon, Professor Charles Andrews, and the University of Iowa Physics Department, a suit that drags on six years and sets a twenty-first-century precedent for libel, the stress of which results in my developing eczema, an ulcer, asthma, and finally cancer.

I am nominated for an S.F. award for this story and attend WorldCon, where I meet Harlan Ellison, who convinces me to write science fiction, which makes me enormously popular and fulfills my earliest literary desires, previously thwarted by rebelling against my father.

This story is dismissed as the worst in the anthology, signaling the wane of my career, and I end up teaching composition at a small state school I had previously scorned as being beneath me.

The University of Iowa hires me as a full-time professor, but the teaching requires so much effort that after achieving tenure, I cease to publish and join the parade of writers who are known in academic circles as having been quite promising at one time.

I become well known for my nonfiction, which leads to magazine work, and I spend the rest of my life leading an adventurous life reporting from abroad, finally retiring to the south of France.

I suffer a nervous breakdown from lack of sleep due to fear of ghosts, seek professional counseling and get diagnosed as delusional and grandiose, wind up addicted to Ambien, Xanax, Prozac, and Ritalin, and after a full recovery publish a book about the experience that leads to hosting a television talk show.

I find that I enjoy writing something that is fun, hitherto unknown with my bleak and introspective works about Kentucky, and embark on an ambitious campaign to write a novel in each popular genre, which annoys the critics, and mainly serves to confuse bookstore workers, who never know in what section to shelve my books.

Chuck abruptly halted the experiment and I remembered nothing tangible for the next three days. He filled me in later, showing me a videotape of my behavior in the bucket. My feet and hands developed a rhythmic twitching. My breathing became shallow but my heartbeat was highly elevated. My lips moved with incredible velocity, as if forming inaudible words in an unknown tongue. Chuck recognized this as binary code and began converting it to various permutations of software programming.

I spent three weeks at bed rest, although I began sleeping on the couch to avoid my own eerie visits. My body felt depleted in every way, reminding me of all-night study sessions in college, only now I couldn't recover from the fatigue. When I drifted into sleep, the memory of one of the mop strands poured through my mind like pressurized water. After each re-experienced parallel reality, I was enervated for hours by the compressed intensity of a life's worth of sensory perceptions.

Chuck stayed in touch by phone. He ferried me to a medical clinic for a full physical examination, which turned out fine. My preference for lying on the couch indicated possible depression, and the doctor wrote a prescription for SSRI medication but I never had it filled. Chuck also supplied me with two pairs of spectacles and his car economy rig. He believed that my body had reached its limit after enduring twenty-five dunks into the bucket of time. This number corresponded with the number of proposed dimensions in the universe, plus the one I was currently living in, according to recent advances in unifying theory.

I didn't know how to tell him that he was wrong. I may have gone into the bucket twenty-five times, but what chilled me to the marrow was the seemingly infinite number of branches that each reality string had. There were millions of Chris Offutts living simultaneous lives similar to each other. The knowledge of all my alternate lives rendered me powerless to engage in my current reality. I felt as if quicksand closed over my head and I was trapped with no firm footing below, nothing to cling to above, surrounded by a constant flow of information I could not use.

The deadline for the *McSweeney's* story came and went. Michael Chabon delicately nudged me via e-mail, then called when I didn't respond. I explained that the story was dead, and asked if he could let me off the hook. He said no because the space was already allotted, and I told him I'd cobble something together with a little more time.

The next day I began writing about my screwball childhood in the Appalachian foothills of eastern Kentucky. My memory for the past improved in a phenomenal way—I recalled obscure details with stunning clarity. I returned to my bedroom and slept through the night without any disturbances. When I left the house I felt different, more alert. Slowly I realized that people liked me. I even began to like myself.

Chuck and I met occasionally for awkward lunches during which he refused to talk of the bucket. He ate little and appeared gaunt. He dropped out of contact and I thought nothing of it until reading in the paper that a security guard discovered him dead in his lab. The cause of death was heart trauma. The exact circumstances were not publicly revealed, but campus gossip said he died inside a glass coffin. Members of an unknown government agency removed his equipment. The lab was converted to storage. His faculty records were so thoroughly expunged that there is no longer any reference to him at the university.

I never told anyone about my visit to the physics lab, but I have thought about it often. After using me as a human subject, Chuck probably had a difficult time going back to chimps. If he died while in the bucket, his consciousness would be marooned forever in a reality string. This would make Chuck the first true ghost.

Up the Mountain Coming Down Slowly

By DAVE EGGERS

How much were they willing to sacrifice to prove an uncertain point, to no one in particular, about a mountain that none of them could begin to understand?

She lies, she lies, Rita lies on the bed, looking up, in the room that is so loud so early in Tanzania. She is in Moshi. She arrived the night before, in a jeep driven by a man named Godwill. It is so bright this morning but was so madly, impossibly dark last night.

Her flight had arrived late, and customs was slow. There was a young American couple trying to clear a large box of soccer balls. For an orphanage, they said. The customs agent, in khaki head to toe, removed and bounced each ball on the clean reflective floor, as if inspecting their viability. Finally the American man was taken to a side room, and in a few minutes returned, rolling his eyes to his wife, rubbing his forefinger and thumb together in a way meaning money. The soccer balls were cleared, and the couple went on their way. Outside it was not humid; it was open and clear, the air cool and light, and Rita was greeted soundlessly by an old man, black and white-haired and thin and neat in shirtsleeves and a brown tie. He was Godwill, and he had been sent by the hotel to pick her up. It was midnight and she was very awake as they drove and they had driven, on the British side of the road, in silence through rural Tanzania, just their headlights and the occasional jacaranda, and the constant long grass lining the way.

At the hotel she wanted a drink. She went to the hotel bar alone, something she'd never done, and sat at the bar with a stenographer from Brussels. The stenographer, whose name she did not catch and couldn't ask for again, wore a short inky bob of black coarse hair, and was wringing her napkin into tortured shapes, tiny twisted mummies. The stenographer: face curvy and shapeless like a child's, voice melodious, accent soothing. They talked about capital punishment, comparing the stonings common to some Muslim regions with America's lethal injections and electric chairs; somehow the conversation was cheerful and relaxed. They had both seen the same documentary about people who had witnessed executions, and had been amazed at how little it had seemed to affect any of them, the watchers; they were sullen and unmoved. To witness a death! Rita could never do it. Even if they made her sit there, behind the partition, she would close her eyes.

Rita was tipsy and warm when she said good night to the Brussels stenographer, who held her hand too long with her cold slender fingers. Through the French doors and Rita was outside, and walked past the pool toward her hut, one of twelve behind the hotel. She passed a man in a plain and green uniform with a gun strapped to his back, an automatic rifle of some kind, the barrel poking over his shoulder and in the dim light seeming aimed at the base of his skull. She didn't know why the man was there, and didn't know if he would shoot her in the back when she walked past him, but she did, she walked past him, because she trusted him, trusted this country and the hotel—that together they would know why it was necessary to have a heavily armed guard standing alone by the pool, still and clean, the surface dotted with leaves. She smiled at him and he did not smile back and she only felt safe again when she had closed the hut's door and closed the door to the bathroom and was sitting on the cool toilet with her palms caressing her toes.

M orning comes like a scream through a pinhole. Rita is staring at the concentric circles of bamboo that comprise the hut's round conical roof. She is lying still, hands crossed on her chest—she woke up that way—and through the mosquito net, too tight, terrifying, suffocating in a small way when she thinks too much about it, she can see the concentric circles of the roof above and the circles are twenty-two in number, because she has counted and recounted. She counted while lying awake, listening to someone, outside the hut, fill bucket after bucket with water.

Her name is Rita. Her hair is red like a Romanian's and her hands are large. Eyes large and mouth lipless and she hates, has always hated, her lipless mouth. As a girl she waited for her lips to appear, to fill out, but it did not happen. Every year since her sixteenth birthday her lips have not grown but receded. The circles make up the roof but the circles never touch. Her father had been a pastor.

Last night she thought, intermittently, she knew why she was in Tanzania, in Moshi, at the base of Kilimanjaro. But this morning she has no clue. She knows she is supposed to begin hiking up the mountain today, in two hours, but now that she has come here, through Amsterdam and through the cool night from the airport, sitting silently alone the whole drive, an hour or so at midnight, next to Godwill—really his name was Godwill, an old man who was sent by the hotel to pick her up, and it made her so happy because Godwill was such a . . . Tanzanian-sounding name—now that she has come here and is awake she cannot find the reason why she is here. She cannot recall the source of her motivation to spend four days hiking up this mountain, so blindingly white at the top—a hike some had told her was brutalizing and often fatal and others had claimed was, well, just a walk in the park. She was not sure she was fit enough, and was not sure she would not be bored to insanity. She was most concerned about the altitude sickness. The young were more susceptible, she'd heard, and at 38 she was not sure she was that anymore—young—but she felt that for some reason she in particular was always susceptible and she would have to know when to turn back. If the pressure in her head became too great, she would have to turn back. The mountain was almost 20,000 feet high and every month someone died of a cerebral edema and there were ways to prevent this. Breathing deeply would bring more oxygen into the blood, into the brain, and if that didn't work and the pain persisted, there was Diamox, which thinned the blood and accomplished the same objective but more quickly. But she hated to take pills and had vowed not to use them, to simply go down if the pain grew intolerable—but how would she know when to go down? What were the phases before death? And what if she decided too late? She might at some point realize that it was time to turn and walk down the mountain, but what if it was already too late? It was possible that she would decide to leave, be ready to live at a lower level again, but by then the mountain would have had its way and there, on a path or in a tent, she would die.

She could stay in the hut. She could go to Zanzibar and drink in the sun. She liked nothing better than to drink in the sun. With strangers. To drink in the sun! To feel the numbing of her tongue and limbs while her skin cooked slowly, and her feet dug deeper into the powdery sand!

Her hands are still crossed on her chest, and the filling of the buckets continues outside her hut, so loud, so constant. Is someone taking the water meant for her shower? At home, in St. Louis, her landlord was always taking her water—so why shouldn't it be the same here, in a hut in Moshi, with a gecko, almost translucent, darting across her conical ceiling, its ever-smaller circles never interlocking?

She has bought new boots, expensive, and has borrowed a backpack, huge, and a thermarest, and sleeping bag, and cup, and a dozen other things. Everything made of plastic and Gore-Tex. The items were light individually but together very heavy and all of it is packed in a large tall purple pack in the corner of the round hut and she doesn't want to carry the pack and wonders why she's come. She is not a mountain climber, and not an avid hiker, and not someone who needs to prove her fitness by hiking mountains and afterward casually mentioning it to friends and colleagues. She likes racquetball.

She has come because her younger sister, Gwen, had wanted to come, and they had bought the tickets together, thinking it would be the perfect trip to take before Gwen began making a family with her husband, Brad. But she'd gone ahead and gotten pregnant anyway, early, six months ahead of schedule and she could not make the climb. She could not make the climb but that did not preclude—Gwen used the word liberally and randomly, like some use curry—her, Rita, from going. The trip was not refundable, so why not go?

Rita slides her hands from her chest to her thighs and holds them, her thin thighs, as if to steady them. Who is filling the bucket? She imagines it's someone from the shanty behind the hotel, stealing the hot water from the heater. She'd seen a bunch of teenage boys back there. Maybe they're stealing Rita's shower water. This country is so poor. Is poorer than any place she's been. Is it poorer than Jamaica? She is not sure. Jamaica she expected to be like Florida, a healthy place benefiting from generations of heavy tourism and the constant and irrational flow of American money. But Jamaica was desperately poor almost everywhere and she understood nothing.

Maybe Tanzania is less poor. Around her hotel are shanties and also well-built homes with gardens and gates. There is a law here, Godwill had said in strained English, that all the men are required to have jobs. Maybe people chose to live in spartan simplicity. She doesn't know enough to judge one way or the other. The unemployed go to jail! Godwill had said, and seemed to like this law. The idle are like the devil! he said, and then laughed and laughed.

In the morning the sun is as clear and forthright as a spotlight and Rita wants to avoid walking past the men. She has already walked past the men twice and she has nothing to say to them. Soon the bus will come to take her and the others to the base of the mountain, and since finally leaving her bed she has been doing the necessary things—eating, packing, calling Gwen—and for each task she has had to walk from her hut to the hotel, has had to walk past the men sitting and standing along the steps into the lobby. Eight to ten of them, young men, sitting, waiting without speaking. Godwill had talked about this—that the men list their occupations as guide, porter, salesperson—anything that will satisfy their government and didn't require them to be accounted for in one constant place, because there really wasn't much work at all. She had seen two of the men scuffle briefly over another American's bag, for a $1 tip. When Rita walked past them she tried to smile faintly, without looking too friendly, or rich, or sexy, or happy, or vulnerable, or guilty, or proud, or contented, or healthy, or interested—she did not want them to think she was any of those things. She walked by almost cross-eyed with casual concentration.

Rita's face is wide and almost square, her jaw just short of masculine. People have said she looks like a Kennedy, one of the female Kennedys. But she is not beautiful like that woman; she is instead almost plain, with or without makeup, plain in any light. This she knows, though her friends and Gwen tell her otherwise. She is unmarried and was for a time a foster parent to siblings, a girl of nine and boy of seven, beaten by their birth mother, and Rita had contemplated adopting them herself—had thought her life through, every year she imagined and planned with those kids, she could definitely do it—but then Rita's mother and father had beaten her to it. Her parents loved those kids, too, and had oceans of time and plenty of room in their home, and there were discussions and it had quickly been settled. There was a long weekend they all spent together in the house where Rita and Gwen were raised, Rita and her parents there with J.J. and Frederick, the kids arranging their trophies in their new rooms, and on Sunday evening, Rita said goodbye, and the kids stayed there. It was easy and painless for everyone, and Rita spent a week of vacation time in bed shaking.

Now, when she works two Saturdays a month and can't see them as often, Rita misses the two of them in a way that's too visceral. She misses having them both in her bed, the two little people, seven and nine years old, when the crickets were too loud and they were scared of them growing, the crickets, and of them together carrying away the house to devour it and everyone inside. This is a story they had heard, about the giant crickets carrying away the house, from their birth mother.

* * *

Rita is asleep on the bus but wakes up when the road inclines. The vehicle, white and square with rounded edges—it reminds her vaguely of something that would descend, backward, from a rocket ship and onto the moon—whinnies and shakes over the potholes of the muddy road and good Christ it's raining!—raining steadily on the way to the gate of Kilimanjaro. Godwill is driving, and this gives her some peace, even though he's driving much too fast, and is not slowing down around tight curves, or for pedestrians carrying possessions on their heads, or for schoolchildren, who seem to be everywhere, in uniforms of white above and blue below. Disaster at every moment seems probable, but Rita is so tired she can't imagine raising an objection if the bus were sailing over a cliff.

"She's awake!" a man says. She looks to find Frank smiling at her, cheerful in an almost insane way. Maybe he is insane. Frank is the American guide, a sturdy and energetic man, from Oregon, medium-sized in every way, with a short-shorn blond beard that wraps his face as a bandage would a man, decades ago, suffering from a toothache. "We thought we'd have to carry you up. You're one of those people who can sleep through anything, I bet." Then he laughs a shrill, girlish laugh, forced and mirthless.

They pass a large school, its sign posted along the road. The top half: DRIVE REFRESHED: COCA-COLA; below: MARANGU SEC. SCHOOL. A group of women are walking on the roadside, babies in slings. They pass the Samange Social Club, which looks like a construction company trailer. Farther up the road, a small pink building, the K&J Hot Fashion Shop, bearing an enormous spray-painted rendering of Angela Bassett. A boy of six is leading a donkey. Two tiny girls in school uniforms are carrying a bag of potatoes. A driveway leads to the Tropical Pesticides Research Institute. The rain intensifies as they pass another school—COCA-COLA: DRIVE REFRESHED; ST. MARGARET'S CATHOLIC SEC. SCHOOL.

That morning, at the hotel, Rita had overheard a conversation between a British woman and the hotel concierge.

"There are so many Catholic schools!" the tourist had said. She'd just gotten back from a trip to a local waterfall.

"Are you Catholic?" the concierge had said. She was stout, with a clear nasal voice, a kind of clarinet.

"I am," the tourist said. "And you?"

"Yes please. Did you see my town? Marangu?"

"I did. On the hill?"

"Yes please."

"It was very beautiful."

And the concierge had smiled.

The van passes a FEMA dispensary, a YMCA, another social club called Millennium, a line of teenage girls in uniforms, plum-purple sweaters and skirts of sports-coat blue. They all wave. The rain is now real rain. The people they pass are soaked.

"Look at Patrick," Frank says, pointing at a handsome Tanzanian man on the bus, sitting across the aisle from him. "He's just sitting there smiling, wondering why the hell anyone would pay to be subjected to this."

Patrick smiles and nods and says nothing.

There are five paying hikers on the trip and they are introducing themselves. There are Mike and Jerry, a son and father in matching jackets. Mike is in his late twenties and his father is maybe sixty. Jerry has an accent that sounds British but possesses the round vowels of an Australian. Jerry owns a chain of restaurants, while the son is an automotive engineer, specializing in ambulances. They are tall men, barrel-chested and thin-legged, though Mike is heavier, with a loose paunch he carries with some effort. They wear matching red jackets, scarred everywhere with zippers, their initials embroidered on the left breast pockets. Mike is quiet and seems to be getting sick from the bus's jerking movements and constant turns. Jerry is smiling broadly, as if to make up for his son's reticence—a grin meant to introduce them both as happy and ready men, as gamers.

The rain continues, the cold unseasonable. There is a low fog that rises between the trees, giving the green a dead, faded look, like most of the forest's color had leaked into the soil.

"The rain should clear away in an hour or so," Frank announces, as the bus continues up the hills, bouncing through the mud. The foliage everywhere around is tangled and sloppy. "What do you think, Patrick?" Frank says. "This rain gonna burn off?"

Patrick hasn't spoken yet and now just shrugs and smiles. There is something in his eyes, Rita thinks, that is assessing. Assessing Frank, and the paying hikers, guessing at the possibility that he will make it up and down this mountain, this time, without losing his mind.

Grant is at the back of the bus, watching the land pass through the windows, sitting in the middle of the bus's backseat, like some kind of human rudder. He is shorter than the other two men but his legs are enormous, like a power lifter's, his calves thick and hairy. He is wearing cutoff jean shorts, though the temperature has everyone else adding layers. His hair is black and short-shorn, his eyes are small and water-cooler blue.

He is watching the land pass through the window near his right cheek, and the air of outside waters his small blue eyes.

Shelly is in her late forties and looks precisely her age. She is slim, fit, almost wiry. Her hair, long, ponytailed, once blond, is fading to gray and she is not fighting it. She has the air of a lion, Rita thinks, though she doesn't know why she thinks of this animal, a lion, when she sees this small woman sitting two seats before her, in an anorak of the most lucid and expectant yellow. She watches Shelly tie a bandanna around her neck, quickly and with a certain offhand ferocity. Shelly's features are the features Rita would like for herself: a small thin nose with a flawless upward curve, her lips with the correct and voluptuous lines, lips that must have been effortlessly sexual and life-giving as a younger woman.

"It's really miserable out there," Shelly says.

Rita nods.

The bus stops in front of a clapboard building, crooked, frowning, like a general store in a Western. There are signs and farm instruments attached to its side, and on the porch, out of the rain, there are two middle-aged women feeding fabric through sewing machines, side by side. Their eyes briefly sweep over the bus and its passengers, and then return to their work as the bus begins again.

Frank is talking about the porters. Porters, he says, will be accompanying the group, carrying the duffel bags, and the tents, and the tables to eat upon, and the food, and propane tanks, and coolers, and silverware, and water, among other things. Their group is five hikers and two guides, and there will be thirty-two porters coming along.

"I had no idea," Rita says to Grant, behind her. "I pictured a few guides and maybe two porters." She has a sudden vision of servants carrying kings aboard gilt thrones, elephants following, trumpets announcing their progress.

"That's nothing," Frank says. Frank has been listening to everyone's conversations and inserting himself when he sees fit. "Last time I did Everest, there were six of us and we had eighty sherpas." He holds his hand horizontally, demonstrating the height of the sherpas, which seems to be about four feet or so. "Little guys," he says, "but badasses. Tougher than these guys down here. No offense, Patrick."

Patrick isn't listening. The primary Tanzanian guide, he's in his early thirties and is dressed in new gear—a blueberry anorak, snow-boarding pants, wraparound sunglasses. He's watching the side of the road, where a group of boys is keeping pace with the bus, each in a school uniform and each carrying what looks to be a small sickle. They run alongside, four of them, waving their sickles, yelling things Rita can't hear through the windows and over the whinnies of the van going up and up through the wet dirt. Their mouths are going, their eyes angry, and their teeth are so small, but by the time Rita gets her window open to hear what they're saying the van is far beyond them, and they have run off the road with their sickles. They've dropped down the hillside, following some narrow path of their own making.

There is a wide black parking lot. MACHAME GATE reads a sign over the entrance. In the parking lot, about a hundred Tanzanian men are standing. They watch the bus enter the lot and park and immediately twenty of them converge upon it, unloading the back-packs and duffel bags from the bus. Before Rita and the rest of the hikers are off, all of the bags are stacked in a pile nearby, and the rain is falling upon them.

Rita is last off the bus, and when she arrives at the door, Godwill has closed it, not realizing she is still aboard.

"Sorry please," he says, yanking the lever, trying to get the door open again.

"Don't worry, I'm in no hurry," she says, giving him a little laugh.

She sees a man between the parking lot and the gate to the park, a man like the man at her hotel, in a plain green uniform, automatic rifle on his back.

"Is the gun for the animals, or the people?" she asks.

"People," Godwill says, with a small laugh. "People much more dangerous than animals!" Then he laughs and laughs and laughs.

It's about forty-five degrees, Rita guesses, though it could be fifty. And the rain. It's raining steadily, and the rain is cold. Rita hadn't thought about rain. When she had pictured the hike she had not thought about cold, cold, steady rain.

"Looks like we've got ourselves some rain," Frank says.

The paying hikers look at him.

"No two ways about it," he says.

Everything is moving rapidly. Bags are being grabbed, duffels hoisted. There are so many porters! Everyone is already wet. Patrick is talking with a group of the porters. They are dressed in bright colors, like the paying hikers, but their clothes—simple pants and sweatshirts—are already dirty, and their shoes are not large and complicated boots, as Rita is wearing, but instead sneakers, or track shoes, or loafers. None wear rain gear, but all wear hats.

Now there is animated discussion, and some pointing and shrugging. One porter jumps to the ground and then lies still, as if pretending to be dead. The men around him roar.

Rita ducks into her poncho and pulls it over her torso and backpack. The poncho was a piece of equipment the organizers listed as optional; no one, it seems, expected this rain. Now she is thrilled she bought it—$4.99 at Target on the way to the airport. She sees a few of the porters poking holes in garbage bags and fitting themselves within. Grant is doing the same. He catches Rita looking at him.

"Forgot the poncho," he says. "Can't believe I forgot the poncho."

"Sorry," she says. There is nothing else to say. He's going to get soaked.

"It's okay," he says. "Good enough for them, good enough for me."

Rita tightens the laces on her boots and readjusts her gaiters. She helps Shelly with her poncho, spreading it over her backpack, and arranges her hood around her leonine hair, frayed and thick, blond and white. As she pulls the plastic close to Shelly's face, they stare into each other's eyes and Rita has a sharp pain in her stomach, or her head, somewhere. She wants them here. They are her children and she allowed them to be taken. People were always quietly taking things from her, always with the understanding that everyone would be better off if Rita's life were kept simplified. But she was ready for complication, wasn't she? For a certain period of time, she was, she knows. It was the condominium that concerned everyone; she had almost bought one, in anticipation of adopting the kids, and she had backed out—but why?—just before closing. The place wasn't right; it wasn't big enough. She wanted it to be more right; she wanted to be more ready. It wasn't right, and they would know it, and they would think she would always be insolvent, and they would always have to share a room. Gwen had offered to cosign on the other place, the place they looked at with the yard and the three bedrooms, but that wouldn't be right, having Gwen on the mortgage. So she had given up and the kids were now in her old room, with her parents. She wants them walking next to her asking her advice. She wants to arrange their hoods around their faces, wants to pull the drawstrings so their faces shrink from view and stay dry. Shelly's face is old and lined and she grins at Rita and clears her throat.

"Thank you, hon," she says.

They are both waterproof now and the rain tick-ticks onto the plastic covering them everywhere. The paying hikers are standing in the parking lot in the rain.

"Porters have dropped out," says Frank, speaking to the group. "They gotta replace the porters who won't go up. It'll take a few minutes."

"Are there replacements close by?" Grant asks.

"Probably get some younger guys," Frank says. "The younger guys are hungry."

"Like the B-team, right?" Jerry says. "We're getting the B-team!" He looks around for laughs but no one's wet cold face will smile. "Minor leaguers, right?" he says, then gives up.

It is much too late to go home now, Rita knows. Still, she can't suppress the thought of running all the way, ten miles or so, mostly downhill, back to the hotel, at which point she would—no matter what the cost—fly to warm and flat Zanzibar, to drink and drink until half-blind in the sun.

Nearby in the parking lot, Patrick seems to settle something with the man he's speaking to, and approaches the group.

"Very wet," he says, with a grimace. "Long day."

T he group is going to the peak, a four-day trip up, two down, along the Machame Route. There are at least five paths up the mountain, depending on what a hiker wants to see and how quickly he wants to reach the peak, and Gwen had promised that this route was within their abilities and by far the most scenic. The group's members each signed up through a website, EcoHeaven Tours, dedicated to adventure travel. The site promised small group tours of a dozen places—the Scottish Highlands, the Indonesian lowlands, the rivers of upper Russia. The trip up this mountain was, oddly enough, the least exotic-sounding. Rita has never known anyone who had climbed Kilimanjaro, but she knew people who knew people who had, and this made it just that small bit less intriguing. Now, standing below the gate, this trip seems irrelevant, irrational, indefensible. She's walking the same way thousands have before, and she will be cold and wet while doing so.

"Okay, let's saddle up," Frank says, and begins to walk up a wide dirt path. Rita and the four others walk with him. They are all in ponchos, Grant in his garbage bag, all with backpacks beneath, resembling hunchbacks, or soldiers. She pictures the Korean War Memorial, all those young men, cast in bronze, eyes wide, waiting to be shot.

Rita is glad, at least, to be moving, because moving will make her warm.

B ut Frank is walking very slowly. Rita is behind him; his pace is elephantine. Such measured movements, such lumbering effort. Frank is leading the five of them, with Patrick at the back of the group, and the porters are now distantly behind them, still in the parking lot, gathering the duffels and propane tanks and tents. They will catch up, Patrick said.

Rita is sure that this pace will drive her mad. She is a racquetball player because racquetball involves movement, and scoring, and noise, and the possibility of getting struck in the head with a ball moving at the pace of an airplane. And so she had worried that this hike would drive her mad with boredom. And now it is boring; here in Tanzania, she is bored. She will die of a crushing monotony before she even has a chance at a high-altitude cerebral edema.

After ten minutes, the group has traveled about two hundred yards, and it is time to stop. Mike is complaining of shoulder pain. His pack's straps need to be adjusted. Frank stops to help Mike, and while Frank is doing that, and Jerry and Shelly are waiting with Patrick, Grant continues up the trail. He does not stop. He goes around a bend in the path and he is out of view. The rain and the jungle make possible quick disappearances and before she knows why, Rita follows him.

Soon they are up two turns and can no longer see the group. Rita is elated. Grant walks quickly and she walks with him. They are almost running. They are moving at a pace she finds more fitting, an athletic pace, a pace appropriate for people who are not yet old. Rita is not yet old. She quit that 10k Fun Run last year but that didn't mean she couldn't do it if it wasn't so boring. She had started biking to work but then had decided against it; at the end of the day, when she'd done as much as she could before 5:30, she was just too tired.

They tramp through the mud and soon the path narrows and bends upward, more vertical, brushed by trees, the banana leaves huge, sloppy, and serrated. The trail is soaked, the mud deep and grabbing, but everywhere the path is crosshatched with roots, and the roots become footholds. They jump from one root to the next and Grant is relentless. He does not stop. He does not use his hands to steady himself. He is the most balanced person Rita has ever known, and she quickly attributes this to his small stature and wide and powerful legs. He is close to the ground.

They talk very little. She knows he is a telephone-systems programmer of some kind, connects "groups of users" somehow. She knows he comes from Montana, and knows his voice is like an older man's, weaker than it should be, wheezy and prone to cracking. He is not handsome; his nose is almost piggish and his teeth are chipped in front, leaving a triangular gap, as if he'd tried to bite a tiny pyramid. He's not attractive in any kind of way she would call sexual, but she still wants to be with him and not the others.

The rain forest is dense and twisted and drenched. Mist obviates vision past twenty yards in any given direction. The rain comes down steadily, but the forest canopy slows and a hundred times redirects the water before it comes to Rita.

She is warmer now, sweating under her poncho and fleece, and she likes sweating and feels strong. Her pants, plastic pants she bought for nothing and used twice before while skiing, are loud, the legs scraping against each other with a constant, violent swipping sound. She wishes she were wearing shorts, like Grant. She wants to ask him to stop, so she can remove her pants, but worries he won't want to stop, and that anyway if he does and they do, the other hikers will catch up, and she and Grant will no longer be alone, ahead of the others, making good time. She says nothing.

There are no animals. Rita has not heard a bird, or a monkey, or seen even a frog. There had been geckos in her hut, and larger lizards scurrying outside the hotel, but on this mountain there is nothing. Her guidebook had promised blue monkeys, colobus monkeys, galagos, olive baboons, bushbacks, duikers, hornbills, turacos. But the forest is quiet and empty.

Now a porter is walking down the path, in jeans, a sweater, and tennis shoes. Rita and Grant stop and step to one side to allow him to pass.

"Jambo," Grant says.

"Jambo," the man says, and continues down the trail.

The exchange was quick but extraordinary. Grant had lowered his voice to a basso profundo, stretching the second syllable for a few seconds in an almost musical way. The porter had said the word back with identical inflection. It was like a greeting between teammates, doubles partners—simple, warm, understated but understood.

"What does that mean?" Rita asks. "Is that Swahili?"

"It is," Grant says, leaping over a puddle. "It's . . . well, it means 'Hello.'"

He says this in a polite way that nevertheless betrays his concern. Rita's face burns. She's traveled to Tanzania without learning any Swahili; she didn't even learn "hello." She knows that Grant considers her a slothful and timid tourist. She wants Grant to like her, and to feel that she is more like him—quick, learned, seasoned—at least more so than the others, who are all so delicate, needy, and slow.

They walk upward in silence for an hour. The walking is meditative to an extent she thought impossible. Rita had worried that she would either have to talk to the same few people—people she did not know and might not like—for hundreds of hours, or that, if the hikers were not so closely grouped, that she would be alone, with no one to talk to, alone with her thoughts. But already she knows that this will not be a problem. They have been hiking for two hours and she has not thought of anything. Too much of her faculties have been devoted to deciding where to step, where to place her left foot, then her right, and her hands, which sometimes grip trees for balance, sometimes touch the wet earth when a fall is likely. The calculations necessary make unlikely almost any other thinking—certainly nothing of any depth or complexity. And for this she is grateful. It is expansive and well fenced, her landscape, the quiet acres of her mind, and with a soundtrack: the tapping of the rain, the swipping of her poncho against the branches, the tinny jangle of the carabiners swinging from her backpack. All of it is musical in a minimal and calming way, and she breathes in and out with the uncomplicated and mechanical strength of a bear—plodding, powerful, robust.

"Poly poly," says a descending porter. He is wearing tasseled loafers.

"Poly poly," Grant says.

"I got here a few days before the rest of you," Grant says, by way of explanation and apology, once the porter has passed. He feels that he's shamed Rita and has allowed her to suffer long enough. "I spent some time in Moshi, picked up some things."

"'Jambo' is 'Hello,'" he says. "'Poly poly' means 'Step by step.'"
A porter comes up behind them.

"Jambo," he says.

"Jambo," Grant says, with the same inflection, the same stretching of the second syllable, as if delivering a sacred incantation. Jaaaahmmmmboooow. The porter smiles and continues up. He is carrying a propane tank above his head, and a large backpack sits between his shoulders, from which dangle two bags of potatoes. His load is easily eighty pounds.

He passes and Grant begins behind him. Rita asks Grant about his backpack, which is enormous, twice the size of hers, and contains poles and a pan and a bedroll. Rita had been told to pack only some food and a change of clothes, and to let the porters take the rest.

"I guess it is a little bigger," he says.

"Is that your tent in there, too?" she asks, talking to his back.

"It is," he says, stopping. He shakes out from under his pack and zippers open a compartment on the top.

"You're not having a porter carry it? How heavy is that thing?"

"Well, I guess . . . it's just a matter of choice, really. I'm . . . well, I guess I wanted to see if I could carry my own gear up. It's just a personal choice." He's sorry for carrying his things, sorry for knowing "hello." He spits a stream of brown liquid onto the ground.

"You dip?"

"I do. It's gross, isn't it?"

"You're not putting that sucker in there, too."

Grant is unwrapping a Charms lollipop.

"I'm afraid so. It's something I do. Want one?"

Rita wants something like the Charms lollipop, but now she can't separate the clean lollipops in his Ziploc bag—there are at least ten in there—from the one in his mouth, presumably covered in tobacco juice.

Minutes later, the trail turns and under a tree there is what looks like a hospital gurney crossed with a handcart. It's sturdy and wide, but with just two large wheels, set in the middle, on either side of a taut canvas cot. There are handles on the end, so it can be pulled like a rickshaw. Grant and Rita make shallow jokes about the contraption, about who might be coming down on that, but being near it any longer, because it's rusty and terrifying and looks like it's been used before and often, is unpleasant, so they walk on.

When they arrive at a clearing, they've been hiking, quickly, for six hours. They are at what they assume to be their camp, and they are alone. The trees have cleared—they are above treeline—and they are now standing on a hillside, covered in fog, with high grass, thin like hair, everywhere. The rain has not subsided and the temperature has dropped. They have not seen any of the other hikers or guides for hours, nor have they seen any porters. Rita and Grant were hiking quickly and beat everyone up the trail, and were not passed by anyone, and she feels so strong and proud about this. She can tell that in some way Grant is also proud, but she knows he will not say so.

Within minutes she is shaking. It's no more than forty degrees and the rain is harder here; there are no trees diverting its impact. And there are no tents assembled, because they have beaten the porters to the camp. Even Grant seems to see the poor reasoning involved in their strategy. The one thing Grant doesn't have is a tarp, and without it there is no point in pitching his tent on earth this wet. They will have to wait, alone in the rain, until the porters arrive.

"It'll be at least an hour," Grant says.

"Maybe sooner for the porters?" Rita suggests.

"We sure didn't think this one through," he says, then spits a brown stream onto a clean green banana leaf.

Under a shrub no more than four feet tall, offering little protection, they sit together on a horizontal and wet log and let the rain come down on them. Rita tries not to shiver, because shivering is the first step, she remembers, to hypothermia. She slows her breathing, stills her body, and brings her arms from her sleeves and onto her naked skin.

Frank is furious. His eyes are wild. He feels compromised. The paying hikers are all in a cold canvas tent, sitting around a table no bigger than one meant for poker, and they are eating dinner—rice, plain noodles, potatoes, tea, orange slices.

"I know a few of you think you're hotshots," Frank says, blowing into his tea to cool it, "but this is no cakewalk up here. Today you're a speed demon; tomorrow you're sore and sick, full of blisters and malaria and God knows what."

Grant is looking straight at him, very serious, neither mocking nor confronting.

"Or you get an aneurysm. There's a reason you have a guide, people. I've been up and down this mountain twelve times, and there's a reason for that."

He blows into his tea again. "There's a reason for that, you . . . people."

He shakes his head as if suddenly chilled. "I need to know you're gonna act like adults, not like . . . yahoos!" And with that he burrows his thumb and forefinger into his eye sockets, a man with too much on his mind.

The food before the group has ostensibly been cooked, by the porters, but within the time it took to carry it from the tent where it was heated to this, their makeshift dining tent, the food has gone cold, as cold as if it had been refrigerated. Everyone eats what they can, though without cheer. The day was long and each hiker has an injury, or an issue of some sort. Mike's stomach is already feeling wrong, and at some point Shelly slipped and cut her hand open on a sharp stick. Jerry is having the first twinges of an altitude headache. Only Rita and Grant are, for the time being, problem-free. Rita makes the mistake of announcing this, and it seems only to get Frank angrier.

"Well, it'll happen sooner or later, ma'am. Something will. You're probably better off being sick now, because in a few days, it'll hit you harder and deeper. So pray to get sick tonight, you two."

"You sit over there, you'll get dead," Jerry says, pointing to a corner of the tent where a hole is allowing a drizzle to pour onto the floor. "What kinda equipment you providing here anyway, Frank?" Jerry's tone is gregarious, but the message is plain.

"Are you dry?" Frank asks. Jerry nods. "Then you're fine."

They're sitting on small canvas folding stools, and the paying hikers have to hunch over to eat; there is no room for elbows. When they first sat down they had passed around and used the clear hand-sanitizing fluid provided—like soft soap but cool and stinging lightly. Rita had rubbed her hands and tried to clear the dirt from her palms, but afterward found her hands no cleaner. She looks at her palms now, after two applications of the sanitizer, and though they're dry their every crevice is brown.

The man who brought the platters of rice and potatoes—Steven—pokes his head into the tent again, his smile preceding him. He's in a purple fleece pullover with a matching stocking cap. He announces the coming of soup and everyone cheers. Soon there is soup finally and everyone devours the soup. The heat of the bodies of the paying hikers slowly warms the canvas tent and the candles on the table create the appearance of comfort. But they know that outside this tent the air is approaching freezing, and in the arc of night will dip below.

"Why are there no campfires?"

It's the first thing Mike has said at dinner.

"Honey collectors," Frank says. "Burned half the mountain."

Mike looks confused.

"They try to smoke out the bees to get the honey," Frank explains, "but it gets out of control. That's the theory anyway. Might have been a lot of things, but the mountain burned and now they won't allow fires."

"Also the firewood," Patrick says.

"Right, right," Frank says, nodding into his soup. "The porters were cutting down the trees for firewood. They were supposed to bring the firewood from below, but then they'd run out and start cutting whatever was handy. You're right, Patrick. I forgot about that. Now they're not even allowed to have firewood on the mountain. Illegal."

"So how do clothes get dry?" This from Jerry, who in the candle-light looks younger, and, Rita suddenly thinks, like a man who would be cast in a soap opera, as the patriarch of a powerful family. His hair is white and full, straight and smooth, riding away from his forehead like the back of a cresting wave.

"If there's sun tomorrow, they get dry," Frank says. "If there's no sun, they stay wet," he says, then sits back and waits for someone to complain. No one does, so he softens. "Put the wet clothes in your sleeping bag. Somewhere where you don't have to feel 'em. The heat in there will dry 'em out, usually. Otherwise work around the wet clothes till we get some sun."

"This is why those porters dropped out," Jerry says, with certainty.

"Listen," Frank says, "porters drop out all the time. Some of them are superstitious. Some just don't like rain. Doesn't mean a thing. We'll be fine."

Rita cannot get a grip on how this will work. She doesn't see how they can continue up the mountain, facing more rain, as it also becomes colder, the air thinner, and without their having any chance of drying the clothes that are surely too wet to wear. Is this not how people get sick or die? By getting wet and cold and staying wet and cold? Her concern, though, is a dull and almost distant one, because almost immediately after the plates are taken away, she feels exhausted beyond all measure. Her vision is blurry and her limbs tingle.

"I guess we're bunking together," Shelly says, suddenly behind her, above her. Everyone is standing up. Rita rises and follows Shelly outside, where it is still drizzling the coldest rain. The hikers all say good night, Mike and Jerry heading toward the toilet tent, just assembled—a triangular structure, three poles with a tarp wrapped around, a zipper for entry and a three-foot hole dug below. Father and son are each carrying a small roll of toilet paper, protecting it from the rain with their plastic baggies containing their toothbrushes and paste. Their silhouettes are smudges scratched by the gray lines of the cold rain.

Shelly and Rita's tent is small and quickly becomes warm. Inside they crawl around, arranging their things, using their headlamps—a pair of miners looking for a lost contact lens.

"One day down," Shelly says.

Rita grunts her assent.

"Not much fun so far," Shelly says.

"No, not yet."

"But it's not supposed to be, I suppose. The point is getting up, right?"

"I guess."

"At all costs, right?"

"Right," Rita says, though she has no idea what Shelly is talking about.

Shelly soon settles into her sleeping bag, and turns toward Rita, closing her eyes. Shelly is asleep in seconds, and her breathing is loud. She breathes in through her nose and out through her nose, the exhalations in quick effortful bursts. Shelly is a yoga person and while Rita thought this was interesting an hour ago, now she hates yoga and everyone who might foster its dissemination. Yoga people are loud breathers and loud breathers are selfish and wicked.

The rain continues, tattering all night, almost rhythmic but not rhythmic enough, and Rita is awake for an hour, listening to Shelly's breathing and the rain, which comes in bursts, as if deposited by planes sweeping overhead. She cannot help but concentrate on Shelly's breathing. She worries that she will never sleep, and that she will be too tired tomorrow, that this will weaken her system and she will succumb to the cerebral edema that is ready, she knows, to leap. She sees the aneurysm in the form of a huge red troll, like a Kewpie doll, the hair aflame, though with a pair of enormous scissors, like those used to open malls and car dealerships—that the troll will jump from the mountain and with its great circus scissors, sever Rita's medulla oblongata and her ties to this world.

Gwen is to blame. Gwen had wanted, she guesses, to help Rita do something great. Gwen had been ruthlessly supportive for decades now, sending money, making phone calls on her behalf, setting Rita up with job interviews and divorced men who on the first date wanted to hold hands after an Olive Garden dinner. Their hands were rough and fat always, and Rita wanted no more of Gwen's help. Rita loved Gwen in an objective way, in an admiring way totally separate from her obligations to sibling affection. Gwen was so tall, so narrow, could not wear heels without looking like some kind of heron in black leggings, but her laugh was round and rolling, and it came out of her, as everything did, with its arms wide and embracing. She could be president if she'd wanted that job, but she hadn't—she'd chosen instead to torment Rita with her thoughtfulness. Baskets of cheese, thank you notes, that long weekend in Puerto Vallarta when they'd rented the convertible Beetle. She even bought Rita a new mailbox and installed it, with cement and a shovel, when it was stolen in the night. This is what Gwen did, this and humor Brad, and await her baby, and run a small business, as fruitful as she could hope, that provided closet reorganization plans to very wealthy people in Santa Fe.

Rita knows she can't ask Shelly to share her sleeping bag but she wants a body close to her. She hasn't slept well since J.J. and Frederick went away because she has not been warm. No one ever said so but they didn't think it appropriate that the kids slept in her bed. Gwen had found it odd when Rita had bought a larger bed, but Rita knew that having those two bodies near her, never touching anywhere but a calf or ankle, her body calming their fears, was the only indispensible experience of her life or anyone else's.

As her heart blinks rapidly, Rita promises herself that the next day will be less punishing, less severe. The morning will be clear and dry and when the fog burns off, it will be so warm, maybe even hot, with the sun coming all over and drying their wet things. They will walk upward in the morning wearing shorts and sunglasses, upward toward the sun.

T he morning is wet and foggy and there is no sun and everything that was wet the night before is now wetter. Rita's mood is a slashing despair; she does not want to leave her sleeping bag or her tent, she wants all these filthy people gone, and wants her things dry and clean. She wants to be alone, for a few minutes at least. She knows she can't, because outside the tent are the other hikers, and there are twenty porters, and now, a small group of German hikers, and at the far side of the camp, three Canadians and a crew of twelve—they must have arrived after dark. Everyone is waking up. She hears the pouring of water, the rattle of pots, the thrufting of tents. Rita is so tired and so awake and she comes close to crying. She wants to be in this sleeping bag, not awake but still sleeping, for two and a half hours more. In two and a half hours she could regather her strength, all of it. She would have a running start at this day, and could then leap past anyone.

There is conversation from the next tent. The voices are not whispering, not even attempting to whisper.

"You're kidding me," one voice says. "You know how much we paid for these tickets? How long did we plan to come here, how long did I save?"

It's Jerry.

"You know you didn't have to save, Dad."

"But Michael. We planned this for years. I talked to you about this when you were ten. Remember? When Uncle Mark came back? Christ!"

"Dad, I just—"

"And here you're going down after one freaking day!"

"Listen. I have never felt so weak, Dad. It's just so much harder than—"

"Michael. Yesterday was the hardest day—the rest will be nothing. You heard what's-his-face . . . Frank. This was the hard one. I can see why you're a little concerned, but you gotta buck up now, son. Yesterday was bad but—"

"Shhh."

"No one can hear us, Michael. For heaven's sake. Everyone's asleep."

"Shh!"

"I will not have you shushing me! And I won't have you—"

There is the sound of a sleeping bag being adjusted, and then the voices become lower and softer.

"I will not have you leaving this—"

And the voice dips below audibility.

Shelly is awake now, too. She has been listening, and gives Rita a raised eyebrow. Rita reciprocates, and begins searching through her duffel bag for what to wear today. She has brought three pairs of pants, two shorts, five shirts, two fleece sweatshirts, and her parka. Putting on her socks, wool and shaped like her foot, the ankle area reinforced and double-lined, she wonders if Mike will actually be going down so soon. There is a spare garbage bag into which she shoves her dirty socks, yesterday's shirt, and her jogging bra, which she can smell—rain and trees and her.

"You'd have to break my leg," Shelly whispers. She is still in her sleeping bag, only her face visible. Rita suddenly thinks she looks like someone. An actress. Jill Clayburgh. Jane Curtin? Kathleen Turner.

"Break my leg and cut my tendons. You'd have to. I'm doing this climb."

Rita nods and heads toward the tent's door flap.

"If you're going outside," Shelly says, "give me a weather report."

Rita pokes her head through the flaps and is facing fifteen porters.

They are all standing in the fog, just across the campsite, under the drizzle, some holding cups, all in the clothes they were wearing yesterday. They are outside the cooking tent, and they are all staring at her face through the flap. She quickly pulls it back into the tent.

"What's it like?" Shelly asks.

"Same," Rita says.

Breakfast is porridge and tea and orange slices that have been left in the open air too long and are now dry, almost brown. There is toast, cold and hard and with hard butter needing to be applied with great force. Again the five paying hikers are hunched over the small card table, and they eat everything they can. They pass the brown sugar and dump it into their porridge, and they pass the milk for their coffee, and they worry that the caffeine will give them the runs and they'll have to make excessive trips to the toilet tent, which now everyone dreads. Rita had wondered if the trip might be too soft, too easy, but now, so soon after getting here, she knows that she is somewhere else. It's something very different.

"How was that tent of yours?" Frank asks, directing his chin toward Grant. "Not too warm, eh?"

"It was a little cool, you're right, Frank." Grant is pouring himself a third cup of tea.

"Grant thinks his dad's old canvas army tent was the way to go," Frank says. "But he didn't count on this rain, didja, Grant? Your dad could dry his out next to the fire, but that ain't happening up here, friend."

Grant's hands are clasped in front of him, as if arm-wrestling with himself. He is listening and looking at Frank without any sort of emotion.

"That thing ain't dry tonight, you're gonna be bunking with me or someone else, Grant." Frank is scratching his beard in a way that looks painful. "Otherwise the rain and wind will make an icebox of that tent. You'll freeze in your sleep, and you won't even know it. You'll wake up dead."

The trail winds like a narrow river up through an hour of rain forest, drier today, and then cuts through a hillside cleared by fire.

Everyone is walking together now, the ground is bare and black. There are twisted remnants of trees straining from the soil, their extremities gone but their roots almost intact.

"There's your forest fire," Frank says.

The fog is finally clearing. Though the pace is slow, around a field of round rocks knee-high, it is not as slow as the day before, and because Rita is tired and her legs are sore in every place, from ankle to upper thigh, she accepts the reduced speed. Grant is behind her and also seems resigned.

But Mike is far more ill today. The five paying hikers know this because it has become the habit of all to monitor the health of everyone else. The words "How are you?" on this mountain do not form an innocuous or rhetorical question. The words in each case, from each hiker, give way to a distinct and complicated answer, involving the appearance or avoidance of blisters, of burgeoning headaches, of sore ankles and quads, shoulders that still, even with the straps adjusted, feel pinched. Mike's stomach feels, he is telling everyone, like there is actually a large tapeworm inside him. Its movements are trackable, relentless, he claims, and he's given it a name: Ashley, after an ex-girlfriend. He looks desperate for a moment of contentment; he looks like a sick child, lying on the bathroom floor, bent around the toilet, exhausted and defeated, who only wants the vomiting to stop.

Today the porters are passing the paying hikers. Every few minutes another goes by, or a group of them. The porters walk alone or in packs of three. When they come through they do one of two things: If there is room around the hikers, when the path is wide or there is space to walk through the dirt or rocks beside them, they will jog around them; when the path is narrow they will wait for the hikers to step aside.

Rita and Grant are stepping aside.

"Jambo," Grant says.

"Jambo," the first porter says. He is about twenty, wearing a CBS News T-shirt, khaki pants, and cream-colored Timberland hiking shoes, almost new. He is carrying two duffel bags on his head. One of them is Rita's. She almost tells him this but then catches herself.

"Habari," Grant says.

"Imara," the porter says.

And he and the two others walk past. Rita asks Grant what he's just said. "Habari," Grant explains, means "How are you," and "Imara" means "strong."

"Blue!" Jerry yells, pointing to a small spot of sky that the fog has left uncovered. It's the first swatch of blue the sky has allowed since the trip began, and it elicits an unnatural spasm of joy in Rita. She wants to climb through the gap and spread herself out above the cloud line, as you would a ladder leading to a tree fort. Soon the blue hole grows and the sun, still obscured but now directly above, gives heat through a thin layer of cloud cover. The air around them warms almost immediately and Rita, along with the other paying hikers, stops to remove layers and put on sunglasses. Frank takes a pair of wet pants from his bag and ties them to a carabiner; they hang to his heels, filthy.

Mike now has the perpetual look of someone disarming a bomb. His forehead is never without sweat beaded along the ridges of the three distinct lines on his forehead. He is sucking on a silver tube, like a ketchup container but larger.

"It's a kind of energy food," he explains.

They are all eating the snacks they've brought. Every day Steven gives the paying hikers a sack lunch of eggs and crackers, which none of them eat. Rita is eating peanuts and raisins and chocolate. Jerry is gnawing on his beef jerky. They are all sharing food and needed articles of clothing and medical aid. Shelly loans Mike her Ace bandage, to wrap around his ankle, which he thinks is swollen. Jerry loans Rita a pair of Thinsulate gloves.

Fifteen porters pass while the paying hikers are eating and changing. One porter, more muscular than the others, who are uniformly thin, is carrying a radio playing American country music. The porter is affecting a nonchalant pride in this music, a certain casual ownership of it. To each porter Grant says "Jambo" and most say "Jambo" in return, eliciting more greetings from Jerry—who now likes to say the word, loudly.

"Jahm-BO!" he roars, in a way that seems intended to frighten.

Shelly steps over to Frank.

"What do the porters eat?" she asks.

"Eat? The porters? Well, they eat what you eat, pretty much,"

Frank says, then reaches for Shelly's hips and pats one. "Maybe without the snacking," he says, and winks.

There is a boom like a jet plane backfiring. Or artillery fire. Everyone looks up, then down the mountain. No one knows where to look. The porters, farther up the trail but still within view, stop briefly. Rita sees one mime the shooting of a rifle. Then they continue.

N ow Rita is walking alone. She has talked to most of the paying hikers and feels caught up. She knows about Shelly's marriages, her Ph.D. in philosophy, her son living in a group home in Indiana after going off his medication and using a pizza cutter to threaten the life of a coworker. She knows Jerry, knows that Jerry feels his restaurants bring their communities together, knows that he fashioned them after Greek meeting places more than any contemporary dining model—he wants great ideas to be born over his food—and when he was expanding on the subject, gesturing with a stick he carried for three hours, she feared he would use the word *peripatetic,* and soon enough he did. She knew she would wince and she did. And she knows that Mike is unwell and is getting sicker and has begun to make jokes about how funny it would be for a designer of ambulances to lie dying on a mountain without any real way of getting to one.

The terrain is varied and Rita is happy; the route seems as if planned by hikers with short attention spans. There has been rain forest, then savannah, then more forest, then forest charred, and now the path cuts through a rocky hillside covered in ice-green ground cover, an ocean floor drained, the boulders everywhere huge and dripping with lichen of a seemingly synthetic orange.

The porters are passing her regularly now, not just the porters from her group but about a hundred more, from the Canadian camp, the German camp, other camps. She passes a tiny Japanese woman sitting on a round rock, flanked by a guide and a porter, waiting.

The porters are laboring more now. On the first day, they seemed almost cavalier, and walked so quickly, that now she is surprised to see them straining, plodding and unamused. A small porter, older, approaches her back and she stops to allow him through.

"Jambo," she says.

"Jambo," he says.

He is carrying a large duffel with Jerry's name on it, atop his head, held there with the bag's thick strap, with cuts across his forehead. Below the strap, perspiration flows down the bridge of his nose.

"Habari?" she says.

"Imara," he says.

"Water?" she asks. He stops.

She removes her bottle from her backpack holster and holds it out to him. He stops and takes it, smiling. He takes a long drink from the wide mouth of the clear plastic container, and then continues walking.

"Wait!" she says, laughing. He is walking off with the water bottle. "Just a sip," she says, gesturing to him that she would like the container back. He stops and takes another drink, then hands it to her, bowing his head slightly while wiping his mouth with the back of his hand.

"Thank you," he says. He continues up the trail.

They have made camp. It's three in the afternoon and the fog has returned. It hangs lightly over the land, which is brown and wide and bare. The campground looks, with the fog, like a medieval battleground, desolate and ready to host the deaths of men.

Rita sits with Jerry on rocks the size and shape of beanbags while their tents are assembled. Mike is lying on the ground, on his backpack, and he looks to Rita much like what a dead person would look like. Mike is almost blue, and is breathing in a hollow way that she hasn't heard before. His walking stick extends from his armpit in a way that looks like he's been lanced from behind.

"Oh Ashley!" he says to his tapeworm, or whatever it is. "Why're you doing this to me, Ashley?"

Far off into the mist, there is a song being sung. The words sound German, and soon they break apart into laughter. Closer to where she's sitting, Rita can hear an erratic and small sound, a tocking sound, punctuated periodically by low cheers.

The mist soon lifts and Rita sees Grant, who has already assembled his tent, surrounded by porters. He and a very young man, the youngest and thinnest she's seen, are playing a tennis-like game, using thin wooden paddles to keep a small blue ball in the air. Grant is barefoot and is grinning.

"There he is," says Jerry. "Saint Grant of the porters!"

At dinner the food is the same—cold noodles, white rice, potatoes, but tonight, instead of orange slices there is watermelon, sliced into neat thin triangles, small green boats with red sails on a silver round lake.

"Someone carried a watermelon up," Mike notes.

No one comments.

"Well, it didn't fly up," Frank says.

No one eats the watermelon, because the paying hikers have been instructed to avoid fruit, for fear of malaria in the water. Steven, the porter who serves the meals and whose smile precedes him always, soon returns and takes the watermelon back to the mess tent. He doesn't say a word.

"What happens to the guy who carried up the watermelon?" Jerry asks, grinning.

"Probably goes down," Frank says. "A lot of them are going down already—the guys who were carrying food that we've eaten. A lot of these guys you'll see one day and they're gone."

"Back to the banana fields," Jerry says.

Rita has been guessing at why Jerry looks familiar to her, and now she knows. He looks like a man she saw at Target, a portly man trying on robes who liked one so much he wore it around the store for almost an hour—she passed him twice. As with Jerry, she's both appalled by and in awe of their obliviousness to context, to taste.

The paying hikers talk about their dreams. They are all taking Maladrone, an antimalarial drug that for most fosters disturbing and hallucinogenic dreams. Rita's attention wanes, because she's never interested in people's dreams and has had none of her own this trip.

Frank tells a story of a trip he took up Puncak Jaya, tallest peak in Indonesia, a mountain of 16,500 feet and very cold. They were looking for a climber who had died there in 1934, a British explorer named Frankon whom a dozen groups had tried to locate in the decades since. Frank's group, though, had the benefit of a journal of the climber's partner, recently found a few thousand feet below. Knowing the approximate route Frankon had taken, Frank's group, once at the elevation believed to be where Frankon expired, found the man within fifteen minutes. "There he is," one of the climbers had said, without a trace of doubt, because the body was so well preserved that he looked precisely as he did in the last photograph of him. He'd fallen at least two hundred feet; his legs were broken but he had somehow survived, was trying to crawl when he'd frozen.

"And did you bury him?" Shelly asks.

"Bury him?" Frank says, with theatrical confusion. "How the heck we gonna bury the guy? It's eleven feet of snow there, and rock beneath that—"

"So you what—left him there?"

"Course we left him there! He's still there today, I bet in the same damned spot."

"So that's the way—"

"Yep, that's the way things are on the mountain."

Somewhere past midnight Rita's bladder makes demands. She tries to quietly extricate herself from the tent, though the sound of the inner zipper, and then the outer, is too loud. Rita knows Shelly is awake by the time her head makes its way outside of the tent.

Her breath is visible in compact gusts and in the air everything is blue. The moon is alive now and it has cast everything in blue. Everything is underwater but with impossible black shadows. Every rock has under it a black hole. Every tree has under it a black hole. She steps out of the tent and into the cold cold air. She jumps. There is a figure next to her, standing still.

"Rita," the figure says. "Sorry."

It's Grant. He is standing, arms crossed over his chest, facing the moon and also—now she sees it—the entire crest of Kilimanjaro. She gasps.

"It's incredible, isn't it?" he whispers.

"I had no idea—"

It's enormous. It's white-blue and huge and flat-topped. The clarity is startling. It is indeed blindingly white, even now, at 1 A.M. The moon gives its white top the look of china under candlelight. And it seems so close! It's a mountain but they're going to the top. Already they are almost halfway up its elevation and this fills Rita with a sense of clear unmitigated accomplishment. This cannot be taken away.

"The clouds just passed," Grant says. "I was brushing my teeth."

Rita looks out on the field of tents and sees other figures, alone and in pairs, also standing, facing the mountain.

Now she is determined to make it to its peak. It is very much, she thinks, like looking at the moon and knowing one could make it there, too. It is only time and breath that stand between her and the top. She is young. She'll do it and have done it.

She turns to Grant but he is gone.

Rita wakes up strong. She doesn't know why but she now feels, with her eyes opening quickly and her body rested, that she belongs on this mountain. She is ready to attack. She will run up the path today, barefoot. She will carry her own duffel. She will carry Shelly on her back. She has slept twice on this mountain but it seems like months. She feels sure that if she were left here alone, she would survive, would blend in like the hardiest of plants—her skin would turn ice-green and her feet would grow sturdy and gnarled, hard and crafty like roots.

She exits the tent and still the air is gray with mist, and everything is frozen—her boots covered in frost. The peak is no longer visible. She puts on her shoes and runs from the camp to pee. She decides en route that she will run until she finds the stream and there she will wash her hands. Now that this mountain is hers she can wash her hands in its streams, drink from them if she sees fit, live in its caves, run up its sheer rock faces.

It's fifteen minutes before she locates the stream. She was tracking and being led by the sound of the running water, without success, and finally just followed the zebra-pattern shirt of a porter carrying two empty water containers.

"Jambo," she says to the man, in the precise way Grant does.

"Jambo," the porter repeats, and smiles at her.

He is young, probably the youngest porter she's seen, maybe eighteen. He has a scar bisecting his mouth, from just below his nose to just above the dimple on his chin. The containers are the size and shape of those used to carry gasoline. He lowers one under a small waterfall and it begins to fill, making precisely the same sound she heard from her bed, in her Moshi hut. She and the porter are crouching a few feet apart, his sweatshirt lashed with a zebra pattern in pink and black.

"You like zebras?" she asks.

He smiles and nods. She touches his sweatshirt and gives him a thumbs-up. He smiles nervously.

She dips her hands into the water. Exactly the temperature she expected—cold but not bracing. She uses her fingernails to scrape the dirt from her palms, and with each trowel-like movement, she seems to free soil from her hand's lines. She then lets the water run over her palm, and her sense of accomplishment is great. Without soap she will clean these filthy hands! But when she is finished, when she has dried her hands on her shorts, they look exactly the same, filthy.

The sun has come through while she was staring at them, and she turns to face the sun, which is low but strong. The sun convinces her that she belongs here more than the other hikers, more than the porters. She is still not wearing socks! And now the sun is warming her, telling her not to worry that she cannot get her hands clean.

"Sun," she says to the porter, and smiles.

He nods while twisting the cap on the second container.

"What is your name?" she asks.

"Kassim," he says.

She asks him to spell it. He does. She tries to say it and he smiles.

"You think we're crazy to pay to hike up this hill?" she asks. She is nodding, hoping he will agree with her. He smiles and shakes his head, not understanding.

"Crazy?" Rita says, pointing to her chest. "To pay to hike up this hill?" She is walking her index and middle fingers up an imaginary mountain in the air. She points to the peak of Kilimanjaro, ringed by clouds, curved blades guarding the final thousand feet.

He doesn't understand, or pretends not to. Rita decides that Kassim is her favorite porter and that she'll look out for him. She'll give him her lunch. When they reach the bottom, she'll give him her boots. She glances at his feet, inside ancient faux-leather basketball shoes, and knows that his feet are much too big. Maybe he has kids.

He can give the shoes to the kids. It occurs to Rita then that he's at work. That his family is at home while he is on the mountain. This is what she misses so much, coming home to those kids. They would just start in, a million things they had to talk about. She wants to sign more field trip permission slips. She wants to quietly curse their gym teacher for upsetting them. She wants to clean the gum out of J.J.'s backpack or wash Frederick's urine-soaked sheets.

Kassim finishes, his vessels full, and so he stands, waves goodbye and jogs back to the camp.

I n the sun the hikers and porters lay their wet clothes out on the rocks, hang them from the bare limbs of the trees. The temperature rises from freezing to sixty in an hour and everyone is delirious with warmth, with the idea of being dry, of everything being dry. The campsite, now visible for hundreds of yards, is wretched with people— maybe four hundred of them—and the things they're bringing up the mountain. There are colors ragged everywhere, dripping from the trees, bleeding into the earth. In every direction hikers are walking, toilet paper in hand, to find a private spot to deposit their waste.

Rita devours her porridge and she knows that she is feeling strong just as a few of the others are fading. They are cramped around the card table, in the tent, and the flaps are open for the first time during a meal, and it is now too warm, too sunny. Those facing the sun are wearing sunglasses.

"Lordy, that feels good," Jerry says.

"It's like being at the beach," Shelly says, and they laugh.

"I don't want to spoil the mood," Frank says, "but I have an announcement. I wanted to make clear that you're not allowed to give porters stuff. This morning, Mike thought it was a good idea to give a porter his sunglasses, and what happened, Mike?"

"Some other guy was wearing them."

"How long did it take before the sunglasses were on this other guy?"

"Fifteen minutes."

"Why's that, Mike?"

"Because you're supposed to give stuff to Patrick first."

"Right. Listen, people. There's a pecking order here, and Patrick knows the score. If you have a wave of generosity come over you and wanna give someone your lunch or your shoelaces or something, you give it to Patrick. He'll distribute whatever it is. That's the only way it's fair. That understood? You're here to walk and they're here to work."

Everyone nods.

"Why you giving your sunglasses away anyway, Mike? You're sure as hell gonna need 'em these next couple days. You get to the top and you're—"

"I'm going down," Mike says.

"What?"

"I have to go down," Mike says, staring at Frank, the sun lightening his blue eyes until they're sweater-gray, almost colorless. "I don't have the desire anymore."

"The desire, eh?"

Frank pauses for a second, and seems to move from wanting to joke with Mike, to wanting to talk him out of it, to accepting the decision. It's clear he wants Jerry to say something, but Jerry is silent. Jerry will speak to Mike in private.

"Well," Frank says, "you know it when you know it, I guess. Patrick'll get a porter to walk you down."

Mike and Frank talk about how it will work. All the way down in one day? That's best, Frank says. That way you won't need provisions. Who brings my stuff? You carry your pack; a porter will carry the duffel. Get in by nightfall, probably, and Godwill will be there to meet you. Who's Godwill? The driver. Oh, the older man. Yes. Godwill. He'll come up to get you. If the park rangers think it's an emergency, they'll let him drive about half the way up. So how much of a hike will we make down? Six hours. I think I can do that. You can, Mike, you can. You'll have to. No problem. Thanks for playing. Better luck next time.

Jerry still hasn't said anything. He is eating his porridge quickly, listening. He is now chewing his porridge, his face pinched, his eyes planning.

After breakfast Rita is walking to the toilet tent and passes the cooking tent. There are six porters inside, and a small tight group outside—younger porters, mostly, each holding a small cup, standing around a large plastic tub, like those used to bus dishes and silverware. Kassim is there; she recognizes him immediately because he, like all of the porters, wears the same clothes each day. There is another sweatshirt she knows, with a white torso and orange sleeves, a florid Hello Kitty logo on the chest. Rita tries to catch Kassim's eye but he's concentrating on the cooking tent. Steven steps through the flaps with a silver bowl, and overturns it into the tub. The young porters descend upon it, stabbing their cups into the small mound of porridge until it's gone in seconds.

The trail makes its way gradually upward and winds around the mountain, and Mike, groaning with every leaden step, is still with them. Rita doesn't know why he is still with the group. He is lagging behind, with Patrick, and looks stripped of all blood and hope. He is pale, and he is listing to one side, and is using hiking poles as an elderly man would use a cane, unsure and relying too heavily on that point at the end of a stick.

The clouds are following the group up the mountain. They should stay ahead of the clouds, Frank told them, if they want to keep warm today. There has been talk of more rain, but Frank and Patrick believe that it won't rain at the next camp—it's too high. They are hiking in a high desert area called the Saddle, between the peaks of Mawenzi, a mile away and jagged, and Kibo above. The vegetation is now sparse, the trees long gone. Directly above the trail stands the mountain, though the peak is still obscured by cloud cover. She and Grant are still the only ones who have seen it, at midnight under the bright small moon.

Two hours into the day, Rita's head begins to throb. They are at 11,200 feet and the pain comes suddenly. It is at the back of her skull, where she was told the pain would begin and grow before one suffered from a cerebral edema. She begins to breathe with more effort, trying to bring more oxygen into her blood, her brain. Her breathing works for small periods of time, the pain receding, though it comes back with ferocity. She breathes quickly, and loudly, and the pain moves away when she is walking faster, and climbing steeper, so she knows she must keep going up.

S he walks with a trio of South Africans who have driven to Tanzania from Johannesburg. She asks them how long it took, the drive, and guesses at sixteen, eighteen hours. They laugh, no, no—three weeks, friend, they say. There are no superhighways in East Africa! they say. They walk along an easy path, a C-shape around the mountain, through a field of shale. The rocks are the color of rust and whales, shards that tinkle and clink, loudly, under their feet.

The path cuts through the most desolate side of Kilimanjaro, an area that looks like the volcano had spewed not lava but rusted steel. There is a windswept look about it, the slices of shale angled away from the mountaintop as if still trying to get away from the center, from the fire.

T hey descend into a valley, through a sparse forest of lobelia trees, all of them ridiculous, each with the gray trunk of a coconut tree topped by an exuberant burst of green, a wild head of spiky verdant hair. A stream runs along the path, in a narrow and shallow crack in the valley wall, and they stop to fill their water bottles. The four of them squat like gargoyles and share a small vial of purification pills. They drop two of the pills, tiny and the color of steel, into the bottles and shake. They wait, still squatting like gargoyles, until the pills have dissolved, then they drop in small white tablets, meant to improve the water's taste. They stand.

She decides she will jog ahead of the South Africans, down the path. Weighing the appeal of learning more about the economic situation in sub-Saharan Africa against the prospect of running down this trail and making it to camp sooner, she chooses to run. She tells them she'll see them at the bottom and when she begins jogging, she immediately feels better. Her breathing is denser and her head clears within minutes. Exertion, she realizes, must be intense and constant.

There is a man lying in the path just ahead, as it bends under a thicket of lobelias. She runs faster, toward him. The body is crumpled as if it had been dropped. It's Mike. She is upon him and his skin is almost blue. He is asleep. He is lying on the path, his pack still strapped to his back. She dumps her pack and kneels beside him. He is breathing. His pulse seems slow but not desperate.

"Rita."

"You okay? What's wrong?"

"Tired. Sick. Want to go home."

"Well, I'm sure you'll get your wish now. You're a mess."

He smiles.

Rita helps him stand and they walk slowly down the valley to the camp. It is spread out in a wide valley, the tents on the edge of a cliff—the camp this third day is stunning. It's late afternoon when they arrive and the sun is out and everywhere. This is the Great Barranco Valley, sitting high above the clouds, which lie like an ocean beyond the valley's mouth, as if being kept at bay behind glass.

The tents are assembled and she helps him inside one, his head on a pillow of clothes, the sun making the interior pink and alarming. When Jerry, already at camp and washing his socks in the stream, notices that his son is present, he enters the tent, asks Rita to leave, and when she does, zips the tent closed.

In her own tent Rita is wrecked. Now that she's not moving the pain in her head is a living thing. It is a rat-sized and prickly animal living, with great soaring breaths and a restless tail, in her frontal lobe. But there is no room for this animal in her frontal lobe, and thus there is great strain in her skull. The pain reaches to the corners of her eyes. At the corners of her brow someone is slowly pushing a pen or pencil, just behind her eyes and through, into the center of her head. When she places her first and second fingers on the base of her skull, she can feel a pulsing.

The tent is yellow. The sun makes the tent seem alive; she's inside a lemon. The air seems to be yellow, and everything that she knows about yellow is here—its glory and its anemia. It gets hotter, the sun reigning throughout the day, giving and giving, though with the heaviest heart.

* * *

The night goes cold. They are at 14,500 feet and the air is thin and when the sun disappears the wind is cruel, profane. The rain comes again. Frank and Patrick are amazed by the rain, because they say it is rare in this valley, but it begins just when the sun descends, a drizzle, and by dinner is steady. The temperature is plunging.

At dinner, tomorrow's hike—the final ascent—is mapped out. They will rise at six A.M., walk for eight hours and stop at the high camp, where they'll eat and then sleep until eleven P.M. At eleven, the group will get up, get packed, and make the final six-hour leg in the dark. They will reach the peak of Kibo at sunrise, take pictures and dawdle for an hour before making the descent, eight hours to the final camp, halfway down the mountain, the path shooting through a different side this time, less scenic, quicker, straighter.

Shelly asks if all the porters go up with the group.

"What, up to the top? No, no," Frank says. About five do, just as guides, basically, he says. They come with the group, in case someone needs help with a pack or needs to go down. The rest of the porters stay at camp, then break it down and head out to meet the group at the final camp, on the long hike down.

After she's eaten, very little, Rita exits the tent and bumps her head against the ear of a porter. It's the man with the water by the stream.

"Jambo," she says.

"Hello," he says. He is holding a small backpack. There are about twenty porters around the dining tent, though only three are carrying dishes away. With the tent empty, two more are breaking down the card table and chairs. The tent is soon empty and the porters begin filing in, intending, Rita assumes, to clean it before disassembling it.

Rita lies down. She lies down slowly, resting her head so slowly onto the pillow Shelly has created for her from a garbage bag full of soft clothes. But even the small crinkling sound of the garbage bag is thunderously loud. Rita is scared. She sees the gravestone of the young man who died here six months before—they had a picture of it, and him—a beautiful young man grinning from below a blue bandanna—

at the hotel, laminated on the front desk, to warn guests about pushing themselves too far. She sees her body being taken down by porters. Would they be careful with her corpse? She doesn't trust that they would be careful. They would want to get down quickly. They would carry her until they got to the rickshaw gurney and then they would run.

She listens as the paying hikers get ready for bed. She is in her sleeping bag and is still cold—she is wearing three layers but she feels flayed. She shivers but the shivering hurts her head so she forces her body to rest; she pours her own calm over her skin, coating it as if with warm oil, and she breathes slower. Something is eating her legs. She is awake when a panther comes and begins gnawing on her legs. She is watching the panther gnawing and can feel it, can feel it as if she were having her toes licked by a puppy, only there is blood, and bone, and marrow visible; the puppy is sucking the marrow from her bones, while looking up at her, smiling, asking, What's your name? Do you like zebras?

S he wakes up when she hears the rain going louder. She shakes free of the dream and succeeds in forgetting it almost immediately. The rain overwhelms her mind. The rain is strong and hard, like the knocking of a door, the knocking getting louder, and it won't end, the knocking—sweet Jesus will someone please answer that knocking? She is freezing all night. She awakens every hour and puts on another article of clothing, until she can barely move. She briefly considers staying at this camp with the porters, not making the final climb. There are photographs. There is an IMAX movie. Maybe she will survive without summitting.

But she does not want to be grouped with Mike. She is better than Mike. There is a reason to finish this hike. She must finish it because Shelly is finishing it, and Grant is finishing it. She is as good as these people. She is tired of admitting that she cannot continue. For so many years she has been doing everything within her power to finish but again and again she has pulled up short, and has been content for having tried. She found comfort in the nuances between success and failure, between a goal finished, accomplished, and a goal adjusted.

She puts on another T-shirt and another pair of socks. She falls back to sleep. She wakes up at dawn and Shelly is holding her, spooning. She falls to sleep.

The light through the vent is like a crack into a world uninterrupted by shape or definition. There is only white. White against white. She squints and reaches for her sunglasses, reaches around to no avail, feels only the rocks beneath the tent, and every rock beneath her fingers somehow makes its way into her head, every rock beneath her fingers is knocking against her head. She is breathing as deeply as she can but it has no effect. She knows her head is not getting enough blood. Her faculties are slipping away. She tries to do simple mental tasks, testing herself—the alphabet, states of the Union, Latin conjugations—and finds her thoughts scattered. She inhales so deeply the air feels coarse, and exhales with such force her chest goes concave. Shelly is still asleep.

It's the first light of morning. If there is sun the rain must have passed. It will not be so cold today—there is sun. Already she is warmer, the tent heating quickly, but the wind is still strong and the tent ripples loudly.

What is that? There is a commotion outside the tent. The porters are yelling. She hears Frank, his tent so close, unzip and rezip his tent's door, and then she can hear his steps move toward the voices. The voices rise and fall on the wind, fractured by the flapping of the tent.

There is someone trying to enter the tent.

"Shelly," Rita says.

"Yes, hon."

"Who is that?"

"That's me, dear."

Hours or seconds pass. Shelly is back. When did she leave? Shelly has entered the tent, and is now slowly rezipping the doorflap, trying not to bother her. Hours or seconds?

"Rita, honey."

Rita wants to answer but can't find her tongue. The light has swept into her, the light is filling her, like something liquid pushing its way into the corners of a mold, and soon she's fading back to sleep.

"Rita, honey, something's happened."

Rita is now riding on a horse, and she's on a battlefield of some kind. She is riding sidesaddle, dodging bullets. She is invincible, and her horse seems to be flying. She pats her horse and the horse looks up at her, without warmth, bites her wrist, and keeps running, yanking on its reins.

And then it's hours later. She opens her eyes and it doesn't hurt. Something has changed. Her head is lighter, the pain is diminished. Shelly is gone. Rita doesn't know what time it is. It's still bright. Is it the same day? She doesn't know. Everyone could be gone. She has been left here.

She rises. She opens the tent door. There is a crowd around two men zipping up a large duffel bag. The zipper is stuck on something pink, fabric or something, a striped pattern. Now they have the duffel over their shoulders, the duffel connecting their left shoulders, and there are men around them arguing. Patrick is pushing someone away, and pointing the porters with the duffel down the path. Then there is another huge duffel, carried by two more porters, and they descend the trail. Grant is there. Grant is now helping lift another duffel bag. He hoists his half onto his shoulder while another porter lifts the other side, and they begin walking, down the trail, away from the summit.

Rita closes her eyes again and flies off. There are bits of conversation that make their way into her head, through vents in her consciousness. "What were they wearing?" "Well, think about it like the cabbies again. It's a job, right? There are risks. . . ." "Are you bringing the peanuts, too?" "Sleeping through it all isn't going to make it go away, honey."

J.J. and Frederick are in electric chairs. The Brussels stenographer is there, standing next to Rita, and they are smiling at the children. It is apparent in the logic of the dream that J.J. and Frederick are to be executed for losing a bet of some kind. Or because they were just born to be in the chair and Rita and the Brussels stenographer were born to hold their hands. J.J. and Frederick turn their eyes up to her and sing. They are singing to her in unison, their voices falsettos, cool and strong:

> One two
> We always knew
> Three four
> You'd never give us more

Rita is holding their hands as the vibrations start. She is resigned, knowing that there are rules and she is not the person to challenge them. But their teeth begin to chatter, and their eyes rise to her and she wonders if she should do something to stop it.

"How you feel, sweetie?"

Her head is clear and without weight. It again feels like part of her.

"You just needed time to acclimate, I bet."

Rita raises her head and there is no pain. Lifting her head is not difficult. She is amazed at the lightness of her head.

"Well, if you're coming, I think you'll have to be ready in a few minutes. We're already very late. We gotta get a move on."

Rita doesn't want to be in the tent anymore. She can finish this and have done it, whatever it is.

The terrain is rocky, loose with scree, and it is steep, but otherwise it is not the most difficult of hikes, she is told. They will simply go up until they are done. It will be something she can tell herself and others she has done, and being able to say yes when asked if she summitted will make a difference, will save her from explaining why she went down when two hikers over fifty years old went up.

Rita packs her parka and food, and stuffs the rest into her duffel bag for the porters to bring down to the next camp. The wind picks up and ripples the tent and she is struck quickly by panic. Something has happened. She remembers that Shelly had said something happened while she was asleep—but what? What was—

Mike. Oh, Christ. Her stomach liquifies.

"Is Mike okay?" she asks.

She knows the answer will be no. She looks at Shelly's back.

"Mike? Mike's fine, hon. He's fine. I don't think he'll be joining us today, but he's feeling a little better."

Rita remembers Grant going down the trail. What happened to Grant?

"I'm honestly not sure why he left," Shelly says, applying a strip of white sunblock to her nose. "He's not the most normal guy, though, is he?"

The sky is clear and though the air is still cold, maybe 45 or so, the sun is warm to Rita's face. She is standing now, and almost can't believe she is standing. She steps over the shale to the meal tent, the thin shards of rock clinking like the closing of iron gates.

Mike is at breakfast. It's eight A.M., and they are two hours behind schedule. They quickly eat a breakfast of porridge and hard-boiled eggs and tea. Everyone is exhausted and quiet. Grant has gone down the mountain and Mike is not going up. She smiles to Mike as he bites into an egg.

The remaining paying hikers—Rita, Jerry, Shelly—and Frank and Patrick say goodbye. They will see him again in about twelve hours, they say, and he'll feel better. They'll bring him some snow from Kibo, they say. They want to go and drag their bodies to the top, from which they can look down to him.

From the peak Rita can see a hundred miles of Tanzania, green and extending until a low line of clouds intercepts and swallows the land. She can see Moshi, tiny windows reflecting the sun, like flecks of gold seen beneath a shallow stream. Everyone is taking pictures in front of a sign boasting the altitude at the top, and its status as the highest peak in Africa, the tallest freestanding mountain in the world. Behind the signs is the cavity of Kibo, a great volcanic crater, flat, paisleyed with snow.

On the Moshi side of the mountain, the glaciers are low and wide, white at the top and striped from her viewpoint, above. She sees the great teeth of a white whale. Icicles twenty feet tall extend down and drip onto the bare rock below.

"They're disappearing," Jerry says. He is standing behind Rita, looking through binoculars. "They melt every year a few feet. Coming down slowly but steadily. They'll be gone in twenty years."

Rita shields her eyes and looks where Jerry is looking.

"No more snows of Kilimanjaro, eh?" he says, and sighs in a theatrical way.

There are others at the top of Kibo, a large group of Chinese hikers, all in their fifties, and a dozen Italians in light packs and with sleek black gear. The hikers who have made it here nod as they pass each other. They hand their cameras to strangers to take their pictures. The wind comes over the mountain in gusts, like ghosts.

The hike up had been slow and steep and savagely cold. They rested ten minutes every hour and while sitting or standing, eating granola and drinking water, their bodies cooled and the wind whipped them. After four hours Shelly was faltering and said she would turn back. "Get that pack off!" Frank yelled, tearing it off her as if it were aflame. "Don't be a hero," he'd said, giving the pack to one of the porters. Shelly had continued, refreshed without the weight. The last five hundred yards, when they could see the crest of the mountain just above, had taken almost two hours. They'd reached the summit as the sun crested through a band of violet clouds.

Now Rita is breathing as fast and as deeply as she can—her headache is fighting for dominion over her skull, and she is panting to keep it at bay. But she is happy that she walked up this mountain, and cannot believe she almost stopped before the peak. Now, she thinks, seeing these views in every direction, and knowing the communion with the others who have made it here, she would not have let anything stop her ascent. She knows now why a young man would continue up until crippled with edema, why his feet would have carried him while his head drained of blood and reason. Rita is proud of herself, and loves her companions, and now feels more connected to Shelly, and Jerry, Patrick, and even Frank, than to Mike, or even Grant. Especially not to Grant, who chose to go down, though he was strong enough to make it. Grant is already blurry to her, someone she never really knew, a friend she knew as a child but who moved away before they could grow up together.

Rita finds Shelly, who is sitting on a small metal box chained to one of the signs.

"Well, I'm happy anyway," Shelly says. "I know I shouldn't be, but I am."

Rita sits next to her, panting to keep her head clear.

"Why shouldn't you be happy?" Rita asks.

"I feel guilty, I guess. Everyone does. But I just don't know how our quitting would have brought those three porters back to life."

Last night, Shelly says. Or the night before last. The last night we slept, when you were sick, Rita. Remember? The rain? It was so cold, and they were sleeping in the mess tent, and there was the hole, and the tent was so wet. They just didn't wake up, Rita. You didn't know? I know you were asleep but really, you didn't know? I think part of you knew. Who do you think they were carrying down? Oh lord, look at the way the glaciers sort of radiate under the sun. They are so huge and still but they seem to pulse, don't they, honey? Where are you going?

A ll the way down Rita expects to fall. The mountain is steep for the first hour, the rock everywhere loose. None of this was her idea. She was put here, in this place, by her sister, who was keeping score. Rita had never wanted this. She dislikes mountains and peaks meant nothing to her. She's a boat person; she likes to sit on boats in the sun, or in the sun with her feet in the powdery sand! As the mountain is still steep she runs and then jumps and runs and then jumps, flying for twenty feet with each leap, and when she lands, hundreds of stones are unleashed and go rolling down, gathering more as they descend. She never would have come this far had she known it would be like this, all wrong, so cold and with the rain coming through the tents on those men. She makes it down to the high camp, where the porters made her dinner and went to sleep and did not wake up. This cannot be her fault. Patrick is responsible first, and Frank after him, and then Jerry and Shelly, both of whom are older, who have experience and should have known something was wrong. Rita is the last one who could be blamed; but then there is Grant, who had gone down and hadn't told her. Grant knew everything, didn't he? How could she be responsible for this kind of thing? Maybe she is not here now, running down this mountain, and was never here. This is something she can forget. She can be not-here—she was never here. Yesterday she found herself wanting something she never wanted, and she became something else and why go up when everything is wrong? Every day the porters walked ahead, helping them to get to some frigid place with a view and a savage wind, carrying watermelons and coffee for Christ's sake, and it felt wrong and she was hollow and shamed. She wanted to be able to tell Gwen that she'd done it, and she wanted to bring J.J. and Frederick a rock or something from up there, because then they'd think she was capable of anything finally and someday they would come back to her and—oh God, it was a mess and she keeps running, sending scree down in front of her, throwing rocks down the mountain, because she cannot stop running and she cannot stop bringing the mountain down with her.

At the bottom, ten hours later, she is newly barefoot. The young boy who now has her boots, whom she gave them to after he offered to wash them, directed her into a round hut of corrugated steel, and she ducked into its cool darkness. Behind a desk, flanked by maps, is a Tanzanian forest ranger. He is very serious.

"Did you make it to the top?" he asks.

She nods.

"Sign here."

He opens a log. He is turning the pages, looking for the last names entered. There are thousands of names in the book, with each name's nationality, age, and a place for comments. He finds a spot for her, on one of the last pages, at the bottom, and after all the names before her she adds her own.

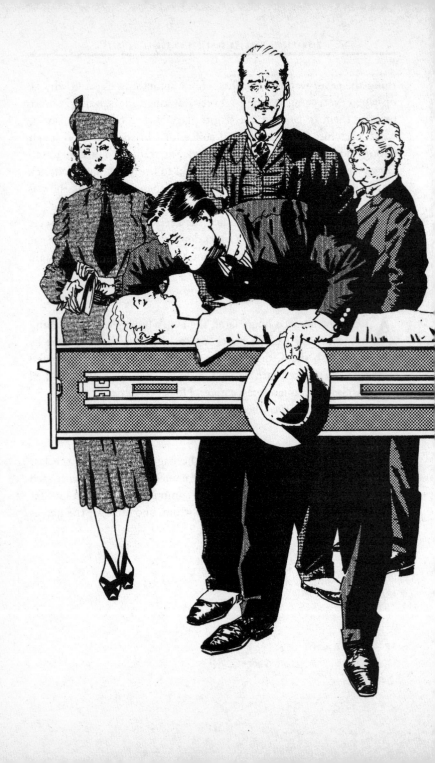

The Nazis entrusted the future of their party to the capable hands of Sir Seaton Begg, Metatemporal Detective—the only man who could possibly destroy them!

The Case of the Nazi Canary

A SEATON BEGG MYSTERY

By MICHAEL MOORCOCK

AUTHOR OF

THE MASKED BUCKAROO, THE WHITE WOLF'S LEGEND, THE AFFAIR OF THE SEVEN VIRGINS, LOST SORCERESS OF THE SILENT CITADEL, KANE OF OLD MARS, THE MOON HAWK, CALLING JERRY CORNELL!, THE CARIBBEAN CRISIS, THE METATEMPORAL DETECTIVE, AGAIN, SEATON BEGG! THE ADVENTURE OF THE TEXAN'S HONOUR, BUCHAN OF WHITEHALL, THE "SIR MILK AND BLOOD" CASE, THE CASE OF THE PRINTER'S DEVIL, THE CASE OF THE CHINESE AGENT, THE WAR LORD OF THE AIR, THROUGH THE SHAVING MIRROR, THE TAROT MURDER CASE, THE CASE OF THE DREAMTHIEF'S DAUGHTER, AND MANY OTHER BEST-SELLING "THRILLERS" OF CRIME AND THE SUPERNATURAL.

CHAPTER ONE
MESSAGE FROM MUNICH

It was, or would be, the misty autumn of 1931. A suite of comfortable bachelor apartments in the highest tower of London's exclusive Sporting Club Square.

Sir Seaton Begg, former MI5 special operator now metatemporal investigator, reached across the fire-grate, singeing the sleeve of his smoking jacket. As he examined the silk, his aquiline, unconventionally handsome features were illuminated by the fire.

"What d'you make of that, Taffy?"

John "Taffy" Sinclair, Begg's best and oldest friend, and the leading Home Office pathologist, accepted the rectangle of yellow paper. The balding giant had the mild but sturdy rectitude of an East End bishop. Balancing a cup of Darjeeling in one hand, he sank back into the depths of his armchair to read. Moments later, with an impatient expression, he set the telegram aside.

"The National Socialists?" Taffy frowned. "Sort of German Mussolini-ites? Aren't they even worse than the commies for going around beating up honest citizens? And, of course, there's that lunatic anti-Jewish muck."

Begg smiled a familiar, almost sly, smile. "I gather they will restore 'German pride' and so forth, meaning, no doubt, the military. A very attractive message to the heavy industrialists, naturally, who find more profit in swords than ploughshares." He lifted delicate bone china to his full, masculine lips. "The armorers and their jackals."

Like Sinclair, Begg supported world disarmament under the League of Nations and was disappointed when Woodrow Wilson had been forced to placate the parochial exigencies of his Congress by quitting the League.

Begg continued with some emphasis. "Look here, Taffy, read that thing again and let me know any other names you recognize, apart from their Little Corporal destined to become their German Napoleon."

"You mean that awful oik who looks like Charlie Chaplin? Musso's effeminate pal Mr. Hitler? The Nazi general secretary or whatever he styles himself. Nothing new, is it?"

"I'd agree he seems to be preaching a familiar line of l'intoxication special." Sinclair reached a taper into the fire and relit his pipe. "These chaps have been getting more dangerous since the successes of Primo Riviera and Mussolini, of course." He puffed heroically on his briar.

"I agree, old man." Begg glanced into the fire. For an instant his eyes burned an angry red. "Come on, Taffy. Be a pal and glance at that wire again."

Reluctantly, Sinclair adjusted his spectacles. "Well, Hess is a pretty common German name. But don't you know a Baron von Hess? Some sort of relative of your cousin, Count von Bek?"

"Von Bek?" Begg laughed at this mention of his old sparring partner, known to the British public as Monsieur Zodiac, the Albino, Count of Crime. "I doubt if my cousin would deign to involve himself in this. It's not what you call an epicurean crime, eh? What about this Fräulein Raubal?"

"Her first name, Geli, is short for Angela, I believe. Raubal's a fairly common name in southern Germany and Austria. Who is she, do you know?"

"Herr Hitler's mistress, my dear chap." Begg smiled self-indulgently, at once mocking and forgiving his own relish for scandal. "They are also, one hears, close relatives."

Sinclair shook his head. "Afraid I don't follow the German gossip columns."

"You should, old boy." The lean detective sprang from his chair. He tapped out his own pipe against the fireplace. "You'd learn a lot more from them, Taffy, than from any piece of biased front-page news." He waved at the untidy stacks of *Der Spiegel, Svenske Dagbladet, Berliner Poste,* and *Munchener Telegraf* which shared not always agreeable space with *Le Figaro, Les Temps, Al Misr, The Times of India, The Cape Times, El Pais, La Posta,* and the Berlin-published *Munda Veritas.* Few were open at the early pages. "Now, anything else?"

"Well, the thing's from Briennerstrasse. Seems to be genuine. That's a pretty posh avenue in the salubrious bit of Munich. Papal Nuncio's there and all that. So these chaps seem to have some powerful backers, as you say. Naturally, Begg, you wouldn't consider working for such people!"

"Well, I agree it might be a bit unsavory to take their money, but I'm curious. Fascinating, eh, the dreams of power of failed shopkeepers and frustrated shipping clerks?"

"That's downright perverse, Begg!" exclaimed the sensitive Celt. "Keep 'em away with a ten-foot pole, I say."

"Currently President Stalin's favorite foreign policy strategy, the ten-foot Pole." Sir Seaton referred to Lenin's successor, who led the Bolshevik Party in the Duma and was spouting nationalistic rubbish every day, winning votes from Monsieur Trotsky, the liberal internationalist. "Poland as a buffer zone in case civil war breaks out in Germany. Could be the touch paper for another world conflict."

"Germany's safe enough," Taffy insisted. "She has the best and most just political constitution in the world. Certainly better than ours. Even sturdier than the American."

Like so many old Harrovians, but unlike his former schoolfellow Begg, Sinclair had a comfortable, phlegmatic belief in the sense of the commons and their strong survival instinct both as social democrats and as self-interested individuals with jobs and businesses to ensure. War made economic sense for a couple of years at most and then began impoverishing the participants. It was the one lesson learned from the recent beastliness ending with the Treaty of Versailles.

Begg took back the German wire and read it aloud, translating swiftly. "*My dear Sir Seaton: Here in Germany we have long admired the exploits of your famous English detectives. We are sufficiently impressed with your national virtues as a detecting folk to inquire if you, paramount in your specialized profession, would care to come at once to Munich, where you will have the satisfaction of rescuing a reputation, bringing the guilty to justice, and also knowing you have saved a noble and betrayed nation. The reputation is that of our country's most able philosopher-general. I refer, of course, to our Guide Herr Adolf Hitler, author of* Mein Kampf *and bearer of the Iron Cross, who has been devastated by the murder of his ward, Fräulein 'Geli' Raubal, and whose reputation could be ruined by the scandal. With a view to seeing the triumph of justice, could we, the National Socialist Party, enjoin you to lose no speed in taking the earliest zeppelin from Manchester to Munich? While B.O.A.C. provides an excellent run from Croydon and appears quicker, there is a long delay making stops at Berlin and Frankfurt. Therefore we recommend you take the modern German vessel which leaves Manchester Moss Side field at five PM and arrives at ten AM the next morning. An excellent train leaves Kings Cross at two PM and connects with the airship, the* Spirit of Nuremberg. *Please excuse the brevity of this telegram. My inner voices tell me you are destined to save not merely Germany but the entire Western world from an appalling catastrophe and become the best-loved Englishman our country has ever known. On the presumption that you will accept our case, as you accept your historic destiny, I have sent, via courier, all necessary first-class travel documents for yourself and an assistant, together with documents enabling you to bring any personal transport you favor. We are, you see, familiar with your foibles. I will personally be at Munich International Aerodrome to meet the ZZ.700. I look forward to the honor of shaking your hand. Writing in all admiration and expectation that your famous sense of fair play will move your conscience, I am, Yours Most Sincerely, Rudolf Hess, Deputy Leader, The N.S.D.A.P., Briennerstrasse, Munich, Bavaria, Germany.*

"Rum style, eh?"

"About as laconic as his countryman Nietzsche," reflected Sinclair with a snort. "No doubt the poor blighter's trench-crazy. Harmless enough, I'm sure, but still barking barmy. I mean to say, old sport, you are our leading metatemporal snooper. There's all sorts of ordinary 'tecs could do this job. This case is merely about a particularly grubby murder of a girl, who was probably no better than she ought to be, by a seedy petit bourgeois who sets himself up as the savior of the world. He'll likely find his true destiny, if not on the gallows, among the sandwich-board men of Hyde Park Corner, warning against the dangers of red meat and Asian invasion. A distinct case of an undersatisfied libido and an overstimulated ego, I'd say."

"Quite so, old man. I know your penchant for the Viennese trick cyclists. But surely you wouldn't wish to see the wrong cove found guilty of such an unpleasant crime?"

"There's no chance he's guilty, I suppose?" Sinclair instantly regretted his words. "No, no. Of course we must assume his innocence. But there are many more deserving cases around the world, I'm sure."

"Few of them cases allowing me to take the very latest in aerial luxury liners and even put yourself and Dolly on the payroll without question."

"It's no good, Begg, the idea's unpalatable to me. . . ."

With an athlete's impatient speed, Begg crossed to his vast, untidy bureau, and tugged something out of a pigeonhole. "Besides, our tickets arrived not ten minutes before you turned up for tea. Oh, say you'll do it, old man. I promise you, the adventure will be an education, if nothing else."

Taffy began to grumble, but by midnight he was on his feet, phoning down for his Daimler. He would meet Begg, he promised, at Kings Cross, where they would travel to Manchester that afternoon on the high-speed *M & E Flyer,* so as to be safely aboard the zep by four-thirty.

Begg was delighted. He trusted and needed his old comrade's judgment and cool head. Their personalities were complementary, like a couple of very different fives players. This time Begg felt he had involved himself in a job that would have him holding his nose for longer than he cared.

As for the Presbyterian Taffy, he would still be debating the morality of accepting the tickets when they met the next day and began the journey to Munich.

CHAPTER TWO
HOMICIDE OR SUICIDE?

Sir Seaton and Taffy had fought the "pickle-fork brigade" for too long to hate them. They understood that your average Fritz wasn't so very different from your average Tommy and that it took self-interested and foolish politicians to make men kill one another. Yet for all his certainty that the War to End War had done its work, Begg knew that vigilance was forever the price of freedom. Few threats to our hard-won rights came from the expected sources. The unexpected angle of attack was generally successful. Authority is by nature conservative and therefore never truly prepared for surprises. It was Seaton Begg's job always to be prepared for the unexpected. That was why the Admiralty, the War Office, the Home Office, and the Foreign Office all continued to pay him substantial retainers to investigate any affair that, in their opinion, required the specialized services of one versed in the subtleties of alternative time-lines, which he was able to cross with rare ease. It was also why they encouraged him to take the occasional foreign case.

The service aboard the *Spirit of Nuremberg* was impeccable. This made Taffy a little nervous.

"Sort of military feel about it, if you know what I mean. Sometimes I think I prefer the old, sloppy cockneys we get on the Croydon-Paris run."

Begg was amused by this. "Sit back and enjoy it, old man," he said. He had asked for that morning's Munich newspapers, which were full of the recently averted bomb attack on the new Miami-Havana rail tunnel. After quickly scanning the headlines, Begg ignored this news, and concentrated his attention on the newspapers' interiors, especially the back sections.

"I see a well-known hater of Hitler and Co. is leading a new orchestra at the Carlton Tea Rooms. Though wisely he has adopted another name. Margarita Sarfati remains Mussolini's most trusted art advisor, and the Nazis berate the Duce for keeping a Jewish mistress with decadent modernist tastes. Roosevelt is proclaimed the new Mussolini by some American papers and the new Stalin by the Hearst press, who are supporting Hitler. And Marion Davies, Hearst's long-time mistress, is secretly keeping a liason with Max Peters, the Jewish cowboy star who is such a close friend of Mussolini. Ah, the intrigues of the powerful. . . . The Raubal murder case has proved meat and drink for the left-wing press. They are thirsty for any sign of Hitler's downfall, it seems. But the public still expects evidence if it's going to change its loyalties now!"

Taffy hated gossip. Deprived of his *Times,* he contented himself with the *Frankfurter Allgemeine*'s crossword puzzle, which he found surprisingly straightforward.

The wind and rain thudded hard against the huge airship's canopy as she swayed at anchor between forward and stern masts. In spite of the stirring waltz tunes coming over the Tannoy, there was still an air of adventure about boarding an airship, especially in bad weather when you realized how much you were at the mercy of elemental nature. Outside the windows, Moss Side Field was obscured by mist and even Manchester's famous chimneys were hardly visible, wrapped, as they were, in cloaks of their own making. Begg had been pleased to see the smoke.

"Those chimneys are alive, Taffy," he had said upon boarding. "And a live chimney means a living wage for those poor devils in the factory towns."

Since Begg needed to make notes, they had ordered cabin service. At seven PM sharp, as the lights of London faded on their starboard bow and they saw below the faint white flecks of waves, there came a discreet knock on their door. At Begg's command, a short, jolly, red-faced waiter entered their little sitting room. They had already decided on their menu and the efficient waiter soon converted a writing table to a dining table and laid it with a bright, white cloth. He then proceeded to bring the first courses, which, while of the heavy German type, were eaten by the pair with considerable zest. A good white wine helped the meal down.

The signs of dining magically removed, Taffy took up a light novel and read for an hour while Begg continued to make notes and refer to the newspapers. Eventually, the pathologist could stay awake no longer and, with a yawning "Good night, old man," decided to turn in. He took the sleeping cubicle to the left of the main room. He knew from experience not to compete with Seaton Begg, who needed at most five hours' sleep in twenty-four.

Indeed, when Sinclair rose to use the well-designed hidden amenities, it seemed Begg had done no more than change into his pajamas while retaining his place and posture from the previous night.

Only the scenery below had changed. They had crossed the North Sea and were now making their way above the neat fields of the German lowlands. In another two hours they would berth in Munich, the *Spirit*'s home port. Meanwhile there was a full English breakfast to consume and wash down with what, even Sinclair admitted, was a passable cup of Assam.

Munich Aerodrome had the very latest in winching masts. Disembarking from the fully grounded zeppelin, Begg and Sinclair descended the ship's staircase. They were greeted at the bottom by a tall, rather cadaverous individual in a poorly fitting Norfolk jacket of chocolate brown, two swastika armbands in the German colors of black, red, and white, rather baggy riding breeches, and highly polished polo boots. He offered them a *Quo Vadis* Roman salute, made famous in the popular film drama, then immediately began to pump Begg's hand.

"This is such an honor, Sir Seaton. I have read about you so much. I myself have a natural affinity with the British aristocracy. I so admire your Prince of Wales. The best of English and German blood breed fine specimens of humanity, eh?" Then his affable manner turned abruptly anxious. "Might I know your eating habits?"

Begg, as Sinclair could tell, was a little taken aback by Herr Hess's intensity.

"Eating habits?"

"I ask because of lunch," Hess confided.

Begg gave every appearance of insouciance as he replied. "A plate of weisswürst and a pint or two of your marvelous beer will suit us down to the ground, old chap."

Hess frowned. "Both Alf"—he coughed, anxious to let the investigators know he was on such intimate terms with Hitler—"I mean Herr Hitler and myself are convinced vegans. We are firmly opposed to the cruel treatment of animals and understand the dangers to health involved in eating their slaughtered meat." He shuddered. "Adolf Hitler is a man of considerable feeling. He would not harm a fly, let alone another human being. I hope you don't judge us all by Berlin decadence or aggression, which is largely a foreign and alien invention, anyway."

As they talked, they strolled through the passenger foyer of the great modern aerodrome. Over a dozen pairs of steel masts held ships, or awaited vessels from all over southern and eastern Europe. The 'drome was one of Munich's very latest monuments to municipal pride.

The weather was much improved and a warm, golden sun was reflected in the silvery hulls of the airships. Through massing white clouds, rays of sunlight struck the distant outlines of Munich herself, her twisted gables and glittering spires. As they reached the exit, Begg was delighted to see Dolly waiting for them at the curbside.

Dolly was Begg's massive, supercharged Duesenberg touring car, custom-made, powered by a V-12 engine tuned to take the great automobile up to two hundred miles an hour if necessary.

Sinclair slipped discreetly into the shadows of the backseats, leaving Hess to sit next to Begg as the detective engaged the engine and gears. With a mighty purring roar, they were soon on their way to Munich, following Hess's precise directions. In what seemed a quixotic request, Begg asked Hess to give him a quick tour of the city and take them to the Nazi HQ, familiarly known as the Brown House, before lunch. Knowing the ways of English detectives to be mysterious and circuitous, Hess did not hesitate in obeying.

Sinclair had visited the city several times and had an affection for it, but Begg knew Berlin much better. He remarked on Munich's pleasant architecture, the broad tree-lined avenues and parks, her well-appointed public galleries and museums, her extraordinary Grimmelshausen Museum, which warned of the horrors of war, the little landing fields, right on the edge of the city, where the autogyro buses came and went.

Hess had lived here for much of his life. He pointed out the various sights. Munich was a busy provincial metropolis with an excellent public transport system, chiefly trams and buses, though increasingly the autogyro companies were taking business from the main lines. As her many churches indicated, she was predominantly Catholic by religion. Her almost Italian embrace of modernity was striking, especially since so much of her new architecture was in the vein of Gaudi and the Viennese moderns. The Nazis, Hess informed them primly, would tear down all decadent architecture and replace it with impressive classical designs. Meanwhile the old Bavarian capital had the baroque quaintness usually associated with German provinces, tributes to the taste and vision of her princes and governors.

Dolly was soon purring through the old quarter of the city, making a circuit of the huge, covered market, then driving along another avenue, sparsely occupied by large mansions and official buildings, some flying the flags of other nations. Here Hess gave the order to stop. They had arrived at the Brown House, the N.S.D.A.P. headquarters. The respectable surroundings made one think twice about the party's violent image. The huge silk Nazi "hooked cross" banners were very striking as they stirred in the faint, westerly breeze.

Once at the Brown House, Hess's status was confirmed. Smartly uniformed SA men in their odd ski-cap headgear and brown uniforms sprang to open the doors of the car, and the three occupants were greeted with a barrage of "Heil Hitlers" and lifted arms, as they entered the busy vestibule decorated in the very latest "Folkic" style. Bustling as it was, the place had a mournful, depressed quality, as if everyone in it grieved for their leader's loss and feared for his safety in the face of slander and scandal.

Now Hess became a different man. He took on the authority and manner of a high-ranking officer as he led the two Englishmen through the simple, quasi-rustic foyer and up the low, wide staircase.

"This is the Führer's own office."

Hess guided them into a large, triangular room dominated by a portrait of Hitler himself, his hands in Napoleonic pose, his stern, cool eyes fixed on the problems of the Nation and those who would threaten Germany's security again. Outside there appeared to be a large amount of building work going on.

"We are making a barracks for the SA boys," explained Hess. "This place, of course, is a natural target for Sozie attack." Sozie was the slang for Socialist, just as Nazi was slang for National Socialist. The street clashes between the two groups had become endemic and notorious throughout Germany.

"I'd be obliged, Herr Hess," said Begg, "if you wouldn't mind telling us again exactly what you know about the circumstances surrounding the discovery of poor Fräulein Raubal's body. I know you were the first party member on the scene."

"Naturally the Winters called me first," agreed Hess. His black, bushy eyebrows twitched as if with a life of their own. He pulled at his earlobes and, grinding his teeth, stared into a middle distance where he seemed to be looking at a cinema screen presenting the events he described.

"Geli is Alf's ward, you know. His niece. His half sister's child. When he moved into his new apartment in Prinzregensburgstrasse he needed someone to look after the place, so he invited his sister to come and be his housekeeper. He insisted she bring her daughter Geli, too. He was, I will admit, a little infatuated, but more in the way a childless man might yearn for a daughter. He doted on the girl. He bought her whatever she wanted. He paid for drama lessons. Singing lessons. Dancing lessons. He took her with him everywhere he went."

"Even to political meetings?" asked Begg, making a note.

"Even to those. His career had begun to prosper. The SA were glad to see him with a girl from time to time. He paid for the singing lessons, because she had a talent for operetta, which Adolf loves. Of course there were more puritanical party comrades, such as Heinrich Himmler, who disapproved of this relationship. Himmler felt it detracted from Hitler's seriousness, and it made him vulnerable to the anti-Nazi press. There were vile rumors, of course, but those are always attached to successful politicans.

"Geli caused the odd scene in public, and Alf seemed unable to control her. Alf knew how Himmler felt, but he ignored him. Geli fired his political engine, he told Himmler. Without Geli he could not give the speeches which swayed the crowds.

"But it was not only Himmler who noticed," Hess said, "how much less the rich ladies would give to party funds when they saw their beloved Herr Hitler, who on other occasions had laid his head in their laps, with his niece. They had influence over their husbands. And the industrialists Adolf wanted to win over were not too sure about a man who took his niece everywhere he went.

"I know there were strong arguments in this very room. Once Adolf became so incensed by what he said was interference in his private life that he fell to the floor and began to tear at the carpet with his teeth. He can be very wearing sometimes. That is why few of us ever wish to upset him. . . ."

"The carpet?" declared Sinclair. "With his teeth?"

"I wasn't there on that occasion, but Röhm, Strasser, and Doctor Göbbels were, as I recall."

"You have told us about Captain Röhm, but have not explained about Herr Strasser and Doctor Göbbels."

"Personally, I prefer Röhm, for all his predilections. He is at least an honest soldier and as loyal to Hitler as I am. Gregor Strasser is the leader of our party in the Reichstag. He's a bit of a left-winger. A very distinguished man, but rather at odds with Adolf over the direction of the party. Strasser is more socialist than nationalist. Doctor Göbbels is the intellectual of the party. A frail little man with a club-foot. He represents what I call 'the Berlin faction'—those who have more recently attached themselves to our party's destiny."

"And would any of these think the death of Geli Raubal would benefit Herr Hitler and the party?" Begg enquired, staring out at the construction in what had once been a rather pretty garden.

"Oh, all of them would probably say something like it." Hess nodded absently, looking about the room, its sparse furniture, rather as if he saw it for the first time. "But saying and doing are very different things. I can't see Röhm, who thought Geli a bit of a doxy, or Strasser, who was the last one to want scandal, or Göbbels, who is our chief propagandist, threatening either Hitler's career or the party's prospects by killing Geli. And Captain Göring has no interest in such things. Göbbels might have made her an offer she couldn't refuse. Röhm might have frightened her away. Strasser would have told her to keep her nose clean and not embarrass the Führer."

"And this Herr Himmler?"

"He's a cold fish. He has Hitler's ear. He has wheedled his way into the Führer's confidences in recent years. I thought he might have been behind that sniper's assassination attempt. They tried to kill me, you know. But I heard the rifle shot in time and flung myself flat. I still live in fear in case the sniper should try again—"

"You were telling us about Herr Himmler."

"Head of Hitler's personal bodyguard. Big rival of Röhm, who runs the SA, our storm troopers. He did hate the relationship. But he, too, knows that the party is on the very brink of sweeping the country. As far as I know he is in Berlin. Why would he jeopardize his own career? You see, there are no real suspects within the party. This is the work of communists and their backers. Our self-interest would not be served by scandal."

"True," agreed Begg. "So you believe there was perhaps a political motive for her death. And what about a personal one?"

"You will have to ask others about that." Hess was suddenly very subdued.

Under Begg's clever prompting, Hess revealed all he knew of the Geli Raubal murder case.

Hitler was becoming increasingly jealous of Geli, who grew steadily bored with his prolonged absences from the flat. His political career took him farther and farther from Munich for longer periods. She, being a young, spirited woman, had wanted more gaiety in her life and eventually had asked her uncle Alf if he would pay for her to go to Vienna, where she had more friends and where she could get far better voice lessons than in Munich.

Hitler had objected to this. He had not wanted her to go to Vienna. He had not wanted her to leave their flat. He was becoming even more suspicious of her. He threatened and wheedled, and it seemed she calmed down. Then, on the morning he was due to leave for an important speaking tour, there was another row. "It was to involve some crucial secret meetings, for there are those in our party who do not believe Alf should be courting the rich at all. Yet without them, we are nothing." Hess paused, his voice taking on an increasingly retrospective tone.

"That same morning, Geli had found one of her pet canaries dead on the floor of its cage. She had become hysterical. She threatened Hitler. She said that if he did not let her go to Vienna she would kill herself. Then she threatened to spill the beans about 'everything.'"

"Everything?" Begg lifted an eyebrow.

Hess did not know what "everything" was, he said. But Sinclair recognized Begg's sudden alertness.

"Well, Hitler's car was to call for him early that morning, after breakfast. He could not cancel his engagements. But Geli demanded that he either stay with her or let her go to Vienna. Again Hitler refused. Even as he got into the car, Geli appeared on the balcony above. 'So you won't let me go to Vienna?' she had shouted.

"Hitler's reply had been a terse 'No.' Then the automobile had driven away."

Hours later Hitler was meeting his new backers. He stayed overnight at the Deutscherhof in Nuremberg. There were many witnesses. At eight-thirty the next morning, the housekeeper, Annie Winter, arrived at Prinzregensburgstrasse to begin work. The flat was silent. Frau Winter knocked several times, without getting a response.

Eventually she sent for her butler husband, to force it. They found Geli.

"She appeared to have shot herself. Beside her lay the dead canary, spattered with her blood. She was shot in the heart."

Hitler's Walther 9.5 mm automatic pistol lay near her hand. She had been dead for some hours. Hess had been called. Eventually, he called the police.

"You have to be certain who you call, Sir Seaton. The Munich police have a decided anti-Nazi bias and would love to use something like this against the Führer."

The police had soon decided Fräulein Raubal could not easily have shot herself at that angle and that she had probably been murdered. Nobody believed it was suicide.

"And it could not have been Alf, Sir Seaton, however it seems. Alf was miles away, in Nuremberg, when the crime occurred. You can see how easy it will be, perhaps, to prove he paid someone to kill her. But he loved Geli, Sir Seaton. He lived for her. He is too gentle. Too idealistic. I fear that if the case isn't cleared up rapidly, by one such as yourself, it will mean the end of Alf's career and, because he is our most important spokesman, the dissolution of the Nazi Party. Please stop this from happening, Sir Seaton. Please say you will help us!"

Begg's features were hidden from Hess and the astonished Sinclair as he spoke reassuringly.

"Of course I will, Mr. Hess. It's not the sort of problem one solves every day. And we do love a challenge—don't we, Taffy?"

The pathologist was taken aback. "If you say so, old boy."

Sometimes even Taffy Sinclair found his friend's game very hard to follow.

CHAPTER THREE
LEADING THE MASTER RACE

Begg's first stop after lunch was to the murder scene itself. Prinzregensburgstrasse was the smart area where "Führer" Hitler now lived. On the way, Hess explained how the Winters had called him and he in turn had tried to telephone Hitler in Nuremberg. But

Hitler had already left Nuremberg and was traveling to his next appointment. Apparently he was singing snatches of song, entertaining the other occupants of the car with jokes, impressions of people they had just met.

"Many people, Sir Seaton, have no idea what a marvelous entertainer Alf is. He used to keep us in fits of laughter on those long tours. He could impersonate anyone. Pompous innkeepers, party officials, intense old maids, famous politicians! He could have gone onstage as a comedian if he had not been chosen to lead his people."

Hess recollected the question. "Well, the hotel sent a boy after Herr Hitler's car, and when he got the message Alf almost collapsed. Everyone says it was completely unexpected. Indeed the first words from his lips, I understand, were 'Who has done this?' He had the car turned, his appointments canceled, telephoned me the first chance he got, and came back at once to Munich. It was my suggestion I next call the Munich Police Headquarters and he assented. And then I sent you a telegram. My staff arranged your tickets and so on."

"The police weren't suspicious concerning the time you waited before telephoning them?"

"I explained that I myself had been in a state of some shock after seeing poor Geli's body." He paused and then looked with a strange, new innocence into Begg's face. "I know I am a suspect, Sir Seaton, but I seek peace and security and pride from the Nazi Party, not violence. This is what most of us in Germany want. The thought of killing a mouse makes me sick. The thought of killing some poor, foolish creature who had been flattered and cajoled into waters well above her natural depth, that is abominable. You must not judge us all by those who 'goose-step' through the main streets of our towns with banners and bludgeons. Yet remember those poor lads were boys when they went to war, and what they saw in the trenches and learned to do in the trenches never left them, especially when they found they had no jobs. . . ."

Rudolf Hess continued this apologia all the way to the flat in Prinzregensburgstrasse, an imposing modern classical building built on the corner of a broad, quiet avenue. Hitler's flat was on the second floor. It was light, airy, and luxurious in a subdued, up-to-date way. Doors led in several directions from the main vestibule, suggesting servants' quarters and guest apartments. Certainly there was every way in which Hitler, his half sister, and niece could live together in such a flat very respectably indeed.

Minutes later, Sir Seaton was interviewing Herr and Frau Winter themselves. The couple had found Geli on the carpet in her bedroom, only partially dressed, as if she had been disturbed at her toilet.

The Winters were clearly shaken by what had happened. At that moment Frau Winter resembled a bewildered mole, in her gray cardigan, gray blouse, skirt, and stockings. This dour appearance was not, Begg guessed, natural to her. Herr Winter's features, on the other hand, seemed habitually surly, yet his voice was agreeable enough. Neither man nor woman was of very high intelligence. They both confirmed, under Begg's questioning, that Hitler and his niece had quarreled increasingly as his political career made demands on his time. But the party needed Hitler.

"Even I have fallen under his oratorical spell," said Winter seriously. "It is almost impossible to escape his charm when he wants something from you. Crowds love him. Without him the party would be lost. But as a result, he spent even less time with Geli. You couldn't really blame her. She grew restless; he grew jealous."

"He had plenty to be jealous about, too," Frau Winter interjected with an angry twitter. "She was not a good girl, Sir Seaton."

Herr Winter reluctantly conceded. "I think she had plenty of company when Herr Hitler was gone. In particular that tall, blond SS man who wanted her to run off to Vienna with him . . . Himmler's chap."

"You saw them?" Begg demanded.

"Just as we saw the whips and the blood after one of Herr Hitler's 'sessions,'" she said primly.

"Whips?" asked a startled Begg. "Blood?"

Herr Winter interrupted hastily, too late to silence his wife. "It was Herr Hitler's way of relaxing. He carries heavy responsibilities. It is often the way with important men, not so? We are people of the world here. We all know what goes on in Berlin."

Having verified with the Winters the events of the recent past, Sir Seaton Begg thanked them gravely and made to leave. Taffy Sinclair in particular seemed glad of some fresh air.

Back in the Duesenberg, Begg asked a further question of Hess.

"Tell me, old boy, did Herr Hitler ever have his niece watched? And was he ever blackmailed?"

"Aha! I knew I had approached the right detective. You realized. Unfortunately, since the blackmail, he's grown suspicious of everyone. Yes, he did have a couple of SA men in plainclothes keeping an eye on her, but they were incompetent. Himmler wanted to use SS people. He thinks they're more efficient. So yes, he watched her, but you can't really blame him for that."

"Blackmail?" said Sinclair from the shadows in the back, unable to contain himself. "Your leader was being blackmailed?"

"A couple of years ago. That's not what the blackmailer called it, of course, Herr Sinclair. But Putzi, Hitler's foreign-press secretary, handled the details of that. Putzi's half-American, a great source of vitality, you know. We all love him. Only his jokes and piano playing can cheer Alf up when he's really depressed. . . ."

Begg had begun to realize Hess had to be kept on course or he would wander off down all kinds of twists and turns in the story. He slowed the car behind a stopping tram, then indicated that he was going to pass. Slowly he increased pressure on the accelerator. "Putzi?"

"A nickname, naturally. Putzi Hanfstaengl was at Harvard. He's an art expert. Has a gallery in Munich. His firm publishes the official engraved portraits of Hitler, Strasser, Röhm, Göring, myself, and the other eminent Nazis. Anyway, Putzi took the money to the blackmailer—we weren't rich in those days and it was hard to scrape together—and got the material back. Probably nothing especially bad. But, of course, Alf became much less trusting after that."

"Does Herr Hanfstaengl usually enjoy a drink at the Hotel Bavaria?"

Hess's enormous eyebrows almost met his hairline.

"Mein Gott, Sir Seaton! You are indeed the genius they say you are. That is remarkable deduction. Putzi's natural American vitality has been drained, it seems, by recent events. He has never really been at ease since we began to gain real power. A little bit of a playboy, I suppose, but a good fellow and a loyal friend."

After that, Begg asked no more questions. He darted Sinclair a vindicated glance, for he had gotten that information from one of his much-loved "gossip columns." He told Hess he would like to drive around and think the case through for a while. Hess showed some impatience, but his admiration for the English detective soon reminded him of his manners. Heels were clicked as Hess was dropped off at the Brown House. Then Begg had touched the feather-light wheel of the superb roadster and turned her back toward central Munich.

CHAPTER FOUR

FEAR AND TREMBLING

As usual, Sinclair was amazed at Begg's extraordinary retentive memory, which had drawn itself a precise map of the town and was able to thread Dolly's massive bonnet through the winding streets of old Munich as if the driver had lived there all his life.

Soon they were leaving the Duesenberg in the safekeeping of the Hotel Bavaria's garage and strolling into the plush and brass of the old-fashioned main bar. Clearly the Bavaria was more popular with those who preferred to be in bed with a good book by eight PM. The bar was large, but sparsely occupied, save for one middle-aged couple dancing to the strains of Franz Lehar played by an ancient orchestral ensemble half-hidden by palms and curtains on the distant dais. At a shadowed table two smart young men upon second glance turned out to be smart young women. Against the walls leaned a couple of sleepy-eyed old waiters and at the bar sat two young couples from the local "cocktail set" who had lost their way to the latest jazz party. Slumped alone, as far away from the couples as possible, wearing a great, bulky English tweed overcoat, sat a giant of a man nursing a drink which seemed tiny in his monstrous hands.

With his huge, pale head and irregular features, an expression of solemn gloom on his long face, the lone drinker looked almost comical. He glanced up in some curiosity as they entered. Begg wasted no time in introducing himself and his colleague. "You are Herr Hitler's foreign-press secretary, I understand. Too often in Berlin, these days, I suppose. We've been hired to prove your boss's innocence."

Herr "Putzi" Hanfstaengl did not seem greatly surprised that

Begg knew his name. He lifted his hand in a salute before returning it to the glass. "You guys from the *Times,* are you?" He spoke in English with an educated American accent. He was clearly drunk. "I told your colleagues—when the *Times* turns up, that'll be a sign this is actually an international story." He let out an enormous sigh and drew himself to his full six and a half feet.

"You've been trying to keep all this speculation out of the papers, I suppose."

"What do you think, sport?" Hanfstaengl tossed back his drink and snapped his fingers for a refill. "It's not doing anyone much good, least of all Alf himself. He's gone under the bed, as we say, and won't come out. And I'm talking too much. Have a schnapps!" Again he snapped for the waiter, who disappeared through a door and a little later appeared behind the bar to serve them. Begg and Sinclair modified their orders to beers, but Hanfstaengl hardly noticed.

"We're not from the newspapers," Begg told him before the drinks arrived. "We're private detectives employed by Herr Hess. Anything you tell us we will use in the processes of justice."

The lumbering half-American seemed relieved to hear this. He loosened his big coat and made himself more comfortable. As he listened to the tunes of Strauss and Lehar, he relaxed. "This isn't for publication. I have your word on it?"

"Our word as English gentlemen," said Begg.

For a while "Putzi" chatted about the old days of the Nazi Party when there were only a few of them, when Hitler had been released from prison a hero, the author of *Mein Kampf,* which was published here in Munich by Max Amman. "We have a concession on pictures of the Nazi hierarchy and Amman publishes what they write. It's pretty much our only business. This scandal could wreck us." Since the party's success in elections, sales had climbed. *Mein Kampf* was now a best-seller and it was money from royalties, Hanfstaengl insisted, not from secret financiers, which was paying for the Mercedes and the place in Prinzregensburgstrasse. He seemed to be answering questions neither Begg nor Sinclair had asked. And when Sir Seaton threw the big query at him, he was rather surprised, glad that he did not have to hide something from the detective. It was dawning on him at last who Begg and Sinclair were.

"You really are the ace sleuths they say you are," he said. "I know those Sexton Blake things are heavily sensationalized, but it's surprising how like him you are. Do you remember *The Affair of the Jade Skull?*"

Blake was, of course, the name said to disguise the identity of Sir Seaton Begg in a long series of stories written for *The Union Jack, The Sexton Blake Library,* and other popular British publications known as tuppenny skinnies and four-penny fats.

"I'm surprised they're read at all beyond the London gutters," said Begg, who made a point of never reading the "bloods." "Speaking of which—what about that material itself? I've seen some of it, of course. The stuff Hitler was being blackmailed with? Weren't you the middleman on that?"

Only Taffy Sinclair knew that his friend had just told a small, deliberate lie.

"What earthly need is there for you to know more? If you've seen how dreadful that stuff is—?" Hanfstaengl's brow cleared. "Oh, I get it. You have to eliminate suspects. You're looking for an alibi." He sipped his drink. "Well, I, too, dealt through a middleman. An SA sergeant who had got himself mixed up in something he didn't like. Called himself Braun, I think. Nobody ever proved it, but he pretty much confirmed who the blackmailer was and nobody was surprised. It was that crazy old Heironymite. Stempfle. I'm not sure how a member of an order of hermits, like Father Stempfle, can spend quite so much time drinking in the seedier Munich beer halls, but there you are. He has a certain following, of course. Writer and editor, I think. He worked for Amman once."

"The publisher?"

"Do you know him? Funny chap. Never really took to him. He's putting Hitler up at the moment. My view is that Amman could be cheating Hitler of his royalties. What if he's covering his tracks? Could Geli have found something out, do you think?"

"You mean she knew too much?"

"Well," said Hanfstaengl, glancing up at the big clock over the bar, "she wasn't exactly an innocent, was she? Those letters! Foul. But his pictures were worse. It was my own fault. I was curious. I wish I'd never looked." He let out a great sigh. "Party funds paid the blackmailer, you know. The stuff was impossibly disgusting. I said I'd burn it—but he—Alf—wanted it back."

The orchestra had begun to play a polka. The couple on the dance floor were having difficulty keeping time. Begg studied the musicians for any sign of cynicism but found none.

Hanfstaengl's tongue, never very tight at the best of times, it seemed, was becoming looser by the moment. "After that, things were never the same. Hitler changed. Everything turned a little sour. You want to ask crazy old Stempfle about it. I'm still convinced only he could have had the inside knowledge. . . ."

"But where could I find this hermit?"

"Well, there's a chance he'll be at home in his cottage. It's out in the Munich woods there." He jabbed his hand toward the door. "Couple of miles or so. Do you have a map?"

Sinclair produced one and Hanfstaengl plotted their course for them. "I'd go with you myself, but I'm a bit vulnerable at the moment. I think someone's already had a potshot at me with a rifle. Be a bit careful, sport. There are lots of homeless people in the woods these days. They could spell danger for a stranger. Even some of our locals have been held up at gunpoint and robbed."

Begg shook hands with Hanfstaengl and said that he was much obliged. "One last question, Herr Hanfstaengl." He hesitated.

"Fire away," said "Putzi."

"Who do you think killed Geli Raubal?"

Hanfstaengl looked down.

"You have an idea, I know," said Begg.

Hanfstaengl turned back, offering Begg a cigarette from his case, which Begg refused. "Killed that poor little neurotic girl? Almost anyone but Hitler."

"But you have an idea, I know."

Hanfstaengl drained his glass. "Well, she was seeing this SS guy. . . ."

"Name?"

"Never heard one, but I think they planned to go to Vienna together. Hitler knew all about it, of course. Or at least he guessed what he didn't know."

"And had her killed?"

Hanfstaengl snorted sardonically. "Oh, no. He doesn't have the guts." His face had turned a terrible greenish white.

"Who does—?" Begg asked, but Hanfstaengl was already heading from the room, begging his pardon, acting like a man whose food had disagreed with him.

"Poor fellow," murmured Begg, "I don't think he has a taste for the poison or the antidote. . . ."

CHAPTER FIVE
THE POLITICS OF EXCLUSION

An hour or so later, Taffy Sinclair was shining the hand-torch down onto their map, trying to work out what Hanfstaengl had shown them. All around them in the woods were the camps of people who had been ruined by Germany's recent economic troubles. While Munich herself seemed wealthy enough, the homeless had been pushed to the outlying suburbs and woodlands, to fend for themselves as best they could. The detectives saw fires burning and shadows flitting around them, but the forest people were too wary to reveal themselves and would not respond when Begg or Sinclair called out to them.

"I suppose it's fair enough that a follower of Saint Heironymous the Hermit makes himself hard to find," declared Sinclair, "but I think this place was less populated and with fewer caves when—aha!" His torchlight had fallen on the penciled mark. "Just up this road and stop. Should be a cottage here."

The car's brilliant headlamps made day of night, picking up the building ahead as if lit for the cinema, with great, elongated black shadows spreading away through the moonlit forest. An ancient, thatched, much-buttressed cottage was revealed. The place had two main chimneys, three downstairs windows and three up, including the dormer, which had its own chimney. The whole place leaned and declined in a dozen different directions, so that even the straw resembled a series of dirty, ill-fitting wigs.

"This has got to be it." Noting shadows moving in the nearby trees, Sir Seaton climbed from the car and walked across the weed-grown path to the old door of Gothic oak and black iron, hammering on it heavily and calling out in his most authoritative tone: "Open up! Metatemporal detectives! Come along, Father Stempfle, sir! Let us in."

A grinding of locks and rattling chains confirmed Sir Seaton's inspired guess. A face that looked as if it had been folded, stretched, and refolded many times regarded them in the light of the lamp it held over the chink in the door, still latched by a massive row of steel links.

"Open up, sir."

Seeing their faces seemed to weaken the old man's resolve, for another bolt turned and the door creaked slowly open.

Begg followed Stempfle into the hermit's horrible candlelit den, which stank of mold, old food, woodsmoke, and dust. Everywhere were piles of books, manuscripts, scrolls. There was no doubt the man was a scholar, but whether he followed God or the Devil was hard to determine. In a small grate, a sparse, damp fire emitted a little heat.

"You're a close friend of Adolf Hitler, I gather, Father?" Begg hardly gave the unshaven old man in the filthy cassock a chance to catch his breath.

Father Stempfle stuttered. "I wouldn't say that. I have very little to do with him, these days."

"You helped him write his book—*Mein Kampf*, is it?"

Now Begg's long hours of reading and study were coming to his aid as usual. Sinclair remembered how impressed he so often was with his friend's ability to put together a jigsaw with pieces from so many apparently disparate sources.

Father Stempfle began to turn scarlet. He fumed. In his mephitic cassock and sandals, he stamped about his paper-strewn study until it seemed the unevenly stacked piles of books would fall and bury them all alive. "Helped him, my good sir? Helped that illiterate little trench terrier, that scum of Vienna's pervert's quarter? Helped him? I wrote most of it. The manuscript was unreadable until his publisher asked me to work on it. Ask Max Amman. He'll confirm everything. He and Hitler fell out over it. Or perhaps he has now been persuaded to lie by Röhm and his apes. My arguments are the purest and the best. You can tell them because I offer a much more sophisticated analysis of the Jewish problem. Hitler's contribution was a whine of self-pity. For years Amman didn't publicize the book widely enough. Now, of course, it's selling very well. And do I get a pfennig in royalties?" The squalid old monk shuffled to a stop, his face breaking into something which might have been a grin. "Of course, it'll sell even better once they know about the murder. . . ."

Begg had no stomach for this. He drew a large handkerchief from his pocket and blew his nose. "You think Hitler killed her?"

"Nobody seems to think he's up to it," murmured Sinclair. "Not a strong man, physically at least. A pacifist, we were learning today . . ."

Stempfle crushed old parchment in his hands as he moved toward the fire. Something had made him feel the cold. "He says he hates violence. But you should see how cruelly he treats that dog of his. Wulf? He calls it such a name so that he can demonstrate his own masculinity the better. I think he is capable of any violence."

Sinclair stepped forward. "What about those pictures—those letters—the blackmail attempt?"

"Oh, he's calling it blackmail now, is he? I simply wanted fair reimbursement for the work I'd done. . . ." Stempfle glowered into the fire, which seemed to flicker in sympathy.

"If you still have some of that stuff, I could see that it got into the appropriate hands. Would it not strengthen the case against Hitler?"

Stempfle snorted. The sound was almost gleeful. "It would top and tail him nicely, true. . . ."

"That material is here?"

Stempfle grew cunning. "The originals are elsewhere, in safekeeping. Still, I don't mind showing you the copies."

"I am prepared to pay one hundred pounds for the privilege," declared Sir Seaton.

At this the old man moved with slightly greater alacrity, ascending a ladder, moving a picture, rattling a combination, then going through the whole process backward again. When he came down, he had an envelope in his hands. Begg paid him in the four crisp twenty-five-pound notes he held ready, and Sinclair accepted the envelope, casually drawing out the first photograph and then blanching at what he saw. He returned the photograph to the envelope and covered his mouth. "Great Jehovah, Begg! I had no idea! Why would any woman involve herself in this? Or any man demand it?" Now he knew why Angela Raubal could not help being a disturbed young woman and why Hanfstaengl had left the bar so swiftly.

Stempfle's crooked body shook with glee. "Not how Adolf might wish to be remembered, eh? They would make excellent illustrations for certain works of the Marquis de Sade, no? I think I've been very modest in my request for my share of the royalties. Since I suspect you are already representing him, you can tell him that the originals of these are much more expensive!"

"I've yet to become a blackmailer's runner, Father Stempfle," Begg protested mildly. "Good night to you."

He ducked beneath the warped lintel and began to make for his car, Sinclair slightly ahead of him. Only then did the two men realize that someone was beside their car, trying to force the lock. With a roar of rage Sinclair seized and grappled with the ill-smelling thieves. But there were at least a dozen of them. Others slipped out of the shadows, clubs and fists flailing as they came to their companions' assistance.

Begg was skilled in most forms of unarmed combat.

"Hold them for me for a moment, old man!" He carefully removed his hat and then weighed in.

Several of the assailants soon lay on the ground. The others began to regroup, still a threat.

Then, suddenly, Begg heard a sharp thud against the tree nearest his head and the distinctive crack of a high-powered Mauser rifle. Almost immediately, as if familiar with the sound, the vagrants melted back into the trees. Sinclair paused, ready to pursue them, but with a smile Begg retrieved his hat and hurried his friend into the car. "No one else intends us any harm, Taffy. But it might be wise to keep moving."

Within the wholesome comfort of the great automobile, Sinclair was still more upset by the photographs than afraid of the gunshot. He continued to vent his disgust. "How could he make her—? I mean—?"

"Not a position any sane creature would volunteer for," Begg agreed. He began to reverse the car back down the short drive. "I think it's time we paid a call on the local cop shop, don't you?"

CHAPTER SIX
THE FEDERAL AGENT

As it happened, there was no need to visit the police station. Arriving back at their hotel's foyer and collecting their keys, they were immediately confronted by an extraordinarily beautiful young woman who rose from a couch and came toward them smiling. Her full red lips and dark red hair worn in a fashionable wave were complemented by her green evening dress as she stretched a gloved hand toward Sir Seaton.

He bent to kiss it. Of course they had immediately recognized the woman. Once a ruthless adventuress whose love affair with Begg had resulted in her decision to make herself his ally, she was now a freelancer. Unlike Begg she took retainers from any government that valued her skill.

From her reticule the woman took a small book on which was fastened a metal badge. After they had glanced at it, she returned it swiftly to its place.

"My dear Countess von Bek," exclaimed Sir Seaton, "I had no idea you were in Munich. Are you staying here?"

"Nearby, Sir Seaton. I wondered if you had seen my cousin lately?" This was prearranged code. Countess Rose von Bek wanted to speak urgently and privately. Begg immediately led them into the deserted sitting room, ordered some tea, and closed the doors.

Once they were settled and the tea served, Sir Seaton relaxed. "So, my dear Rose, we appear to be working on the same case? Can you say who your client is?"

The adventuress responded with her usual charm. "I have made no more a secret of it than have you, Seaton. The German Federal Government Special Political Service. They sent me down from Berlin to give support to the local cops—the ones who don't actually believe Herr Hitler to be the next world savior and that Jews are damned to hell for not accepting the Messiah. So far I've met a good number of decent cops and some very clever newspapermen."

"So we find ourselves on different sides in this case. I take it, therefore, you know who killed Geli Raubal?"

She took an ironic sip from her Dresden cup. "We've been working on the broader political associations."

"But surely everything we need to know hinges on the circumstances and solution of this case?" Taffy Sinclair chipped in.

"No doubt, Mr. Sinclair. But the government's priorities aren't always our own." She spoke softly, anxious not to offend him. "I agree it is possible to argue that Fräulein Raubal's death is emblematic, if not symptomatic, of her times, but at the moment we're worrying that the National Socialists have a sizable representation in Parliament. And a large amount of armed support. We are thinking 'civil war' here. *Cherchez la femme* is not a game we often play in my section."

Taffy mumbled some polite apology and said he thought it was time he turned in, but Begg insisted he stay. "I think I'm going to need your help tonight, old man."

"Tonight?"

"Afraid so."

Sinclair rather reluctantly poured himself a fresh cup of Earl Grey.

"Was the corpse still in the apartment when you arrived on the scene?" Begg asked his old paramour.

"Hinkel of the Taggeblat called us. He's our best man down here. So I caught the express from Berlin and was here in time to have a look at the body."

"You're certain she was murdered? How? Did some expert sniper shoot her through the window?"

Rose was certain. "Nothing so complicated. Someone's made a clumsy attempt to make it look as if she'd shot herself through the heart. Hitler's gun—easy accessibility. Dead canary nearby—she'd been carrying it around all day—no doubt adding to the impression that she was suicidal. But the angle of entry was wrong. Someone shot her, Seaton, while she was lying on the rug—probably during an amorous moment. Half-undressed. Evidently an intimate. And Hitler was certainly an intimate. . . .

"You've seen these pictures?" He handed her the envelope.

"No wonder the poor girl was confused." Even the countess winced at what she saw. "They might have tried to push her toward suicide but she wouldn't fall. Eventually someone shot her at close range, then put the gun in her hand so it seemed suicide. Only there were too many clues to the contrary."

"Any chance of taking a look at the corpse?" Taffy's dry, decisive tone was unexpected.

"Engaging your gears at last, are we, Taffy?" said Begg jumping to his feet. "Come on, Countess. Get us to the morgue, posthaste!"

Responding with almost gleeful alacrity, Countess von Bek allowed Sinclair to open the door for her. Dolly was still outside, so within moments the investigators were on their way to the Munich police headquarters.

The countess had already established her authority there. She led the way directly through the building to a door marked "Inspector Hoffmann." The round, red-faced inspector assured them that he knew them all by reputation and had the greatest respect for their skills. He was grateful, he said, for their cooperation.

"However," said the bluff Bavarian when they were all seated, "I ought to tell you that I'm convinced Hitler killed her during quite a nasty fight. Fortunately for your client, Sir Seaton, he has the best possible alibi—with dozens of witnesses to show he could not possibly have committed the murder. Hess? What do you think? Was it Hess who contacted you, Sir Seaton?"

They all agreed Hess was an unlikely suspect. Indeed, not one of the party hierarchy had an evident motive. All had perfect alibis. A hired killer? Begg put the notion to Hoffmann, who remained convinced that Hitler was the murderer. Another lover? Vaguely mysterious figures had been reported as coming and going, but Geli, of course, had not advertised them. "Coffee?" Hoffmann touched an electric bell.

After coffee, Hoffman led them down to the morgue, a clean, tiled, up-to-date department with refrigerated cabinets, dissecting tables, and the latest in analytical instruments. Taffy was impressed, unable to hold back his praise for the splendid facilities. "I can't tell you how old-fashioned Scotland Yard looks in comparison. You can't beat the Germans at this sort of thing."

Herr Hoffman was visibly flattered.

"Practical science and sublime art," murmured Taffy.

Inspector Hoffmann rather proudly crossed the mortuary. "Wait until you see this, my friend." He went to a bank of switches, each with a number. He flipped a toggle and then, magically, one of the drawers began to open!

"The wonders of 'electronics'!" cried Begg. Then he moved quickly toward the projecting steel box, where he knew he would find the mortal remains of Hitler's mistress.

Begg's expression changed to one of deep pity as he studied the contents. Even Sinclair stood back, paying some sort of respect to the corpse. Begg touched the skin, inspected the wound, and then, frowning, bent as if to kiss the frozen lips.

A shocked word froze on Sinclair's tongue as Begg straightened up, his nose wrinkling almost in disgust. "See what you think, Taffy."

After Sinclair had inspected the corpse, Hoffmann turned the switch to send the temporary coffin back into its gleaming, stainless-steel housing.

"I know we're on opposite sides in this, Sir Seaton," Hoffman said, "but I have to insist the obvious suspect is the masochist. Herr Hitler. Hired killers? Communists? Mysterious lovers? How could we find them? The Winters noted only one lover but hinted at many others. They would not be on our side in court. I suppose I shouldn't be saying this. But I know your analytical powers, Sir Seaton. And your thirst for justice."

"And you know something of the science of psychiatry?" chimed in Taffy.

"Of course, I first studied in Vienna. To me this Hitler matter seems a classic case of the father figure and the bored young protégée. The father becomes obsessively possessive. The more he grows like that, the more she seeks to break free in the only way she knows— affairs of the heart. One after another. The father, unable to watch her hourly, pretends it isn't happening. The daughter grows bolder. No one can ignore what is going on. Her affairs become common gossip. Eventually his ego can be suppressed no longer. . . ." He turned to Begg. "You saw the marks on her face and shoulders?"

"Indeed I did," said the detective.

"He had beaten the poor little thing black and blue!" Sinclair barely controlled his anger. "They were fighting, as you say, and brought Hitler's gun into play. Next thing, 'Bang,' and the girl's dead on the carpet."

"Lovers' quarrel?" said Rose von Bek. "Maybe. But I prefer to believe the girl knows too much about our suspect's sex life as well as political plans. Election coming up. She tries blackmail. Second time it's happened. Could she have been behind the first attempt? He snaps." She spread her hands, palms out. "Open and shut." She made fists. "This isn't the first time Herr Adolf Hitler has been involved in some sadistic business or other, I take it."

Hoffmann nodded. "But, if it could be proven, Hitler's enemies would be dancing in the streets. His chances of wheedling any more concessions from Hindenburg would disappear at once. Hindenburg already considers him a parvenu. So he has to go to great lengths to build an alibi."

Begg became uncomfortable at this. "You seem to hate Hitler," he suggested. "Yet you seem to be a conservative yourself. . . ."

"I hate Bolshevism." Hoffmann searched through a gleaming filing cabinet for the documents he needed. "But I am also a Catholic, and all the Nazis' antireligious talk, especially against the Jews, who are amongst the most law-abiding people in the nation, is too much for me to stomach. I know Hitler did this murder, but that alibi . . ."

"No way he could have come back, committed the crime, then returned to Nuremberg?" asked Sinclair.

"Too many people know him in Nuremberg. He is very popular there. They would have noticed something. Of course, he could have used another car altogether, and a disguise. I think you'll agree the bruises might have been delivered earlier than the gunshot?"

All three nodded.

"So," continued Hoffmann, "she knew too much. There was a fight. The gun. A shot. I don't say it was premeditated. Then he gets into the car and heads for Nuremberg, guessing nobody would want to disturb her until the next morning. He locked her door with his own key. No doubt he had had it made long before."

Begg smiled almost apologetically, adding: "And then she appears on the balcony. No doubt she has at last got Hitler's message.

Stemming the blood from her wounded heart she calls: 'So you won't let me go to Vienna?'"

"Pretty clear, I'd say." The countess recognized Begg's rather inappropriate black humor.

"I think Hitler beat her up. Then one of his henchmen went back and shot her. Maybe some kind of 'Murder in the Cathedral' situation? I gather that's how Mussolini learned he was responsible for his first murder. Overzealous followers. So who shot her? Röhm? He's ruthless enough and he doesn't much like women. Himmler? A cold fish, but too far away at the time. Same with Göring or Göbbels, if we assume they didn't come to Munich incognito."

"I think our people would have known about it," said the countess.

"Ours, too, most likely," confirmed Hoffmann, rubbing at his red jowls. "They have orders to keep track of who goes in and out of the Brown House."

"So we have a dozen suspects and nothing which leads to any of them." Sinclair lifted his eyebrows. "But two of you at least are convinced Hitler did it. What about you, Begg? What do you think?"

"I'm beginning to get an idea of who killed Geli Raubal, and I think I can guess why. But there is another element here." Begg frowned deeply. "I think in the morning we'll set off for Berchtesgaden, for Herr Amman's little hideaway. You, presumably, have already interviewed Hitler, Inspector Hoffmann?"

"As soon as he arrived back from Nuremberg, of course. He seemed in a state of shock, but, as stated, his alibi was airtight. Of course, you will wish to prove he didn't do it, Sir Seaton, and I admit the cards are stacked in your favor."

"Not exactly, old boy. But I agree with you that as things stand, any case against Herr Hitler couldn't be proven in a court of law."

With a courteous good night to the policeman, Begg escorted his two friends outside. In the street his car was being guarded by a uniformed constable, who saluted as soon as he recognized Countess von Bek and opened the doors for them.

It was only a short drive to the hotel and most of it was spent in silence as the three investigators thought over what they had learned.

"I suppose there's no chance of me coming down with you?" asked the countess. "Since Herr Hitler isn't my client."

"Exactly," murmured Begg, concentrating on the unfamiliar streets. "And I think even you'd agree, Rose, that client confidentiality, at least at this stage, is sacrosanct."

While Begg waited with the engine running, Sinclair saw the beautiful adventuress through the doors of her hotel. As they drove off, Sinclair said: "She wants our Mr. Hitler hanged, no doubt about it. She's afraid you'll get him off the hook. Are you sure he didn't do it?"

"I merely noted," said the detective with what seemed inappropriate cheerfulness, "that there was no evidence directly linking Hitler with the murder of his niece. Nothing to convince a jury. Don't worry, Taffy. One way or another justice will out. I have a feeling we will meet at least one more old acquaintance before this business is over."

CHAPTER SEVEN
INTERVIEW WITH A SAVIOR

Hess now took the Duesenberg's backseat. They had been driving for some hours, making for the lodge at Berchtesgaden where Adolf Hitler had retreated, apparently in deep mourning for the loss of his niece. The surrounding scenery was both dramatic and beautiful, with high hills and pinewoods, giving the air a rich, invigorating quality.

"The Führer is very sensitive. His mind is of a higher order than most. He always comes here when things go wrong. Here he collects himself and makes something of his experience." The hero worship in Hess's tone was tangible and had become extremely familiar to the two Englishmen.

Sinclair's expression, could Hess have seen it, would have revealed that he had already had far too much of this sort of talk. But Begg remained apparently affable. "Bit like Mr. Gandhi, I suppose," he suggested.

"Perhaps." Hess seemed uncomfortable with the comparison.

They turned another corner of the winding road. Ahead was a pleasant, rustic hunting chalet of the kind many Germans built for their summer season. As they drove up a tall, thickset, grim-faced man with a head so thoroughly bald it might have been shaven hurried from the door to greet them. They were, of course, already expected.

"Ah," declared Sir Seaton Begg, climbing from his car, "I take it I have the pleasure of addressing Reichstag Leader Strasser?" He put out his hand and it was firmly shaken.

Gregor Strasser's face was clouded, but he knew his manners. He spoke in a soft, well-educated voice. "We are so glad you have come to help us, Sir Seaton, though I am not sure Herr Hitler is in any real condition to speak to you." He was almost disapproving. "Hitler has gone into one of his hysterical states again. Always been one to hide under the blankets during a crisis. Hasn't been out of bed since he got here. Won't talk to me. Will hardly talk to Röhm."

"Captain Röhm is here also." Begg was clearly pleased. "Excellent. You, I presume, don't believe that Herr Hitler's guilty?"

"I speak, of course, from loyalty as well as conviction. But Herr Hitler loved his niece. He was, of course, very possessive. Even when my brother Otto expressed willingness to take her to a dance, Hitler furiously forbade it. I felt sorry for her. A bit of a bird in a gilded cage, you know. But while Hitler might speak rather fiercely in public, he rarely exposed Geli to that side of himself. It was Himmler who hated her. Even Alf knew that! But I really think she must have killed herself."

"The police evidence suggests she was killed, as you probably know." Now all three men had paused on the veranda outside the front door.

"Surely you don't believe—?" The big politician purpled.

Begg put a reassuring hand on Strasser's arm. "Fear not, old sport. I think we are going to be able to tell you something about the real killer soon. But I really must speak to your Führer, you know."

The house was decorated like a typical hunting lodge, though without the usual trophies of animal heads and skins. Hitler hated such signs of violence against animals, and his host pandered to him. Otherwise, with its hat stands and gun racks of antlers and its heavy rugs and old, comfortable furniture, it felt familiar and secure. Off the main reception room a broad staircase rose up into the darkness of a landing where, no doubt, the bedrooms were. A big fire burned in the grate. The surround was carved with bears, stags, and other game. Leaning against it was a short, stocky individual with a hideous scar marring half his rather pudgy face. He was dressed in what, apart from its brown color, resembled the regular uniform of a Wehrmacht officer, with Nazi emblems on collar, cuffs, and sleeves. Knocking back a ballon of brandy, he came forward, greeting them in a surprisingly hearty rich Bavarian accent. In private, none of these men used the Hitler salute. "Grüss Gott, Sir Seaton. Just as we're at the point of real power someone's trying to sabotage the party's chances. What can you do for us?"

"A miracle would help," said Strasser, pouring schnapps for the two men.

Captain Röhm helped himself to another large cognac.

Only Hess did not join them in a drink. He almost immediately made an excuse and disappeared upstairs, presumably to report to his old friend and leader.

Röhm was the worse for drink. He leaned easily, excessively relaxed as the habitual drunkard usually is. In spite of his hideous appearance, his tightly buttoned and belted uniform, there was an almost sensitive set to his features, a haunted look to his eyes which suggested he knew and rather approved of the arguments against almost every statement he made. His rough charm, his loyalty, his bluntness allowed him to survive. Not long after he had returned from Bolivia, affectionate Spartan letters from Röhm to a young cadet had been published in the yellow press. Yet somehow Röhm had survived the scandal, and even today made no secret of his Greek tendencies.

"I gather Herr Hitler has taken his niece's suicide to heart." Begg strolled to the gun rack and casually examined the rifles. He was interrupted by a gusty, brandy-laden laugh at once sardonic and angry.

"Suicide! Absolutely, my dear Sir Seaton! Suicide! Certainly! And I'm the bloody Virgin of Lourdes." Still chuckling, the Brown-shirt leader, considered by many to be the most powerful man in Germany, turned to throw his cigar butt into the flames.

"Perhaps if we had a word with Herr Hitler himself?"

Again the Herculean snort. "Good luck, my friend. He's a wreck. Maybe you can get more sense out of him than we can. He's a classic

Austrian. All talk and trousers and useless in a crisis. Feckless as they come. Yet he's my leader, and I live with it. I am an infantile man, at heart, and a wicked one. I offer my loyalty to whichever leader best serves my interest. I have too many weaknesses to be more than an ordinary soldier taking orders."

"You've known him a long time?" Begg asked quietly.

"I threw in with Alf, as we knew him in the trenches, soon after the Stab in the Back of the Armistice. Just as we were on the verge of winning, victory was stolen from us by Jews and Socialists at home. I didn't need to explain anything to Alf. We had a lot in common. He was a great infiltrator. Used to get in with the Commies, find out what they were up to, then report back to me. They say he won the Iron Cross for bravery, as a runner in the trenches, but that's not his talent. My guess is that he was terrified the whole time. No choice. Run the lines or be shot as a coward. He's always managed to slip away from the violence. Bad precedent, of course, in a soldier. Learns the wrong lessons." Röhm shrugged. "I doubt if he ever had to shoot anyone personally in his life. Good luck to you, my dear sir."

Strasser was sober and collected. He put down his glass half-finished. "Let me see if the Führer is ready."

As he walked up the staircase, Sinclair murmured to Begg, "Classic case of manic depression, eh?"

From the landing above, Rudolph Hess peered down. "I have very good hearing, Mr. Sinclair. We reject the debased jargon of the Jew Freud. We have perfectly good German words and good German precedents to describe our leader's state of spirit. Goethe, himself, I believe coined several . . ."

"Our Anglo-Saxon phrase would be 'barkingbarmy,' Herr Hess." Sinclair craned to look at their customer. "Would that be better?"

Hess adopted a haughty manner. "Perhaps," he said. "Herr Strasser. Would you like to bring them now?"

With a somewhat theatrical movement of his hand, Gregor Strasser motioned for the two Englishmen to follow him up the stairs.

Hitler's room was at the far end of the landing. There was only faint flickering candlelight issuing from it. When, at Hess's knock, they entered, they found a dark, ill-smelling room in which guttered a few church candles of yellow wax, placed here and there on dressing table and nightstands. The Englishmen were immediately reminded of Father Stempfle's den. The mirror of the dressing table reflected a man's naked legs, scrawny feet. The knees were bare. The man had hastily pulled on a raincoat in lieu of a dressing gown.

Adolf Hitler sat at the end of his bed. Clearly he had just allowed himself to be coaxed out of bed. He sat hunched with his hands folded in front of him and did not look up as Begg and Sinclair were introduced. Then a thin whine, like a distant turbine, started in the man's throat. "No, no, no. I can't. I can't. I can't."

Strasser stepped forward. "Just a few minutes, Alf. They want to find out who killed Geli. This means you'll be able to punish the culprit and put an end to suspicion within the party. It will save your career."

"What do I care for my career now that my angel is dead?" The soft, Austrian accent was unexpected.

When the man looked up, a ghastly intelligence in his sleepless eyes, even Begg was shocked. Hitler had the familiar red blotches on his cheekbones, the drawn lines of anxiety, a face so mad and yet so utterly without redeeming character that one might have been looking at a damned soul in Limbo. It was all the two men could do not to turn away in disgust.

Now Hitler began to mumble in a monotone. "She loved life. She loved her Uncle Alf. We had so much in common. She would never have killed herself. Somebody shot her!"

"It is a possibility we're looking into, Herr Hitler. Do you have any suspicions?"

"Naturally, I am convinced who killed her, but how can we hope to bring them to justice? They are masters of this kind of conspiracy. Oh, Geli, Geli, my perfect angel." He began to weep then, with tears streaming from those mad eyes. He spoke with sudden clarity and force. "They'll get me next, you know. They killed her with my gun. It was to make it seem as if I had done it. And where are they now, these traitors and saboteurs? Returned to Berlin and Moscow. You'll never catch them. They come and go like poisoned gas. They couldn't kill me, so they killed poor Geli. You waste your time, Englishman. Already there have been serious attempts on my life. I am doomed. I carry too great a burden on my shoulders. I am a lone voice against chaos and Bolshevik Jewry."

"Quite a responsibility!" agreed Sir Seaton, backing toward the door. "We'll take up no more of your time, Herr Hitler."

As they walked down the stairs, strange, mewling noises continued to come from Hitler's room. Hess had remained with his master. Strasser shook his head, speaking softly. "You wouldn't believe it, gentlemen. Hitler's a different creature on a public platform."

They had returned to the fireplace, where Röhm still lounged, and he agreed vigorously. "It's as if the crowd feeds its energy to him. He stands there sometimes for minutes before he speaks, drawing in that energy. He's a kind of vampire, I suppose." The SA leader drained his glass and sighed.

Strasser interrupted. "He's our best bet for chancellor. We all know that. He has something the crowd responds to. But once we are in power, we'll find him a more suitable position—head of propaganda, perhaps." He started as, softly, upstairs, a door closed.

Strasser dropped his voice still lower. "In a few days Hitler has an appointment with Chancellor Hindenburg. It looks as if, so long as we keep our noses clean, old Hindenburg will name Alf as his successor. But if Alf remains like—like what you saw upstairs—he won't make any other impression than the obvious one. So you don't have much time, I'm afraid, Sir Seaton."

"I'll do my best, Captain Röhm. And, of course, I'll be grateful for any help." Sir Seaton reached to shake hands, but Röhm was taking his cap and greatcoat down from the antlered peg.

"Give me a lift back to Munich. I might have a lead for you." Sinclair was astonished at how rapidly Röhm had sobered.

Hess decided that he should remain at his leader's side, and Strasser had also decided to spend the night, so Röhm joined Sir Seaton in the front while Taffy again found himself in the profoundly comfortable leather of the back. Against his will, he began to doze and did not hear the whole exchange between Röhm and Begg.

"She had only one lover, you know that?" announced Röhm. "I think he might have been assigned to guard her. My chaps were keeping a watch. She had a lot of guards, but this one was special. I think she was infatuated with him. A tall SS captain, by all accounts. Blond. Always wore dark glasses. He's disappeared out of the picture since the shooting. They say he was Himmler's spy, but he didn't seem to be following anyone's orders much. Himmler hated old Geli, you know. I had a soft spot for her. Bit of a whore, like myself. Maybe she died because she knew too much. Maybe that's what'll happen to me, too." Again that monstrous, grunting laugh, far too big for the size of the soft, battle-scarred face.

Captain Röhm was staying at the Brown House that night. His own flat, he reported with a laugh, was full. It was dusk as they dropped him off. "Where to, now, Seaton? Bed?" Sinclair asked hopefully.

"I'm afraid not, Taffy. There's just time to catch the last few musical numbers and get a decent glass of Russian tea at the Carlton Tea Rooms! You remember I was studying the entertainment pages on the way over. This will help take the taste of that schnapps out of your mouth, eh?"

CHAPTER EIGHT
THE VIOLINIST OF THE CAFÉ ORCHESTRA

As Taffy Sinclair enjoyed the strange mixture of black Russia tea and a plate of small weisswürst, he relaxed to the strains of Ketalby's "In a Persian Market," played by the group of musicians on the stand. It was their last performance of the evening. All the players were seated save for their leader, a tall man with close-cropped hair and wearing impeccable evening dress. He stood in the shadows of the curtain and played the violin with extraordinary beauty and skill. When Begg tipped the waiter heavily and put a folded note on the plate, Sinclair thought his friend was asking for one of his favorite sentimental tunes, such as "The Gypsy" or "The Merry Widow Waltz," but neither of these was played before the musicians brought their performance to an end.

Sinclair was surprised when the tall violinist, having replaced his instrument in its case, strolled over to their table. Then, when the albino removed his dark glasses, Sinclair realized with a shock that he sat across the table from Sir Seaton Begg's cousin and archenemy, the notorious Count Zodiac, wanted for countless daring crimes throughout the Empire. More than once the two had crossed swords on the

Continent and only a few months earlier Count Zodiac had been thwarted by Begg in his daring attempt to rob the New York–bound aerial express. In London, where Zodiac commanded an almost fanatical loyalty from the crooks of Smith's Kitchen, the most notorious den of thieves in Christendom, they had fought many times. A year earlier Zodiac had succeeded in stealing the British Crown Jewels, only to have them snatched back by Begg as he tried to make his underwater escape from the city.

The red-eyed albino had a charming, crooked smile. "So, gentlemen, you have discovered how I earn my living, these days. . . ."

Begg grinned almost boyishly at this. "Good evening, Count Zodiac. Perhaps I am too familiar with your aliases. The Tarot Tea Orchestra rather betrayed you? But I hear you work for Heinrich Himmler now. . . ."

For a split second Zodiac's expression changed to one of anger. Then again he was all urbane affability. "Is Himmler claiming that? Scum like him can't employ me, Sir Seaton." He sat back in his chair, lighting a pungent, black cigarette. "However, you might find that Himmler and the others have all been playing my game. . . ." He chuckled with deep pleasure.

Sinclair, who had been up for too long and drunk too much schnapps, lost his usual discretion then. He leaned across the table. "Look here, Count von Bek, did you kill Geli Raubal? You seem to be the only one who had the opportunity, if not the motive! You are the mysterious SS man, eh?"

"Captain Zeiss," said Begg.

Zodiac drew a deep, ennui-ridden sigh. Ignoring Sinclair, he addressed Begg directly, reaching across the table and handing him a pasteboard card. "I was at this address until yesterday. You might find it interesting. Even useful." He turned, bowing, to Sinclair. "We all work in the ways which best suit our temperaments, I think, Mr. Sinclair? Who is to say in our good or our evil intentions we unknowingly serve the causes of law or chaos?"

With that, the albino turned on his heel, picked up his violin case, and disappeared into the night.

Sinclair, stunned for a moment, leapt to his feet and pursued the albino, but he soon returned, shaking his head: lost him. Begg continued to sip his tea, studying the card. "We don't need to follow him, Taffy. He has left us his most recent address."

Begg frowned down at the card in his hand. "Do you feel like making a visit to the Hotel Rembrandt? It's just around the corner. We can walk."

"Oh, good heavens, Begg! This is unbelievable!" Taffy Sinclair was staring aghast at a handful of papers and photographs. He had just opened the writing bureau in Room 25. Count Zodiac's room at the Hotel Rembrandt looked as if it had been hastily vacated.

Sir Seaton Begg was inspecting the wardrobe. He picked up and put back a black Mauser rifle with a telescopic sight. "There's our red herring. Zodiac was no doubt trying to sow further suspicion amongst the Nazis. And look at this!" On hangers hung a complete SS captain's uniform. The metatemporal detective offered it to his friend. "And look here, Taffy. Bloodstains. They fit perfectly with the suspected shooting."

"And these—these—letters from Himmler to Captain Zeiss, asking him to seduce that poor girl, compromise her, then kill her, so that Himmler could continue his blackmailing of Hitler through a third party. There's a note here that even suggests Himmler was responsible for the initial blackmail a couple of years ago! The most damning evidence! So your cousin, von Bek, is a common murderer, after all! And in Captain Himmler's employ?"

"It certainly appears so." Begg looked around for a bag. "Come on, Taffy. We'd better take these togs to Hitler."

"Surely we should get them to Inspector Hoffmann as soon as possible? Zodiac must be captured!"

"I remind you again, Taffy, that Herr Hitler is our paying client and it is our duty to show him the evidence before it is presented to the police."

"But Great Jehovah, Begg, this overrides any client loyalty!"

"I'm afraid not, Taffy. I remember the way to Berchtesgaden. You'd better come with me, old man, whatever your scruples. I need a witness and someone at my shoulder if the client decides to kill the messenger."

Only this persuaded the pathologist to accompany his friend, but he did so in brooding silence. Begg seemed completely insouciant, whistling fragments from musical comedies as the great car bore them relentlessly up toward Hitler's retreat.

Only because Rudolf Hess was convinced they had good news for Hitler were the Englishmen allowed into the fusty stench of the Nazi leader's lair. Again he greeted them in nothing but his mackintosh, his eyes as mad as ever. He moved between gross self-pity and rage against his niece's killers, sometimes in seconds. But when he at last looked at the evidence Begg and Sinclair had brought with them, he was stunned into a cold, sudden pseudo-sanity.

"Himmler! He was behind the assassination attempts. Failing to kill any of us, he made his victim an innocent young girl! He always hated her. He has grown closer and closer to me, building up the SS on my behalf, he says. They warned me he had Jewish blood, but I laughed at them. And all the time he plotted against me in this subtle way, getting at me through Geli, using one of his own men to— ugh!" He stood up suddenly, bowing with both hands at his sides, and brought his bare heels together. "I am most grateful to you gentlemen. You have done everything Hess promised. Naturally you will receive your fee. Herr Hess will take you to the Brown House at once."

Even Hess seemed surprised by this sudden volte-face.

"No need, old boy." Sir Seaton Begg lifted his hat. "Have this one on me. I am happy to serve the cause of justice."

Though dressed only in a mackintosh, Hitler visibly grew an inch or two. "You have served not only my interests and those of my great party, Sir Seaton. You have served the interests of the entire free world. Hess. We shall need the Mercedes. There is something I must take care of at once. Thank you again." He lifted his arm in his familiar salute.

"Only too happy to oblige, old chap." And with that Begg steered an open-mouthed Sinclair into the fir-rich air of the sub-Alpine forests.

"Take a good gulp, Taffy," he murmured.

"Are you out of your mind, Begg? That chap's about as unbalanced as it's possible to be without falling off the planet. You've no idea what notions you've given him."

"Oh, I think the ones he was meant to be given, Taffy. Perhaps you already suspect the truth? In this case we served a client other than we thought!"

By now Dolly's headlights were piercing the dark shadows of the German night. Taffy, still deprived of his usual amount of sleep, began to doze in the seat beside his friend. He was awakened to realize that Begg was driving far slower than usual and that the headlamps of another car were coming from behind. He watched in some astonishment, as if dreaming. The great Mercedes swept past them, overtaking at almost one hundred miles an hour. Sinclair made out Herr Hitler in the backseat. Hess was with him. Strasser appeared to be driving. Before he began to fall back to sleep, he remembered noticing that Hitler appeared to be wearing a suit and a tie and asking Begg where Hitler was going at this time of night.

"Berlin, I'd guess." Sir Seaton kept Dolly at a steady pace.

"We're going to Berlin?"

"Good Lord no, old boy. Our work's done here. We're going home. If I put on a little speed at the crossroads, we should be just in time to catch the dawn zeppelin for London."

Without Sinclair's knowledge, Begg had already stowed the luggage. There had been no hotel bill to settle. By dawn they reached the great Munich Aerodrome and were soon installed in a comfortable suite. Through the portholes came floods of intermittent sunshine caused by the movement of the ship in her cables. A radio bulletin playing on the State Radio took on a rather excited air, and as soon as he had disrobed, washed, and settled in his seat, Begg turned the volume up.

He listened in some amusement, but Sinclair was aghast at the news. He even failed to notice the almost effortless lifting of the huge liner as she uncoupled from her masts and began her journey to London.

There had effectively been a complete disintegration of the Nazis. Already the Reichstag party seemed divided into opposing camps headed by Strasser and Göring. Nazi officials were issuing contradictory statements since the arrest earlier that morning of Adolf Hitler, self-confessed murderer of the man he termed the "Jew Fifth Columnist Himmler," hitherto his trusted aide and an ex–chicken farmer. Hitler understood that he could no longer hope to be vice-chancellor, but now it scarcely mattered, since he had in his own words "torn out the heart of the hydra sucking the life from Germany, keeping the nation safe against injustice and horror for a thousand years."

"You effectively put the gun into Hitler's hand and killed Himmler!" cried Sinclair. "Really, Begg, sometimes . . ."

"I told you, Taffy, that I did what I was supposed to do. Zodiac knew only too well that there are few better and more trustworthy messengers than you and me. So he sent us to Hitler with the evidence he had carefully manufactured over months. Those papers were enough to convince almost anyone and in a bad light they were even harder to detect. But they were forgeries, old man. Planted for someone to find. Just as those apparent sniper shots which always missed their targets were intended to distract attention from what was actually being accomplished. Zodiac had been looking for a good way to make the Nazi leadership fall out. When he knew we were on to him, he simply made us his cat's-paws. Pretty audacious, eh."

"But Zodiac killed that poor creature, Fräulein Raubal," insisted Taffy.

"Not at all, Taffy, though you could argue Hitler effectively drove her to her death. She killed herself, as everyone insisted. She tested the poison first. You smelled that distinctive odor as readily as I did."

"Cyanide!"

"Exactly. The smell of cyanide, if taken by mouth, lingers on the lips long after the taker has gone to the hereafter. That dead canary the young lady carried around all day. She had already tried the stuff on the bird and saw that it worked. She took a pretty heavy dosage, I'd say. The police remained deceived by the gunshot. The way she lay on the floor made it seem to others that she had died in the throes of passion. But I believe she died in the throes of death."

"But she was shot, Begg. Shot by Zodiac!"

"True."

"So Zodiac is the real murderer. . . ."

"No."

There was a knock at their door and Begg called, "Come in!" A busboy with a salver presented him with a card which he glanced at; then he smiled and tucked it into his upper waistcoat pocket. He offered the boy a silver coin. "Ask Countess von Bek to join us at her pleasure." He beamed across at a bewildered Taffy.

"No?"

"No. Zodiac was, of course, Fräulein Raubal's lover. He played the violin by night and courted her by day. By whatever clever devices, he had provided himself with the assignment of keeping guard on her, knowing that he planned to seduce her. But I think he also planned to save her. He took some conventional 'glamour' pictures of her. He made those Himmler forgeries we showed Hitler. I don't think he had any plan to kill the girl. But he did want her to run away with him. So he suggested they go to Vienna together. He told her to demand of Hitler that she be allowed to stay with her relatives and study singing there. It was a plan she had already toyed with. So she did as she was told. But Hitler, as we know, had reached the end of his tolerance." Begg rose to his feet to open their door, bowing Countess Rose into their rather cramped quarters. Offering her his chair, he brought her rapidly up-to-date and then, leaning beside the porthole, continued.

"Someone, probably an SA spy, had reported the 'secret lover,' even if they had not been able to say who it was. So Hitler refused. Under no circumstances could she go to Vienna. She again threatened suicide. He did not believe her. Neither, I suspect, would 'Captain Zeiss' have believed her. But when he let himself into the apartment late that night, he found poor Geli Raubal on the floor, having tasted the torments of cyanide. She had left a note, no doubt. This went against his plans, but he had to go through with the rest of it. He pocketed the note. He found Hitler's gun, shot the already dead Geli through the heart in a way deliberately to draw suspicion on someone, placed the gun in her hand with equally deliberate clumsiness, then left the police and investigators, like ourselves, to conclude that the young woman had been murdered, either by Hitler or one of his lieutenants."

The Countess Rose sat back in her seat, her eyes gleaming with admiration. "So Hoffmann and myself were completely fooled. Only the fact that Hitler had an ironclad alibi stopped us from arresting him."

"Zodiac already had his original plan, which he modified. He knew that Hitler could not be 'framed.' So he planned to let his men discover the clothing and documents at the Hotel Rembrandt. Since I caught up with him so much sooner than he expected, he merely decided to use me as his messenger! He was always a clever customer. Even those pictures, released to the press, would be enough to threaten the fortunes of Hitler and his party. But Zodiac wanted to be dead certain. That was why he had forged some Himmler documents to make sure all in the party were suspect. He hoped they would find their way to Hitler. I made sure that they did. The consequences then followed like clockwork. Leading to a satisfactory resolution, I think you'll agree, Taffy. Sometimes it is just about possible for two wrongs to make a right."

Rose von Bek clapped her hands together as another knock came at the door. "Ah. That will be our breakfast champagne!"

But Sinclair's Presbyterian soul was not yet ready to accept the full burden of these unwelcome demonstrations. He rose gracefully, so that Begg might have his chair.

"If you'll forgive me, I'll take a stroll up to the dining hall and avail myself of the full English breakfast. I think an occasion like this calls for some honest fried bread, fried tomatoes, mushrooms, and black pudding. Traditional fortification."

"Very well, old boy. To each his own poison. I trust you'll rejoin us as soon as you can." Begg lifted a victorious glass.

Declaring that he would probably take a turn or two about the observation deck before he rejoined them, Sinclair stepped into the corridor and closed the door on his colleagues.

Once in the corridor, the pathologist stared thoughtfully at the tranquil, dreaming German fields and villages passing below. A man trained to follow the law and to play the game by the regular rules, Sinclair mused that this was not the first time that his association with his friend Seaton Begg troubled him.

He shook his head, the delicious scent of frying bacon drawing his attention back to breakfast. He put the problem behind him. For all his moral dilemma, Taffy Sinclair was forced to admit that his friend had assured, by the most unconventional, even cynical methods, by the most circuitous path, that justice had again been done.

NOTE: While originally scheduled for the May 1932 issue of *The Thriller Library,* Amalgamated Press, London, this story is said to have been withdrawn from publication at the request of Buckingham Palace and Downing Street. The author and high-ranking civil servant John Buchan is said to have been involved. It is published here for the first time.

The Case of the Salt and Pepper Shakers

By AIMEE BENDER

*The murdered couple was matched as perfectly as the salt and
pepper shakers they so passionately collected. But the murderer
of their passion for each other was the greatest mystery of all.*

I found the dead bodies face-to-face, cold, on the living room carpet
of the suburban household. One was a husband, sprawled in a fetal
position; the other his wife, tilting forward, her head butting into
his stomach. The carpet beneath them was soaked through with
blood and saliva. I took the necessary samples and marked off the area
while the usual team came in to check for fingerprints and clues. I
myself have never been a proponent of walking around and instead
sat quietly in one of the taller chairs and tried to take in the room.
Ivory-colored carpet, ivory walls, brown sofa, wooden chairs. Ordi-

nary. The faintest smell of rosemary drew my focus to the kitchen, visible through an open countertop, and lining its walls I could see copper pots and pans, a hanging chain of garlic, and rows upon rows of salt and pepper shakers. Fourteen pairs in total. While the team used their equipment to make sure every piece of furniture revealed its underbelly, I wrote down one word on my yellow pad: *Shaker.* I have a feel for such things; it's the only reason I've held on to this job for so long, since I have no patience for the details and am clumsy with the props.

I made ten calls that afternoon. My phone manners are fair to poor. To my surprise, no one I spoke to seemed particularly shocked by the double murders. No windows were broken, I told them. No key was forced. They sat silent as schoolchildren, on the other line, waiting for me to push the issue.

"Any idea of suspects?" I asked. "Motives? Suspicious behavior?"

No, no, no.

"Might you know," I asked at the end, "why these two collected so many salt and pepper shakers?"

I spoke with the neighbor, the bosses, the doctor, and a friend, but no one could explain to me why they were dead, or why two people who paid a live-in chef to the very edge of their budget, and whose blood pressure kept climbing up the ladder into the red zone, would collect so many salt and pepper shakers, in ceramic, wood, glass, and metal.

"I ate there for dinner several times," said the friend, "and as far as I can recall, they only used one ordinary set."

I spent that night in their house while the bodies were being examined at the morgue. The cook was away for the night, and I slept in the guest bedroom, on top of the comforter, not moving any evidence but just resting and listening, as the only way to get a true feel of a house and its residents is to stay in it overnight. This model was fairly standard for the neighborhood: one story, ranch style, two bedrooms and an office. The pictures on the walls were easy landscapes, and in the guest room, I slept beneath a watercolor of horses running.

Every piece of furniture and decor was slippery to the mind and would not stick. I can hardly recall the sofa or the chairs, so unobtrusive was their style, and so involved was I with examining those shakers. Several pairs were masterfully crafted, with zigzag patterns of mahogany and oak, or cut diamonds of crystal, and must have cost quite a pile. One was a humorous set, each a green ceramic frog: salt with a cane, pepper with a hat. One pair was built of very modern and angular chrome and glass. Each held varying levels of grain. The house grew so quiet I could hear the movement of cats next door, paws treading softly on the sidewalk.

I awoke to a call from the coroner. He explained that the husband was knifed in the stomach at five PM, while the wife had been poisoned at a quarter to three, with a poison that took exactly 2.5 hours to kick in. They both died within about a minute of each other. Her late lunch had been a small chicken pot pie, unsalted, a green salad, peppered, and a glass of freshly squeezed grapefruit juice. The poison had been discovered in sedimentary bits inside her water bottle. Her fingertips were cut at the tip, and covered neatly with bandages.

"Any fingerprints on the knife?" I asked.

"Not in yet," he said.

"Any records of who was out buying poison in town?" I asked. He said that was not his area. My team would report on that soon. Today they would scour all the nearby pharmacies, compiling records of purchase times.

The coroner is an upstanding fellow. He fought in Vietnam and raises orchids. I thanked him repeatedly but he gets embarrassed by gratitude and hung up.

After ordering in a bowl of chicken soup and a sandwich, I spent several hours in the living room, sitting with the stain from his wound. It spread over the carpet in a curling line, as if he'd put his arm around her with his blood.

The reports came in around six PM. The wife's middle finger and thumb prints were all over the knife handle, being the two unbandaged fingers, and the husband had bought the poison just four days before at the local pharmacy under his regular name. When I got on the phone and called back the silent people, they all, suddenly, spoke up. The two hated each other, they confessed. Hated enough to murder? I asked. They grunted toward a yes. By the end, said the friend, she would hardly talk to him anymore, and he took so many long frustrated walks that all the neighbors expected to see him pass by their window, head down, at least twice a day.

"We do not understand," said a neighbor. "But we are not surprised."

Now, here's what got me. If it's true that they killed each other, then she could not have known she was poisoned when she knifed him, as he had chosen a poison that is silent and causes no suffering, and he had hidden the bottle somewhere very difficult to find, as we had not yet found it. In fact, their greatest difference here was revealed through their choice of murder weapon, in that she wanted to make him suffer and be aware of her murderous inclinations, choosing the overt and physical technique, while he selected the secretive, one of the few methods available where she would die without fully realizing what was happening. He perhaps was more ashamed of his loathing, and also he did not want her to feel pain. Their greatest similarity, however, was revealed in their choice of occasion, since each seemed to have conceived of the exact month and moment of death fully independent of the other. Certainly that was something. Even with their differing methods, they still timed it in perfect unison. I could hardly get my mind around it. And I imagine that as they lay on the carpet next to each other, one bleeding from the gut, the other foaming from the mouth, they saw something meaningful and linked in the eyes of the other. The nature of hate is as elusive as love's. I am just relieved they never had children.

Back to the dilemma of the spices. I finished my dinner and called up both their hairdressers, and spoke to one very unfriendly sibling, and no one had any interest in discussing these salt and pepper shakers, and in fact I could feel a stirring annoyance in the voices of the questioned, one which I am used to but still resent. I went home to shower, and spoke briefly with my girlfriend, who was half-asleep and seemed distracted, and only right before I dozed off in my own bed did a phone call come in and tell me that the missing bottle of poison had been discovered in the chef's quarters, underneath her bathroom sink. "Has anyone questioned her?" asked my boss, and I coughed in embarrassment. I had tried repeatedly to contact her, but she had taken off several days to grieve, and was returning for the first time the following morning to begin the slow process of packing up her bags. This couple had not been exceedingly wealthy, but the luxury of a live-in cook was something both felt was important to their happiness. So they shared a car, and rarely ate out or vacationed.

I found the cook in the kitchen, making afternoon snacks. Nothing was packed yet, and the house was just as I had left it. The couple had been married for twenty-five years and the cook was older than I expected, with a head of silver hair, although her fingers were still swift and nimble. She seemed saddened by the loss of her employers, but perhaps not sad enough. I was not ready to rule her out as a possible suspect, particularly now with the poison bottle, wrapped in plastic, sitting bulbous on the coroner's desk. While we were talking she made us a perfect turkey sandwich, on a triangle of bread, grilled lightly on the stove.

"The wife liked salt and the husband liked pepper," she said, "and the salt and pepper pair served as a symbol of their relationship." She briskly flipped the sandwich on the grill and then scooped it onto one yellow plate and one red plate, which she handed over to me.

"Thank you," I said. The bread had crisped to a fine golden color around the edges. I waited until she took a bite of hers until I tried mine. "How so?"

"Well," she said, swallowing carefully, "they used salt and pepper as their model union. In their wedding vows, they said she was salt—she intensified the existing flavor—and he was pepper—he added a new angle—and that every fine table needed both.

"In fact," she said, leaning in, "instead of a man and woman atop their wedding cake, they had a pair of miniature salt and pepper shakers."

"No kidding," I mumbled, chewing.

She nodded. "I can show you photos." She started toward the

living room, and before I could take another bite, she had the white wedding album open, full of smiling attractive faces, and there was the cake, with those shakers on top. "It was a white cake with strawberry cream filling," she said. "Quite light."

"Did you have any reason to dislike them?" I asked casually. "Were they good employers?"

"Yes," she said. "I liked them just fine. Isn't the case solved?"

"Seems to be," I said. "It's just that no one else remembered the shakers." I tried to keep sandwich crumbs off the photos. "This is delicious, by the way."

She shrugged. "I've been here since the wedding," she said, pointing to herself in the photo album, serving plates of cake with a full head of very brown hair, "and salt and pepper shakers were their gift to each other every single anniversary."

She shut the book. "Case closed," she said.

I opened the book back up. "Except," I said, pointing to the date on the invitation, "there are only fourteen pairs of shakers, and I believe they were married for twenty-five years. . . ."

"Twenty-six," she said, pulling a clear bag of lemons up from the floor. "Well."

I waited.

"What happened," the cook said, now slicing lemons in half, "was that after about fourteen years of marriage, he, as people do, grew allergic to spicy food, and her blood pressure went up so high that she had to abandon salt. She could only use pepper, he only salt. He did not like the salt, it seemed to him redundant, which hurt her feelings. She did not like the pepper, as it seemed to distract from the true nature of the dish. This made him feel discounted.

"After some time, she grew less vibrant, and he less stimulating."

"Truly?"

"From my perspective," said the cook, "it actually seemed to be true."

I pressed my finger into the plate to pick up the last crumbs of sandwich.

"And did this fill you with a strange hatred?" I asked.

She smiled at me. "No," she said. "Why, you don't believe they killed each other?"

"We found the bottle of poison in your room," I said.

She sat back down in her chair. I said nothing. At moments like this, it is always best to say nothing. Her eyes faded and lost focus.

"I'm not so surprised," she said softly after a while. "I'm sure he put it there on purpose. He had always hoped that I would be able to fix it all. I tried," she said. "It is a chef's job, this," she said, squeezing lemon juice into a pitcher.

She sighed now, with some elegance in her shoulders, and stirred the growing lemonade with a wooden spoon.

"But a good chef must let go of the salt/pepper ratios," she said. "It's uncontrollable. It is a chef's nightmare to see the salt shaker dump itself all over a perfectly salted piece of meat or to see the pepper dirty up what is an ideal wave of béchamel. It is a chef's sleeplessness, right there," she said.

"So let it go," she said. "I cannot worry about it excessively. I simply Can Not." She poured herself half a glass of lemonade and took a sip. "Too sweet," she said, cutting four more lemons precisely in half. "And if lemonade is too sweet," she said, "then we are somehow lost to the crush of anonymity."

Her face struck against itself, and her eyebrows folded in.

"Sir," she said. "I was here for twenty-six years. Had they both trusted my expertise, perhaps none of this would have happened."

I found I wanted to comfort her but her eyes had shut down, and after I finished spiking the last crumb, I tried to thank her sincerely, but she had lost herself in thought, at the kitchen table, stirring four grains of sugar at a time into the pitcher, and tasting, repeatedly, with the large wooden spoon.

"Thank you for your time," I said, then, to no one.

It was not the chef; I believed her fully. It was not the neighbor. It was no outside job. The evidence was in. So then if the mystery was solved, both big and small, why was I still on it? That was what my boss kept asking. He had a new case for me involving a homicide over on the west end of town, of a very old rich codger who had seven children, and it seemed likely that one of the seven had killed him. But I was bored by that one. It would solve itself, like a hose releasing its pinch and letting the water flow. I bought some orchid food instead, and went to see the coroner again, because my mind would not stop thinking of that end, when the husband and wife realized they were dying together, each by the hand of the other. In a way, they actually had swapped personalities, by killing the other in the manner of his or her favorite spice. The wife chose knifing, which is certainly "pepper-like" in its spicy attack on the body, and the coroner thanked me for the orchid food and confirmed my suspicions about the poison, by explaining how the one the husband had chosen killed by increasing the saline level of the bloodstream to such a degree that the person essentially dehydrated.

I myself have a girlfriend, as I have mentioned, which is perhaps why the salt and pepper pair do not leave my mind. The case is closed and the file cabinet locked but I still think of them all the time. The ranch-style house sold for cheap to a small family who moved here from Michigan and didn't hear the history. I believe the cook retired from family work, and now is doing private catering on her own, and if I ever get married, I will surely hire her, although my superstitious girlfriend might not approve. I do love my girlfriend, for her differences and her similarities, but I do not know if one day the item that defines me in her eyes will no longer work. If my body will fail. If I will face her in bed and not know what to do, when now her body still seems infinite. If she will stop having that bright look in her eye at the parrot store, and instead lose herself circling letters in word searches. There are couples who commit suicide together and they are in line with Shakespeare's greatest lovers, but those who murder each other precisely at the same minute are written up in all the papers as crazy. Even their family members coughed and got off the phone as fast as they could. They would like to erase the whole rigamarole. I picked up more than one tone of disgust and superiority in my many interviews. But it seems to me beautiful. How right at the end, when everything was over, they realized they had reached the ultimate gesture of compromise, that their union had come full circle, and perhaps it was the sting of that bittersweetness that killed them most, crueler than any knife or poison.

Ghost Dance

By SHERMAN ALEXIE

The Cheyenne woman came to him in a dream, with death in her kiss. But the nightmarish Seventh Cavalry came in waking life—with a taste for human flesh.

Two cops, one big and the other little, traveled through the dark. The big cop hated Indians. Born and raised in a Montana that was home to eleven different reservations and over 47,000 Indians, the big cop's hatred had grown vast. Over a twenty-two-year law enforcement career he'd spent in service to one faded Montana town or another, the big cop had arrested 1,217 Indians for offenses ranging from shoplifting to assault, from bank robbery to homicide, all of the crimes committed while under the influence of one chemical or another.

"Damn redskins would drink each other's piss if they thought there was enough booze left in it," the big cop said to the little cop, a nervous little snake-boy just a few years out of Anaconda High School.

"Sure," said the little cop. He was a rookie and wasn't supposed to say much at all.

It was June 25th, three in the morning, and still over 100 degrees. Sweating through his polyester uniform, the big cop drove the patrol car east along Interstate 90, heading for the Custer Memorial Battlefield on the banks of the Little Big Horn River.

"But you want to know the worst thing I ever saw?" asked the big cop. He drove with one hand on the wheel and the other in his crotch. He felt safer that way.

"Sure," said the little cop.

"Out on the Crow rez, I caught these Indian boys," the big cop said. "There were five or six of them scalp-hunters, all of them pulling a train on this pretty little squaw-bitch."

"That's bad."

"Shoot, that ain't the bad part. Gang rape is, like, a sacred tradition on some of these rez ghettoes. Hell, the bad part ain't the rape. The bad part is the boys were feeding this girl some Lysol sandwiches."

"What's a Lysol sandwich?"

"You just take two slices of bread, spray them hard with Lysol, slam them together, and eat it all up."

"That'll kill you, won't it?"

"Sure, it will kill you, but slow. Make you a retard first, make you run around in a diaper for about a year, and then it will kill you."

"That's bad."

"About the worst thing there is," said the big cop.

The little cop stared out the window and marveled again at the number of visible stars in the Montana sky. The little cop knew he lived in the most beautiful place in the world.

The big cop took the Little Big Horn exit off I-90, drove the short distance to the visitors' center, and then down a bumpy road to the surprisingly simple gates of the Custer Memorial Cemetery.

"This is it," said the big cop. "This is the place where it all went to shit."

"Sure," said the little cop.

"Two hundred and fifty-six good soldiers, good men, were murdered here on that horrible June day in 1876," said the big cop. He'd said the same thing many times before. It was part of a speech he was always rehearsing.

"I know it," said the little cop. He wondered if he should say a prayer.

"If it wasn't for these damn Indians," said the big cop, "Custer would've been the president of these United States."

"Right."

"We'd be living in a better country right now, let me tell you what."

"Yes, we would."

The big cop shook his head at all of the injustice of the world. He knew he was a man with wisdom and felt burdened by the weight of that powerful intelligence.

"Well," said the big cop. "We've got some work to do."

"Sure," said the little cop.

The cops stepped outside, both cursing the ridiculous heat, and walked to the back of the car. The big cop opened the trunk and stared down at the two Indian men lying there awake, silent, bloodied, and terrified. The cops had picked them up hitchhiking on the Flathead Reservation and driven them for hours through the limitless dark.

"Come on out of there, boys," said the big cop with a smile.

The Indians, one a young man with braids and the other an older man with a crew cut, crawled out of the trunk and stood on unsteady legs. Even with already-closing eyes and broken noses, with shit and piss running down their legs, and with nightstick bruises covering their stomachs and backs, the Indians tried to stand tall.

"You know where you are?" the big cop asked the Indians.

"Yes," said the older one.

"Tell me."

"Little Big Horn."

"You know what happened here?"

The older Indian remained silent.

"You better talk to me, boy," said the big cop. "Or I'm going to hurt you piece by piece."

The older Indian knew he was supposed to be pleading and begging for mercy, for his life, as he'd had to beg for his life from other uniformed white men. But the older Indian was suddenly tired of being afraid. He felt brave and stupid. The younger Indian knew how defiant his older friend could be. He wanted to run.

"Hey, chief," said the big cop. "I asked you a question. Do you know what happened here?"

The older Indian refused to talk. He lifted his chin and glared at the big cop.

"Fuck it," said the big cop as he pulled his revolver and shot the older Indian in the face, then shot him twice more in the chest after he crashed to the ground. Though the big cop had lived and worked violently, this was his first murder, and he was surprised by how easy it was.

After a moment of stunned silence, the younger Indian ran, clumsily zigzagging between gravestones, and made it thirty feet before the big cop shot him in the spine, and dropped him into the dirt.

"Oh, Jesus, Jesus, Jesus," said the younger cop, terrified. He knew he had to make a decision: Be a good man and die there in the cemetery with the Indians or be an evil man and help disappear two dead bodies.

"What do you think of that?" the big cop asked the little cop.

"I think it was good shooting."

Decision made, the little cop jogged over to the younger Indian lying there alive and half-paralyzed. His spine was shattered, and he'd die soon, but the Indian reached out with bloodied hands, grabbed handfuls of dirt, rock, and grass, tearing his nails off in the process, and pulled himself away in one last stupid and primal effort to survive. With his useless legs dragging behind him, the Indian looked like a squashed bug. Like a cockroach in blue jeans, thought the little cop and laughed a little, then retched his truck stop dinner all over the back of the dying Indian.

There and here, everywhere, Indian blood spilled onto the ground, and seeped down into the cemetery dirt.

The big cop knelt beside the body of the old Indian and pushed his right index finger into the facial entrance wound and wondered why he was doing such a terrible thing. With his damn finger in this dead man's brain, the big cop felt himself split in two and become twins, one brother a killer and the other an eyewitness to murder.

Away, the little cop was down on all fours, dry heaving and moaning like a lonely coyote.

"What's going on over there?" asked the big cop.

"This one is still alive," said the little cop.

"Well, then, finish him off."

The little cop struggled to his feet, pulled his revolver, and pressed it against the back of the Indian's head. Maybe he would have found enough cowardice and courage to pull the trigger, but he never got the chance. All around him, awakened and enraptured by Indian blood, the white soldiers in tattered uniforms exploded from their graves and came for the little cop. As he spun in circles, surrounded, he saw how many of these soldiers were little more than skeletons with pieces of dried meat clinging to their bones. Some of the soldiers still had stomachs and lungs leaking blood through jagged wounds, and other soldiers picked at their own brains through arrow holes punched into their skulls, and a few dumb, clumsy ones tripped over their intestines and ropy veins spilling onto the ground. Dead for over a century and now alive and dead at the same time, these soldiers rushed the little cop. Backpedaling, stepping side to side, the little cop dodged arms and tongueless mouths as he fired his revolver fifteen times. Even while panicked and shooting at moving targets, he was still a good marksman. He blasted the skull off one soldier, shot the arms off two others and the leg off a third, had six bullets pass through the ribs of a few officers and one zip through the empty eye socket of a sergeant. But even without arms, legs, and heads, the soldiers came for him and knocked him to the ground, where they pulled off his skin in long strips, exposed his sweet meats, and feasted on him. Just before two privates pulled out his heart and tore it into halves, the little cop watched a lieutenant, with a half-decayed face framing one blue eye, feed the big cop's cock and balls to a horse whose throat, esophagus, and stomach were clearly visible through its ribs.

That night, as the Seventh Cavalry rose from their graves in Montana, Edgar Smith slept in his bed in Washington, D.C., and dreamed for the first time about the death of George Armstrong Custer.

Inside the dream, it was June 1876 all over again, and Custer was the last survivor of his own foolish ambitions. On a grassy hill overlooking the Little Big Horn River, Custer crawled over the bodies of many dead soldiers and a few dead Indians. Seriously wounded, but strong enough to stand and stagger, then walk on broken legs, Custer was followed by a dozen quiet warriors, any one of them prestigious enough to be given the honor of killing this famous Indian Killer, this Long Hair, this Son of the Morning Star. Crazy Horse and Sitting Bull walked behind Custer, as did Gall, Crow King, Red Horse, Low Dog, Foolish Elk, and others close and far. But it was a quiet Cheyenne woman, a warrior whose name has never been spoken aloud since that day, who stepped forward with an arrow in her hand and stabbed it through Custer's heart. After Custer fell and died, the Cheyenne woman stood over his body and sang for two hours. She sang while her baby son slept in the cradleboard on her back. She sang an honor song for the brave Custer, for the great white warrior, and when she ended her song, she kneeled and kissed the general. But Custer was no longer Custer. The quiet Cheyenne woman kissed Edgar Smith lying dead in the greasy grass of his dream.

A ringing telephone pulled Edgar from sleep. Reflexively and professionally, he answered, heard the details of his mission, grabbed a bag that was always packed, and hurried for the airport. Brown-eyed, brown-haired, pale of skin, and just over six feet tall, he was completely unremarkable in appearance, a blank Caucasian slate. Measured by his surface, Edgar could have been a shortstop for the New York Yankees, a dentist from Sacramento, or the night shift manager at a supermarket. This mutability made him the ideal FBI agent.

Two hours after the phone call, after his Custer dream, Edgar sat in a window seat of the FBI jet flying toward the massacre site in Montana. All around him, other anonymous field agents busied themselves with police reports and history texts, with biographies and data on Native American radicals, white separatists, domestic terrorists, religious cultists, and the other assorted crazies who lived within a five-hundred-mile radius of the Custer Memorial Battlefield.

"Can you imagine the number of men it took to pull this off?" asked one agent. "Over two hundred graves looted and sacked. How big a truck do you need to haul off two hundred bodies? You'd need a well-trained army. I'm thinking militia."

"But it's two hundred dead bodies buried for a hundred years, so that's about two million pieces of dead bodies," said another agent. "Hell, you'd be hauling loose teeth, ribs, some hair, a fingernail or two, and just plain dust. You'd need a vacuum for all this. It's not the size of the job; it's the ritual nature of it. You have to be crazy to do this, and you have to be even crazier to convince a bunch of other people to do it with you. We're looking for the King of the Crazy People."

"You want my opinion?" asked the third agent. "I'm thinking these two dead Indians, along with a bunch of other radical Indians, were desecrating these graves. I mean, it is the anniversary of Custer's Last Stand, right? They were trying to get back at Custer."

"But Custer isn't even buried there," said a fourth agent. "He's buried at West Point."

"So maybe these were stupid Indians," said yet another agent. "These Indians were pissing and shitting on the graves, digging them up, and piling the bones and shit into some old pickup. And along come our local boys, Mr. Fat Cop and Mr. Skinny Cop, who shoot a couple of renegades before the rest of the tribe rises up and massacres them."

"That's well and good," said the last agent, "but damn, the local coroner says our cops were chewed on. Human bite marks all over their bones and what's left of their bodies. Are you saying a cannibal-istic army of Indian radicals ate the cops?"

All of the agents, hard-core veterans of domestic wars, laughed long and hard. They'd all seen the evil that men do, and it was usu-ally simple and concise, and always the result of the twisted desire for more power, money, or sex. Perhaps the killers in this case were new and unusual. The FBI agents thrilled at the possibility of discovering an original kind of sin and capturing an original group of sinners. The local cops had described the massacre scene as the worst thing they'd ever seen, but each FBI agent was quite confident he'd already seen the worst death he would ever see. One more death, no matter how ugly, was just one more death.

In his seat apart from the other agents, Edgar wondered why he had dreamed about Custer on the same night, at the very same moment, these horrible murders were happening on the battlefield that bore Custer's name. He didn't believe in ESP or psychics, in haunted houses or afterlife experiences, or in any of that paranormal bullshit. Edgar believed in science, in cause and effect, in the here and now, in facts. But no matter how rational he pretended to be, he knew the world had always contained more possibilities than he could imagine, and now, here he was, confronted by the very fact of a dream killing so closely tied with real killings. Edgar Smith was scared.

He was even more scared after he and the other agents walked over a rise and stood before the Little Big Horn massacre site. Three of the agents immediately vomited and could only work the perimeter of the scene. Another agent, who was the first rescuer at the bombing of the U.S. military barracks in Beirut and had searched the rubble for bodies and pieces of body, turned back at the cemetery gate and retired on half-pension. Everybody else ran back to their cars and donned thick yellow haz-mat suits with oxygen tanks. Trembling with terror and nausea, the agents worked hard. They had a job to do, and they performed it with their customary grace and skill, but all along, the agents doubted they had enough strength to face an enemy capable of such destruction.

Edgar counted two hundred and fifty-six open graves, all of them filled with blood, pieces of skin, and unidentifiable body parts. Witches' cauldrons, thought Edgar as he stared down into the worst of them. The dirt and grass were so soaked with blood and viscera that it felt like walking through mud. And then there was the dead. One of the state cops, or what was left of him, was smeared all over his cruiser. He was now a pulp-filled uniform and one thumb dark with fingerprint powder. The other cop was spread over a twenty-foot circle, his blood and bones mixing with the blood and bones of one Indian. The other Indian, older, maybe fifty years old, was largely untouched, except for twenty or thirty tentative bite marks, as if his attackers had tasted him and found him too sour. One tooth, a human molar, was broken off at the root and imbedded in the old Indian's chin. This was all madness, madness, madness, and Edgar knew that a weaker person could have easily fallen apart here and run screaming into the distance. A weaker person might have looked for escape, but Edgar knew he would never truly leave this nightmare.

And yet, Edgar could only know the true extent of this nightmare after he followed the blood trails. There were two hundred and fifty-six blood trails, one for each grave, and they led away from the cemetery in all directions. Occasionally, five or ten or fifteen blood trails would merge into one, until there were only forty or fifty blood trails in total, all of them leading away in different directions. Eventually all of these trails faded into the grass and dirt, and became only a stray drop of blood, a strip of shed skin, or small chip of bone, then a series of footprints or single hoofprint before they disappeared altogether. Edgar had no idea what humans, animals, or things had left these blood trails, but they were gone now, traveling in a pattern that suggested they were either randomly fleeing from the murder scene or beginning a carefully planned hunt.

E arly the next morning, in Billings, Montana, Junior Estes sat on the front counter of the Town Pump convenience store, where he'd worked graveyard shift for two years. He worked alone that night because his usual partner, Harry Quakenbrush, had called in sick at the last moment.

"Jesus," Junior had cursed. "You know I can't get nobody to work graveyard at the last sec. Come on, Harry, if you ain't got cancer of the balls, then you better get your ass in here."

"It is cancer of the nuts, and you should feel sorry for bringing it up," Harry had said as he'd hung up the phone and crawled back into bed with his new girlfriend.

So Junior was all by himself in the middle of the night, and knew he couldn't cashier, stock the coolers, and disinfect the place all at the same time, so he decided to do nothing. He might get fired when the boss man showed up at 6 A.M., but he knew Harry would get fired, too, and that would be all right enough. Most nights, twenty or thirty insomniacs, other night shift workers, and the just plain crazy would wander into the store, but only two hookers had been in that night and had pointedly ignored Junior. Poor Junior wasn't ugly, but he was lonely, and that made him stink.

At 3:17 A.M., according to the time stamped on the surveillance tape, Junior noticed a man staggering in slow circles around the gas pump. Junior grabbed a baseball bat from beneath the counter and dashed outside. The external cameras were too blurry and dark to pick up much detail as he confronted the drunken man. A few years earlier, up north in Poplar, a drunk Indian had set a gas pump on fire and burned down half a city block, so Junior must have remembered that as he pushed the man away from the store. Then, at the very edge of the video frame, the drunken man grabbed Junior by the head and bit out his throat. As the video rolled, the drunken man fell on Junior and ate him. Later examination of the videotape revealed that the drunken man was horribly scarred and that he was wearing a Seventh Cavalry uniform, circa 1876.

Edgar and another agent were on the scene twenty minutes after Junior was killed. In the parking lot, as Edgar kneeled over Junior's mutilated body, he felt like he was falling; then he did fall. In a seizure, with lightning arcing from one part of his brain to another, Edgar saw a series of mental images, as clear as photographs, as vivid as film. He saw death.

On Sheep Mountain, near the Montana-Wyoming border, six members of the Aryan Way Militia were pulled out of an SUV and dismembered.

Edgar saw this and somehow knew that Richard Usher, the leader of the Aryan Way, was the great-grandson of a black coal miner named Jefferson Usher.

On an isolated farm near Jordan, Montana, a widowed farmer and his three adult sons fought an epic battle against unknown intruders. Local police would gather five hundred and twelve spent bullet shells, five shotguns with barrels twisted from overheating, two illegal automatic rifles with jammed firing mechanisms, and six pistols scattered around the farm and grounds. The bodies of the farmer and his sons were missing.

But Edgar saw their stripped skeletons buried in a shallow grave atop the much deeper grave of a one-thousand-year-old buffalo jump near the Canadian border. Edgar saw this and somehow knew the exact latitude and longitude of that particular buffalo jump. He knew the color of the grass and dirt.

Outside Killdeer, North Dakota, a few miles from the Fort Berthold Indian Reservation, five Hidatsa Indians were found nailed to the four walls and ceiling of an abandoned hunting cabin.

Edgar saw these bodies and suddenly knew these men's names and the names of all of their children, but he also knew their secret names, the tribal names that had been given to them in secret ceremonies and were never said aloud outside of the immediate family.

All told, sixty-seven people were murdered that night and Edgar saw all of their deaths. Somehow, he knew their histories and most personal secrets. He saw their first cars, marriages, sex, and fights. He suddenly knew them and mourned their butchery as if he'd given birth to them.

And then, while still inside his seizure and fever-dream, and just when Edgar didn't know if his heart could withstand one more murder, he saw survival.

At a highway rest stop off Interstate 94, a trucker changing a flat tire was attacked and bitten by a soldier, but he fought him off with the tire iron. He jumped into his truck and ran over twelve other soldiers as he escaped. Throwing sparks by riding on one steel rim and seventeen good tires, he drove twenty miles down the freeway and nearly ran down the Montana State Patrolman who finally stopped him.

Edgar saw an obese white trucker weep in the arms of the only black cop within a one-thousand-mile radius.

In the Pryor Forest, Michael X, a gold-medal winner in downhill bicycling at the last ESPN X Games, escaped five soldiers on horseback by riding his bike off a cliff and dropping two hundred feet into Big Horn Lake. With a broken leg and punctured lung, Michael swam and waded north for ten miles before a local fisherman pulled him out of the river.

Edgar could taste the salt in the boy's tears.

At Crow Agency, a seven-year-old Indian girl was using the family outhouse when she was attacked. While the soldiers tore off the door, she sneaked out the moon-shaped window and crawled onto the outhouse roof. On the roof, she saw she was closer to a tall poplar tree than to her family's trailer, and there was nobody else home anyway, so she jumped to the ground and outran two soldiers to the base of the tree. She climbed for her life to the top and balanced on a branch barely strong enough to hold her weight. Again and again, the two soldiers climbed after her, but their decayed bones could not support the weight of their bodies, and so they broke apart, hands and arms hanging like strange fruit high in the tree, while their bodies kicked and screamed on the ground below.

Here, Edgar pushed himself into his vision, into the white-hot center of his fever, and attacked those two soldiers with his mind.

"Go away," he screamed as he seized in the convenience store parking lot. The other agents thought Edgar was hallucinating and screaming at ghosts. But Edgar's voice traveled through the dark and echoed in the soldiers' ears. The little Indian girl heard Edgar's disembodied voice and wondered if God was trying to save her. But the soldiers were not afraid of God or his voice. Edgar watched helplessly as the soldiers leaned against the tree, pushed it back and forth, and swung the girl at the top in an ever-widening arc. Edgar knew they were trying to break the tree at the base.

"Leave her alone," he screamed.

But the soldiers ignored him and worked against the tree. Up high, the Indian girl cried for her mother and father, who had gone to a movie and were unaware that the baby-sitter had left their daughter alone in the house.

"Stop, stop, stop," Edgar screamed. He was desperate. He knew the girl would die unless he stopped the soldiers, and then he knew, without knowing why he knew, exactly how to stop them.

"Attention," he screamed.

The two soldiers, obedient and well trained, immediately stood at full attention.

"Right face," Edgar screamed.

With perfect form, the two soldiers faced right, away from the tree.

"Forward march," Edgar screamed.

Stunned, the little Indian girl watched the two soldiers marching away from her. They marched into the darkness. Edgar knew the soldiers would keep marching until they fell into a canyon or lake, or until they crossed an old road where a fast-moving logging truck might smash them into small pieces. Edgar knew these two soldiers would never stop. He knew all of these soldiers, all two hundred and fifty-six of them, would never quit, not until they had found whatever it was they were searching for.

Sixty miles away from that little girl, Edgar burned with vision-fever as he saw the world with such terrible clarity. In that filthy Town Pump parking lot, illuminated by cheap neon, his fellow agents kneeled over him, held his arms and legs, and shoved a spoon into his mouth so he wouldn't swallow his tongue. Edgar pushed and pulled with supernatural strength. Six other men could barely hold him down. Then it was over. Edgar quickly awoke from his seizure, stood on strong legs, rushed to a dispatch radio transmitter, and told his story. On open channels, Edgar told dozens of police officers and FBI agents exactly where to find dead bodies and survivors. And once those doubtful police officers and agents traveled all over Montana, Wyoming, North and South Dakota, and across the border into Canada, and found exactly what Edgar had said would be found, he was quickly escorted to a hospital room, where he was first examined and found healthy, and then asked again and again how he had come to know what he knew. He told the truth, and they did not believe him, and he didn't blame them because he knew that it sounded crazy. He'd interviewed hundreds of people who claimed to see visions of the past and future. He'd made fun of them all, and now he wondered how many of them had been telling the truth. How many of those schizophrenics had really been talking to God? How many of those serial killers had really been possessed by the Devil? How many murdered children had returned to; haunt their surviving parents?

"I don't know what else to say; it's the truth," Edgar said to his fellow agents, who were so sad to see a good man falling apart, and so they left him alone in his hospital room. In the dark, Edgar listened hard for the voices he was sure would soon be speaking to him, and he wondered what those voices would ask him to do and if he would honor their requests. Edgar felt hunted and haunted, and when he closed his eyes, he smelled blood and he didn't know how much of it would be spilled before all of this was over.

Goodbye to All That

By HARLAN ELLISON

*At the end of a grand adventure, the answer to all the
riddles of existence—with fries and a large Coke.*

"Like a Prime Number, the Ultimate Punchline stands alone."
—DANIEL MANUS PINKWATER

He knew he was approaching the Core of Unquenchable Perfection, because the Baskin-Robbins "flavor of the month" was tuna fish–chocolate. If memory served (served, indeed! if only! but, no, it did nothing of the sort . . . it just lay about, eating chocolate truffles, whimpering to be waited on, hand and foot) he was now in Nepal. Or Bhutan. Possibly Tanna Touva.

He had spent the previous night at a less-than-opulent b & b in the tiny, forlorn village of Moth's Breath—which had turned out to be, in fact, not a hostelry, but the local abbatoir—and he was as yet, even this late in the next day, unable to rid his nostrils of the stultifying memory of formaldehyde. His yak had collapsed on the infinitely upwardly spiraling canyon path leading to the foothills that nuzzled themselves against the flanks of the lower mountains timorously raising their sophomore bulks toward the towering ancient massif of the thousand-peaked Mother of the Earth, *Chomolungma,* the pillar of the sky upon which rested the mantle of the frozen heavens. Snow lay treacherously thick and deep and placid on that celestial vastness; snow blew in ragged curtains as dense as swag draperies across the summits and chasms and falls and curved scimitar-blade sweeps of icefields; snow held imperial sway up here, high so high up here on this sacred monolith of the Himalayas that the natives called the Mother-Goddess of the Earth, *Chomolungma.*

Colman suffered from poriomania. Dromomania was his curse. From agromania, from parateresiomania, from ecdemonomania, from each and all of these he suffered. But mostly dromomania.

Compulsive traveling. Wanderlust.

Fifty United States before the age of twenty-one. All of South America before twenty-seven. Europe and most of Africa by his thirtieth birthday. Australia, New Zealand, the Antarctic, much of the subcontinent by thirty-three. And all of Asia but this frozen nowhere as his thirty-ninth birthday loomed large but a week hence. Colman, helpless planomaniac, now climbed toward the Nidus of Ineluctable Reality (which he knew he was nearing, for his wafer-thin, solar-powered, internet-linked laptop advised him that Ben & Jerry's had just introduced a new specialty flavor, Sea Monkey—which was actually only brine-shrimp-flavored sorbet) bearing with him the certain knowledge that if the arcane tomes he had perused were to be believed, then somewhere above him, somewhere above the frozen blood of the Himalayan icefalls, he would reach The Corpus of Nocturnal Perception. Or The Abyss of Oracular Aurochs. Possibly The Core of Absolute Discretion.

There had been a lot of books, just a *lot* of books. And no two agreed. Each had a different appellation for the Ultimate. One referred to it as the Core of Absolute Discretion, another the Intellectual Center of the Universe, yet a third fell to the impenetrable logodædelia of: The Foci of Conjunctive Simultaneity. Perhaps there had been too *many* books. But shining clearly through the thicket of rodomontade there *was* always the ineluctable, the inescapable truth:

there *was* a place at the center of it all. Whether Shangri-la, or Utopia, Paradisaical Eden or the Elysian Fields, whether The Redpath of Nominative Hyperbole or The Last and Most Porous Membrane of Cathexian Belief, there was a valley, a greensward, a hill or summit, a body of water or a field of grain whence it all came.

A place where Colman could travel to, a place that was the confluence of the winds of Earth, where the sound of the swaying universe in its cradle of antiquity melded with the promise of destiny.

But where it might be, was the puzzle.

Nepal, Katmandu, Bhutan, Mongolia, Tibet, the Tuva Republic, Khembulung . . . it *had* to be up here, somewhere. He'd tried everywhere else. He'd narrowed the scope of the search to a fine channel, five by five, and at the end he would penetrate that light and reach, at last, The Corpus of Nocturnal Perception, or *whatever*; and then, perhaps only then, would his mad unending need to wander the Earth reach satiation.

Then, so prayed Colman deep in the cathedral of his loneliness, then he might begin to lead a life. Home, family, friends, purpose beyond *this* purpose . . . and perhaps no purpose at all, save to exist as an untormented traveler.

His yak had died, there on the trail; he presumed from sheer fright at the prospect of having to schlep him up that great divide, into the killing snowfields. The yak was widely known to be a beast of really terrific insight and excellent, well at least pretty good, instincts.

Death before dishonor was not an unknown concept to the noble yak.

Colman had tried several simple, specific, and sovereign remedies to resucitate the imperial beast: liquor from toads boiled in oil to help reduce the fever; leaves of holly mixed with honey, burned to ash in oast ovens and rendered into syrup; the force-feeding of a live lizard tongue, swallowed whole in one gulp (very difficult, as the yak was thoroughly dead); tea made from tansy; tea made from vervain.

Absolutely no help. The yak was dead. Colman was afoot in the killing icefields. On his way to Utopia, to Shangri-la, or, at least, The Infinitely Replenishing Fountain of Mythic Supposition. There had been just a *lot* of books.

He reconciled the thought: *I'll never make it with all this gear.* Then, the inevitable follow-up: *I'll never make it* without *all this gear.* He unshipped the dead noble beast and began, there on the slope, to separate the goods into two piles, seeing his chances of survival diminish with every item added to the heap on his right. He lifted his tinted goggles onto his forehead and stared with naked eye at the massif looming above him. There were more than a few hysterical flurries of snow. Naturally: there was a storm coming.

He knew he was nearing the Heart of Irredeemable Authenticity because the happily buzzing laptop informed him that not only had geomancy been declared the official state religion of Austria, but that Montevideo had been renamed Happy Acres. An investment banker in Montreal had been found dismembered, parts of his body deposited in a variety of public trash bins and Dumpsters, but Colman didn't think that had anything of the significant omen about it.

The storm had broken over him, sweeping down from the pinnacles; less than two hours after he had crossed the great divide, broached the slope, and begun his ascent toward the summit now hidden by thunderheads. Abrading ground-glass flurries erupted out of crevasses; and the swirling lacelike curtains of ice and snow were cruelly driven by a demented wind. He thought he had never known cold before, no matter how cold he had ever been, never anything like this. His body moaned.

And he kept climbing. There was no alternative. He would either reach the Corporeality of the Impossible Metaphor, or he would be discovered eons hence, when this would all be swampy lowland, by whatever species had inherited the planet after the poles shifted.

Hours were spent by Colman coldly contemplating the possible positions his centuries-frozen (but perfectly flash-frozen) corpse might assume. He recalled a Rodin sculpture in a small park in Paris, he thought it was an *hommage* to Maupassant or Balzac, one or the other, and remembered the right hand, the way it curled, and the position of the fingers. He envisioned himself entombed in just that way, sculptural hand with spread fingers protruding from the ages of ice. And so, hours were spent trudging with ice-axe in hand, up the killing icefields, dreaming in white of death tableaux.

Until he fell forward and lay still, as the storm raged over him. There was silence only in that unfrozen inner place beyond the residence of the soul.

When he awoke, not having frozen to death at all, which eventually struck him as fairly miraculous (but, in fact, easily explained by the storm having blown itself out quickly, and the escarpment just above him providing just enough shelter), he got to his feet, pulled the staff loose from the snowpack, and looked toward the summit.

High above him, blazing gloriously in the last pools of sunlight whose opposite incarnations were fields of blue shadow, he beheld the goal toward which he had climbed, that ultimate utopian goal he had sought across entire continents, through years of wandering. There it was, as the books had promised: The Singular Scheme of Cosmic Clarity. The center, the core, the hub, the place where all answers reside. He had found lost Shangri-la, whatever its real name might be. He saw above him, in the clearness of the storm-scoured waning day, what appeared to be a golden structure rising from the summit, its shape a reassuring and infinitely calming sweep of dual archlike parabolas. He thought that was what the shapes were called, parabolas.

Now there was no exhaustion. No world-weariness. He was not even aware that inside his three pairs of thermal socks, inside his crampon'd boots, all the toes of his left foot and three of his right had gone black from frostbite.

Mad with joy, he climbed toward those shining golden shapes, joyfully mad to enter into, at last, The Sepulchre of Revealed Truths. There may have been a great many books but, oh frabjous day, they were all, every last one of them, absolutely dead on the money. The Node of Limitless Revealment. Whatever.

It was very clean inside. Sparkling, in fact. The tiles underfoot were spotless, reflective, and calming. The walls were pristine, in hues of pastel solicitude that soothed and beckoned. There were tables and chairs throughout, and at one end a counter of some magnificent

gleaming metal that showed Colman his ravaged reflection, silvered and extruded, but clearly wan and near total exhaustion. Patches of snowburned flesh had peeled away on both cheeks, chin, nose. The eyes somewhat unfocused as if coated with albumin. The Sanctum of Coalesced Revelations was brightly lit, scintillant surfaces leading the eye toward the shining bar of the magic metal counter. Colman shambled forward, dropping his ice staff; he was a thing drawn off the mountain barely alive, into this oasis of repose and cleanliness, light and succor.

There was a man in his late thirties standing behind the gleaming metal counter. He smiled brightly at Colman. He had a nice face. "Hi! Welcome to The Fountainhead of Necessary Perplexity. May I take your order, please?"

Colman stood rooted and wordless. He knew precisely what was required of him—each and every one of the arcane tomes had made it clear there was a verbal sigil, a password, a phrase that need be spoken to gain access to the holiest of holies—but he had no idea what that *open sesame* might be. The Gardyloo of Ecstatic Entrance. Wordless, Colman looked beseechingly at the counterman.

He may have said, "Uh . . ."

"Please make your selection from the menu," said the man behind the counter, who wore a classic saffron robe and a small squared-off cardboard hat. Colman remembered a film clip of The Andrews Sisters singing "Boogie Woogie Bugle Boy," wearing just such "garrison caps." The counterman pointed to the black-on-yellow signage suspended above the gleaming deck. Colman pondered the choices:

THE OXEN ARE SLOW, BUT THE EARTH IS PATIENT

CHANCE FAVORS THE PREPARED MIND

IT TAKES A HEAP O' LIVIN' TO MAKE A HOUSE A HOME

DEATH COMES WITHOUT THE THUMPING OF DRUMS

I LIKE YOUR ENERGY

THE AVALANCHE HAS ALREADY STARTED; IT'S TOO LATE
FOR THE PEBBLES TO VOTE

EVERY CLOUD HAS A SILVER LINING

DON'T LOOK BACK. SOMETHING MAY BE GAINING ON YOU

YES, LIFE IS HARD; BUT IF IT WERE EASY, EVERYBODY WOULD BE DOING IT

LIFE IS A FOUNTAIN

TRUST IN ALLAH, BUT TIE YOUR CAMEL

THE BARKING DOG DOES NO HARM TO THE MOON

THE MAN WHO BURNS HIS MOUTH ON HOT MILK
BLOWS ON HIS ICE CREAM

NO ONE GETS OUT OF CHILDHOOD ALIVE

SO NEAR, AND YET SO FAR

MAN IS COAGULATED SMOKE FORMED BY HUMAN PREDESTINATION . . .
DUE TO RETURN TO THAT STATE FROM WHICH IT ORIGINATED

French fries are à la carte.

Colman drew a deep, painful breath. To get to this point, and to blow it because of a few words . . . unthinkable. His mind raced. There were deep thoughts he could call up from a philosophy base on the laptop, the aphorisms and rubrics of six thousand years of human existence, but it was only one of them, only one—like a prime number—that would stand alone and open to him the portals of wisdom; only one that would be accepted by this gatekeeper of *Universal* Oneness; only one unknown core jot of heart-meat that would serve at this moment.

He tried to buy himself a cæsura: he said to the saffron-robed counterman, "Uh . . . one of the those . . . 'Life is a fountain'? I know that one; you've got to be kidding, right? 'Life is a fountain . . .'"

The counterman looked at him with shock. "Life *isn't* a fountain?"

Colman stared at him. He wasn't amused.

"Just fooling," the counterman said, with a huge smile. "We always toss in an old gag, just to mix it up with the Eternal Verities. Life should be a bit of a giggle, a little vaudeville, whaddaya think?"

Colman was nonplussed. He was devoid of plus. He tried to buy another moment: "So, uh, what's your name?"

"I'll be serving you. My name's Lou."

"Lou. What are you, a holy man, a monk from some nearby lamasery? You look a little familiar to me."

Lou chuckled softly again, as if he were long used to the notoriety and had come to grips with it. "Oh, heck no, I'm not a holy man; you probably recognize me from a bubble gum card. I used to play a little ball. Last name's Boudreau." Colman asked him how to spell that, and he did, and Colman went to his rucksack, dropped on one of the tables, and he pulled out the laptop and did a Google search for the name *Lou Boudreau.*

He read what came up on the screen.

He looked at what he had read on the screen for a long time. Then he went back to the counter.

"You were the player-manager of the World Champion 1948 Cleveland Indians. Shortstop. 152 games, 560 at bats, 199 hits, 116 runs. You were the all-time franchise leader with a .355 batting average, slugging and on-base percentages, and a .987 OPS! What are you doing here, for gawdsakes?!"

Boudreau removed the little paper hat, scratched at his hair for a moment, sighed, and said, "Rhadamanthus carries a grudge."

Colman stared dumbly. Zeus had three sons. One of them was Rhadamanthus, originally a judge in the afterlife, assigned the venue of the Elysian plain, which was considered a very nice neighborhood. But sometime between Homer and Virgil, flame-haired Rhadamanthus got reassigned to Tartarus, listed in all the auto club triptychs as Hell. Strict judge of the dead. No sin goes unpunished. From which the word "rhadamanthine" bespeaks inflexibility.

"What did you do to honk him off?"

"I went with Bearden instead of Bob Lemon in the first game of the series against the Boston Braves. We lost one to nothing. Apparently he had a wad down on the game."

A slim black man, quite young, wearing a saffron robe and cardboard garrison cap, came out of the back. Lou aimed a thumb at him. "Larry Doby, left fielder. First Negro to play in the American League." Doby smiled, gave a little salute, and said to Colman, "Figure it out yet?"

Colman shook his head.

"Well, good luck." Then, in Latin, he added, *"Difficilia quae pulchra."* Colman had no idea what that meant, but Doby seemed to wish him well with the words. He said Thank you.

Lou pointed toward the rear. "That's our drive-thru attendant, Joe Gordon, great second baseman. Third baseman Ken Keltner on the grill with our catcher, Jim Hegan; Bob Feller's working maintenance just till his arm gets right again, but Lemon and Steve Gromek'll be handling the night shift. And our fry guy is none other than the legendary Leroy 'Satchel' Paige . . . hey, Satch, say hello to the new kid!"

Lifting the metal lattice basket out of the deep fryer filled with sizzling vegetable oil, Satchel Paige knocked the basket half-full of potatoes against the edge of the tub to shake away excess drippings, and grinned hugely at Colman. "You see mine up there?" he said, cocking his head toward the signage of wise sayings. Colman nodded and smiled back.

"Well," said Lou Boudreau, saffron-robed counterman shortstop manager of the 1948 World Series champion Cleveland Indians, who had apparently really pissed off Rhadamanthus, "are you ready to order?"

Time had run out. Colman knew this was it. Whatever he said next would be either the gate pass or the bum's rush. He considered the choices on the menu, trying to pick one that spoke to his gut. It had to be *one* of them.

His mind raced. It *had* to be one of them.

He paused. It was the moment of the cortical-thalamic pause. *Why* did it have to be one of them?

Life *wasn't* a fountain.

There was only one thing to say to God, if one were at the Gate. At the Core, the Nexus, the Center, the Eternal Portal. Only one thing that made sense, whether this was God or just a minimum-wage, part-time employee. Colman straightened, unfurrowed his brow, and spoke the only words that would provide entrance if one were confronting God. He said to Lou Boudreau:

"Let me talk to the Head Jew."

The peppy little shortstop grinned and nodded and said, "May I super-size that for you?"

The mummy's eyes gazed out of the ancient past . . . and into the depths of his soul!

Private Grave 9

By KAREN JOY FOWLER

Every week Massoud takes our trash out and buries it. Yesterday's was chicken bones, orange peels, a tin that cherries had come in and another for peas, a comb I sat on and broke, two prints I overexposed, and several discarded drafts of Mallick's letter to Lord Wallis about our progress. Meanwhile, at G4 and G5, two bone hairpins and seven clay shards were unearthed, one of which was painted with some sort of dog, or so Davis says, though I would have guessed a lion. There was more in other sectors, but too recent—anything Roman or later is still trash as far as we are concerned. G4 and G5 are along the deep cut and we pull our oldest stuff from them.

I spent the morning in the darkroom, feeling lucky that my work affords me such privacy; the constant companionship of the expedition house can be hard sometimes. I was printing photographs of infant skeletons. There is an entire level of these, all laid out identically on their sides with their legs pulled into their stomachs. My pictures were of all different children, but all my pictures looked the same. Davis had cleared each tiny skull and rib cage with his breath and I wondered if that had given him any attachment to one more than another, but it seemed a rude thing to ask. I had some philosophical thoughts that I shared at lunch, on how much sadder a single child would have been and how odd that it should be like that, you feeling less with each addition. Mallick, our director, said when I'd put in a few more seasons I'd find I didn't think of them as dead people at all, but as the bead necklace or the copper bowl or whatever else might be found with the body. Mallick's eyes are all rimmed in red like a basset hound's; it gives him a tragic demeanor, though he's really quite a cheerful sort. The whole time he was speaking, Miss Jackson, his secretary, was shaking her head at me behind his back. Miss Jackson lost her husband in the trench war and her son to the flu after. She has come here specifically to be with dead people.

Ferhid carved us a cold lamb for lunch and had the mail lying under our forks. Ferhid has the profile of a film star, but a mouthful of rotted teeth. I often wish he smiled less; his mouth is a painful thing to confront while eating. We each had a letter or two, which was fair and companionable, though most of them mentioned Howard Carter's dig, which was not. Mine was from my mother, who pretends not to miss me as unpersuasively as she can. I was kept out of the military as I'm her sole support, but it's a role I've found burdensome since the war ended. Last month I wrote to her that a man must have a vocation and if nothing comes to him, then he must go looking. Today she responded by wondering if it was necessary to travel half a globe and 4500 years away. She said that Mesopotamia must be about as far from Indiana as it's possible to get. How wonderful it must be, she said, to be so unattached that you can pick up and go anywhere and never mind the people you've left behind. And then she assured me she was not complaining.

Patwin read bits of the *Times* aloud while we had our coffee.

Apparently reporters are still camped at the Tut-ankh-Amen tomb, cataloguing gold masks and lapis lazuli scarabs and ebony effigies as fast as Carter can haul them out. These *Times* accounts have Lord Wallis and everyone else in a spin, as if we're playing some sort of sporting match against Carter and losing badly. Our potsherds, never mind how old they are, have become an embarrassing return on Wallis's investment, though they were good enough before. Our skeletons are too numerous to be tasteful. I'm betting Wallis won't be whimsical about paintings of dogs, nor will anyone else at his club.

As he read, Patwin's tone conveyed his disapproval. He has an anarchist's face, but is actually a French Marxist and, though he'll tell you slavery was a necessary historical phase, shards of good clay working-class pots suit him better than golden bowls put by for the afterlife.

"We had a lovely morning in PG9," Mallick said stoutly. PG stands for private grave and PG9 is the largest tomb we've found so far, four chambers in all, and never plundered, which is the really exciting bit. A woman is laid out in the second of these chambers— a priestess or a queen in a coffin of clay. There is a necklace of gold leaves, a gold ring, and several of the colored beads she once wore in her hair have fallen into her skull. The bodies of seven other women kneel about her. There are two groomsmen and two oxen and a musician with what I imagine, when we've reconstructed the missing bits, will be a lyre. Once upon a time Wallis would have been entirely content with this. A royal tomb. A sleeping priestess. But that was before Carter began to swim in golden sarcophagi.

I took her picture that afternoon, but two days passed before I developed it.

A nother American, a girl from Rapid City, had come to visit us at the expedition house. Her name was Emily Whitfield and she was a cousin of Mallick's wife or a second cousin or some such thing, some relative Mallick found impossible to send away. She was twenty-nine years old, which is two years younger than I, unremarkable looking, with short black hair and blue eyes. Because of our similar ages there'd been some mild teasing before she arrived. "High time you met the right girl," Mallick had said, but the minute I saw Miss

Whitfield I knew she wasn't that. I've never known if I believe in love at first sight, but I've had a fair amount of experience with the opposite.

Patwin had not looked forward to Miss Whitfield's visit, despite the obvious appeal of a new face in a confined set. "She will need to be taken everywhere and her feelings will often be hurt by one thing or another," Patwin had predicted. Patwin prided himself on knowing women, although when that would have happened I really could not say. "She'll find it all very dirty and our facilities insupportable. She'll never have stood before." And then Patwin had a coughing fit; it was such a rude thing to have said in Miss Jackson's presence.

But Miss Whitfield was proving entirely game. Davis took her to see the baby skeletons and he said she made no comment, lit an unmoved cigarette. She was actually an authoress and quite success-ful, according to Mallick, who learned it from his wife. Five books so far, books in which people are killed in clever and unusual ways, mur-derers unmasked by people even cleverer. She was about to set a book at a dig such as ours; it's why she'd come. Mallick told me to take her along and show her the tomb, so she was there when I took my picture. I pointed out an arresting detail or two—the way the workmen chant as they haul the rubble out of the chamber, the rags they tie around their heads, their seeping eyes. She didn't seem terri-bly interested.

We brought the smell of sweat and flesh with us into the tomb. Most people would have instinctively known to whisper. Not Miss Whitfield. "I thought it would be grander," she said when we were inside the second chamber. "I didn't picture mud." She lifted a hand to her hair and when she lowered it again there was a streak of dust running from the hairline down her temple. It gave her a friendlier, franker look, but like Mallick's eyes, this proved deceiving. What she really wanted to know was whether there were tensions in the expe-dition house. "You all live so cheek-to-jowl. It must drive you crazy sometimes. There must be little, annoying habits that send you right around the bend."

"Actually things go very smoothly," I told her. "Sorry to disap-point." I set up for the picture. I dragged a stool over and stood on it. Miss Whitfield was at my elbow. Davis was in a corner of the cham-ber on his knees, pouring wax and covering it with cloth. Bits of shell and stone had been found there in a pattern; when the wax dried he would lift them out without disturbing their placement.

Miss Whitfield softened her voice so he wouldn't hear her. She was so close I could smell the cigarette smoke lingering on her skin. "But if you did murder someone," she said, "would it more likely be Mr. Patwin or Mr. Davis?" She might have been asking this at the exact moment I got my shot. Afterward she looked closely at the priestess's skull. "I hear Tut-ankh-Amen's skull was bashed in at the back," she said.

Later that night Patwin complained that I was blocking his light while he tried to read. I told him it was interesting that he thought the light belonged to him. I said, That's an interesting point of view for a Marxist to take, and I saw Miss Whitfield pull out her notebook to write the whole thing down.

A cylindrical seal was found on the bier and Davis deciphered a name from it. Tu-api, along with a designation for a highborn woman. A princess, not a priestess, then. We also found a golden amulet, carved in the shape of a goat standing on its hind legs. There'd been a second goat, a matching partner, but that one was crushed beyond mending. Pictures of all the ornaments had to be finished in a rush and sent off to Lord Wallis. The goat is really lovely and my photograph showed it well; no one need feel apologetic for that find.

But best of all were the stones and shells that Davis had been excavating. Mallick believed there'd once been a wooden box with pictures pressed into its sides. The box had disintegrated and the two sides fallen together, but Davis was slowly putting them to rights. One side showed scenes from ordinary life. There was a banquet with guests and musicians, farmers with wood on their backs, oxen and sheep. The second side was all armies, prisoners of war, chariots, men with weapons. Before and After, Miss Jackson called it, but Mallick called it Peace and War to clarify that it represented two parts of a cycle, and not a sequence, that peace would follow war as well as precede it. The artist must have been remarkable as the people were quite detailed, down to the sorry look on the prisoners' faces.

Patwin criticized me for taking more pictures of Tu-api than of the kneeling girls or the poor musician. Tu-api, he guessed, had the good fortune to die of natural causes. He said that I must fight the bourgeois impulse to care more about the princess than about the slave. It would be even harder, he conceded, now that the princess had a name.

"Does he always lecture at you like that?" Miss Whitfield asked.

Because I was busy developing pictures of golden goats and verdigris bowls, because we'd already sent Lord Wallis plenty of photographs of skeletons, I left my shot of Tu-api untouched for a couple of days. It was late at night when I put it through the wash and hung it up. I didn't look at it closely until the following morning. In my photograph, Tu-api had a face. This wasn't part of the picture exactly, but a cloudy, ghostly spot superimposed over the skull. It made my skin crawl up the back of my neck and I took it to the dig to show the others. It was a hot day and the air so dry it stung to breathe. I found Mallick, Davis, and Miss Jackson all together in the third chamber.

They were not as unnerved as I was. A human face is an easy thing to find, Davis pointed out, in the paint on a ceiling, the grain in a wooden board. "I once saw the face of God in the clouds," Miss Jackson agreed. "I know how that sounds, but it was sharp and perfect, like a Michelangelo. Sober and very beautiful. Thin Chinese sort of beard. I got down on my knees and watched until it melted and blew away."

This sudden display of fancy from solid, cylindrical Miss Jackson obviously embarrassed Mallick. He came over scholarly in response, with his dry voice and those sad eyes. "I've heard of places where bodies are naturally preserved right down to the facial expression," he said. "In the Arctic ice, for example. At very high altitudes. I've always thought those discoveries must be rather grim."

"Buried in the bogs," Patwin said. He had arrived with Miss Whitfield while Mallick was speaking. He held out his hand for my photograph and looked it over silently. He handed it to Miss Whitfield. "I knew a man who'd met a man who'd found a thousand-year-old woman while digging for peat. He said you can't look into a thousand-year-old face and not find yourself just a little bit in love. You can't look into a thousand-year-old face and think, I bet you were an annoying old nag."

"You've just put your thumb here on the print," Miss Whitfield suggested to me. As if I were eight years old and playing with my father's camera.

I imagined myself with my hands about her throat. It came on me all of sudden and shocked me even more than the photograph had. I took my imaginary hands off her and gave her an imaginary and forgiving handshake instead.

In fact, I was angry at them all for refusing to believe the evidence of their own eyes. The woman's face was indistinct, I granted that. But so beautiful. So filled with longing. I looked into her eyes and I could see that she had been frightened. I could see that she hadn't wanted to die alone, had surrounded herself with other people, but it hadn't helped. I thought I knew something about that.

O n payday there were forgeries to be exposed. A number of intriguing little carvings had begun to show up, all found by the same pair of brothers. The recent ones were simply too intriguing. Mallick made a show of dismissing the culprits as a lesson to the rest. It was all very good-natured. Even the brothers laughed at their exposure, left with a cheerful round of goodbyes. It was, no doubt, a great disappointment to Miss Whitfield, who had been looking forward to the confrontation ever since Mallick showed us the tiny forged bear.

None of the workmen would be back until their money ran out, which meant that we would start again in two days with a whole new group. Yusef, who'd found the golden goat, had been paid its weight in gold and wouldn't be back for weeks. This was a shame as he was one of our most skilled workers and a natural diplomat as well. Diplomats were always needed on our mixed crew of Armenians, Arabs, and Kurds.

The site was sadly quiet with everyone gone. I missed the rhythmic chanting, the scraping of stone on stone, the frequent pleasure of dim and distant laughter.

Davis and I used the day off to drive Miss Whitfield to the holy shrine of the Yezedis. The Yezedis worship Lucifer and represent him with the symbol of the peacock. We bounced along the road, the dust so thick I had to stop every fifteen minutes and wipe down the car windows. The last few miles can only be done on foot, but by this time you've risen into the pure air and walking is a pleasure. The shrine is breathtakingly beautiful, white and intricate as a wedding cake. Streams pour through descending basins in the cool courtyard and acolytes tiptoe in to bring you tea. Clearly their Lucifer is not the same as our Lucifer.

Still we had done our best to work Miss Whitfield up with stories of Satan worshippers so that the peaceful, bucolic scene would be a nasty surprise. I fancied I was getting to know what Miss Whitfield wanted. I whispered to her that the priest, whom we did not see, was said to be kept drugged so that his aunt could rule in his name; I didn't want the trip to be a complete disappointment.

"Tell me," Davis said to Miss Whitfield. He sat holding his small, black cup of tea in two hands and smiling sweetly. I was across from him, sleepy from the sun and the sound of water. Miss Whitfield had knelt by the lowest of the fountain pools. She broke the surface with her hand, so her submerged fingers seemed larger than the dry hand to which they were attached. "When you come to a place like this," Davis asked, "even at a place like this, do you find yourself imagining a murder?"

And I thought how easy it would be to push Miss Whitfield's head under and hold it. It wasn't even a complete thought, just a flicker, really, with no emotional content, no actual desire. I put it out of my mind at once, which was easy enough since it had hardly been there to begin with.

"Would you think me a ghoul if I said yes?" Miss Whitfield's black hair shivered in the slight breeze. She smoothed it back with her wet fingers, dipped her hand, and wet her hair again.

"I'd think you the complete professional," Davis said politely. "But it's a ghoulish profession."

"So's yours," she answered. And then to me, "So's yours," even though I hadn't said a thing.

On our way back we stopped in town to buy bread and chocolate to add to our supper of mutton and goat cheese and tankards of wine. Davis had taken the sun during our outing; he was as pink as if he'd been boiled. When he came to the table he sat on a chair that wasn't solidly beneath him and fell to the floor with a great cry of alarm. I had never seen Patwin enjoy anything so much. He could hardly chew he was laughing so hard.

Miss Whitfield was too tired to eat. Ferhid took her untouched plate back to the kitchen, where he dropped knives and slammed pots onto tables to communicate his disapproval until Mallick went out to mollify him.

Before the light went, and when there was no one else about, I slipped away and took six more pictures of Tu-api. I developed them that night, quietly so that no one would hear me up and about. None of the new ones showed her face. I took another print off my original exposure and her face didn't show up there either. Perhaps this should have persuaded me that the image was not to be trusted, was a fault of the paper and therefore unreal. Instead it had the opposite effect. I was more than ever persuaded in the event, which had proved so singular and so intimate. Tu-api had shown her face only once and only to me.

"I have a bone to pick with you." Patwin caught me as I came out of the bathroom. "You're always riding me about my politics." Patwin didn't often use the sort of English idioms these two sentences contained so I imagined he was merely repeating what some more native speaker had said to him and I imagined I knew who that would be. I was outraged by the collusion, but also by the sentiment.

"You must be joking," I said. "The way you lecture me . . ."

"Live and let live is all I'm saying." And he brushed by without another word.

I passed Davis on the way to my bedroom. "That really hurt when I fell," he said. "I may have cracked a bone."

"I didn't laugh as hard as Patwin did," I told him.

Miss Whitfield asked us all what it was about a dig that we liked. We were sitting in the courtyard in the middle of the expedition house and only Mallick was missing, trapped in town by a heavy rain that had turned the roads to mud. The air outside was washed and wonderful and the sky an ocean of cool, gray clouds. Davis and Miss Jackson were playing a game on a stone board more than four thousand years old. Four thousand years ago they would have played with colored stones, but they were making do with buttons. Seven such boards had been found in Tu-api's tomb and the rules were inscribed in cuneiform though not in our dig, but back in Egypt at Carter's. This same game had been played as far away as India. Ferhid was a demon at it.

"Not the fleas," Patwin said. He was scratching at his ankles.

"Not the dust." That was Miss Jackson.

"Not the way the workmen smell," I said.

"Not the way you smell," Patwin added. And then placatingly, "Not the way I smell."

"I like a routine," Davis told her. "I actually enjoy picky, painstaking work. And, of course, I like a puzzle. I like to put things together, guess what they mean."

"I like that it's backwards." Miss Jackson won a free turn and then a second. All six of her buttons were on the board now. "You dig down from the surface and you move backwards in time as you go. Have you ever wanted, desperately wanted, to go backwards in time?"

"Yes, of course," Miss Whitfield said. "Erase your mistakes, the stupid things you say without thinking."

"I like the monotony of it." Patwin had his eyes closed and his face turned up to the cool sky. "Day after day after day with nothing at all but your own thoughts. You begin to think things that surprise you."

Davis bumped one of Miss Jackson's buttons back to the beginning. "There you go backwards in time," he said, but Miss Jackson was speaking too, only quieter so it took a moment longer to hear. "You have to be in love with the dead to like a dig," she said. She took two of her buttons off the board in a single turn and bumped one of Davis's. A third button occupied a safe square, leaving Davis no move.

He shook his fist at her, smiling. "You are a lucky woman," he said.

"Do you know how many bodies we've found on this site?" Miss Jackson asked Miss Whitfield. "Almost two thousand. And every single one of those left someone behind, begging their gods to undo it. Bargaining. Screaming. Weeping. You can only manage a dig if you already feel so much you can't take in another bit."

A long silence followed. "Excuse me," Miss Jackson said and left the courtyard.

Miss Jackson seldom made speeches. She never, ever referred to her losses and I only knew about them because Patwin, who'd worked with her three seasons now, had heard from gossipy Mallick. Patwin had hinted that she was sleeping with Mallick, but I'd seen no signs and hoped it wasn't true. Miss Jackson was not a young woman, nor a pretty one, but she was too young and too pretty for Mallick. Few women would not be.

I thought back on how she'd also told us she'd seen the face of God in the sky and how that speech too had been uncharacteristic. Perhaps we'd come up on the anniversary of something or other. Or perhaps Miss Whitfield was responsible. Miss Whitfield might make me edgy and snappish, but perhaps Miss Jackson had melted in the sympathetic presence of another female.

"Well," said Miss Whitfield. "I hope it wasn't something I said." She wrote a few words in her notebook and then addressed me. "You're very quiet. Are you in love with the dead?"

Since I'd been thinking about Miss Jackson and not about myself, I had nothing prepared to say. "I'm not sure I do like a dig," I answered. "I'm still deciding." My heart was thudding oddly; the question had unnerved me more than I could account for. So I kept talking, just to demonstrate a steadier voice. "I wanted to see some things I wouldn't see in Indiana. Mallick gave a lecture at the university and I asked some questions that he liked and he said if I could make my own way here, he could use me."

Miss Whitfield was staring at me through little eyes. I could see that she didn't believe me and, from that vantage point, I could also see how defensive I'd sounded, how unresponsive to the actual question, and how unlikely my sequence of events was. Mallick in Indiana! Me, asking such good questions from the audience that I was hired on the spot. In fact, it was all true, but pointing that out would be the most suspicious move of all. I felt unjustly accused, but also terribly, visibly guilty. There was a letter opener on a table by the doorway. I pictured myself picking it up and opening Miss Whitfield's throat in one clean swipe.

All of a sudden Patwin laughed.

"What?" Davis asked him. "What's so funny?"

"I was just remembering when you fell off your chair," Patwin said. He was still laughing. "How your arms flew up!"

I had begun visiting Tu-api's tomb at night when no one would know. I would like to say that there was nothing at all odd in this, but how defensive would that sound? Let's just skip that part.

In fact I was disturbed by the murderous images coming over me and the tomb seemed a quiet place to figure things out. I wasn't the sort to hurt anyone. People rarely upset or angered me. I'd never been a bully at school, didn't fight, didn't really engage much with people at all. Didn't care about anyone but myself, my mother had said once after my father died. She'd never said it again, but she hinted it. Buried it in the subtext of every letter. Her own grief had been an awful thing for an eight-year-old boy to see.

But I thought of myself simply as a typical photographer. A watcher, a recorder. Transparent. And I thought how these violent images had begun shortly after Miss Whitfield's arrival, so they might be put to her account. But they'd also begun shortly after Tu-api had shown me her face. In fact, if I remembered correctly, at the moment I had taken my picture the word *murder* had been hanging in the air. There was the smell of smoke. "If you were to murder someone," Miss Whitfield had been asking, "who would it be?" Was it possible that the word itself had brought Tu-api back? Perhaps what I saw in her face wasn't longing after all, but remorse. Patwin was always pointing out how she was a murderess.

Yet I found it easier to think Miss Whitfield was to blame than that Tu-api wished me ill. I'd begun to carry the print of her face in my pocket so I could pull it out and look at it whenever I was alone. At night I would sit on the bricks by her coffin and stare until I had conjured her face out of the darkness.

One night as I was walking as silently as possible back to my bedroom I collided with Mallick. He was wearing a nightshirt that left his saggy old knees bare. "Going to the lavatory," he explained, unnecessarily, so that I knew it was true what Patwin had told me, that he'd been visiting Miss Jackson. I tried to see the good in that, but really, what comfort could sleeping with Mallick have been?

"Me, too," I said with an equal lack of conviction.

We stood a moment, carefully not meeting each other's eyes. "So, Miss Whitfield leaves tomorrow," Mallick offered finally. "She's been a lively addition." I realized then that he thought I'd been visiting Miss Whitfield. As if that wouldn't be worth your life!

A woman's face appeared in a doorway, white and sudden. When my heart began beating again, I recognized Miss Whitfield. She didn't speak to me; merely noted my suspicious, nighttime ramblings, my covert meeting with Mallick, and disappeared as quickly as she'd come, no doubt to write it all down before she forgot. "Taking my own sort of pictures," she called it once, as if what she did and what I did were the same, as if her imposed judgments could be compared to my dispassionate records. If I'd wished to murder her this would have been my last opportunity.

I went to my room and into a night of troubled dreams. Miss Whitfield left the next morning. I took pictures of everyone before she left, at Patwin's insistence. Patwin was always reminding me to document the work as much as the artifacts. "Take some pictures of live people today," he would say. "Take some pictures of me."

Everyone lined up in the expedition house courtyard, staring into the morning sun. Davis had his hand on Patwin's shoulder, but no one else was touching. Miss Whitfield could not stand still and ruined three exposures before I got one that showed her clearly.

"Was there a curse on Tu-api's tomb?" she'd asked us shortly after her arrival. According to the newspapers Carter had a curse; it was one more way in which we disappointed. (According to Mallick, who had his own sources, no one could find the actual site or text of this alleged curse. Other tombs had them so, of course, Carter couldn't do without.)

The very day Carter found the entrance to Tut-ankh-Amen's tomb a cobra ate his pet canary. "Some curse," Patwin scoffed when we read this, but Davis had reminded us of the function canaries served in mines, their deaths a warning that death had entered a room. And then, just last week, we had a telegram from Lord Wallis that Lord Carnarvon, who sponsored Carter's dig, had suddenly died in Cairo. The cause was indeterminate, but might have been a fever carried by an insect bite on his cheek. Back in England his dog also died—this curse was most unkind to pets.

It was the dog that did it for Miss Whitfield. She cared little for mountains of copper, gold, and ebony. She was, as Patwin had once noted, being nothing but fair, no materialist. But she loved a suspicious death. She left us for Egypt just as quick as an invitation could be wrangled and transport arranged.

I believe we were all a bit disappointed to realize that none of us was to be either the murderer nor the victim in her next book. All those murderous thoughts I'd obligingly had, all the probing we'd withstood, all the petty disputes we'd engaged in, and all for nothing. Carter would reap the benefit.

We stood at the entry to the expedition house and waved. She was turned around to us, her face in the window, smaller and smaller until it and then the car that carried her vanished entirely. "A dangerous woman," Patwin said.

"A pot-stirrer," said Davis.

"A terrible eater," said Ferhid. His tone was venomous. "A picky eater."

"I can't put my finger on exactly what it was about her," said Miss Jackson. "But there were times when she was watching us, taking notes on everything we said and did, as if she knew what we really meant and we didn't—there were times when I could have happily strangled her."

So we were all glad to see the last of her. It didn't mean she wasn't missed. It was hard to go back to how we'd been before; there was a space left where she'd been and nothing else would fit inside it. Ferhid continued to set her plate at the table for four days after she'd gone.

The night of her departure I went again to Tu-api's tomb. The silhouette of the ruined ziggurat shone in the moonlight. There was the hum of bugs; a dog barked sleepily in the distance; my footsteps thudded in the dust. The wind was cool and carried the smell of cooked chicken. My relief was enormous. The only reason I'd thought of murdering Miss Whitfield was that she was an annoying woman who often talked about murder. There was nothing supernatural at work here; it was all perfectly normal and everyone had felt the same.

The moon had risen, round as an opened rose. I walked away

from it into the perfect stillness of the tomb. I owed Tu-api an apology. How could I ever have thought, even for a minute, that she would curse me? I asked her for forgiveness. It was the first time I'd spoken to her aloud.

She was not the only one listening. Mallick had apparently told Patwin his suspicions regarding me and Miss Whitfield, and Patwin, being more discerning and trained to read puzzles far older and more mysterious than I, came upon the truth of it. He'd followed me and when I spoke, he responded. "What's this about?" he asked, and what could I possibly say?

"I took a picture of her face."

"You didn't. You can't be coming here anymore at night by yourself." Patwin stepped toward me. "You can't be thinking this way." He took me by the arm. "Come back with me."

I allowed him to lead me over the moonlit dust to the expedition house, our footsteps padding softly. As we went he analyzed the errors in my thinking. I was guilty of romanticism, of individualism. I was guilty of ancestor worship. I had entertained the superstition of an ancient, powerful curse. I wasn't even bourgeois; I had barely made it to primitive.

Then he put me to bed as tenderly as if he were my own mother. He sat beside me for a while, pretending nothing was wrong, just the way my mother would have pretended. "You need a girlfriend," he suggested. "It's too bad Miss Whitfield has gone. It's too bad Miss Jackson is already—spoken for."

I agreed with everything. I agreed that my infatuation with Tu-api was at an end. I agreed that, circumstances being different, I would have considered Miss Jackson or even, God forbid, Miss Whitfield. I agreed that when the weather grew too hot and we all went to our separate homes for the summer, I would put serious effort into finding a girlfriend who was alive. I agreed that love could be usefully examined with the tool of Marxist analysis. I handed over the photograph and watched Patwin tear it up, both of us pretending there was someplace he could put those pieces where they wouldn't last forever.

Albertine, solace of a city in ruins.
Any memory you wanted, anytime you wanted
it. All for the low, low price of—history itself.

The Albertine Notes

By RICK MOODY

The first time I got high all I did was make sure these notes came out all right. I mean, I wanted the girl at the magazine to offer me work again, and that was going to happen only if the story sparkled. There wasn't much work then because of the explosion. The girl at the magazine was saying, "Look, you don't have to like the assignment, just do the assignment. If you don't want it there are people lined up behind you." And she wasn't kidding. There really were people lined up. Out in reception. An AI receptionist, in a makeshift lobby, in a building on Staten Island, the least-affected precinct of the beleaguered City of New York. Writers spilling into the foyer, shouting at the robot receptionist. All eager to show off their clips.

The editor was called Tara. She had turquoise hair. She looked like a girl I knew when I was younger. Where was that girl now? Back in the go-go days you could yell a name at the TV and it would run a search on the identities associated with that name. For a price. Credit card records, toll plaza visits, loan statements, you set the parameters. My particular Web video receiver, in fact, had a little pop-up window in the corner of the image that said, *Want to see what your wife is doing right now?* Was I a likely customer for this kind of snooping based on past purchases? Anyway, recreational detection and character assassination, that was all *before* Albertine.

Street name for the buzz of a lifetime. Bitch goddess of the over-whelming past. Albertine. Rapids in the river of time. Skin pop a little bit, or take up the celebrated Albertine eyedropper, and any memory you've ever had is available to you all over again. That and more. Not a memory like you've experienced it before, not a little tremor in some *presque vu* register of your helter-skelter consciousness: Oh yeah, I remember when I ate peanut butter and jelly with Serena in Boston Commons and drank rum out of paper cups. No, the actual event itself, completely renewed, playing in front of you as though you were experiencing it for the first time. There's Serena in blue jeans with patches on the knee, the green Dartmouth sweatshirt that goes with her eyes, drinking the rum a little too fast and spitting up some of it, picking her teeth with her deep red nails, shade called "lycanthrope," and there's the taste of super-chunky peanut butter, in the sandwiches, stale pretzel rods. Here you are, the two of you, walking around that part of the Commons with all those willows. She lets slip your hand because your palms are moist. The smell of a city park at the moment when a September shower dampens the pavement, car exhaust, a mist hanging in the air at dusk, the sound of kids fighting over the rules of softball, a homeless dude, scamming you for a sip of your rum.

Get the idea?

It almost goes without saying that Albertine appeared in a certain socioeconomic sector not long after the blast. When you're used to living a comfortable middle-class life, when you're used to going to the organic farmers' market on the weekend, maybe a couple of dinners out at that new Indian place, you're bound to become very uncomfortable when fifty square blocks of your city suddenly looks like NASA photos of Mars. You're bound to look for some relief when you're camped in a school gymnasium pouring condensed milk over government-issued cornflakes. Under the circumstances, you're going to prize your memories, right? So you'll skin pop some Albertine, or you'll use the eyedropper, hold open your lid, and go searching back through the halcyon days. Afternoons in the stadium, those stadium lights on the turf, the first roar of the crowd. Or how about your first concert? Or your first kiss?

Only going to cost you twenty-five bucks.

I'm Kevin Lee. Chinese-American, third generation, which doesn't mean my dad worked in a delicatessen to get me into MIT. It means my father was an IT venture capitalist and my mother was a microbiologist. I grew up in Newton, Mass., but I also lived in northern California for a while. I came to New York City to go to Fordham, dropped out, and started writing about the sciences for the one of the alternative weeklies. It was a start. But the offices of the newspaper, all of its owners, a large percentage of its shareholders, and nine-tenths of its reporting staff were incinerated. Not like I need to bring all of that up again. If you need to assume anything, assume that all silences from now on have grief in them.

One problem with Albertine was that the memories she screened were not all good, naturally. Albertine didn't guarantee good memories. In fact, Albertine guaranteed at least a portion of pretty awful memories. One guy I interviewed, early on when I was chasing the story, he spoke about having only memories of jealousy. He got a bad batch, probably too many additives, and all he could see in his mind's eye were these moments of intense jealousy. He was even weeping when we spoke. On the comedown. I'd taken him out to an all-night diner. Where Atlantic Avenue meets up with Conduit. Know that part of the city? A beautiful part of the city, a neglected part. Ought to have been a chill in the early autumn night. Air force jets were landing at the airport in those days. The guy, we'll say his name is Bob, he was telling me about the morning he called a friend, Nina, to meet her for a business breakfast. In the middle of the call Nina told him that his wife, Maura, had become her lover. He remembered everything about this call, the exact wording of the revelation. *Bob, Maura has been attracted to me as far back as your wedding.* He remembered the excruciating pauses. He could overhear the rustling of bedclothes. All these things he could picture, just like they were happening, and even the things he imagined during the phone call, which took place seventeen years ago. What Nina had done to Maura in bed, what dildo they used. It was seventeen years later on Atlantic and Conduit, and Maura was vaporized, or that's what Bob said, "Jesus, Maura is dead and I never told her I regretted all of that, I never told her what was great about the years together, and I'll never have that chance now." He was inconsolable, but I kept asking questions. Because I'm a reporter. I put it together that he'd spent fifty bucks on two doses of Albertine. Six months after the thyroid removal, here he was. Bob was just hoping to have one sugary memory—of swimming in the pond in Danbury, the swimming hole with the rope swing. Remember that day? And all he could remember was that his wife had slept with his college friend, and that his brother took the girl he liked in high school. Like jealousy was the single color of his life. Like the atmosphere was three parts jealousy, one part oxygen.

That's what Albertine was whispering in his ear.

Large-scale drug dealing, it's sort of like beta-testing. There are unscrupulous people around. Nobody knows how a chemical is going to behave until the guinea pigs have lined up. FDA thinks it knows, like when it rubber-stamps some compound that makes you grow back hair you lost during chemotherapy. But the feds know nothing. Try giving your drug to a hundred and fifty thousand disenfranchised members of the new middle-class poor in a recently devastated American city. Do it every day for almost a year. Allow people to mix in randomly their favorite inert substances.

There were lots of stories. Lots of different experiences. Lots of fibs, exaggerations, innuendoes, rumors. Example: not only did Albertine cause bad memories as frequently as good memories—this is the lore—but she also allowed you to *remember the future.* This is what Tara told me when she assigned me the 2500 words. "Find out if it's true. Find out if we can get to the future on it."

"What would you do with it?"

"None of your business," she said, and then like she was covering her tracks, "I'd see if I was ever going to get a promotion."

Well, here's one example. The story of Deanna, whose name I'm also changing for her own protection: "I was going to church after the blast, you know, because I was kind of feeling like God should be doing something about all the heartache. I mean, maybe that's simpleminded or something. I don't care. I was in church and it was a beautiful place. Any church still standing was a beautiful place, when you had those horrible clouds overhead all the time and everybody getting sick. Fact of the matter is, while I was there in church, during what should have been a really calm time, instead of thinking that the gospels were good news, I was having a vision. I don't know what else to call it. It was like in the movies, when the movie goes into some kind of flashback. Except in this vision, I saw myself driving home from church, and I saw a car pulling ahead of me out onto the road by the reservoir, and I had this feeling that the car pulling out toward the reservoir, which was a twenty-year-old model of one of those minivans, was some kind of bad omen, you know? So I went to my priest, and I told him what I thought, that this car had some bad intention, at least in my mind's eye, you know, I could see it, I could see that Jesus was telling me this, *Better watch out at the reservoir. Some potion is going to be emptied into the reservoir. I have seen it, I have seen it.* The guys doing it, they're emptying jugs in and they definitely have mustaches. They're probably from some desert country. The priest took me to the bishop, and I repeated everything I knew, about the Lord and what he had told me, and so I had an audience with the archbishop. The archbishop said, 'You have to tell me if Jesus really told you this. Did Jesus tell you personally? Is this a genuine message from the Christ?' In this office with a lot of dusty books on the dusty shelves. You could tell that they were all really hungry to be in the room with the word of the Christ, and who wouldn't feel that way? Everybody is desperate, right? But then one of them says, 'Roll up your sleeves, please.' "

Deanna was shown the door. Because of the needle tracks. Now she's working down by the Gowanus Expressway.

The archbishop did give the tip to the authorities, however, just to be on the safe side, and the authorities did stop a Ford Explorer on the way to the reservoir in Katonah. And Deanna's story was just one along these lines. Many Albertine users began reporting "memories" of things that were yet to happen. Outcomes of local elections, declines in various international stocks, the intensity of the upcoming hurricane season. The dealers, whether skeptical or believing on this point, saw big profits in the mythology. Because garbage heads and gamblers often live right next door to one another, know what I mean? One vice is like another. Soon there were those scraggly guys that you used to see at the track. These guys were all looking to cop from the man in Red Hook, or East New York, and they were sitting like autistics in a room with Sheetrock torn from the walls, no electricity, no running water, people pissing themselves, refusing food, and they were in search of the name of the greyhound that was going to take the next race. Maybe they could bet the trifecta? Teeth were falling out of the heads of these bettors, and their hair falling out, because they believed if they just hung on long enough, they would receive the vision.

Now that's marketing.

Logically speaking, there were some issues with a belief system like this. On Albertine, the visions of the past were mixed up with the alleged future, of course. And sometimes these were nightmarish visions. You had to know where to cast your gaze. There was no particular targeting of receptors. The drug wasn't advanced. It was like using a lawn mower to harvest wildflowers. I shook one girl awake, Cassandra, down in the Hot Zone in Bed-Stuy. I knew Cassandra was a bullshit name, the kind of name you'd tell a reporter. It was a still night, coming on toward December, bitter cold, because the debris cloud had really fucked with global warming, and I was walking around dictating into a digital recorder, okay? The streets were uninhabited. I mean, take a city from eight million down to four and a half million, suddenly everything seems kind of empty. And this is a pedestrian town anyhow. Now more than ever. I was on my way to interview an epidemiologist who claimed that while on Albertine he'd had a memory of the proper way to eradicate the drug. He'd tell me if I would remunerate him. And maybe Tara would reimburse me, because I had run through most of the few hundred dollars I had in cash before my bank was wiped off the map. And I'd already sold blood and volunteered for a dream lab.

But on the way to the epidemiologist, I saw this girl nodding out on a swing, an old wooden swing, the kind that usually gets stolen in the projects. Over by the middle school in the Hot Zone. I picked up her arm; she didn't even seem to notice at first. I lifted up her arm; I turned it over. Like I couldn't tell from the rings under the eyes, those black bruises that say, *This one has remembered too much.* I checked her arms anyway. Covered with lesions.

I said, "Hey, I'm doing a story for one of those tits-and-lit mags. About Albertine. Wondering if I can ask you a few questions."

Her voice frail at first, almost as if it was the first voice ever used: "Ask me any question. I'm like the oracle at Delphi, boyfriend."

Sort of a dark-haired girl, and she sort of reminded me of Serena. Wearing this red scarf on her head. A surge from her voice, like I'd heard it before, like maybe I was almost verging on something from the past. I figured I'd try out Cassandra, see what kind of a fact-gathering resource she could be, see where it led. It beat watching the Hasidim in Crown Heights fighting with the West Indians. Man, I'd had enough with the Hasidim and the Baptists and their rants about *end times.* The problem was that Albertine, bitch goddess, kept giving conflicting reports about which end times we were going to get.

"What's my name?" I said.

"Your name is Kevin Lee. You're from Massachusetts."

"Okay, uh, what am I writing about?"

"You're writing about Albertine, and you're way in over your head already. And the batteries on your recording device are going to run out soon."

"Thanks for the tip. Are we going to kiss?"

A reality-testing question, get it?

No inflection at all, Cassandra said: "Sure. We are. But not now. Later."

"What do you know about the origins of Albertine?"

"What do you want to know?"

"Are you high now?"

Which was like asking if she'd ever seen rain.

"Are you high enough to see the origins from where you are sitting?"

"I'd need to have been there to have a memory of it."

"What have you heard about it?" I said.

"Everybody's heard something."

"I haven't."

"You aren't listening. Everybody knows."

"Then tell me," I said.

"You have to be *inside.* Take the drug; then you'll be inside."

Up at the corner, a blue-and-white sedan—NYPD—as rare as the white tiger in this neighborhood. The police were advance men for the cartels. They had no peacetime responsibility any longer, except that they made sure the trade proceeded without any interference. For this New York's Finest got a cut, a portion of which they tithed back to the city. So the syndicate was subsidizing the City of New York, the way I saw it. Subsidizing the rebuilding, subsidizing the government, so that government would have buildings, underground bunkers, treatment centers, whole departments devoted to Albertine, to her care and protection.

Fox, a small-time dealer and friend of Bob, one of my sources, was the first person I could find who'd float these conspiratorial theories. Right before he disappeared. And he wasn't the only one who disappeared. Bob stopped returning my calls too. Not that it amounted to much, a disappearance, here and there. Our city was outside of history now, beyond surveillance. People disappeared.

"I don't buy the conspiracy angle," I said to Cassandra. "Been there, done that."

Her eyes fluttered like she was fighting off an invasion of butterflies.

"Well, actually . . ." she said.

"Government isn't competent enough for conspiracy. Government is a bunch of guys in a subbasement somewhere, in Englewood, waiting for the war to blow over. Guys hoping they won't have to see what everyone out on the street has seen."

I helped her from the swing. She was thin like a greyhound, just as distracted. The chains on the swing clattered as she dismounted.

It wasn't that hard to be at the center of the Albertine story, see, because there was no center. Everywhere, people were either selling the drug or using the drug, and if they were using the drug, they were in its thrall, which is the thrall of memory. You could see them lying around everywhere. In all public places. Albertine expanded to fill any container. If you thought she was confined to Red Hook, it seemed for a while like she *was* only in Red Hook. But then if you looked in Astoria, she was in Astoria too. As if it were the activity of observing that somehow turned her up. More you looked, more you saw. A city whose citizens, when outdoors, looked preoccupied, or vacant. If inside, almost paralytic. I couldn't tell you how many times that week I happened to gaze in a ground-floor window and saw people staring at television screens that were turned off.

"People think the government has the skills to launch conspiracies. But if they were good enough, then they'd be good enough to track some guy who brings a suitcase detonator into the country across the Canadian border and has the uranium delivered to him by messenger. Some messenger on a bike! They'd be good enough to avoid having a third of Manhattan blown up! Or they'd be able to infiltrate the cartels. Or they'd be able to repair all of this. So are we going to kiss now?"

"Later," she said.

I was thinking maybe this conversation had come to an end, that there was no important subtext to the conversation, that Cassandra was just another deep-fried intelligence locked away in the past, and maybe I should have gone on my way to pay off the epidemiologist with the new angle. But then, like she was teasing out a little bit of insider information, she said, "Brookhaven."

Meaning what? Meaning the laboratory?

Of course, the Brookhaven theory, like the MIT theory, like the Palo Alto Research Center theory. These rumors just weren't all that compelling, because everyone had heard them, but for some reason I had this uncanny recognition at the sound of the name of the government facility on Long Island. Then she said that we should *go see the man.*

"I don't know exactly about the beginning, the origin," Cassandra said, "but I've been with someone who does. He'll be there. Where we're going."

"What are you seeing right now?"

"Autumn," she whispered.

It was a coming-down thing. The imagery of Albertine began to move toward the ephemeral, the passing away, leaves mulching, pumpkin seeds, first frost. Was there some neurotransmitter designated as the seat of memory that necessarily had autumn written into it? A chromosome that contained a sensitivity to fall? When I was a kid there were a couple years we lived in northern California, a charmed place, you know, during the tech boom. Those words seem quaint. Like saying *whore with a heart of gold*. I couldn't forget northern California, couldn't forget the redwoods, seals, rugged beaches, the austere Pacific, and when I heard the words I knew what memory I would have if I took the drug, which was the memory of the first autumn that I didn't get to see the seasons change. In northern California, watching the mist creep into the bay, watching the Golden Gate engulfed, watching that city disappear. In northern California, I waited till evening; then I'd go over to the used bookstores in town, because there was always someone in the used bookstores who was from back east. So this would be my memory, a memory of reading, of stealing time from time itself, of years passing while I was reading, hanging out in a patched armchair in the used bookstore in northern California and later on, back in Mass. Maybe I was remembering this memory, or maybe I was constructing it.

We were going over the bridge, the Kosciusko, where there was only foot traffic these days. Down Metropolitan Ave, from Queens to Brooklyn, over by where the tanks used to be. Not far from the cemetery. You know what you might have seen there? Right? Used to be the skyline, you used to see it there every day, caught in traffic, listening to the all-news format, maybe you got bored of the skyline rising above you, maybe it was like a movie backdrop, there it was again, you'd seen it so many times that it meant nothing, skyscrapers like teeth on the insipid grin of enterprise, cemetery and skyscrapers, nice combination. The greatest city in the world? Once my city was the greatest, but this was not the view anymore, on the night that I walked across there with Cassandra. No more view, right? Because there were the debris clouds, and there was the caustic rain that fell on all the neighborhoods, a rain that made everybody sick afterward, a rain that made people choke and puke. People wore gas masks on the Kosciusko. Gas masks were the cut-rate fashion statement. South of Citicorp Center, whose tampon-applicator summit had been blown clean off. There was nothing. Show over. Get it? You could see all the way to Jersey, during the day. If the wind was blowing right. Edgewater. You could see the occasional lights of Edgewater. There was no Manhattan to see, and there was no electricity in Manhattan, where the buildings remained. The generating plant downtown had been obliterated. Emergency lights, not much else.

People just turned their backs on Manhattan. They forgot about that island, which was the center of nothing, except maybe the center of society ladies with radiation burns crowding the trauma units at the remaining hospitals. Manhattan was just landfill now. And there are no surprises in a landfill. Unless you're a seagull.

Outer boroughs, that was where the action was. Like this place we were going. It'd been a smelting plant, and the police cars were lined up around it, the cops were all around it like they were the blue border of imagination. It was a ghost factory, and I dictated these impressions, because the digital recorder was still recording. When I played back my notes, there was a section of the playback that was nothing but a sequence of words about autumn, soaping windows, World Series, school supplies, yellow jackets, presidential elections, hurricane season. Who was I trying to kid? I was pretending I was writing a story about Albertine. I was writing nothing.

Cassandra was mumbling: "They were fine-tuning some interrogation aids, or they had made a chemical error with some antidepressants. Or they made progress with ECT therapies, or they saw it in the movies and just duplicated the effects. They figured out how to do it with electrodes, or they figured out how to prompt certain kinds of memories, and then they thought perhaps they could coerce certain kinds of testimony with electrodes. They could torture certain foreign nationals, force confessions from these people, and the confession would be freely signed, because the memories would be true. Who's going to argue with a memory?"

"How do you know all of this?"

We stood in front of a loading dock elevator, and the cops were frozen around us, hands on holsters, cops out front, nervous cops, cops everywhere, and the shadows in the elevator shaft danced, because the elevator was coming for us. The elevator was the only light.

"I can see," Cassandra said.

"In the big sense?"

It was the only time she smiled in the brief period when I knew her. When I was up close enough to see her lesions. People were so busy firing chemicals into their bodies, so busy in the past that they didn't notice. Their cancers were blossoming. They stopped worrying about whether the syringe was dirty or not. And they stopped going to the clinics or the emergency rooms. They let themselves vanish out of the world, like by doing so they could get closer to some point of origin: your mom on your fourth birthday, smiling, holding out her hands, *Darling, it's your birthday!*

She said, "Think biochemistry," and she had the eyedropper out again. "Think quantum mechanics. What would happen if you could harness some of the electrical charges in the brain by bombarding it with certain kinds of free particles?" Her eyes were hopelessly blood-shot. She had a mean case of pink eye. And her pupils were dilated.

"And because it's all about electrical charges, it's all about power, right? And about who has the power."

I was holding her hand, don't know why. Trying to stop her from dribbling more of that shit in her eye. I wasn't under any particular illusion about what was happening. I was lonely. Why hadn't I gone back up to Massachusetts? Why hadn't I called my cousins across town to see if they were okay? I was hustling. I knew things, but I didn't know when to stop researching and when to get down to work. There was always another trapdoor in the history of Albertine, another theory to chase down, some epidemiologist with a new slant. Some street addict, who will tell you things, if you pay.

I knew, for example, that a certain Eduardo Cortez had consolidated himself as a kingpin of the Albertine trade, at least in Manhattan and Brooklyn, and that he occasionally drove his confederates around in a military convoy. Everyone claimed to have seen the convoy, jeeps and hummers. Certain other dealers in the affected neighborhoods, like Mnemonic X in Fort Greene, the 911 Gang in Long Island City, a bunch of them had been *neutralized,* as the language goes, in the gangland style. I knew all of this, and still I walked into the ghost factory in Greenpoint, like I was somebody, not an Asian kid sent by a soft-core porn mag, who rode up in the elevator with a girl whose skin looked like a relief map, a prostitute in a neighbor-hood where almost everyone was a prostitute. As Fox, Bob's dealer, told me, before he disappeared, You'd be amazed what a woman will do for a dealer.

"When Cortez tied off, you know, everything changed," Cassandra said. It was one of those elevators that took forever. She'd been thinking what I was thinking before I even got to saying it. Her lips were cracked; her teeth were bad. She had once been brilliant, I could tell, or maybe that's just how I wanted it to be. Maybe she'd been brilliant, maybe she'd been at a university once. But now we used different words of praise for those we admired, *shrewd, tough.* And the most elevated term of respect: *alive.* Cortez was Dominican, alive, and thus he was part of the foul-is-fair demographics of Albertine. He was from nowhere, raised up in a badly depressed economy. Cortez had been a bike messenger, and then a delivery truck driver, and some of his associates insisted that his business was still about message delivery. *We just trying to run a business.*

I'd seen the very site of Cortez's modest childhood recently, took me almost ten hours to get there, which tells you nothing. It's a big mistake to measure space in time, after all. Because times change. Still, Cortez had the longest subway ride of anyone in the drug trade. If he wanted to go look after his operatives in Brooklyn, he had to get all the way from northern Manhattan to Brooklyn, and most of those lines didn't run anymore. Under the circumstances, a military convoy was just a good investment.

Washington Heights. Kids playing stickball in the street using old-fashioned boom microphones for baseball bats. There were gang-sters with earpieces on stoops up and down the block. What were the memories of these people like? Did they drop, as the addicts put it? Did they use? And what were Cortez's memories like? Memories of middleweight prizefighting at the gym up the block? Maybe. Some drinking with the boys. Some whoring around with the streetwalk-ers on Upper Broadway. Assignations with Catholic girls in the neighborhood? Cortez had a bad speech impediment, everybody said. Would Albertine make it so that he, in memory, could get as far back as the time before speech acquisition, to the sweet days before the neighborhood kids made fun of him for the way he talked? Could he teach his earlier self better how to say the "s" of American English? To speak with authority? One tipster provided by my magazine had offered sinister opinions about the appearance of Cortez, this Cortez of the assumed name. This tipster, whispering into that most rare landline, had offered the theory that the culture of Albertine itself changed when Cortez appeared, just like with the appearance of the original Cortez, great explorer, bearer of a shipload of smallpox. This was, of course, a variation on the so-called *diachronous theory of abuse patterns* that has turned up a lot in the medical journals recently.

There were traditional kinds of memories before the appearance of Albertine, namely *identity builders,* according to these medical theorists. Like that guy at Brooklyn College, the government anthropologist of Albertine, Ernst Wentworth, Ph.D. Even repressed memory syndrome, in his way of thinking, was an identity builder, because in repressed memory syndrome you learn ultimately to empower yourself, in that you are identifying past abusers and understanding the ramifications of their misdeeds. I hate the word *empowerment,* but this is the terminology Wentworth used. A repetition of stressful memories is, according to his writing, an attempt by an identity to arrive at a solution to stress. Even a calamity, the collapse of a bridge, when remembered by one who has plunged into an icy river, is an identity builder, in that it ultimately engenders the reassurance of the remembering subject. The here and now puts him in the position of being alive all over again, no matter how painful it is to be alive. The Wentworth identity-building theory was the prevailing theory of memory studies, up until Albertine.

Since Albertine arrived on the scene after the blast, theorists eventually needed to consider the blast in all early Albertine phenomena. Figures, right? One night I felt like I started to understand these theories in a dramatic way, in my heart, or what was left of it. I was at the armory, where I slept in a closet, really—used to be a supply closet, and there were still some supplies in there, some rug-cleaning solvents, some spot removers, extra towels. You never know when you might need this stuff. Anyway, the halls outside the supply closet echo; you could hear every whisper, in the halls of the armory. You could hear people coming and going. It wasn't and isn't a great place to live, when you consider that I used to have a studio in the

East Village. But compared to living in the great hall itself, where mostly people tried to erect cubicles for themselves, cubicles made out of cardboard or canvas or Sheetrock, the supply closet was not so bad. The process of doling out closets had fallen to an Albertine addict called Bertrand, and when I fixed up Bertrand with Fox and a few other dealers, I got bumped up to the supply closet right away. When moths came after my remaining shirts and sweaters, I had all the insecticide I'd need.

This night I'm describing, I had a breakthrough of dialectical reasoning: I was hearing the blast. You know the conventional wisdom about combat veterans, loud noises suggesting the sharp crack of submachine-gun fire, all that? I thought just the opposite. That certain silences re-created the blast, because there's something about fission, you know it's soundless in a way, it suggests soundlessness, it's a violence contained in the opposite of violence, big effects from preposterously small changes. Say you were one of the four million who survived, you were far enough away that the blast, heat, and radiation could do their damage before the sound reached you, wherever you were. So it follows that the sound of the explosion would be best summoned up in no sound at all. The pauses in the haggard steps of the insomniacs of the armory walking past the door to my closet, this sound was the structured absence in what all our memories were seeking to suppress or otherwise avoid: the truth of the blast.

I'm not a philosopher. But my guess was that eventually people would start *remembering the blast.* You know? How could it be otherwise? I'm not saying I'm the person who came up with the idea; maybe the government mole did. Maybe Ernst Wentworth did. I'm saying, I guess, that all memories verged on being memories of the blast, like footsteps in the echoing corridor outside my supply closet. Memories were like downpours of black raindrops. All noises were examples of the possibility of the noise of the blast, which is the limit of all possibilities of sound, and thus a limit on all possibilities of memory. For a lot of people, the blast was so traumatic they couldn't even remember where they were that day, and I'm one of those people, in case you were wondering. I know I was heading out to Jersey for a software convention in the New Brunswick area. At least, that's what I think I was doing. But I don't know how I got back. When I came to, Manhattan was gone.

People began to have memories of the blast while high. And people began to die of certain memories on the drug. Makes perfect sense. And this is part of the *diachronous theory of abuse patterns* that I was just talking about. First, Conrad Dixon, a former academic himself, was found dead in his apartment in the Flatbush section of Brooklyn, no visible sign of death, except that he'd just been seen scamming a bunch of dealers in Crown Heights. Was the death by reason of poisonous additives in the drug cocktail? That'd be a pretty good theory, if he were the only person who died this way, but all at once, a lot of people started dying, and it was my contention, anyhow, that they were remembering the blast. There were the bad memories in an ordinary fit of Albertine remembering, and then there was the memory of this moment of all moments, a sense of the number of people eliminated in the carnage, a sense of the kind of motive of the guy or guys, men or women, who managed to smuggle the dirty uranium device into the country and then have it delivered, etc. An innocent thing when Conrad Dixon, or the others like him, first did what they did. In the early curve of the epidemic, everybody used Albertine alone, because memories are most often experienced alone. And the recitation of them, that's like dull plot summaries from movies: Oh, let me tell you about the time that I was in Los Angeles, and I saw such and such a starlet at the table next to me, or about the time I broke my arm trying to white-water raft, whatever your pathetic memory is. It's all the same, the brimming eyes of your daughter when she was a toddler and accidentally got a bump on her head, I don't give a fuck, because I know what happened with Conrad Dixon, which is that he put the needle in his arm, and then he was back in midtown and looking down at the lower part of the island where he had spent his entire youth. A good thing, sure, that Conrad, that day, had to take that programmer's certification test up at Columbia, because instead of becoming a faint shadow on the side of some building on Union Square, he could see the entire neighborhood that he worked in subsumed in perfect light, and he could feel the nausea rising in him, and he could see the cloud's outstretched arms, and all the information in him was wiped aside, he was a vacuum of facts, a memory vacuum, and again and again, he could see the light, feel the incineration, and he knew something about radiation that he hadn't known before, about the light on the surface of the stars, giver of all things. He knew that he was sick, knew that again he was going to have to live through the first few days, when everyone was suffering the poisoning of cells, the insides of them liquifying. Don't make me walk you through it, the point is that Albertine gave back the blast, when Conrad had hoped never to experience the blast again, and Conrad was so stuck in the loop of this recollection that he could do nothing else, but die, because that was the end of the blast; whether in actual space, or on the recollected plane, whether in the past, or the present or the future, whether in ideas or reality, the blast was about death.

What's this have to do with Eduardo Cortez? Well, it has to do with the fact that Cortez's play for control of the Albertine cartel came exactly at the moment of highest density of deaths from Albertine overdose or drug interaction. I refer you back again to the *diachronous theory of abuse patterns.* See what I mean? The big question is how does Cortez, by his presence, affect the way that Albertine was used? The mixture of the chemical, if it's even a chemical, certainly didn't change all that much, had not changed, during the course of the twelve months that it grew into a street epidemic. Can we attribute the differences in abuse patterns to any other factors? Why is it Cortez who seemed to be responsible for the blast intruding into everybody's memory?

My notes for the magazine are all about skepticism. I knew I was holding Cassandra's hand now, prostitute in rags, woman with the skeletal body, while she was using the eyedropper, and I know this might seem like a hopeful gesture. Like some good could come out of it all. I heard her sigh. The cage of the elevator, at a crawl, passed a red emergency light on the wall of the shaft. Hookers were always erotic about noerotic things. Time, for example. The elsewhere of time amok was all over her, like she was coming to memories of a time before prostitution. I was holding her hand. I was disoriented. I checked my watch. I mean I checked what day it was. I had been assigned to the Albertine story for two weeks, according to my Rolex knockoff—which had miraculously survived the electromagnetic pulse—but I could swear that it had just been two days before that I'd been hanging out in the offices of the soft-core porn mag, the offices with the bulletproof glass and the robot receptionist out front. When had I last been back to the supply closet to sleep? When had I last eaten? Wasn't it last night, the evening with the footsteps in the corridor, and the revelation about the blast? I was holding Cassandra's hand, because she had this tenuous link to the facts of Albertine, and this seemed like the last chance to master the story, to get it down somehow, instead of being consumed by it.

This is my scoop then. The scoop is that, suddenly, *I saw what she was seeing.*

Cassandra said, "Watch this."

Pay close attention. I saw a close-up, in my head I saw it, like from some Web movie, a guy's arm, a man's arm, an arm covered with scars, almost furry, it was so hairy, and then a hand pulling tight a belt around a bicep, jamming in a needle, depressing the plunger, a grunt of initial discomfort. Then the voice of the guy, thick accent, maybe a Puerto Rican accent, announcing his threats, "I'm going back to the Lower East Side, and I'm going to cap the motherfucker, see if I don't." Definite speech impediment. A problem with sibilance. Then this guy, this dude was looking over at Cassandra, she was in the scene, not in the stairwell, where we were at least theoretically standing, but she was someway associated with Eduardo Cortez. She was his consort. He was taking her hand, there was a connection of hands, a circular movement of hands, and then we were on a street, and I saw Cortez, in Tompkins Square Park, which doesn't exist anymore, of course, and it was clear that he was searching out a particular white guy, and now, coming through the crowd, here was the guy, looked like an educated man, if you know what I mean, one of those East Village art slumming dudes. Cortez was searching out this guy, kinda grungy, wearing black jeans and a T-shirt, and it was all preordained, and now Cortez had found him.

Lights associated with the thrall of Cassandra's recollection, phantom lights, auras. The particulars were like a migraine. Things were solarized, there were solar flares around the streetlamps. We were bustling in and around the homeless army of Tompkins Square. I could hear my own panicky breathing. I was in a park that didn't exist anymore, and I was seeing Cortez, and I was seeing this guy, this white guy, he had that look where one side of his face, the right side, was different from the other side, so that on the right side, he seemed to be melancholy and placid, whereas on the left side of the face, there was the faintest smirk at all times. The left side was contorted and maybe there were scars there, some kind of slasher's jagged line running from the corner of his mouth to his ear, as if his face too were divided in certain ways, as if his face were a product of erosion, and Cassandra, I guess, was saying, "Let's not do this, okay? Eduardo? Please? Eduardo? We can fix the problem another way." Except that at the same moment what she was saying to me, somehow outside of memory, outside of the memory belonging to someone else, she was saying, "Do you understand what you're seeing?"

I said, "He's going to—"

"—Kill the guy."

"And that guy is?"

"Addict Number One."

"Who?"

"That guy is the first user," she said. "The very first one."

"And why is he important?"

Cassandra said, "For the sake of control. You don't get it, do you?"

"Tell me," I said.

"Addict Number One is being killed *in a memory.*"

Something coursed in me like a flash flood. A real perception, maybe, or just the blunt feelings of sympathetic drug abuse. When I tried to figure out the enormity of what Cassandra was telling me, I couldn't. I couldn't understand the implications, couldn't understand why she would tell me, because to tell me was to die, far as I could tell, because Fox was dead, Bob was dead, the Mnemonic X boys had been completely wiped out, probably fifty guys, all disappeared, same day, same time, reporters from my old paper were dead. Chasing the story was to chase time itself, and time guarded its secrets.

"How's that possible? That's not possible! How are you going to kill someone in a memory? It doesn't make any sense."

"Right. It doesn't make any sense, but it happened. And it could happen again."

"But a memory isn't a place. It's nowhere but in someone's head. There's not a movie running somewhere. You can't jump up into the screen and start messing with action."

"Just watch and see."

I was thinking about the diachronous theory. The pattern of abuse and dispersal was widest and most threatening at the instant of the murder of Addict Number One, I was guessing, which was about to be revealed as a murder, the first and only murder, I hoped, that I ever needed to witness, because even if he was a smirking guy, someone unliked or ridiculed, even if he was just a drug addict, whatever, Addict Number One was a prodigious rememberer. As the first full-scale Albertine addict, I learned later, he had catalogued loads of memories, for example, light in the West Village, which in July is perfect at sunset on odd-numbered streets in the teens and twenties. It was true. Addict Number One had learned this. If you stood on certain corners and looked west in June and July, at dusk, you would see that the City of New York had sunsets that would have animated the great landscape painters. Or how about the perfect bagel? Addict Number One had sampled many of the fresh bagels of the City of New York, and he compiled notes about the best hot bagels, which were found at a place on University and Thirteenth Street. They were large, soft, and warm. Addict Number One devoted pages to the taste of bagel as it went into your mouth.

Sadly, instead of illuminating the life of Addict Number One, it's my job now to describe the pattern of the dispersal of his brains. The pattern of which was exactly like the pattern of dispersal of radioactive material in lower Manhattan. Cortez held the revolver to the head of Addict Number One, whose expression of complete misunderstanding and disbelief was heartrending, enough so to prove that he had no idea what his murder meant, and Cortez pulled the trigger of the revolver, and Addict Number One fell over like he had never once been a living thing. *Fucking punk-ass junky,* Cortez intoned. Were the baroque memories of Addict Number One now part of all that tissue, splattered on the dog run in Tompkins Square? Was that a memory, splashed on that retriever there, gunking up its fur, an electrical impulse, a bit of energy withering in a pool of gore in a city park? I saw it, because Cortez saw it, and Cortez gave the memory to Cassandra, who gave it to me: corpus callosum and basal ganglia on the dogs, on the lawn, and screaming women, the homeless army drawn up near, gazing, silent, as Addict Number One, slain by a drug dealer in memory only, weltered, gasping. His memories slain with him.

It was like this. Even though the memory was just a memory, its effect was real. As real as if were all happening now. This is like saying that nine-tenths of the universe is invisible, I know. But just bear with me. Cortez's accomplishment was that, according to Cassandra, he'd learned from informers that Addict Number One was once a real person, with a real past (went to NYU, and his name was Paley, and he wanted to make movies), after which he'd located a picture of Addict Number One by reading an obituary from the time when Addict Number One was already dead.

Must have been pretty tempting to try to fabricate a memory about Addict Number One. Oh yeah, I saw him on the Christopher Street pier that time. Or, I saw him on my way to Forest Hills to visit my grandma. Cortez may have tried this, perhaps a dozen times, skin popping Albertine in an unfurnished room in East Harlem, vainly attempting put a bullet in the head of an imagined encounter with Addict Number One, but no. Cortez had to go through every face in every crowd, all the imagined crowds of which he had ever been a part, every faced passed on Broadway, every prone body on the Bowery, every body in the stands of Yankee Stadium. He shot more, spent most of the money from his bike messenger job on this jones for narrative, and then one day, he was certain.

He was killing roaches in his empty apartment, when he knew. He was prying up a floorboard to look for roaches, and he knew. As certainly as he knew the grid of his city. He'd walked by Addict Number One, one day, when he was sixteen, in Tompkins Square. On his way to a game of handball. He'd walked by him, he knew it. Not someone else, but him, Addict Number One. Guy looked like a faggot, the way Cortez told Cassandra later. All white guys looked like faggots as far as he was concerned, and he'd just as soon kill the punk-ass motherfucker for looking like a faggot as any other reason, although there were plenty of other reasons. Main thing was that if he could figure out a way to kill Addict Number One in his memory, then a whole sequence of events failed, like when Addict Number

One hooked up with certain black guys in his neighborhood who had been fronting heroin up until that time, gave to them the correct chemical compound of Albertine, the secrets of the raw materials needed for the manufacture, the apparatus. If Cortez killed his ass this future would not turn out to be the real future. If Cortez killed his ass, then Cortez would control the syndicate.

It would take even more time and money, more time, doping, a solid six months, in fact, in his room, going through that whole sequence of his life, like that time with Eduardo's neighbor, he told Cassandra. Over and over again, Eduardo had to deal with that *drunken fuck neighbor,* not even gonna say his name here, Cortez would say to Cassandra, fighting off that memory when the guy, Eduardo's alleged uncle, in the rubble of an abandoned building, exposed himself to little Eduardo, his droopy uncut penis, fucking guy couldn't get hard no more, looked like a gizzard, and the uncle drunkenly pronounced that he was lonelier than any man had ever been, didn't belong in this country, couldn't go back to the island nation of his birth, no reason for a man to be as lonely as this man, no reason for this surfeiting of loneliness, every day in every way, and would Eduardo just make him feel comfortable for just this one day, just treat him like a loving man, this one time, because he was so lonely, had an aching in his heart that nothing could still, wouldn't ask again, he swore, and took Eduardo, just a little compadre, just a wisp, couldn't even lift up an aluminum baseball bat, couldn't lift a finger against the alleged uncle, took Eduardo for his goddess, you are my priestess, you are my goddess, and now Eduardo vowed that he would never again suffer that way before any man.

The syringe, the eyedropper, the concentric rings of the past. Again and again the uncle would attempt to seduce him. He was willing to go through that, a thousand times if he had to, until he had the gun on his person, in the waistband of his warm-up suit, and he was ready. He was sixteen, with fresh tattoos, and he'd been to mass that morning and he had a gun, and he was going to play handball, and he saw this white faggot in the dog run, and he just walked up to him like they never met. Though in truth it was like Eduardo Cortez knew him inside and out, and Eduardo wanted to make something out of himself, his life that was lost up until then, where he was just a bike messenger, and the desperados of his neighborhood, they were all going to be working for him and if they made one wrong move, he'd throw them off a fucking bridge, whatever bridge is still up, and if they touched the little girls in his neighborhood, that's another crime, for which he would exact a very high price, a mortal price, and the first priority, the long-term business plan was that Eduardo Cortez would be the guy who would make profits from memories, even if his own memories were bad. That was just how it was going to go, and I saw all this with Cassandra, that Cortez had managed by sheer brute force to murder a memory, splatter a memory like it was nothing at all.

One minute Addict Number One was wandering in the East Village, years before he was an addict, years before there even was an Albertine to cop, and he was thinking about how he was going to get funding for his digital video project, and then, right in front of a bunch of dog walkers, the guy disappeared. This is the story, from the point of view of those who were not in on the cascading of memories. It's one of the really great examples of public delusion, when you read it on the on-line police records, like I did. *Witnessses insist that the victim, first referred to as Caucasian John Doe, later identified as Irving Paley of 433 East 9th St., was present on the scene, along with a Hispanic man in his teens, and then, abruptly, no longer present. "It's as if he just vanished," remarked one witness. Others concur. No body located thereafter. Apartment also completely emptied, possibly by assailant.* Good thing those records were stored on a server. Since One Police Plaza is dust.

The guys in the smelting factory were all wearing uniforms. They were the uniforms of bike messengers, as if the entire story somehow turned on bike messengers. Bike messenger as conveyor of meaning. There were these courtiers in the empire of Eduardo Cortez, and the lowest echelon was the beat cop, a phalanx of whom were all encircling the building, sending news of anyone in the neighborhood into command central by radio. And then there were the centurions of the empire, the guys in the bike messenger uniforms, wearing the crash helmets of bike messengers. All done up in Lycra, like this was some kind of superhero garb. When the elevator door swung back, it was clear that we had definitely penetrated to the inner sanctum of Eduardo Cortez, as if by merely thinking. And this inner sanctum was inexplicable, comic, and deadly. Sure it was possible that I had now been researching for two weeks, and no longer needed food or sleep in order to do it. Sure, maybe I was just doing a really great job, and, since I was an honest guy who seemed cool and nonthreatening, maybe I was just allowed into places that the stereotypical Albertine abuser would not ordinarily be allowed. But it seemed unlikely. This was evidently one of the fabled five mansions of Cortez, to which he shuttled, depending on his whim, like a despot from the coca-producing latitudes.

"Eddie," Cassandra sang out into the low lighting of the smelting factory floor, "I brought him like you said."

Which one was Eddie? The room was outfitted with gigantic machines, suspension devices, ramrods, pistons thundering, wheels turning, like some fabulous Rube Goldberg future, and there was no center to it, no throne, no black leather sofa with a leopard-print quilt thrown over it, and none of the bike messengers in the room looked like the Cortez of my memory, the Cortez of Tompkins Square Park, on his way to play handball. Maybe he'd had himself altered by a cosmetic surgeon with a drug problem and a large debt. In fact, in scanning the faces of the dozens of bike messengers in the room it seemed that they all looked similar, all of European extraction with brown hair on the verge of going gray, all with blue eyes, a little bit paunchy. Were they robots? Were they street toughs from the bad neighborhoods? They were, it turned out, the surgically altered army of Eddie Cortez homonyms, who made it possible for him to be in so many places at so many times, in all the fabled five mansions. Eddie was a condition of the economy now, not a particular person.

At the remark from Cassandra, several of the bike messengers gathered in the center of the room. Maybe they were all modified comfort robots, so that Eddie could use them professionally during the day and fuck them later at night. One of them asked, with a blank expression, "His writing any good?"

Cassandra turned to me. "They want to know if you're a good writer."

"Uh, sure," I said, answering to the room. "Sure. I guess. Uh, you wanting me to write something? What do you have in mind exactly?"

More huddling. No amount of time was too lengthy, in terms of negotiation, and this was probably because time was no longer all that important to Cortez and the empire. Time present was now swallowed in the riptide of the past. Since it was now possible that Eddie could disappear, at any moment, like Addict Number One had, when some-one else figured out his technique for dealing with the past, he had apparently moved to ensure an eternal boring instant, where everybody looked the same, and where nothing particularly happened. Events, any kind of events, were dangerous. Eddie's fabled five mansions fea-tured a languid, fixed now. He took his time. He changed his appear-ance frequently, as well as the appearance of all those around him. That way he could control memories. So his days were apparently taken up with dye jobs, false beards, colored contact lenses, all the shopping for items relating to disguise and imposture and disfigurement.

"Funny you should, uh, suggest it," I said. "Because I have been assigned to write a history of Albertine, and that's why I got in con-tact with Cassandra, in the first place. . . ."

Everyone looked at her. Faint traces of confusion.

Have I described her well enough? In the half-light, she too was a goddess, even though I figure addicts always shine in low lighting. In the emergency lighting of Eddie's lair, Cassandra was the doomed forecaster, like her name implied. She was the whisperer of syllables in a tricky meter. She was the possibility of possibilities. I knew that desire for me must have been a thing that was slumbering for a really long time, it was just desire for desire, but now it was ungainly. I felt some stirring of possible futures with Cassandra, didn't want to let her out of my sight. I was guilty of treating women like ideas in my search for Albertine. In fact, I knew so little about her, that it was only just then that I thought about the fact that she was Asian too. From China, or maybe her parents or grandparents were from Hong Kong, or Taiwan. Because now she swept back her black and maroon hair, and I could see her face. Her expression was kind of sad.

They all laughed. The bike messengers. I was the object of hilarity.

"Cassandra," they said. "That's a good one. What's that, like some Chinese name?"

"You did good, girl. You're a first-class bitch, Albertine, and so it's time for a treat, if you want."

A broadcaster's voice. Like Eddie had managed to hire network talent to make his announcements.

"Wait," I said, "her name is . . ."

And then I got it. They named it after her.

"You named the drug after her?"

"Not necessarily," the broadcasting voice said. "Might have named her after the drug. We can't really remember the sequence. And the thing is there are memories going either way."

"She doesn't look like an Albertine to me."

"The *fuck* you know, canary," the broadcaster said, and suddenly I heard Eddie in there, heard his attitude. Canary. A reporter's nickname.

Cassandra was encircled by bike messengers, and hefted up to a platform in the midst of the Rube Goldberg devices. Her rags were removed from her body by certain automated machines, prosthetic digits, and she was laid out like a sacrificial victim, which I guess is what she was, one knee bent, like in classical sculpture, one arm was laid out above her head. No woman is more poignant than the woman about to be sacrificed, but even this remark makes me more like Eddie, less like a lover.

"Your pleasure?" a bike messenger called out.

"Slave Owner, please," said Cassandra.

"Good choice. Four horsepower, fifteen volts, 350 rpms."

I covered my ears with my hands, and except for the glimpse of the steel bar that was meant to raise her ankles over her head, I saw no more—for the simple reason that I didn't want to have to remember.

The bike messengers of the Cortez cartel had a different idea for me. I was led down a corridor, to the shooting gallery. I was finally going to get my taste.

The guy holding my arms said, "Thing is all employees got to submit to a mnemonic background check. . . ."

A week or so before, I'd read a pamphlet by a specialist in medicinal applications of Albertine. There's always a guy like this, right, a Dr. Feelgood, an apologist. He was on the Upper West Side, and his suggestion was that, when getting high, one should always look carefully around a room and eliminate bad energies. Set and setting, in fact, was just as important here as with drugs in the hallucinogenic family:

> If there's any scientific validity at all to the theories of C.G. Jung and his followers, there's genuine cause for worry when taking the drug known as Albertine.
>
> The reason for this is quite simply Jung's concept known as the collective unconsciousness. What do we mean when we invoke this theory? We mean that under certain extraordinary circumstances it is possible that memory, properly thought of as the exclusive domain of an Albertine effect, can occasionally collide with other areas of brain function. As Jung supposed, we each harbor a register of the simulacra that is part of being human. This fantasy register, it is said, can be a repository for symbolisms that are true across cultural and national lines. What kinds of images are these? Some of them are good, useful images, such as the representation of the divine: Christ as the Lamb of God, Buddha under the bodhi tree, Ganesh, with his many arms. Each of these is a useful area for meditation. However, images of the demonic are also collective, as with depictions of witches. The terrors of hell, in fact, have had a long collective history. Now it appears that certain modern phantasms—the CIA operative, the transnational terrorist—are also both "real" and collective.
>
> Therefore, we can suggest that casual users of Albertine make sure to observe some rules for their excursions. It's important to know a little about whom you have with you at the time of ingestion. It's important to know a little bit about their own circumstances. To put it another way, people you trust are a crucial part of any prolonged Albertine experience.
>
> I suggest five easy steps to a rewarding experience with your memories: 1) Find a comfortable place, 2) Bring along a friend or loved one, 3) Use the drug after good meals or rewarding sexual experiences, so that you won't waste all your time on the re-creation of these things, 4) Keep a photo album at hand, in case you want to draw your attention back to less harmful recollections, 5) Avoid horror films, heavy metal music, or anything with occult imagery.

* * *

The advice of the good doctor was ringing in my ears. No matter what happened to my city, no matter how many incarnations of boom and bust it went through, the go-go times, the Municipal Assistance Corporation, didn't seem to matter, shooting galleries persisted in the Hot Zone and elsewhere. The exposed beams, the crumbling walls, the complete lack of electricity, the absence of heat, windows shattered, bodies lying around on mattresses. If it was important to know or trust the people with whom I was going to use, I was in some deep shit. Who wouldn't dread coming here to this place of unwashed men, of human waste and dead bodies?

In the shadows, there was a guy with a stool and a metal folding table. I was motioned forward, as an old hippie collapsed onto the floor. Probably remembering the best night of sleep he ever had.

Behind me, operatives in the Cortez syndicate made sure that my step was sturdy.

"Give me your hand," the Albertine provider said. In a kind of doomed murmur.

I looked at my hand. Laid it out on that cheap table, site of a hundred violent games of poker.

"Don't mind we kinda stay close?" said one of the goons. He used the chokehold. Another guy held my hand. This would be the gentle description. If they were worried about my getting away, they shouldn't have, because I was a reporter. But that wasn't the motive, it dawned on me. They were hoping to come along for the ride, if possible, to see what they needed to know about their collaborator, if that's what I was going to be. The historian of the Empire.

"You don't honestly think you're going to be able to see what I see, do you?" I said. "There's just no way that works according to physics."

The needle went in between the tendons on the top of my right hand. Blood washed back into the syringe. A bead pearling at my knuckle.

"First time, yo?" someone said.

"For sure," I said.

"Goes better if you're thinking about what you want to know.

Chiming. Thinking of bells, bells from a church, that's what you do, things get chiming, the pictures get chiming. Because if you think of stuff you don't want to know, then, *bang—*"

Like I said, what I wanted to know first when I finally got dosed on Albertine was how I did on this assignment. I mean, if you could see the future, which seemed like horseshit, if that was really possible, then I wanted to know how my story turned out. Which I guess makes me a real writer, because a reporter is someone who doesn't care about his own well-being when the story is coming due, he just cares about the story, about getting it done. I just wanted to get the story done, I wanted to get it into the magazine. I wanted to be more than just another guy who survived the blast. So that was the memory where I was bound. But that doesn't describe the beginning at all. One second I was listening to the guy tell me about chiming, next moment there was a world beside the world in which I lived, a world behind the world, and maybe even a sequence of them lined up one behind the other, where crucial narratives were happening. Suddenly the splinter hanging off the two-by-four next to the table seemed to have a world-famous history, where dragonflies frolicked in the limbs of an ancient redwood. And maybe this was the prize promised first by Albertine, that all things would have meaning. Suddenly there was discrimination to events, not all this disjunctive shit, like a million people getting incinerated for no good reason. Instead: discrimination, meaning, value. The solarizing thing again, and I could hear the voices of the people in the room, but like I was paralyzed, I was experiencing language as material, not as words, but as something sludgy like molasses, language was molasses. Like life had been EQ'd badly, and all was high-end distortion, and then there was a tiling effect, and the grinning toothless face of the guy who'd just shot me up was divided into zones, like he was a painting from the Modernist chapter of art history, and zones were sort of rearranged, so he was a literal blockhead, and then I heard this music, like the whole history of sounds from my life had become a tunnel under the present, and I could hear voices, and I could hear songs, I could pluck one out, like I could pluck out some jazz from the 1950s, here's a guy banging on the eighty-eights, stride style, and when I plucked it out of the tunnel I could hear the things beside it, a concert that I had to go to in junior high, school auditorium, where some guys in robes demonstrated some Buddhist overtone singing, they were sitting on an oriental carpet, you know the mysteries of the world always had to have an oriental carpet involved, we were all supposed to be mystical and wearing robes and shit, and beside me there was the voice of my friend Dave Wakabayashi, who whispered, "Man, we could be listening to the game," because there was a day game that day, right. What team? And who was pitching? And then the sound of Mandarin, which was exactly like a song to me, because of all the kinds of intonation that were involved in it, all those words that had the same sound but different intonations.

And after that accretion of songs, a flood of the smells from my life, barely had time to say some of them aloud, while my stool was tipping backward, in the shooting gallery, my stool was tipping backward, and the back of my head was connecting with some hard surface, citronella, cardamom, smell of melting vinyl, smell of a pack of Polaroid film, five kinds of perfume, smell of my grandfather dying, meat loaf prepared from a box, freshly cut lawns, the West Indian Day Parade in New York City, which is the smell of curried goat, ozone right before a storm, diesel exhaust, the smell of just having fucked someone for the first time, the shock of it, more perfumes, a dog that just rolled in something, city streets in July, fresh basil, chocolate chip cookies, ailanthus trees, and just when I was getting dizzy from all the smells, and right about the moment at which I heard the guys from Eddie's team, in their mellifluous slang, saying *Take his damn money,* which they definitely were going to do now, because I could tell that my arms were thrown wide to the world, give me the world, give me your laser light show and your perfect memories, doesn't matter what they are, rinse me in your sanitorium of memories, for I am ready as I have never been, all of my short life. All was rehearsal for this moment as observer of what has come before, my longing was for perception, for the torrents of the senses, the tastes, the languor of skin on skin. I was made for this trip, it felt good, it felt preposterously good, and I noticed absently that my cock was hard, actually, I'm a little embarrassed to say it now, but I realized in that moment that mastery of the past, even when drug-induced, was as sexy as the vanquishing of loneliness, which is really what men in the city fuck against. Think about it, the burden of isolation that's upon us all day and night, and think about how that diminishes in the carnival of sex. It's the same on the Teen, it's the same with *chiming*, and I was actually a little worried that I might come like that lying on the floor of their shooting gallery, with this guy standing over me, reaching into my hip pocket where there used to be a wallet, but there was no wallet now, just a couple of twenties to get me out of trouble, if it came to that. He wanted them and he took them. I wanted to yell Get the fuck off me, but I could feel the blobs of drool detaching from the corner of my mouth, and I knew I could say nothing, I could say only Yes, yes, yes. And when that seemed like that was the lesson of Albertine, bitch goddess, when I thought, Well, this must be what you get for your twenty-five bucks, you get to see the light show of lost time, just then I got up off the floor and walked into the lobby of the tits-and-lit magazine that had hired me, except that they hadn't hired me, I guess, not like I believed. The matter was still up in the air, and I was in the line with a lot of people claiming to be writers, people with their plagiarized clip files, though why anyone would want to pretend to be a writer is beyond me. I was hoping, since I was the genuine article, that I might actually get the call. Out came this girl with blue hair, past the receptionist robot at the desk out front, saying my name, Kevin Lee, like it somehow magically rhymed with *bored,* and I got up, walked past all those people. I realized, yes, that I was going to get the assignment, because I was the guy who had actually written something, I was the genuine article, and maybe fate had it in store for me that I'd get out of the armory where I shared a cardboard box with a computer programmer from Islamabad who despite the unfortunate fact of his nationality in the current global climate was a good guy.

The girl had blue hair! The girl had blue hair! And she looked sort of like Serena, that babe with whom I once skipped school to drink in Boston Commons, and there I was again, like never before, with Serena, slurring the words a little bit when I told her she was the first person who ever took the time to have a real conversation with me. First white chick. Because, I told Serena, people looked at an Asian kid in school they assumed he was a math and science geek, oh he's definitely smarter than everyone else, that's what I told her, such a sweet memory. Well, it was sweet anyway up until she told me that she already had a boyfriend, some college dude, why hadn't she told me before, didn't I deserve to be told, didn't I have some feelings too? No, probably I was an inscrutable kid from the East. Right? She didn't tell me because I was Chinese.

And I was in a bad spot, in a drug dealer's shooting gallery, probably going to be in really deep shit because if I didn't write something for the cartel about the history of Albertine, I was probably a dead Chinese kid, but I didn't care, because I believed I was drunk in the Boston Commons, and I was reciting poetry, for a girl with green eyes who would actually go on to be an actress in commercials, *There's a certain slant of light/Winter afternoons/That oppresses like the heft/Of cathedral tunes.* I could recite every poem I had ever memorized. It was amazing. Serena's face frozen in a kind of convulsive laughter, You are some crazy bastard, Kevin Lee. It was all good, it was all blessed, the trip. But then she said that thing about her boyfriend again, some would-be filmmaker.

And I was back in the office with Tara, girl with the blue hair. "Jesus, Lee, what happened? You don't look so good. Why didn't you call me? When I gave you the assignment, I assumed you were a professional, right? Because there are a lot of other people who would have jumped at the chance to write this piece." Glimpse of myself in the reflection of her office window. The city smoldering out the window, the whole empty city, myself superimposed over it. I looked like I hadn't eaten in two weeks. The part of my face that actually grew a beard had one of those beards that looked like a Vietnamese guy in a rice paddy. My eyes were sunken and red. I had the bruises under my eyes. Whatever viscous gunk was still irrigating my dry mouth had hardened at the corners into a crust. I had nothing to say. Nothing to do but hand over the notes. Twenty-nine thousand words. Tara paged through the beginning with an exasperated sigh. "What the fuck do you think we're going to do with this, Kevin? We're a fucking porn magazine? Remember?" As in dreams, I could feel the inability to do anything. I just watched the events glide by. From this quicksand of the future. I could see Tara with the blue pencil to match her blue hair receding in the reflection in the window.

And then there were a dozen more futures, each as unpleasant. Breaking into the bedroom of Bertrand, the administrator of the armory, stealing his beaker full of Teen, which he kept in his luxury fridge—he was the only guy in the entire armory who got to have a refrigerator—being discovered in the process of stealing his drugs by a woman who'd just recently gone out of her way to ask me where my family was, why I was living here alone. Seeing her face in the light from the fridge, the only light in the room. She was wearing army fatigues, the uniform of the future, everyone in army fatigues, everyone on high alert. And then I jumped a few rich people up in Park Slope, an affluent neighborhood that wasn't obliterated in the blast, I was wearing a warm-up suit, I was jumping some guy carrying groceries, and suddenly I was awake, with my face in my hands.

The guys at the folding table were laughing.

I wiped my leaking nose on my wrists. Stood up, weak-kneed.

"Good time?" said the administerer of poisons. "You need the boost; everybody needs it afterward. Don't worry yourself. You need the boost. To smooth it out."

He handed me a pill.

One of the security experts said to another: "Just the usual shit, man, names of cheap-ass girls kiss his ass when he was just a little Chinese boy eating his mommy's moo goo gai pan. Some shit."

That was it? That was what I was to them? Bunch of sentimental memories? The predictable twenty-five-dollar memories that coursed through here every day? What were they looking for? Later, I knew. They were looking for evidence that I had dropped off files with government agencies, or that I had tipped off rival gangs. Or they were looking to see if I'd had contact with Addict Number One. They were looking to see what I had put together, what I knew, where my researches had taken me, how much of the web of Albertine was already living in me, and therefore how much of it was available to you.

"Okay chump," bike messenger said to me, "free to go."

The door opened, and down a corridor I went, wearing handcuffs, back the way I'd come, like I could unlearn what I had learned—that I had the taste for the drug, and that the past was woefully lost. I'd been addicted by the drug overlord of my city, and now

I was standing on his assembly-line floor again, though now Cassandra, or whoever she was, was missing, and the voice of the Cortez television announcer rang out, observing the following on the terms of my new employment: "We want you to learn the origin of Albertine, we want you to write down this origin, and all the rest of the history of Albertine, from its earliest days to the present time, and we don't want you to use any fancy language or waste any time, we just want you to write it down. And because what you're going to do is valuable to us, we are prepared to make it worth your while. We're going to give you plenty of our product as a memory aid, and we will give you a generous per diem. You'll dress like a man, you'll consider yourself a representative of Eddie Cortez, you'll avoid disrespectful persons and institutions. Remember, it's important for you to write and not worry about anything else. You fashion the sentences, you make them sing, we'll look after the rest."

"Sounds cool," I said, "especially since I'm already doing that for someone else."

"No, you aren't doing it for somebody else; you are doing it for us. Nobody else exists. The skin magazine doesn't exist, your friends don't exist. Your family doesn't exist. We exist."

I could feel how weak my legs were. I could feel the sweat trickling down the small of my back, soaking through my T-shirt. I was just hanging on. Because that's what my family did, they hung on. My grandfather, he left behind his country, never gave it another thought. My father, you never saw the guy sweat. My mother, she was on a plane that had to make an emergency landing once, she didn't even give it a second thought, as far as I could tell. Representatives of the Cortez cartel were tracking me on a monitor somewhere, or on some sequence of handheld computers, watching me, and they were broadcasting their messages to staff people who could be trusted. Who knew how many other people in the Eddie Cortez operation were being treated the way I was being treated today? Bring this guy into the fold, conquer him, if not, neutralize him, leave him out in the rubble of some building somewhere. It was an operation staffed by guys who all had guns, stun guns and cattle prods, real guns with bullets that could make an Abstract Expressionist painting out of a guy like me, and I was trying to get the fuck out of there, before I was dead, and I could barely think of anything else. Now they were taking me down this long hall, and it wasn't the corridor I was in before, because the building had all these layers, and it was hard to know where you were, relative to where you had been before, or maybe this is just the way I felt because of what the voice on the loudspeaker said next.

"Be sure to be vigilant about forgetting."

Which reminds me to remind you of the *diachronous theory of Albertine abuse,* which of course recognizes the forgetting as a social phenomenon coincident, big-time, with a certain pattern of Albertine penetration into the population. The manifestation of forgetting is easy to explain, see, because it has to do with bolstering the infrastructure of memory elsewhere. Like anyone who's a drinker knows, you borrow courage when you're drinking, and you lose it someplace else. Addiction is about credit. That amazing thing you said at the bar last night, that thing you would never say in person to anyone, it's a onetime occurrence, because tomorrow, in the light of dawn, when you are separated from your wallet and your money, when your girlfriend hates you, then you'll be unable to say that courageous thing again, because you are wrung out and lying on a mattress without sheets. You borrowed that courage, and it's gone.

So the thing with Albertine was that at night, under its influence, you remembered. Tonight the past was glorious and indelible—Serena in the park with the rum and the bittersweet revelation of her boyfriend—tonight was the beauty of almost being in love, which was a great beauty, but tomorrow, your memory was full of holes. Not a blackout, more like a brownout. You could remember that you once knew things, but they were indistinct now, and the understanding of them just flew out the window. It was like the early part of jet lag, or thorazine. Why did I come into this room? I was going to get something. Suddenly you had no idea, you stood looking at the pile of clothes in front of the dresser, clothes that were fascinating colors, that old pair of jeans, very interesting. Look at that color. It's so blue. Maybe you needed to do something, but you didn't, and you realized that things were going on in your body, and they were inexplicable to you. You were really thirsty. Maybe you ought to have had some juice, but on the way to the bottle of water on the table, you forgot.

The history of Albertine became a history of forgetting. A geo-metrically increasing history of forgetfulness. Men in charge of its distribution, by reason of the fact that they started using it for orga-nizational reasons, to increase market share, they were as forgetful as the hard-core users, who after a while couldn't remember their own addresses, except occasionally, and who were therefore on the street, asking strangers, *Do you know my name? Do you happen to know where I live?* The history of the drug, requested by Cortez, was therefore important. How else to plan for the future? If the research and devel-opment team at Cortez Enterprises didn't forget how to read, then, as long as they had a hard copy of the history, everything was cool. I would write the story; they'd lock it away somewhere.

Before I had a chance to agree or disagree, I was going down in the industrial elevator, alone, and it was like being shat out the ass of the smelting factory. It was dawn with the light coming up under the lip of that relentless cloud. Dawn, the only time these days there was any glimmer on the horizon, before the debris clouds massed again. But, listen, I have to come clean on something. I missed Cassandra. That's what I was feeling. She'd sold me out to Eddie Cortez, made me his vassal, like she was his vassal. Trust and fealty, these words were just memories. So was Cassandra, just a memory. A lost person. Who'd reassured me for a few minutes. Who'd have sold out anyone for more drugs and a few minutes on a postindustrial sexual machine. Was I right that there was something there? For an Albertine second, the slowest second on the clock. Seemed like she was the threshold to some partially forgotten narrative, some inchoate past, some incomplete sign, like light coming in through window blinds. Boy, I was stupid, getting sentimental about the Asian mistress of a drug kingpin.

Daylight seemed serious, practical. It was the first time I could remember being out in the daylight since I started compiling these notes. On the way back to the armory, I waited on the line up the block for the one pay phone that still worked. Usually there were fifty or sixty people out front. All of them simmering with rage, because the connection was sketchy, the phone disconnected, and everyone listened to the other callers, listened to the conversations. Imagine the sound of the virtual automaton's computerized warmth, We're sorry, the parties you are contacting are unable to accept the call.

Who was sorry exactly? The robot? A guy holding the receiver shouted, "I need to know the name of that prescription! I'm not a well man!" Then the disconnection. A woman begged her husband to take her back. Disconnection. And a kid who has lost his parents, trying to locate his grandparents. Disconnection. The phone booth had that multitude of sad stories hidden spinning around it.

Soon it was my turn, and my father got on. Man of few words.

"We told you not to call here anymore," he said.

"What?"

"You heard me."

"I haven't called in . . ."

I tried to put it all together. How long? Measuring time had become almost impossible. There was nothing to do but make a stab at it.

" . . . three weeks."

"We can't give you anything more. Our own savings are nearly exhausted. You need to start thinking about how you're going to get out of the jam you're in without calling us every time it gets worse. It's you who is making it worse. Understand? Think about what you're doing!"

I could see the people behind me in the pay phone line leaning in toward the bad news, excited to get a few tidbits. Their own bad scrapes were not nearly as bad.

"What are you talking about?"

"I've told you before," he said. "Don't raise your voice with me."

His own voice defeated, brittle.

"Put Mom on the line!"

"Absolutely not."

"Let me talk to Mom!"

Then some more nonsense about how I had caused my mother unending sorrow, that it was her nature only to sacrifice, but I had squandered this generosity, had stamped up and down on it with my callousness, my American callousness, as if my family had not overcome innumerable obstacles to get me where I was. I made the selflessness of my heritage seem like a deluded joke. I had dishonored him, etc. etc., by my shameful activities, etc. etc. It was as good as if I had died during the blast.

A bona fide patriarchal dressing-down, of a sort that I thought I had left behind long ago. I was watching the faces of the people in the line behind me, and their faces were reflecting my own face. Incredulity. Confusion.

"Dad, I have no idea what you're talking about. Listen to me."

"You can't call here every day with your preposterous lies. Your imagined webs of conspiracy. We won't have it. We are exhausted. Your mother cannot get out of bed, and I am up at all hours frantic with worry about you. How are we supposed to live? Get some help!"

I smiled a befuddled smile for my audience, I replaced the receiver. In midstream. Of course, I hadn't called my parents recently, hadn't called them the day before, or the week before, or the week before that. Hadn't called them often at all. My crime, in fact, was that because of shame about where I lived and what I was doing I didn't really call anyone anymore. So what explained the circumstance?

I looked at the next guy in line. A melancholy African-American man, with a fringe of gray hair and eyeglasses patched with some duct tape. It was beginning to rain, of course, and I saw an obsidian blob splatter the surface of his glasses.

"I guess I just called them," I said. "I mean, I guess I forgot that I called them."

He pushed past me.

To forget was threatening now. Nobody wanted to have anything to do with a forgetter. A forgetter meant just the one thing. A forgetter had abscesses in his arm, or a forgetter had sold off the last of his possessions and was trying to sell them a second time, because he had forgotten that the apartment was already empty. The highest respect, the most admiration was accorded those with perfect recall—that was part of the diachronous theory, or if it wasn't yet, I predicted it would soon be part of that theory. Geeks with perfect recall would get up in public settings, with a circle of folding chairs around them, and then, in front of an amazed audience, these geeks would remember the perfect textures of things, Ah yes, the running mates of the losers in of the last eight presidential elections, let me see. And the names of their wives. And weather on election day. Massive fraud would be perpetrated in certain cases, where these perfect-recall geeks would, it turned out, have needle tracks, just like the rest of us. Ohmygod! They were doping, and they would be escorted out into the street, in shame, where again rain was beginning to fall.

Which is why when I got back to the armory, and found the package on my bed, I felt that pornographic thrill. I could manage an eyedropper as good as the next guy, right? I'd work up to the needles. What else was there to hang around for? No one was waiting for me. Maybe I could get back to the night before, when I was talking to Cassandra. I said this little preliminary prayer, May this roll of the dice be the one in which I remember love, or teen sex, or that time when I had a lot of money from a summer job and I was barbecuing out in the back of the subdivision, and everybody was drinking beer and having a good time.

But, no, I would become a junky in a supply closet, and I would use a lantern I'd looted from a camping equipment store after the blast. I held the eyedropper above me, and the droplet of intoxicant was lingering there, and I was the oyster that was going to envelop it and make it my secret. The drop in the dropper was like the black rain of NYC which was like the money shot in a porn film which was like the tears from the Balkan statuary of the Virgin in the naïf style. The lantern shone up from underneath my supply closet shelves, and there was that rush of perfumes that I've already described, which meant that it was all beginning again; I was lucky for the perfumes I've known, other guys just know paperwork, but I've known the smell of people right before being naked with them, what an honor. All junkies are lapsed idealists, falling away from things as they were. I was a murderer of time. I'd taken the hours of my life out back of the armory and shoved them in the wood chipper or buried them in a swamp or bricked them up in the basement. But this thought was overwhelmed by the personal scent of a fashion student who lived near us when I was in California. It was on me like a new atmosphere. Along with the sheets of fog rolling in over the Bay.

It was all a fine movie. At least until something really horrible occurred to me, a bummer of a thought. How could it be? Thinking about that Serena, again, see, in the Boston Commons, drinking rum, remembering that she actually had Cherry Coke, not the soft drink once known as the Real Thing, to which I said, "Cherry Coke, girl, that's not Coke, because no Coke product that occurs, historically, after the advent of the New Coke—held by some to have been a reaction to sugar prices in Latin American countries—no Coke that occurs after that time is a legitimate Coke. Get it? The only Coke product that is genuine with respect to the rum and Cokes you're proposing to drink here is Mexican Coke, which you can still get in bottles, and which still features some actual cane sugar." An impressive speech, a flirtatious speech, but somewhere in the middle of remembering it—and who knew how many hours had passed now, who knew how many days—this thought I'm speaking about occurred to me:

Serena's boyfriend, the guy she was seeing beside me, or instead of me, *was Addict Number One.*

Years before, I mean. Way before he was the actual Addict Number One. Because we were in high school then, and Addict Number One wasn't killed yet, or hadn't vanished. Not in this version of the story. He was a college guy, and he wanted to make movies, went to NYU, lived downtown, wore a lot of black, just like Addict Number One. And he could tell you a lot about certain recordings that hardcore bands from Minneapolis made in the eighties, and he had a lot of opinions about architecture and politics and sitcoms and maybe bagels, I don't know. I could feel that it was true. It was a hunch, but it was a really good hunch. There was an intersection in the story where there hadn't been one before, and the intersection involved me, or at least tangentially it involved me. Before I was an observer, but now I was coming to see that there was no observing Albertine. Because Albertine was looking back into you. The thought was so unsettling that I was actually shaking with terror about it, but I was too high to stop remembering.

Serena said, "You won't have any idea whether this is Coke or Cherry Coke after the first half a cup. I could put varnish in here, you wouldn't know." She smiled and now I felt myself drunk just with the particulars of her smile. It was a humble, lopsided smile, and she was wearing those patched blue jeans, and she pulled off her green Dartmouth sweatshirt, to reveal a T-shirt with the sleeves cut off, the T-shirt advertising a particular girl deejay, and I could see the lower part of her belly underneath the T-shirt. The slope of her breasts. I mean, her smile promised things that never came to be, you know? While I was taking it in, turning over the irrefutable fact of her smile and a tiny series of beautiful lines, like parentheses, at the corners of her fantastic mouth, Serena began to fade. "Don't go," I said, "there's some stuff we need to cover," but it was like those cries in a dream, the cries that just wake you up. They don't actually bring help. They just wake you. I could see her fading, and in her stead, I saw a bunch of bare trees from some November trip to the malls of Jersey. Autumn.

I seized the eyedropper, which, because it had just been sitting on my roach-infested mattress while I was busy remembering, now seemed to have black specks all over the tip of it, and maybe there were some kinds of bugs crawling around on there, I don't know. I held back my eyelids. I was aching in my eye sockets.

The plan was to summon her back, to call her name in the old psychoanalytic way, you know. Names count for something. Strong feelings count for something. And such a beautiful name anyhow, right? Serena, like some ocean of calm lapping against the fucked-up landscape. I would ask her. If I could map the weird voyages of my younger self, that Asian kid trying to declare himself to a Yankee girl through really abstract complicated poetry, *If all time is eternally present,/All time is unredeemable./What might have been is an abstraction.*

Because if it was really true that Cassandra had somehow willed me to see what she knew about Eddie Cortez, just because she wanted me to see it, even if telling me the truth about Eddie was somehow a danger to her position as his mistress, then it was true that love and affection were important orienting forces in the Albertine epidemic. Like Eddie, who chased Addict Number One through the dingy recesses of his brain simply in the breadth of his malice and greed. Maybe the rememberer, in the intoxication of remembering, was always ultimately tempted to reach out the hand, and maybe this rememberer could do so, if his passion was strong enough. How else to look at it? What else did I have to go on? Because a hundred thousand Albertine addicts couldn't be wrong. Because they were all chasing the promise of some lost, glittering, perfect moment of love. Because some of them must have reached that Elysian destination in their floods of memory and forgetfulness. Because I sure loved Serena, because she had a lopsided smile, because she had nails called *lycan-*

thrope, because love is good when you have nothing, and I had nothing, except bike messengers watching my every move.

Instead of access to Serena, though, I got stuck in this fucked-up loop where all I could remember is a bunch of really horrible songs from my childhood. In particular, "Shake Your Bon-Bon," a song that definitely had not aged very well. Sounds tinny, like the sampling rate is bad somehow, you know, those early sampling rates on digital music, really tinny. And here's that little synthesizer loop that's supposed to sound like the Beatles during their sitar phase, girl backup singers, the attempt to make the glamorous leading man sound as though he didn't prefer boys, fine, really, but why pretend, man, knock yourself out. Seven hours, at least, passed in which I went over the minutiae of "Shake Your Bon-Bon." The utterly computerized sound of it, the vestiges of humanness in its barren musical palette, as if the singer dude couldn't be bothered to repeat the opening hook himself, no way, it'd sound better if they just looped it on ProTools, and then the old-fashioned organ, which was a simulated organ, etc., and the relationship between the congas and the guitars, okay, and what about that Latin middle section? Demographically perfect! So twentieth century! I didn't want to think about the trombone solo at the end of "Shake Your Bon-Bon," buried in the back, that sultry trombone solo, but I did think about it, about the singer's Caribbean origins oozing out at the edges of the composition, and his homosexuality. Went on this way for a while, including a complete recollection of a remix that I think I only heard one time in my entire life, which was in some ways the superior version, because the more artificial the better, like when they take out all the rests between the vocal lines, so that the song has effectively become impossible to sing. Nowhere to take a breath. Was anyone on earth thinking about the singer in question, these days after the blast? I bet no one at all was thinking of him, except for certain stalkers from Yonkers or Port Chester. Where was he exactly? Had he managed to find refuge in a completely pink hotel in South Beach before the blast? And were his memories of showbiz dominance so great that the big new export market for Albertine was seducing him now like everyone else? Was South Beach falling into the vortex of memory, like New York before it?

Just when it seemed like I would never cast my eyes on Serena again, just when it seemed like it was all Ricky Martin from now on, she was a vision before me, you know, a thing of ether, a residuum, like lavender, like coffee regular. The odd thing was I got used to remembering that one portion of our time together. I forgot what came later. I forgot that just because she had this boyfriend, this college dude with short eyes, this college man who chased after teens, didn't mean that I stopped talking to her altogether, because the attachments you have then, when you're a kid, at least back before the trouble in the world began, these friendships are the one sustaining thing. I could see myself in some institutional corridor, high school passageway, and there she was, golden in the light of grimy shatterproof windows, as if women and light were as close as lungs and air. I was slumped by a locker. Serena came across the corridor, across speckled linoleum tiles, and it was like I had never looked at those tiles before, because she was wearing a certain sweatshop-manufactured brand of sneakers, and so I saw the linoleum, because the linoleum was improved by her and her sneakers.

"You okay?"

No. I was hyperventilating. Like I did back then. Anything could set me off. College entrance examinations, these caused me to hyperventilate, any dip in my grades. And I didn't tell anyone about it. Only my mother knew. I was an Asian kid and I was supposed to be incredibly smart. I was supposed to have calculus right at my fingertips, and I was supposed to know C++ and Visual Basic and Java and every other fucking computer language, and this all made me hyperventilate.

I said, "Tell me the name of the guy you're seeing. I just want to know his name. It's only fair."

"You really want to talk about this again?"

"Tell me once."

Battalions of teens slithered past, wearing their headphones and their MP3 players all playing the same moronic dirge of niche-marketed neo-grunge shit.

"Paley," she said. "First name, Irving, which I guess is a really weird name. He doesn't seem like an Irving to me. Is that enough?"

God sure put the big curse on Chinese kids, because when the raven of fate flew across their hearts, they just couldn't show it. We were supposed to be shut up in our hearts, because to do otherwise was not part of the collective plan, or maybe that was just how I felt about it. I felt like my heart was an overfilled water balloon, and I was hyperventilating.

"Kevin," she said, "you have to do something about the panic thing. They have drugs for it. You know?"

Do you know how much I think about you? I wanted to say. Do you want to know how you are preserved for all of human history? Because I have written you down, I have gotten down the way you pull your sweater sleeves over your hands, I have gotten down the way your eyeliner smudges. I have preserved the roll-out on the heels of your expensive sneakers, which you don't replace often enough. I know about you and nectarines, I know you like them better than anything else, and I know that you aren't happy first thing in the morning, not without a lot of coffee, and that you think your shoulders are fat, but that's ridiculous. All this is written down. And the times you yelled at your younger sister on the bus, I wrote down the entire exchange, and I don't want anything for it at all. I don't want you to feel that there's any obligation attached, except that you made me want to use writing for preservation, which is so great, because then I started preserving other things, like all the conversations I heard out in front of the Museum of Fine Arts, and I started describing the Charles River, rowboats on the Charles, I have written all of this down too, I have written it all down because of you.

This was enough! This was enough to redeem my sorry ass, because suddenly all the moments were one, this moment and that, lined up like the ducks on some Coney Island shooting game, chiming together, and I said, "Serena, I only got a second here, so listen up, I don't know any other way to put it, so just listen carefully. Something really horrible is going to happen to your friend Paley, so you have to tell him to stay out of Tompkins Square Park, no matter what, tell him never to go to Tompkins Square Park, tell him it's a reliable bet, and that maybe he should do his graduate work at USC or something. I'm telling you this because I just know it, so do it for me. I know, I know, it's crazy, but do like I say."

At which point, I was shaken rudely awake. *Oh, come on.* It was a time-travel moment. It was a memory-inside-a-memory moment, except that it might have been actually happening. I just wasn't sure.

One of the bike messengers from Cortez Enterprises smacked me in the face. In my supply closet. I'd have been happy to talk, you know, but I was too high, and as so many accounts have suggested in the Albertine literature, trying to talk when you are high is like having all the radio stations on your radio playing at the same time. I could just make out the nasty sound of his voice, in the midst of a recollected lecture from my dad on the best way to bet on blackjack. *Lee, you are not attending to your duties.* Not true, no way, I tried to say, I'm a devoted employee, just got back here an hour ago, and I'm doing some more researches, and I'm finding out some very interesting things.

"You haven't produced shit," said the bike messenger. "We need to see some work. You need to be e-mailing us some attachments, Mr. Lee, and so far we haven't seen anything."

"Totally incorrect," I said. "I've been taking some notes. Somewhere around here. There are all kinds of notes."

There was the digital recorder, for example. But the batteries were dead.

"This conversation isn't going very well," replied the bike messenger. "We have also heard that you have been moving product given to you as part of our agreement."

"There's just no way!"

"Don't make us have to remind you about the specifics of your responsibilities."

"Give me a break," I said. "I'm smarter than that."

Now the bike messenger flung open the door that led out of my supply closet. Like I had forgotten there was a world out there. And standing out in the hall was Tara from the tits-and-lit magazine, except she looked really disheveled, like she didn't want to be seen by anyone else, and I said, "Tara, what are you doing here? I thought I had at least another couple weeks—"

"You said you had the dropper. I don't know anything about all this. I gave you the money, so can I please just have the drugs? Then I'll get the fuck out of here."

I made some desperate pleas to the Cortez employee, looking at him looking at Tara, while Tara stood and watched. I stalled, demanded to know if there was a way for me to be sure that these guys, the bike messenger, and Tara weren't just figments of some future event that I was now "remembering," according to that theory about Albertine.

"Did you or did you not assign me an article about Albertine?"

Tara said, "Just set me up and let me get out of here."

And then Bertrand, the guy who doled out the habitable spaces in the armory, he got into the act too. Standing in the doorway, covered in grime, like he'd just come from his job at a filling station, except that as far as I knew it was just that Bertrand was an addict and had given up on personal hygiene, he gazed at me with a make-believe compassion.

"Kevin, listen, we've given you chances. We've looked the other way. We've been understanding for months. We've made excuses for you. We pulled you out of the gutter when you were passed out there. But people living here at the armory are afraid to walk by your apartment now. They're just afraid of what's going to happen. So where does that leave us?"

And even Bob, my early source, was standing behind Bertrand, hands on his hips. Trying to push past the throng of accusers, to get to me.

This was a moment when thinking carefully was more important than hallucinating. But because of the extremely dangerous amount of Albertine that was already overwhelming both my liver and my cerebral activity, reality just wasn't a station that I could tune very well. What I mean is, I went down under again. Right in front of all those people.

Soon I was hanging out on some sun porch in a subdivision in Massachusetts. All the houses, in whichever direction I turned, looked exactly the same. I bet they had electrical fireplaces in every room. It was like CAD had come through with a backhoe, bulldozed the whole region into uniformity. I could remember each tiny difference, each sign that some person, some family, had lived here for more than ten minutes. Serena's folks had a jack-o'-lantern on the porch. And over there was a guy with one arm mowing the common areas. That intoxicating smell of freshly cut grass. The sound of yellow jackets trying to get in through the screen.

Serena was reiterating that I had said something *really scary* to her at school today, and she needed to know if I'd said what I had said because of the panic thing. Were my symptoms causing me to say these crazy things, and if so, wouldn't it be better if I told someone what was happening, instead of carrying it around by myself? She knew, she said, about really serious mental illnesses, she knew about these things and she wanted me to know that I would still be her friend, her special friend, even if I had one of those mental illnesses, so I was not to worry about it. And now would I please try to explain?

"Listen, I know what I said, and there's no reason you should believe me," I tried, "but the fact is that the only reason I can explain to you about the future is because I'm in the future. And in the future I know how much you mean to me. In the future, this four months that we're close, they keep coming back around, again and again, like that day we were in the Boston Commons. It keeps coming back around. I could tell you all this stuff about the future, about New York City and how it gets bombed into rubble, about drugs, about the epidemic that's coming, I could tell you how strung out I'm going to get. But that's not the point. Somehow you're the point. Serena, you're the *trompe l'oeil* in the triptych of the future, and that's because you know that guy. Paley. So you have to believe me, even though I probably wouldn't believe me, if I were you. Still, the thing is, you have to tell him what I've told you. Maybe none of this will happen, this stuff, I sure hope not. Maybe it will all turn out different, just because I'm telling you. But we can't plan on that. What we have to plan on is your telling Paley that he's in danger."

"Actually, Kevin, what I think we need to do is talk to your mom."

The jack-o'-lantern on the porch, of course. It was *autumn,* which was bad news, which meant I was on the comedown, and badly in need of a boost, and the whole scene was swirling away into an electromagnetic dwindling of stories. Serena was gone, and suddenly instead of being back in my room at the armory, where, suspended in a lost present, I was about to be evicted from my supply closet, I was back doing my job, the job of journalist, and what a relief. I had no idea what day it was. I had no idea if I was remembering the past or the future, or if I happened to be in the present. Albertine had messed with all that. I was confused. So was the guy I was interviewing, who happened to be the epidemiologist with the theory about the Albertine crisis, the one I told you about earlier, except that he was no epidemiologist at all. That was just his cover story. Actually, he was the anthropologist, Ernst Wentworth, and we were in his office in Brooklyn College, which wasn't really an office anymore, because there were about thirty thousand homeless people living on the campus of the college. At night there were vigilante raids in which the Arabic people living on one quad would be driven off the campus, out onto the streets of the Hot Zone, where stray gunshots from Eddie Cortez's crew took out at least two or three a night. It was trench warfare. No one was getting educated at Brooklyn College, and Wentworth was crowded into a single room with a half dozen other desks and twice as many file cabinets pushed against the windows.

He was having trouble following the thread of the interview. Me too. I couldn't remember if I had already asked certain questions:

Q: Check. Check. Check. Uh, okay, do you know anything about the origin of Albertine?

A: No one knows the origin actually. The most compelling theory, which is getting quite a bit of attention these days, is that Albertine has no origin. The physicists at the college have suggested the possibility that Albertine owes her proliferation to a recent intense shower of interstellar dark matter. The effect of this dark matter is such that time, right now, has become completely porous, completely randomized. Certain subatomic constituent particles are colliding with certain others. This would suggest that Albertine is a side effect of a space-time difficulty, a quantum indeterminacy, rather than a cause herself, and since she is not a cause, she has no origin, no specific beginning that we know of. She just tends to appear, on a statistical basis.

Q: Given that this is a possibility, why are Albertine's effects only visible in New York City?

A: The more provocative question would be, according to quantum indeterminacy, does New York City actually exist? At least, if you take the hypothesis of theoretical physics to its logical conclusion. This would be a brain-in-the-vat hypothesis. NYC as an illusion purveyed by a malevolent scientist. Except that the malevolent scientist here is Albertine herself. She leads us to believe in a certain

New York City, a New York City with postapocalyptic, posttraumatic dimensions and obsessions. And yet perhaps this collective hallucination is merely a way to rationalize what is taking place: that it is now almost impossible to exist in linear time at all.

Q: So maybe in Kansas City, they have similar hallucinations. Kansas City is the center of some galloping drug epidemic. And the same thing in Tampa or Reno or Harrisburg?

A: Could be. Something like that. (*Pause.*) Can I borrow some of your—?

Q: There's only a little left. But, sure, get a buzz on. (*Getting serious.*) Have you attempted a catalogue of types of Albertine experiences?

A: Well, sociopaths seem to have a really bad time with the drug. We know that. And it's a startling fact, really. Since much of the distribution network is controlled by sociopaths. But at most dosage thresholds, sociopaths have stunted Albertine experiences. They'll remember their Driver Ed exam for hours on end. By sociopaths, I'm referring especially to individuals with poor intrapsychic bonding, poor social skills. Individuals who lack for compassion. It would be hard to imagine them taking much pleasure in Albertine. On the other hand, at the top end of the spectrum are the ambiguous experiences of which you are no doubt aware. People who claim to remember future events, people who claim to remember other people's memories, people who claim to have interacted with their memories. And so forth. At first we believed that these experiences, which characterized many of the people here conducting our studies—myself included—were only occurring, if that's the right word, among the enlightened. That is, we believed that ahistorical remembering was an aspect of wish fulfillment among the healthiest and most engaged personalities. But then we learned that malice, hatred, and murderous rage could be just as effective at creating these episodes. In either case, we became convinced that the frequency of these reports merited our attention. If true, the fact of ahistorical remembering would have to suggest that the fabric of time is not woven together as consistently as we once thought. We tried at first to analyze whether these logically impossible experiences were "true" on a factual level, but now we are more interested in whether or not they are repeatable, visible to more than one person, etc.

Q: Does your catalogue of experiences shed any light on Albertine's origin?

A: One compelling theory that's making the rounds among guys in the sciences here at the college is that Albertine has infinite origins. That she appeared in the environment all at once, at different locations, synchronously, according to some kind of philosophical or metaphysical randomness generator. There's no other perfect way to describe the effect. According to this view, the disorder she causes is so intense that her origin is concealed in an effacement of the moment of her origin, because to have a single origin violates the parameters of non-linearity. Didn't we already do this part about the origin?

Q: Shit. I guess you're right. Okay, hang on. (*Regroups.*) Do you, do you think it's possible to manipulate the origin of Albertine, to actually control the drug, so as to alter a specific narrative? Like, say, the rise of the Albertine crime syndicate?

A: Sure, persons of my acquaintance have done plenty of that. At least on an experimental basis. We have had no choice. But I'm not at liberty to go into that today.

Q: Let's go back to the issue of what to do about the epidemic. Do you have a specific policy formulation?

A: I did have some good ideas about that. (*Ponders.*) Okay, wait just a second. I'm going to look through my papers on the subject here. (*Riffles mounds on desk.*) I'm forgetting so much these days. Okay, my observation is that Albertine finds her allure in the fact that the human memory is, by its nature, imperfect. Every day, in every way, we are experiencing regret over the fact that we can conjure up some minimal part of the past, but not as much as we'd like. This imperfection of memory is built into the human animal, and as long as it's an issue, the Albertine syndicates will be able to exploit it. Strategies for containment have to come from another direction, therefore. Which is to say that the only thing that could conceivably help in the long run would be to make distribution of the drug extremely widespread. We should make sure everybody has it.

Q: How would that help?

A: Since Albertine has forgetfulness as a long-term side effect, it's possible that we could actually make everyone forget that Albertine exists. It would have to be concerted, you understand. But let me make an analogy. At a certain point in heroin addiction, you no longer feel the effects of the opiate; you only service the withdrawal. A similar effect could take place here. At a certain point, everyone would be trying to avoid the forgetting, because they can't work effectively, they can't even remember where work is, and yet soon this forgetting would begin to invade even the drug experience, so that what you remember grows dimmer, because you are beginning to accelerate plaque buildup, and other anatomical effects. With enough of this forgetting everyone would forget that they were addicts, forget that they needed the drug to remember, forget that memory was imperfect, and then we would be back to some kind of lowest common denominator of civic psychology. Damaged, but equal.

Q: How would you go about doing this?

(Ernst Wentworth gives the interviewer the once-over in a way he had not done before.)

A: We're going to put it in the water supply.

Q: Hasn't that been tried already?

A: What do you mean?

Q: I think someone told me that an attack on the water supply was recently thwarted.

A: Are you serious?

Q: Well, unless someone was using disinformation—

A: *(Wentworth shouts.)* Guys, you recording all of this?

The room was bugged, of course, and on this signal a bunch of academics rushed into Wentworth's office, blindfolded me, and carried me out. I didn't struggle. When I was freed, I was in the Brooklyn College Astronomy Lab. It was Ernst Wentworth who gently removed my blindfold.

"You understand we have no choice but to take every precaution. Just a couple of days ago, Claude Jannings, from the linguistics department, watched his wife disappear in front of him. She was there, in the kitchen, talking about the dearth of political writings pertaining to the Albertine epidemic, and then she was gone, just absolutely gone. As if someone were listening to the conversation the whole time. Apparently, her remarks about Albertine, and inchoate plans to write on the subject, were enough to make her a target."

My eyes became accustomed to the dim light of the astronomy lab. The interior was all concrete, functional, except for the platform where you could get up and take a gander at the heavens. Around me, there was a circle of guys in tweed jackets and cardigan sweaters. A couple of bow ties. Khaki slacks.

"Wow, it's Kevin Lee! Right here in our lab!" Some good-natured chortling.

Huh?

Wentworth ventured further explanations. "We've developed a hierarchy for marking events, so we don't forget later. Whenever one of us goes out in public, we bring along a poster or sign indicating the date and time. That way, if we travel backwards on Albertine in search of particular events, we aren't thrown off or beguiled by unimportant days. And we bring clothing of various colors, red for an alert, green for an all-clear. It's a conspiracy of order, you understand, and that's a particularly revolutionary conspiracy right now. What we've additionally found, by cataloguing memories—and we have guys who are medicated twenty-four hours a day thinking about all this—is that there are certain people who turn up over and over. We refer to people who are present at large numbers of essential Albertine nodal points as memory catalysts. Eduardo Cortez, for example, is a *memory catalyst,* and not in a good way. And there are some other very odd examples I could give you. A talk-show host from ten or fifteen years ago seems to turn up quite a bit, perhaps just because his name is so memorable, Regis Philbin. You'd be surprised how close to the inner workings of the Albertine epidemic is Regis Philbin. When we're around Philbin, we are always wearing red. We don't know what he means yet, but we're working on it. And then there's you."

"Me?"

One doctoral candidate, standing by the base of the telescope, nonchalant, spoke up. "If we had baseball cards of the players in the

McSWEENEY'S MAMMOTH TREASURY OF THRILLING TALES

Albertine epidemic, you'd be collectible. You'd be the power hitting shortstop."

"We have a theory," Wentworth said. "And the theory is that you're important because you're a writer."

"Yeah, but I'm not even a very good writer. I'm barely published."

Wentworth waved his plump hands.

"Doesn't matter. We've been trying to find out for a while who originally came up with your assignment. It wasn't your editor there. That we know. She's just another addict. It was someone above her, and if we can find out who it is, we think we'll be close to finding a spot where the Frost Communications holding company connects to Cortez Enterprises. Somewhere up the chain, you were being groomed for this moment. Unless you are simply some kind of emblem for Albertine. That's possible, too, of course."

Wentworth smiled, so that his tobacco-stained teeth shone forth in the gloomy light. "Additionally, you're a hero from the thick, roiling juices of the New York City melting pot. And that is very satisfying to us. Do you want to see? We know so much about you that it's almost embarrassing. We even know what you like to eat, and what kind of toothpaste you use. Don't worry, we won't make a big stink about it."

Later, of course, the constituency of the Brooklyn Resistance was a matter of much speculation. There were women there too, with mournful expressions, like they had come along with the Resistance, though they had grave doubts about its masculine power structure. Women in modest skirts or slightly unflattering pantsuits, like Jesse Simons, the Deconstructionist, who argued that doping the water supply was embracing the nomadic sign system of Albertine, which of course represented not some empirical astrophysical event, but, rather, a symbolic reaction to the crisis of instability caused by American Imperialism. And there were a couple of African-Americanists, wearing hints of kinte cloth with their tweeds and corduroys. They argued for intervention in the economic imperatives that led to drug dealing among the inner city poor. And there was the great postcolonialist writer Jean-Pierre Al-Sadir. He argued that the route to victory over civic chaos was infiltration of the Albertine cartels. However, Al-Sadir, because of his Algerian passport, had been mentioned as part of the conspiracy that detonated the New York City blast. Still, here he was, fighting with the patriots, if that's what they were. It was a testament to the desperation of the moment that none of these academic stars would normally have agreed on anything, you know? I mean, these people *hated* each other. If you'd gone to a faculty meeting at Columbia three years ago, you would have seen Al-Sadir call Simons an arrogant narcissist in front of a college president. That kind of thing. But infighting was forgotten for now, as the Resistance began plotting its strategies. Even when I was hanging around with them, there would be the occasional argument about the semiotics of wearing red, or about whether time as a system was inherently phallogocentric, such that its present adumbrated shape was preferable, as a representation of labial or vaginal narrative space.

"So you guys probably have one of those dials, on a machine, where we can go directly to a particular year and day and hour and second, right?"

"Fat chance," Wentworth said. "In fact, we have a room next door with a lot of cots in it—"

"A shooting gallery?"

"Just so. And we employ a lot of teaching assistants, keep them comfortable and intoxicated for a long time and see what happens. Whatever you might think, what we have here is a lot of affection for one another, so a lot of stories go around like lightning, a lot of conjecture, a lot of despair, a lot of elation, a lot of plans. You know? We see ourselves as junkies for history. Of which yours is one integral piece. Let's go have a look, shall we?"

It would be great if I could report that the shooting gallery of the Resistance was significantly better than the Cortez shooting gallery, but, really, the only difference was that these guys sterilized the needles after each use and swabbed their track marks. No abscesses in this crowd. Otherwise, it was only marginally more inviting. Some of the most important academics of my time were lying on cots, drooling, fighting their way through the cultural noise of fifty years—television programming, billboards, pornography, newspaper advertisements—in order to get back to the origin of Albertine, bitch goddess, in order to untangle the mess she'd made. The other important difference here was that these guys were synthesizing their own batches of the stuff, instead of buying it on the street, and when a bunch of chemists and biologists get into mixing up a drug, that drug *chimes,* let me tell you. They explained the chemical derivation to me, too. Which looks kinda like this:

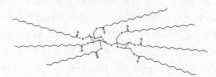

Apparently, the effect had to do with increasing oxygenated blood flow to neurotransmitters, thereby increasing electrical impulses. It wasn't that hard to do at all. Miraculous that no one had done it before now. The only physiognomic problem with Albertine was her tendency to burn out the cells, like in diseases of senescence. Albertine was sort of the neurochemical equivalent of steroid abuse.

I was lucky. Jesse Simons volunteered to be the prefect for my trip, and she and Wentworth stood awkwardly in the center of the room, as a grad student from the Renaissance Studies department pulled the rubber tie around my arm. It was the sweetest thing, tying off again. I didn't care anymore about writing, I only cared about the part where I stunned myself with Albertine. I was dreaming of being ravished by her, overwhelmed by her instruction, where perception was a maelstrom of time past, present, and future. The eons were neon, they were like the old Times Square, first time you ever saw it, first time you felt the rush of its hundreds of thousands of images, and I don't mean the Disney version, I mean the version with hookers and street violence and raving crack fiends. Albertine was like a soup of NYC neon. She was a catalogue of demonic euphonies. I felt the rubber cord unsnap, heard a sigh beside me, felt Jesse's arms around me, and the soft middle of sedentary Ernst Wentworth. Then we were rolling and tumbling in the thick of Albertine's forest. I was back in the armory, and there were a bunch of bike messengers leading me out, and I was screaming to Tara, and to Bertrand, and to Bob, *Save my notes, save my notes,* and the bike messengers were beating on me and I could feel the panic, in my chest, I could feel it, and I said, Where are you taking me? I passed a little circle of residents of the armory, carrying home their government rations of mac and cheese, not a hair on the head of any of them, all the carcinogenic residents of the armory, all of them with appointments for chemo later in the week, and they were all wearing red. I heard a voice, like in voice-over, We're sorry that you are going to have to see this. It was better when you had forgotten all about it. And the bike messengers took me on a tour of Brooklyn in their jeeps, up and down the empty streets of my borough, kicking my ass the whole way, until my lips were split and bleeding, until my blackened eyes were swollen shut. We came to a halt down on the waterfront, on the piers. They dumped me out of the jeep while it was still moving, and my last pair of jeans was shredded from all the broken glass and rubble. My knees and hips were gashed. But the syndicate wasn't through with me yet; some more of Cortez's flunkies took me inside a factory, a creepy institutional place, *where they manufactured the drug.*

Here it was. The Albertine sweatshop. There weren't many buildings left in downtown Brooklyn, you know, because it was within the event horizon of the dirty bomb, a lot of the stuff on the waterfront was rubble. But this building was still here somehow, which implied that Eddie Cortez was subjecting his production staff to radioactive hazards. That was the least of it, of course, because most of the staff was probably high. Maybe that was the one job benefit.

"What are we doing here?" I said to the goons leading me in past the surveillance gate, and in through a front hall that looked remarkably like the reception area of the tits-and-lit magazine that assigned my Albertine story in the first place. There was even one of those remote-control reception robots, just like at the magazine offices.

"Your questions will be answered in due course."

"Really? Because I have a big backlog—"

"Don't get smart, we *will* make it hurt, dig?"

More corridors, linkages of impossible interiors, then into an office. We were waved through without hesitation. The women and men in the typing pool with expressions of abject terror on their faces. Guys in red sweaters in every room, red neckties, matching socks. We passed a troika of potted ferns, and I was congratulating

Eddie, silently, for using his ill-gotten profits for quality-of-life office accessories like potted palms, when I noticed an administrative assistant I recognized.

Deanna. Remember her? If you don't, you should lay off the sauce, gentle reader, because she was the character who told me about the plot to poison the water supply. The character who later became a hooker down by the Gowanus Canal. Have to say, considering the state of most of the people in the boroughs, Deanna was looking really great. I mean, she must have had some reconstructive dentistry, because back when I interviewed her, she had fewer teeth than fingers. Now she had on a slinky silk blouse, and what looked from this angle like a miniskirt. She still had long sleeves, of course. We recognized one another at the same moment, with a kind of disgust. I saw her eyes widen; I saw her glance quickly around herself. To make sure no one noticed. Was she working for Eddie now? Was she another employee drafted into the harem?

Then in the kind of frozen moment that can only happen in an era of completely subjective time, I began to understand that there was a commotion beginning around me, a commotion that had to do, I think, with Jesse Simons and Ernst Wentworth, who had remained so silent during the prior hour of torture and kidnapping that I had forgotten they were orbiting around me at all. They knew, I'd learned, what I knew; they saw what I saw. And I heard Jesse say to Ernst, *No, I have to do it, she's a woman, I don't want to hear about any guys shooting any women.* And Jesse Simons strode out of my memory, giving me a mournful glance on the way. Jesse, turns out, was carrying an enormous pistol, with a silencer on the end, and as soon as she was on the scene, I could see the Cortez guys also moving into position, with their submachine guns, there was a lot of yelling, someone was yelling Get him out of here, get him out of here, as if by removing me from the room, it would take Deanna of the picture, out of the story. I hung onto a desk. They beat on me with the butt ends of submachine guns, and I looked up just in time to see Deanna, whatever her surname was, if she even had a surname, disappear, at the muffled hiss and report of the silencer. The spot where Deanna had been sitting was emptied, and a plastic tape dispenser that she'd been holding in her hand was suspended briefly in midair. It fell to the wall-to-wall with a muffled thud. The men and women in the typing pool sent up a scream, many hands fluttered to gaping mouths. And that was when Cortez's people opened fire on the room. Cleaning out as many witnesses as they could get. As with Jesse and Ernst, who didn't want to leave Deanna alive to inform on their plan, Cortez didn't want any mnemonic jockeys recalling the scene. As if the solution to the disorder of time was the elimination of all possible perceivers of time. I want to allow a dignified space into the story where the Cortez typing pool was massacred, so if I move on with the facts, don't think that I don't know that all those people had families. Because I know.

Someone got hold of my feet, because I tried to make a quick escape myself, and they were swearing at me, dragging me down the corridor toward some blank, faceless office cubicle, where I too would be killed. Meanwhile, Ernst Wentworth, like the angelic presence that he was, again had the job of explanation: "Deanna knew about the trip to the water supply, for which we're embarking now, with many thanks to you for helping us to close the loophole. You were the only person who knew the identity of this informer. Jesse is sticking with you for the last few minutes, because there's one more thing you have to learn before you're done, and then, Kevin, you're a free man, with a load of forgetting in your future. I hope you write comic books or start a rock-and-roll band in your garage. And I hope you do it all somewhere far away from here."

Then the office door opened in.

I guess you already knew that Cassandra was sitting there. Wearing really high-end corporate gear from Italian designers who had managed to stay out of the international backlash against the American export market. Cortez Enterprises was about to have its limited public offering, I learned later, using a brokerage subsidiary that they owned themselves. So they had tarted up the office to impress some analysts. Cassandra was beautiful in a way I probably can't describe, because beauty, ultimately, is outside of language. Though it may have something to do with memory. She was wearing a red bow. One of Cortez's goons, unless it was Eddie himself, said, "Kevin, I guess you don't really remember your own mother?"

"My mother? What the hell are you talking about?"

Cassandra had cleaned up a lot since I saw her. Which I was starting to recognize might have been four months ago. It was hard to tell. Still, she was my age, more or less, maybe a few years younger, so how was she supposed to be my mother?

One thing I'll say for Cassandra, she had the kind of a compassionate expression a mother should have had. She asked if I was all right.

But the goons interfered with this tender moment.

"Okay, shoot 'em up."

"Wait," I said, "I'm already high, I'm already in somebody's memory, I don't even know if it's my own memory anymore, so you're getting me high inside a memory, that's a memory inside a memory, right? When do we come back out to the present, to the part where I'm just a kid trying to make his way?"

"Shut that motherfucker up."

Cassandra volunteered her arm, so I volunteered mine, covered with scars now, so much that they couldn't find a vein.

"Do him in the neck."

So they did. Without asking nicely.

I swirled into the rapture of the deep, far from all the shit that had accumulated since I first found out about Albertine. You know, my very first memory is of my grandfather, the Chinese immigrant patriarch, after his open-heart surgery. I was maybe three and a half years old. I never believed those memories. I never used to believe in the coherence of memory before an age when a kid could understand time. What comes before it? The rapture of the deep is what comes before. Before the scaffolding of time. Memories cartwheeling around in the empty heavens. Anyway, there he was on the stretcher in the living room, where he lived with us, doped on morphine. Doped for a good month anyway. I can remember the implacable smile on his face, I'm suffering now, but I came here for you, so you wouldn't have to suffer. So now go and do something. Make my sacrifices into your day at the beach. It lingered in my consciousness for a moment. From there the howling winds of recollection touched down on my abortive swimming lessons, then a summer on the Cape, walking on the beaches of the seashore, up through childhood, from one associative leap to the next, all memories with beaches in them, then all memories with singing in them, memories featuring varieties of pie, like this was the very last mainline I was going to have, like they were going to make a biopic about my short life from this footage scrolling through my brain. Everything was roses. I was the smartest kid in my elementary school class, I was the class president. I was a shortstop player. Everything was roses. *Until Serena showed up.* Serena, who was exactly contemporary with that nameless dread creeping into my daily life. I was the only Asian kid my parents had ever known who panicked, Asians just didn't panic, or they didn't fucking talk about it, man, that was for sure, like that afternoon when I was supposed to take some government-ordered placement exam and I was sitting in the bathroom puking, my father standing outside the door, telling me, in the severest language, that I was a disgrace. What was I going to do, drop out of society? Go work in a dry cleaner's? Recite poetry to the customers while I was doing alterations? Did I think my grandfather had come from Shanghai, etc. etc., on a boat that almost sank, etc. etc., so that I could . . . etc. etc., and then the sound of my mother's voice telling him to lay off, my mother the microbiologist, or epidemiologist, why couldn't I remember my mother's job, she was never home, actually, she was always working. *Come on.* I called out to the Cortez flunkies, Hey, you guys, give me another shot, because nothing is chiming, I am telling you there is not a chime left in the belfry, you guys, I was still pressing the wet rag against the wound in my neck when the guy slapped me in the back of the head and told me to shut the fuck up, and then I was again on the Ferris wheel of it all, but I could see my father's tassled loafers, and that's when Jesse Simons was talking to me again, suddenly I was recognizing her voice.

"Kevin, this is the end of the story, where you're going now, because your mother is about to lay her hand on yours, across the desk, Kevin, and that will be the signal that I have to let go. Here's what happens. This next ten minutes of your life enables us to dose the reservoir before Eddie Cortez finds out. We have just eliminated the person who informs on the plot to dose the reservoir, and so we are free to go back in time, by virtue of our collective affection for the city, to augment the water supply. And you know what that means, Kevin, it means that Eddie won't have time to drop the bomb, Kevin. *The bomb.* Because we believe Eddie Cortez drops the bomb, to try to keep us from dosing the reservoir, and he drops it on lower Manhattan, because that's where *you* live in the fall of 2008. We believe that Eddie Cortez, not a highly trained sleeper cell of foreign nationals, detonates the uranium bomb, to ensure dominance of Cortez Enterprises and to wipe out a number of key Resistance players living in the East Village at that historical juncture. So take your time in the next few minutes because this gives us the element of surprise we need. Jean-Pierre Al-Sadir is driving a minivan up what's left of the interstate. And I believe he's playing Duke Ellington on the CD player, because he wants to hear something really great before his memory is wiped clean. You're the hero of the story, Kevin. And we're all really sorry we couldn't tell you earlier, and we're sorry you had to learn this way. But we want you to know this. We want you to know that all the traumatic events of the last few months, these were things we knew you could withstand. Like few others. You're the kid who made the story for us. We're proud. We wish you were our son. And in a way you are now. If that's any help at all. When you get to Manhattan, after talking to your mother, if it's still gone, that'll be the sign. Manhattan in ruins. Your ferry driver will be wearing green. That'll mean that Eddie doesn't need to go back in time to try to find you. That'll mean that Eddie has given up trying to control the past, in order to control the present. Well, unless, by poisoning the reservoir, we eliminate the future in which Eddie comes up with the idea of detonating the blast, in which case Manhattan will still be standing and this entire present, with the drug epidemic and the Brooklyn Resistance, will be non-actualizing. And it's also possible that the forgetting will have set in somewhere along the line, we aren't sure where yet, and that you may have forgotten certain important parts of the story. You may have forgotten that Manhattan was ever a city by the time you get home tonight. You might have forgotten all of this, all this rotten stuff, this loneliness, even this speech I'm giving you now. In fact, we have tried to pinpoint forgetting, Kevin, we have targeted it, in such a way as to wipe clean your own memories of the blast. Because you actually had a pretty rotten time that day. You saw some awful things. So if you have forgotten, we believe you are the first locally targeted forgetter. However, if in the future, during this next forgetting, you want to remember this or other events from your life we have a suggestion for the future, Kevin, *just play back your audio recordings.*"

This is where my mom stole into memory of the past. My mom was so beautiful. Every time I saw her. Even when she was Cassandra, on the swing in Brooklyn. So beautiful that I couldn't even see the lines of time carved into her. Here in memory she's young again, she's perfect, young and brilliant, lit in the color of a fading silver halide print. My mom looks Kodak to me, always will, and she leads me out of the bathroom, away from my dad, and she explains that Serena telephoned her, and her syllables are carefully measured like on a metronome. It's not nearly as bad as it seems. If I could redo the color balance in this past, I would make it more ultramarine, because everything's too yellow: my mother taking me into the living room, where my grandfather once slept off his open-heart surgery. She sits me down. And she makes her diagnosis. She says, *I have been doing a lot of research into your chemical problem. And I have talked to a lot of professional friends on the subject. When you have a spare hour or so, later in the week, then we're going in to talk to some of them. But in the meantime, I want you to try something for me.*

So here it was. In a stoppered beaker.

"Just give this a try for me. I think it'll be more interesting than that stuff you and your friends have been smoking."

"Mom," I said. "Do you think I should?"

"I'm your mom."

"What is it?"

"Lithium, some SSRIs, and a memory enhancer we're trying out, in solution. It's supposed to sharpen cognition. Might help with those tests. In an Aspartame sauce."

Just like in the laboratory sequences, you know, from those black-and-white movies of yore. I drank up. And the fact is, I aced that exam. That's what I had forgotten. And I gave some to Serena, and she gave it to her boyfriend, Paley. We called it Albertine, because it sounded like Aspartame. Or so I was remembering. I gave it to the others. We all did well on our tests. Just three kids from the subdivisions fucking up the entire future of the human race, in pursuit of kicks and decent board scores.

I didn't want to open my eyes. I didn't want to know. Didn't want to look across the desk at Cassandra, who may or may not have been my mother, may or may not have been the chief chemist for the

Cortez syndicate, may or may not have been an informer for the Resistance, may or may not have been a young woman, may or may not have been home in Newton, refusing to come to the phone, may or may not have been an older Chinese woman with those sad eyes. I didn't want to hear her voice, from across the room, rationalizing, "Let time show why I've done what I've done." I didn't want to know. I didn't want to know the plans the Cortez operatives had for me, Addict Zero, didn't want to know why I was being put through this exercise—so that they could break me on the rack of information, or because they still wanted me to write down whatever it was that they wanted me to write down. I didn't want to know, finally, which memory was inside of which memory, didn't want to know if there was a truth on top of these other truths. In a few minutes' time, the water supply would be boiling with the stuff, eight weeks back. The cops at the reservoirs would be facedown in pools of blood, and the taps in Brooklyn, Queens, Staten Island, and the Bronx would be running bluer than usual, and there would be dancing in the streets, as though all this stuff I'm telling you hadn't happened at all. I mean, assuming the sweet forgetting didn't come like the instantaneous wave of radiation after the blast. Assuming I didn't forget all of this, how I got where I got, what I'd once known, the order in which I knew it, the cast of characters, my own name, the denouement.

What's memory? Memory's the groove. It's the all-stars laying down their groove, and it's you dancing, chasing the desperations of the heart, chasing something that's so gone, so ephemeral you know it only by its traces, how a certain plucked guitar string summons the thundering centuries, how a taste of fresh cherries calls up the indolent romancers on antebellum porches, all these stories rolling. Memory is the groove, the lie, the story you never get right, the better place. Memory is the bitch, the shame factory, the curse and the consolation. And that's where my journalistic exposé breaks down.

But I can offer a few last tidbits. If you're wondering what the future looks like, if you're one of the citizens from the past, wondering, let me tell you what it's like. First thing I'll tell you, gentle reader, is that the Brooklyn Bridge is gone, probably the most beautiful structure ever built according to the madness of New Yorkers. Brooklyn Bridge is gone, or at least the half of it on the New York

side. The section on the Brooklyn side goes out as far as the first set
of pillars, and after that it just crumbles away. Like the arms of Venus
de Milo. It's a suggestion of an idealized relationship between parts
of a city, a suggestion, not an actual relationship. And maybe that's
why intrepid lovers go there now, lovers with thyroid cancer go up
there at night, because it's finally a time in New York City history
where you can see the night sky. That is, if the wind's blowing toward
Jersey. They go up there, the lovers, they jump the police barriers,
they walk out on that boardwalk, the part that's still remaining, they
look across the East River, they make their protestations of loyalty, *I
don't really have much time, so there's a few things I want to say to you.* I'll
go even further. Because this instant is endless for me, and that's why
I'm dictating these notes. What I do is, I find the ferryman on the
Brooklyn side, out in Bay Ridge, old Irish guy, I pay my fresh coin to
the Irish ferryman with the green windbreaker, pet his rottweiler. I
say, I got some business over there, and the guy says, No can do, pal,
and I point at it and I say, Business, and he says, No one has business
there, but I do, I tell him, and I will make it worth your while, and
he says, There's nothing over there, but in the end he accepts the
offer, and then we are out upon the water, where the currents are stiff,
and the waves treacherous, as if nature wants to wash this experiment
of a city out into the sea, as if nature wants to clean the wound, flush
the leftover uranium, the rubble, the human particulate, we're on the
water, and right there is where that statue used to be, we'll get the
new one from France before too long, and that's where New York
Plaza used to be on the tip there, I tell the ferryman to take me farther up the coast, I want to know every rock and piling, every
remaining I-beam, I want to know it all, so we go past the footprint
of South Street seaport, and here are the things that we lost that
I might have seen from here, the Municipal Building with its
spires, City Hall, the World Financial Center, the New York Stock
Exchange, where did all those bond traders go, what are they doing
now, are they in Montclair or Greenwich, and then it's Chinatown,
bombed almost to China, bombed down to the bedrock, edged by
Canal Street, which is again a canal as it was way back when, and Little Italy is gone, those mobster hangouts are all gone, they're all
working on the Jersey side now, trying to corner the Albertine mar-

ket there, and Soho is gone, New York University is gone, Zeck-
endorf Towers gone, Union Square Park is gone, the building where
Andy Warhol's Factory once was, what used to be Max's Kansas City,
CBGB, and the Empire State Building is gone, which, when it fell
sideways, crushed a huge chunk of lower Fifth Avenue, all the way to
the Flatiron District, the area formerly known as the Ladies' Mile, the
flower district is gone, the Fashion Institute of Technology, in fact,
about the only thing they say is still somewhat intact, like the
Acropolis of Athens, is the Public Library, but I can't see it from here.
The bridges are blown out, the tram at 59th Street, gone, and as we
pull alongside a section of the island where I'm guessing Stuyvesant
Village used to be, I say, *Ferryman, put me down here,* pull your rowboat
with its two-horsepower lawn-mower engine alongside, because I'm
going in, I'm going to Tompkins Square, man, I'm going backward,
through that neighborhood of immigrants, so now I step on the easternmost part of the island, same place the Italians stepped, same
place the Irish stepped, same place the Puerto Ricans stepped, and
I'm going in there now, because as long as it's rubble I don't care how
hot it is, I'm going in, it's like a desert of glass, sand and landfill
burnt into glass, and I can hear the voices, even though it's been a
while now, all those voices layered over one another, in their hundred
and fifty languages, can't hear anything distinct about what they are
saying, except that they're saying, *Hey, time for us to be heard.*

The Martian Agent, a Planetary Romance
BY MICHAEL CHABON

They were the sons of an imperial traitor, marked for life. Their only honor lay in their loyalty to each other. Their sole chance for salvation lay in the empire of the clouds.

'Tis theirs to sweep through the ringing deep where Azrael's outposts are,
Or buffet a path through the Pit's red wrath when God goes out to war,
Or hang with the reckless Seraphim on the rein of a red-maned star.
—RUDYARD KIPLING

CHAPTER ONE
WHELPS

1.

The brothers first encountered a land sloop on the night, late in the summer of 1876, that one hunted their father down. It picked up their trail in Natchitoches country, two miles from

Fort Wellington, at the ragged southwestern border of the Louisiana Territories and of the British Empire itself. The moon, as many sad partisans of the mutineer George Armstrong Custer were to record, hung fat in the sky, stained with an autumnal tinge of blood that, to some diarists, presaged hanging and debacle. Outside the windows of the coach in which the brothers and their parents rode lay the wilderness, flooded in black water and in a steady-flowing hubbub of night birds, insects, and amphibians. The coach bobbed and pitched as if borne on that current of bedlam and black water, down a road already ancient when the ancestors of these very insects had jabbed and goaded DeSoto's men along it to their itching feverish deaths. The boot-heels of the coachman, a big, steady Vermonter named Haseltine, drummed against the front of the coach, just behind the boys' heads, with the random tattoo of a broken shutter in the wind. The timbers of the carriage groaned with each jolt and stone in the road. The respiration of the mosquito-mad team, a pair of spavined drays for which, two days earlier, they had exchanged the last of their sovereigns, rattled out behind the coach like a string of tin cans.

The first shrill call of the steel throat in the distance left a rippling wake of silence.

—Train, said the little one, or—no.

The cry had sounded too forlorn, too lupine for a train. Before the little boy even saw the knot of grief that deformed the hinge of the father's stubbled, powder-burnt jaw, he knew that whatever had uttered it was hungering for them.

—There are no trains, the older brother said. Not this deep into Indian country. Don't be a dolt.

—I'm not a dolt.

—A train.

—Please, the mother said, boys.

The little boy seized his brother's shoulder, gathering a scratchy wool handful of stained cadet gray. *He won't ever be a British officer now, nor will I.* Though he was a good forty pounds lighter and seven years the junior, the little boy sent the older brother lurching clear across the coach, slamming his head against a brass fitting. Before the older brother could retaliate there was another cry from the valve, louder, nearer, a blurred double-reeded blat less like the call of a wolf than of an implacable iron toad. At the sound of it the little boy scooted across the bench and buried his head in the brother's lap. The brother put an arm around him and stroked his hair. He pulled an old Ohio River Company trading blanket with its smell of dog and tallow, amid which they had huddled for most of the past week, up to their chins.

The mother turned to the father.

—Harry, she said. What is it? Could it be a train?

—Not here, said the father. Franklin is right. Not this close to Tejas.

They were less than ten miles now from the border and freedom—another fact which melancholy diarists of the failed rebellion would be inclined, in the days that followed, to record.

The father stood up and went to the door of the coach. The night and its furor of animals and bugs blew in and stirred the damp black strands of the mother's hair. Her cheeks were glinting, febrile. All the way from the Yalobusha River to the Red she had thrashed and dreamed fever dreams that to the little boy, whose name was Jefferson Mordden MacAndrew Drake, were unimaginably cavernous, lit with lamps of blood. The proximity of Tejas seemed to have revived her; reasoning conversely, her younger son was certain that if they did not make it across the Sabine River she would die. They were headed for the ferry at Beurre. Jefferson Drake had been in possession of this fact and little else for the past eleven days. The father hung half out of the door of the rocking coach and called upward into the night. The brothers could not hear what he inquired of the coachman, nor what reply he received. But when he sat down again, he hoisted the canvas haversack that had ridden between his feet all the way from Sulla, in the Ohio Territory, and began to take out his guns.

2.

Every lost cause has its sacred litany, each of whose plaints begins with the words "If only." If only Custer could have waited one week more for the road to Ashtabula to clear. If only Phil Sheridan had not been shot by the jealous husband of Mrs. Delaplane. And if only Cuyahoga Drake had made it to Tejas, surely the guns and gold promised by Lincoln . . .

In a telegram dispatched from Fort Wellington on the Sabine to the C-in-C of Her Majesty's Columbian Army, at Potomac, following the events whose successful conclusion raised him to Command of the Mississippi Army, Lieutenant General H.P.W. Hodge stated that Colonel Harry Drake, fleeing the ruin of the mutiny he had helped to foment, had been spotted by a native Natchitoches scout eleven miles from the Sabine River, eastern border of the Tejas Free Republic. The scout, a half-breed named Victor Piles, turned his mongrel pony toward the squat black turrets of the fort, raising a wild alarm. Word of Cuyahoga Drake's southwestern flight had followed him, more or less delayed by the intermittent drunkenness and indolence of the frontier courier corps, from the moment of his escape from the stockade at Sulla on the Ohio. General Hodge, sad, syphilitic, tormented by hidden sympathy with the mutineers, had been feeding the burners of his shining black pair of Mullock-Treadwell land sloops since early that morning, on the off-chance that Drake and his family might pass through the neighborhood on their way to the rusty yellow Sabine. Wellington was among the last of the southwestern stations to be equipped with steam wagons and had taken delivery of two brand-new Terror-class sloops, the *Dauntless* and the *Princess Louise,* only two weeks before. They had emerged from their crates, to the groaning of hot nails and navvies with crowbars, smelling of fresh paint, leather, packing oil, excelsior. Hodge had fallen in love them at once, with a helpless passion fostered by his remote and lonely billet. When Victor Piles came around crying about the rollicking carriage and dappled nags straining for Tejas down the old Natchitoches road, Hodge agonized over which of his darlings to risk and flaunt in pursuit of the renegade hero of Cleveland and Ashtabula.

In the end Hodge chose the *Dauntless.* She had been among the first wagons rolled out of Mullock-Treadwell's huge new Second Manchester Works, and she more than made up in style and speed what she lacked in seasoning or experience in the field. She was a Model 3 Terror, long and canine, a steel greyhound powered by a hundred-horsepower Bucephalus engine. The relative frailty of her armor-plating was more than compensated for by her maneuverability and by the range and mobility of her big .45 turret-mounted

Gatling. Along with her crew of six she could carry a section of infantrymen, eight troopers of the 27th Cajun Fusiliers whom Hodge assigned to the pursuit. The question of whether there would be sufficient additional room in her acrid sweltering hold for a living prisoner remained unsettled as the *Dauntless* huffed, riveted leather treads clattering against the gangway of pine planking, out through the gates of Fort Wellington into the wilderness. The NCO in command of the Fusiliers, a Sergeant Swindell, had the foresight, in case space was wanting, to bring along a length of stout rope.

3.

In her haste to flee, after her husband's escape from the guardhouse at Sulla, Mrs. Drake, née Catherine Mordden, had endeavored to condense the wealth and history of her family into an Indiaman chest. Clean linens, a strand of Yalu pearls, her wedding dress, a Bible that had been the gift of her brother at their last parting. Mufflers and oilskins for the boys. Biscuit, wine, a small wheel of New York cheese. A plait of Iroquois wampum likely to have no value anywhere that her family might conceivably alight. A hundred-year-old flag of red and white stripes, with a quartered ring of yellowing stars on a blue field, that was her husband's most treasured possession; and a chromolithograph of Lieutenant General George Armstrong Custer, at the time of his accession to the Command of Her Majesty's Army of the Great Lakes, in a rosewood frame, which was her own. (Scurrilous rumors spread by the enemies of the Ohioists, and kept alive for decades afterward by the avid gossip of historians, would link Kitty Drake romantically to the Martyr of American Hopes, and even trace the younger of the two Drake boys to Custer's seed.) Half a mile from the ferry at Beurre Landing the sea chest, strapped to the roof of the rattling coach, worked itself out of its bindings and tumbled to the roadbed. It landed on one corner and split in two with the neat snap of a snuffbox springing open. Starry flag, lace, and biscuits were strewn across the road. Pearls skittered like water on a hot stove lid. The portrait of George Custer lay, glass glinting, in the lovely ill-betokening moonlight. For a moment, the expression of the Martyr in the portrait, that steady, slightly mad blue gaze which had always struck the portrait's owner as summarizing all that was brash, vainglorious, strong, fundamentally and conclusively un-English, about her husband's generation of solitary horsemen and wanderers and Indian fighters, took on a strangely plaintive air. Custer seemed to be remonstrating with the heavens he contemplated. Then, in a half-musical splintering of timber and glass, the *Dauntless*'s left tread nosed its way onto and over the distilled patrimony of the Drakes, flattening what it did not tear or turn to dust and shards.

Then the *Dauntless* spoke.

—Colonel Drake.

It spoke in the voice of its chief engineer, a Sergeant Breedlove, who crouched in the dark roaring stink of its cabin, between the stack of metal rungs that climbed to the gun turret and a small transverse slot that permitted him to peer vaguely out into the Louisiana midnight, clutching a wooden funnel to his lips. The funnel was connected to a length of canvas-covered caoutchouc hose that ran up through a small eye in the roof of the land sloop, where it was joined to the narrow end of a large, slender horn or bell that opened beneath the Gatling like a lily, a black tin corsage.

—Colonel Drake, your mutiny is over. Custer has surrendered to the Crown.

The raspy, rather high-pitched tone of the *Dauntless* and its mushy Yorkshire accent carried easily across the narrowing gap between it and the carriage. The little boy looked at his brother, whose name was Franklin Mordden Evans Drake. Franklin Drake looked at their father.

—It's a trick, he said. Custer would never—

—You will not be permitted to reach the border, said the *Dauntless*. Please, Colonel. Do not force us to open fire.

The father rose from the bench once more to put his grimed face and staring eyes out into the uproar and moonlight of the bayou. He had a measuring gaze that could guess accurately at the weight of bullocks or the height of weather vanes or the wish, however pure or sinful, in the heart of an eight-year-old boy. He hung there for a long moment, leaning on the open door of the coach, estimating the chances and the outcomes. Then he closed the door and sat heavily down.

—Five hundred yards back, he said. A land sloop. Machine gun. A Gatling. A forty-five, I'd say.

—It's a Terror, said Frank with a hint of awe. Semi-amphibious. This late in the summer she could likely swim after us right into the river.

It was all the little boy could do to prevent himself from going to the door to see this marvel. The father noticed.

—No, he said.

The little boy sat back and looked at his brother, who was struggling with his own desire to see the thing that was running them to ground. The carriage rolled on, but its rocking had subsided and there was no question that Haseltine, the coachman, was losing his resolve. He had seen Gatlings and Nordenfeldts used on the Cayugas at Ashtabula and the Lakotas at Poudre and the Russians at Belokonsk. It was all too easy for him to imagine looking down to see the glaucous gray insides of his body lying steaming in his lap.

—Coward, said Cuyahoga Drake.

There was such universal disgust in his voice that for a moment the brothers were unsure whom the epithet was intended to damn. Then the father rose and went to the door once more.

—Haseltine! You damned milk-soaked—

—Harry.

The father turned to find the mother staring at him, her lips pressed together, worrying the worried kerchief tucked into the bodice of her shirtwaist dress.

Colonel Drake opened his mouth. He had sensibly and carefully and with only the most reasoning sort of bravery led the armies of the British Empire in victory after victory against Iroquois and Sioux and Alyeskan Tsarists before taking the first unmeasured step of his career and enlisting for eight brutal and glorious months in Custer's mad attempt to rekindle the extinguished Republic on the shores of Lake Erie. His sons waited for his next words.

—Colonel Drake, said the *Dauntless,* this is the final warning I will make.

In the end, the brothers would remember, their father merely nodded. When he drew his sword it was only to rap with the hilt, twice, against the ceiling of the coach.

Haseltine cursed and forgave the horses in a series of unintelligible barks. The carriage creaked and rumbled. The sand beneath its wheels sighed. Through the windows of the coach the clamor of the bayou, as if their forward progress had tended to slip them past or somehow through it like fingers cupped around a candle, now blew in, a steady, flame-snuffing gust. The mother winced and closed her eyes in pain, as if the discordant productions of nocturnal western Louisiana had triggered one of her megrims. Behind or within that clamor lay the grind of gears, the resolute, dumb, canine chuffing of the Terror's big Bucephalus. Up on the box, Haseltine coughed. There was the scratch of a lucifer.

More to his own surprise, perhaps, than that of those whom he addressed, who knew him better, Jefferson Drake found that he was moved by a spasm of profound outrage.

—We can't just sit here and wait for them to grab us!

Colonel Drake lit his own burled pipe. In more normal circumstances the business with match and tobacco might have served to veil his amusement with his younger son, who disdained generally to sit and wait for anything at all.

—What do you propose, Jefferson?

The boy looked at the two revolvers, two rifles, and eight boxes of cartridges that comprised the family arsenal. There were the pair of Webleys, a balky old single-shot Rigby won in a game of faro by the same seafaring maternal grandfather whose trunk had foundered on the Natchitoches road, and a captured Lebeau-Courally ten-gauge, its stock engraved with (Mrs. Drake had said) scenes from a book called *Atala* by Chateaubriand, and bearing the monogram of the late General Durmanov. It was exquisite but had been designed for the hunting of snipe and woodcock and could not be relied upon to kill a grown man.

Jefferson Drake was an inveterate reader of novels for boys. In these tales there were ever only three possible destinies available to those who found themselves in such a grave predicament. For Heroic Britons, there were the Fighting Martyrdom, guns blazing, and the Impossible Stand, holding out until help arrived. For a noble enemy—Russian, German, Pathan, the odd renegade Frenchman or Iroquois—there was only Defeat Without Surrender, choosing to end one's own life rather than face the ignominy of inevitable capture.

(For "savage" enemies such possibilities rarely arose, for these traveled almost exclusively in Swarms or Hordes, and so never found themselves Surrounded.) Looking at their paltry armaments, and knowing from the grave listening expression on the face of his brother, who was keen on such things, that the approaching Terror must be a formidable piece of machinery indeed, the first two options seemed impracticable, in the first case, and in the second case ridiculous. Then too, they were no longer, for reasons the boy could have just managed to explain without truly understanding, Heroic Britons. They were rebels—mutineers. During those months of rapid victory, barbaric rains, and total failure, the Drake family had passed from that portion of the map of existence tinted proud and homely British red into a blank and hostile territory.

—Take our own lives, the little boy said.

It came out more of a question than he had intended, thin and grave and far too possible. He was hoping to be contradicted, and when the father said, "Nonsense," at once, without even taking his eyes off the glowing bowl of his pipe, the boy was so grateful that he burst into tears.

—Stop that blubbering, the father said.

He turned to the mother with a sharp tone and an air of giving her something useful to do. His tone was not unkind.

—Do button him up.

The mother sat forward and reached across the carriage toward him, trying to draw her son toward her fevered breast. But the boy pulled away, and wiped his eyes on his sleeve.

—I can button myself up.

He saw that his brother was watching him, with a peculiar empty expression that he knew well, and he sat back to wait, feeling obscurely comforted. Frank was always watching him, studying his words and behavior, not with envy or scorn or concern—though these were not unknown elements of his feelings for the little boy—but with a version of their father's measuring gaze that seemed to take Jeff's outbursts and ideas as a form of weather, phenomena that, correctly interpreted, could be exploited as the raw materials to which a masterly hand and chisel might be applied. All the currents of brotherly respect and imitation flowed in the usual direction between them: The younger idolized the older, nearly as devoutly as he did their father. But the impetus for their common undertakings as brothers—for all that it was the older one who arranged and directed them—nearly always derived from some wild remark, from the unreasoned hotheaded dissatisfaction, of the younger of the pair.

—Jeff's right. Give us a gun, Daddy. Let us go. They won't get us. I'll see to that.

—Oh, said the mother, Harry, no.

—We haven't got more than a few miles to go. It's hours yet until daylight. Do you think I can't get myself and one little kid across a few miles of mud and frogs?

—He can, the little boy said. You know he can, Daddy.

The father sat a moment. Each time he drew on his pipe his long nose cast a flaring shadow up the high furrowed dome of his skull. The land sloop was close enough now that they could hear her crewmen shouting at one another to be heard over the racket of the machine they were laboring to control.

—Harry, the mother said. No. They will be cared for. They will not be harmed.

—They will be turned against us, said the father. Perhaps you do not consider this to be a form of harm.

He reached down and picked up one of the Webleys, opened the chamber, and checked it for the third time in ten minutes. Then he snapped it shut, and handed it to his older son.

—Your brother has never had the pleasure of meeting Mr. Lincoln, Franklin. See that you get him to San Antonio.

—Yes, sir. I will look after him, sir.

The boys slid from the bench and crouched down to fill their pockets with boxes of cartridges. Then the little boy went to the door. Afterward he would recall the way his heart pounded with the knowledge that he ought to go and throw his arms around his mother and father and bid them farewell. He was inclined, in later years, to excoriate himself for this omission. The truth, however, was that at the time his mind was such a jumble of agitation, apprehension, and the sheer blind desire to be free at last of that miserable rattletrap box, to be *doing something,* that it was not until he was already out of the coach, and scrambling across the road into a twisted thicket of dwarf-bearded oaks, that it occurred to him that he would never see his parents again. By then the land sloop was less than twenty yards from the coach, and it was too late. He crouched in an inch of sucking water, breathing hard, watching his brother's spidery form in the coach's open door. It was difficult to tell for sure but it looked as though Franklin and their father were gravely shaking hands. No doubt he had kissed their mother as well. Although it was Jefferson who concerned himself with the fine gesture and the act of panache, it was Franklin, who found such things laughable, who was always pulling them off.

There was a thud, a sharp huff of breath, and then Frank came scrambling into the trees, clutching the revolver to his chest. He found Jeff, and they squatted together in the foul-smelling mud, painting their backsides with swamp water, watching as the flame of the land sloop's lantern, mirrored and lensed, reached out to engulf the bayou in a swelling balloon of light.

—Get down, Frank said.

He pushed Jeff facedown into the mud and then lay beside him. The land sloop came, slowing, with a sound like an enormous box of nails and broken crockery falling down a flight of stairs. She stopped. In the moonlight Jeff could read the name, *Dauntless,* picked out in gilt letters on her flank. There was a flat chiming as her rear hatch rolled open, then the scrabble of boots, and then suddenly the roadbed seemed to fill with redcoats. They trotted, rifles aslant, to the carriage. Three of them pulled Haseltine from his seat and threw him to the ground. Several others dragged out Colonel Drake, and then with rough politesse assisted Mrs. Drake to step down. She stood slim and straight-backed, head held up, giving the soldiers a look the boys could not in fact see but could easily imagine. Their father struggled against them and was beaten, once, sharply, with the stock of a Martini. After that he stood, and suffered them to put him in irons.

—Colonel Henry Hudson Drake, in the name of Her Imperial Majesty, Queen Victoria, I place you under arrest on the charge of mutiny and treason against the Crown.

—Shoot! the little boy hissed. Shoot the gun.

—Quiet!

—Let me shoot it, then!

He reached for the revolver, kicking at his brother's shins, blind with rage or with the tears his rage incited. The older brother stuffed the gun into the waist of his pants and wrapped the boy up in his long arms that always seemed capable of encircling the younger one several times around. His left hand he clapped firmly, and for far from the first time in their lives, over the little boy's mouth.

The boy struggled for another moment, then just hung in his brother's embrace, and they watched as their parents and Haseltine were pushed toward the hatch of the *Dauntless*. Their mother was handed up into the hold at once, but the soldiers stood around the two male prisoners for some time, talking in low voices that occasionally broke out into angry hisses and, once, four words, shouted.

—I'll not permit it!

The boys recognized the thick Yorkshire burr in which the land sloop had called to them through the darkness. Then their father and Vernon Haseltine were heaved up into the *Dauntless,* like two buckling sacks of bricks. An order was given, and the iron hatch rolled shut, sealing up their parents within.

The older brother did not relax his grip, or remove his hand from the little boy's mouth, until the glow of the land sloop's lantern, handed from treetop to treetop in the eastern distance, dwindled and finally winked out, and the thump of her engine had been absorbed once more into the universal clangor of the swamp.

4.

At Tir-Na-Nog, the house on a Derbyshire hilltop, fifty miles from the sea, to which their maternal grandfather, Joseph Mordden, had retired at the end of his career as a ship's surgeon, there had stood an oak tree of great age and height. In the branches of this Khyber redoubt, storm-tossed yardarm, donjon, eyrie, pagoda, minaret and pharos, both boys had spent a cumulative total of perhaps twenty-nine full, long August days during the course of their childhoods. And yet in all that time, it had never occurred to either of them—and certainly they would never have been permitted—to attempt to pass a night in the tree. But both of the boys had seen men under their father's command take off into the bush in a boiling cloud of dogs, in pursuit of deserters, fugitives from conscription, runaway spies. Frank suspected that it would be only a matter of time until a squad returned to look for the sons of Cuyahoga Drake. And so, after leading Jeff in a number of elaborate dog-baffling figures and hieroglyphs in and around the shallows of the bayou, he took hold of his younger brother, by the seat and waist of his breeches, and hoisted him up into the branches of a cypress for the night. The moon had set, and it was too dark for them to reconnoiter a way to the Sabine that would keep them off the road. He pulled himself up after Jeff, and they made their way carefully, dizzied by a medicinal odor, into the dark heart of the tree. The branches were coarse and slender and made an unpromising bed. They spent an hour that seemed like five hoping that the dawn would come and proving repeatedly to themselves and to one another that it was impossible to fall asleep while clinging. In the end they chanced the lower, broader boughs, and somehow fell asleep. Jeff's dreams were tormented by lurching and rocking, the creaking of old bones, the ghostly singing of frogs.

Frank hit him.

Jeff opened his eyes. The intervals among the foliage of the tree were filled with luminous needles and clusters of blue, and fringed with Spanish moss and tufts of mist. Jeff sat up, abruptly. If his brother had not caught hold of his arm he would have tumbled into the fly-rippled water below.

—They're coming.

He said it almost without voicing the words, rolling his eyes to the east. Jeff listened. The day lay in an interval of silence between the conversation of the night animals and that of the morning's birds. It was not long before Jeff heard the voices. He could hear that they were irritable and amused; he could hear that some were British and others bayou French. He could hear the labored, happy gasping of a hound. Frank stuck the revolver into the waistband of his uniform trousers, at the back, and lowered himself, hand under hand, down to the shallows. Jeff started after him.

—I thought you said we'd be safe up here, he whispered.

—Safe from alligators. Not redcoats. I just didn't want the dogs to find us before we had a chance to see where we were going.

—Where are we going?

Jeff nearly stumbled over the body of his brother, so quickly did he fall to the soft ground, and threw himself down alongside Frank.

The voices had grown louder, the words intelligible; the men from Fort Wellington were coming their way, their boots sloshing and slurping in the mud. Now Jeff could make out the distant rumble of a steam wagon, idling perhaps, back on the Indian road. Perhaps a pair of wagons. No doubt the troops had been ordered to fan out into the bayou in all directions from the point at which the boys' parents had been taken. Frank was looking wildly around for a place to conceal themselves. The brush was thin, here; now Jeff could make out wavering patches of red moving toward them, beyond the clearing in which they had blindly landed the night before.

The expression on Frank's face was blank, thoughtless.

—Do something, Jeff said. Shoot them, swim for it, do something—

Frank seemed to come out of his fog.

—Give me your penknife, he said.

He cut a pair of the reedy stalks that grew all around them and investigated their cores, which proved to be not quite hollow but filled with a spongy mass through which, as he quickly demonstrated, sucking out his cheeks, a faint but steady breath could be drawn.

—What about the alligators?

—I just made them up.

Jeff looked at him. This was precisely the kind of lie that Frank excelled in; one which claimed that an earlier statement had been a lie. Often such a lie was followed by a third that claimed to invalidate it. Frank handed him a short length of reed, then started to crawl toward a deep pool on the other side of the tree in which they had waited out the night. He stopped and took the revolver from his waist, and tucked it lovingly into a hollow formed by the wild braiding of some thick old roots. Then he lowered himself, wincing broadly to cover the apprehension and disgust he felt at so doing, into the black water with its skin of slime.

5.

Buried in water, Franklin Drake clung to the bottom-mud, clutching a fistful of slick tangling tree roots for an anchor. Water hissed and whispered in his ears. Air came into his lungs only in recalcitrant sips that had a taste of stale bread. His circulatory system was protesting this ill treatment and at first, when he heard the water-muffled gunshots, he thought they were the pulse of his starved heart redounding in his ears. He let go of the roots, burst up into the light and air, and saw that his little brother had killed two men. The dead men lay facedown in an inch of brown water, near the plaiting of roots in which, five minutes earlier, Frank had hidden the gun. And Jeff was still shooting, taking careful aim as their father had taught him, both eyes open, one hand steadying the wrist of the other, as a dozen redcoats rushed him. A third fell backward, clutching his throat; then Jeff was swallowed up in scarlet wool. The gun was twisted from his hands, and he was hoisted into the air by the collar of his shirt.

—Jeff.

He thought they were going to kill his brother for what he had just done. Not five hours and I've already broken my promise, he thought. He waded out of the pool and up onto the slightly firmer mud, then lost his footing and went sprawling forward, hitting his head on an exposed root hard enough to render him almost senseless. There was shouting, and more shouting, red sleeves, spattered gaiters. Then a hand with very cold fingers grabbed him by the back of the neck and jerked him to his feet. Frank stumbled. There was blood in his right eye and then the smell of blood in his nostrils and finally the taste of it, like rawhide, in his mouth.

—Stand up, boy.

—I'm trying.

The soldier's knee found the seat of Frank's britches. Frank stumbled forward a few feet in the direction of his brother, reaching for him though he could no longer see him; though he could no longer see anything at all.

6.

A spatulate darkness, shaped like a shark, poured itself along the rues and alleys of the Vieux Carré. It splashed against the sides of houses and shops, then surged up walls of brick and clapboard to flood the Quarter's rooftops—drowning chimney pots, weather vanes, and tin flues—before brimming over the volutes of a cornice and ladling itself once more down an iron balcony into the street. The shadow, thrust by the angle of the rising sun several hundred feet ahead of its source, drifted west, toward the Place D'Armas and Government House. When it reached the pair of squat bell towers that flanked the dark brick barn or upended ark of the St. Ignatius Boys' Home, the shadow started up the side of the campanile, then hesitated, as if uncertain whether it would clear or be snagged on the tooth of the high black iron cross. After a moment, however, the shadow resumed its progress, inching its immense snout forward. It topped and descended the tower of St. Ignatius, drifted across the dairy and some other outbuildings, and flowed over the high stone wall that separated the home's grounds from those of the old Presbytère, which since the Declaration of Reunion had served as the territorial courthouse and bridewell. Here, as if having at last sniffed out what it sought, the great shadow came to a stop, falling halfway across the broad expanse of the jailyard, where it plunged into gloom the crew of Negro carpenters who were working there, effecting last-minute repairs to the old gallows that had once dangled the hooded carcasses of Andrew Jackson and the pirate Jean Lafitte.

In the office of the rector of St. Ignatius, the inveterate gloom, which served so well to cow the reprobate spirit of boyhood that was the ineradicable plague and evil genius of the institution, deepened to an almost nocturnal pitch. A faint aureole of dust bloomed around the globe of the gaslamp atop the escritoire at which the rector, in his dressing-gown, sat perched on a velvet stool. With his left hand Father Paul Joseph de St. Malo reached to turn up the flame in the lamp. His right hand went on scratching away at the page on his blotter. After a moment he looked up, and contemplated the dull patch on the carpet where, moments before, the morning sunlight slanting in through the leaded window had fallen in bright bars and chevrons. He smiled. He was engaged in the composition of a letter to the parents of an inmate who had died, and though he had written countless such missives over the twenty-odd years of his rectorship, and though the deceased boy had been a sniveler, a liar, and good-for-nothing, Father de St. Malo was nonetheless glad for the interruption, which had been foretold, the previous morning, in a cable from Savannah.

The old priest rose and passed through a stealthy door cut into the Spanish cedar wainscoting of his office. In his small, white bedchamber he washed his hands in the copper basin, emptied his bladder into the pot, and took off his dressing gown. He was still buttoning up his best shoes—from the workshop of Scapelli, the papal cordwainer—when Father Dowd, the rector's secretary, rapped softly on the hidden door.

—Did you put him in the garden?

—As you said.

—Did you offer him tea or coffee? Did you set out the *fraises des bois*?

—He declined them. He was not happy to be made to wait. He wanted to be taken directly to them.

The rector, having smoothed the scant hair of his pate with water and scrutinized his nostrils in the glass, opened the door. Father Dowd looked him over with professional detachment, and nodded. Suitable attire in which to meet a newly made O.B.E., a conqueror of the clouds, a hero of Empire and Science.

—I don't imagine he's very happy about anything just now, the rector said. Do you suppose he can have heard this morning's news?

—He said he has spent the last ten hours on his ship.

—Ah. Then I suppose I shall have to tell him myself.

They hurried, the gangly young priest from Cork and the stout Acadian rector, down the long corridor that led to the garden. The garden was the rector's only vanity, apart from his calfskin boots. He trained and reserved an elite crew of boys to turn its earth and pollard its fruit trees and sweep clean its sandy paths. Naturally these were the only boys ever permitted into its confines. The remainder of the wards of St. Ignatius found employment in the kitchen, the laundry, and in the shops, where they learned the manufacture of such useful items as bandages, laces, dippers and basins, simple furniture, toothpicks, and, lately, coffins. As they walked to the door that opened onto the garden, the priests passed—and inspected the labor of—five little boys on their knees, spread down the length of the corridor, going over the soft marble floor with buckets and chamois and rags.

—His ship, the rector said. You saw it?

—It's lovely, said Father Dowd. Looking at it, Father, I confess, it was difficult not to feel a desire to . . .

—Fly away? From this wonderful place?

They stepped out into the garden. The ponderous late-summer humidity of the last several weeks had diminished and the daylight had a touch of that delicate, wistful clarity that was perceptible only to natives of New Orleans as autumnal. The squash vines were effulgent as a horn section with brass-bright flowers, and a light, lightly rank breeze off the river stripped the petals from the last of the roses. It was, the rector thought, ideal weather for a hanging.

The inventor Sir Thomas Mordden stood beside a white-painted iron chair, his back to the garden door. A silver tray, with tea and coffee and cream from the teat of the home's own cow in silver pots, lay on a white iron table, beside an empty teacup and an appetizing red mound of wild strawberries that looked untouched. The inventor was gazing up at the windows of the dormitory. His hands were clasped behind his back with a suggestion of difficult restraint. He might have been trying to determine if he should call out to the boys he had come to redeem, or if he ought just to scale the wall with his bare hands and climb in through their window. He was a diminutive man, but his shoulders were broad, his legs thick, and the hands that labored to constrain one another behind his back looked capable of governing stone, of discovering fingerholds in the narrowest of chinks. At the sound of the priests' footsteps he spun and showed them a face that was sunburnt and wanted flesh. His pewter hair fell in lank strands, nearly to his collar; the breeze lifted and disarranged it. His suit, though it looked new, fit him poorly, as though it had been chosen in haste or disdain. The hair, the baggy suit, the enormous and snarled sideburns, the irritable cast of his haggard features, were more in accordance with the proctor's notions of a Methodist pamphleteer, unkempt, idealistic, and doctrinaire, than of a savant, a renowned engineer, a man of considerable means.

—Father.

—Sir Thomas. May I say that however tragic and unfortunate the circumstances, you are most welcome in New Orleans.

—Thank you.

The aeronaut briefly weighed the hand the rector had offered him, then discarded it as if it suited no purpose of his.

—And may I say that it is with considerable interest and a sense

of profound pride that I . . . that we all . . . have read of your wonderful experiments over these last several years. The newspapers—

—You may or may not, as you please.

—We read that you anticipate . . .

—Extraordinary things.

This in the same impatient, haughty tone, lips pursed, as if his
nostrils burned with the saltpeter whiff of priestcraft. But Father de
St. Malo saw something kindle in the aeronaut's eyes at the thought
of the outlandish things he and his assistants were verging upon, in
his laboratories in the wolds of Lincolnshire.

—Is it true, said Father Dowd, can it really be true, Sir Thomas,
that you believe that it will one day be possible for men to travel to
the moon?

Sir Thomas did not look at Father Dowd.

—Father, he said to the rector, I have not come four thousand
miles to satisfy the idle curiosity of . . . of anyone. I am here as a private citizen, on personal business.

He gestured up to the windows of the dormitory. They were startling devices, his hands: large, long-fingered, smooth and nimble,
with an unnerving suggestion of self-sentience.

—I wish to see my nephews and then be on our way. We spotted
heavy weather off Biloxi. My weatherman believes it to be headed
this way. I should like to avoid it if I can.

—You do not plan to pass even one night . . .

—Indeed I do not.

—But sir, Mrs. Drake . . .

—Naturally I intend to visit my sister before I leave New
Orleans. Though I confess I fail to see that whether I do so or not is
any affair of yours. Father.

—Sir Thomas. I regret that I must inform you. Mrs. Drake is dead.

Father St. Malo turned to his secretary as if to have him confirm
this information or to solicit further details, though the provost of
the Hôtel-Dieu, Dr. Legac, was a boyhood friend. The rector knew as
much as anyone about the death, that morning, of the traitor Cuyahoga Drake's wife.

—She suffered . . . she underwent a stroke, Sir Thomas. I am
told that her end was swift and painless.

—Swift, perhaps, Sir Thomas said. Not painless. Oh, surely not.

—You have condolences of this house, sir, of the city, and of the whole Empire, I am sure.

Sir Thomas nodded. He took a handkerchief from his vest and dabbed at the corners of his eyes. Then he put the handkerchief away.

—Now I have less reason to tarry in this place than I had five minutes ago, he said.

He consulted his pocket watch, gold, fat as a biscuit, inscribed with tendrils and leaves that entwined the initials V.R.

—The storm may be here in an hour, he said, snapping the watch case shut. Time is short.

—I don't understand.

—It isn't necessary that you do.

—Do you not wish to see—? The, that is . . . the remains? And the arrangements, do you not—

—The arrangements have already been made. I made them by wire before I sailed from England, when it was made known to me that my sister might not survive.

—I see, the rector said. I suppose your work with engines has schooled you to be thorough in your plans.

—You satirize me.

—Not at all, I merely observe. . . .

—You exhibit considerable interest in my affairs, Father. I take it that when I leave New Orleans, you will be careful to report each of my least little actions and statements to the gossips of the town.

—You do me great injustice, Sir Thomas.

—When you do so, Father, make sure you do not fail to report my wishes for the disposition of the second set of remains.

—The second . . . ?

—Say that I wish that the body of Henry Hudson Drake be strung up as food for kites and buzzards, and that crows peck out his eyes.

He took out his handkerchief again, and dabbed a fleck of saliva from his lips.

—Sir Thomas.

—Will you not take that down, Father? Will you not forget?

—No, sir.

—Don't misquote me.

—I will not.

—Good, Sir Thomas said, turning toward the door. Now, take me to the boys.

7.

There was a fat white boy named Zebedee who sat on your head and broke wind into your mouth and nostrils, and a black boy named Hob Pistorus, all of whose modicum of unreasoning love was lavished on the shiv he had crafted from an iron bedslat. It could flay a live pig before the squeal was out the mouth, as he liked endlessly to repeat. Some of the so-called boys had rasp chins and hairy loins and were mean as Ohio keelmen. They drank themselves blind on cloudy stuff concocted from rainwater and sawdust, and boasted of having poisoned the predecessor of Father Dowd with rat bait. To the boys of St. Ignatius, Her Majesty the Queen-Empress was a fat, ancient she-toad who gaped from the wall with Jesus and Loyola as Father de Tant-Malodeur laid a whistling switch across their backs; her Empire was nothing more to them than the back of a constable's hand, the gates of the debtor's prison, the news that your father had succumbed to cholera with his entire troop in a cantonment on the Red River. Nonetheless the boys used the excuse of her betrayal by Cuyahoga Drake to plague the disgraced man's sons with taunts, blows, and wretched tricks, and with constant allusions, enigmatic and stark, to ropes, neck bones, hangman's hoods. Falling asleep at night, if it were not to be a fatal error, must be a work of forbearance and discipline; Jeff learned to distinguish and await the several snores and the varied nocturnal mutterings of every one of the twelve other boys who were locked into C Ward with him and Frank each night. After an early bad surprise from Zebedee Louch, Jeff schooled himself to tell the pattern of that boy's imitation snore from the more erratic trend of his real one. And yet if Jeff had been on his own—if it had been either one of the Drake boys left alone with the toughs, cranks, and arabs of St. Ignatius—he might have suffered a much harder fate than, as befell Frank, encountering with the ball of his naked foot the soft dead rat that someone had placed in his boot or, in Jeff's case, dwelling for an unbearable minute in the hot stench of Zebedee Louch's crotch. Each brother scouted the other's perimeters, stood picket on the other boy's flank, kept vigil, whistling outside the shit-house, as the other underwent his lonely tribulations in the swelter-ing hell of the jakes. They had been assigned to bunks at opposite ends of C Ward, but every night, as soon as the porter snuffed the lamps, Frank would make his way down the long row of iron bed-steads and climb in to lie, tensed, listening to the darkness, alongside Jeff. This was an infraction punishable by a jaunt on the strapping horse. Frank was obliged to rouse himself every morning before light showed in the sky, and creep back in the half-light to his own bare bunk.

The brothers felt themselves and their behavior scrutinized by the priests with a greater than usual degree of intensity, and to the extent that they attempted to baffle or elude inspection they might well have been pleased had they known that the weekly reports on their conduct sent by the Fathers of St. Ignatius to the military tri-bunal at Sulla were replete with puzzled apologies. Though their conversations were indeed diligently monitored, both by the priests and by Hob Pistorus, the usually reliable C Ward telltale, neither of the Drake whelps was ever heard to make reference—not once—to their parents, let alone to any other conspirator, putative accomplice, or hitherto unknown plan of the mutineers. This all-but-inhuman regimen of silence was broken only on Monday mornings at nine, as if according to some privately evolved protocol on the treatment due prisoners of war, when the older brother would appear before Father de St. Malo, shoulders back, head high, and make what he termed a formal petition that he and his co-captive be permitted to visit their mother in hospital, a request that each week, for a different arbitrary reason, was always denied. Beyond this weekly ceremony, however, it was as if the fate and disposition of their imprisoned and ailing par-ents meant nothing to them at all.

It was Jeff who had recalled reading, in the *Boys' Own Paper,* a rip-ping yarn, set in the time of Vortigern and Boadicea, in which shad-owy druids spoke without speaking by means of a manual alphabet; it was Frank who had diagrammed their hands, assigning four letters to the tip, phalanges, and base of the thumb, five to each of the fingers, and Y and Z to the pair of knobby hinges at the heel of the palm. By this cumbersome, intimate means, lying beside each other on Jeff's cot in the gray eternity of a night on C Ward, they communicated slow and feverish plans of escape, itemizing careful lists of necessary materiel, alternate routes, means of creating disruptions. With great difficulty they consolidated geographic information gleaned from other boys to sketch on the flats of their bellies a map of New Orleans, locating at the navel the Presbytère where their father languished and just under the left breast the mournful pile of the Hôtel-Dieu. Against the skin and bones of their hands the boys dwelt constantly, if never at great length, on the physical and emotional state of their mother, and speculated, with urgent jabs of their forefingers, on the chances of their father's obtaining, and the likelihood of his accepting, the mercy of the court-martial. They remembered what they could of the history of Raleigh's first acquittal, and attempted to derive a kind of grim comfort from the stoical grace with which earlier rebels of the frontier, Jackson and Crockett and Clay, had gone to their deaths. If the boys fell asleep too soon or too deeply, they knew, they would be set upon, and so each labored to keep the other awake, quizzing him on the colors and orders of Imperial regiments; the stages, battles, and commanders of the great Yukon and Ohio campaigns; the names of dogs and horses their family had owned over the years; the genealogies of Morddens, MacAndrews, Evanses, and Drakes as far back as either could stretch them. They spoke and fretted and argued far into the stillness of the morning. They lay together on Jeff's narrow cot, holding hands.

On the day when the dogfish shadow came snuffling over the housetops of the Vieux Carré, the Drake boys took the extreme liberty of appearing for morning inspection as they had slept, side by side, sitting on the younger boy's bunk. This was grounds for caning but on this awful morning they sensed that for once they might be excused and if not then rules be damned and it would suit them to be caned. They had dressed themselves in the cadet's uniform and the broadcloth suit, laundered by Jeff and patched by Frank, in which the troop of Cajun Fusiliers had first dragged them onto the ward. Drawers, comb, stockings, and two suits of gray shoddy provided by the home lay rolled with regimental precision into a worn duffel on the floor.

The bolt was thrown back and the door to C Ward swung open. The brothers' gazes remained fixed on the tall windows opposite the younger boy's bunk. These windows overlooked the rector's garden but years of salt breeze and soot and some inherent light-denying property of the glass precluded a view of anything but an ashy residue of the morning. Frank sat perfectly still; Jeff swung his skinny legs back and forth, making a swishing sound with the tips of his boots against the rough canvas top of the duffel.

—Franklin, Jefferson, said the rector. Sir Thomas is here.

Jeff started to look toward the doorway but felt or rather struck against his brother's inertness, the inflexibility of his gaze on that impenetrable gray window. He stopped kicking at the duffel and just sat.

—He has come all the way from England to fetch you. That is far more than either of you deserves.

One of the boys snickered and Jeff could feel the steady hard examining stares of the others. The two men came down between the ranks of cots and stood before them. The black bulk of the uncle eclipsed the gray windows. His watch chain dangled before Jeff's eyes. Frank had met the uncle a few times before, at Tir-Na-Nog, but Jeff only once, and that when Jeff was an infant in a dress. Frank said that their father and the uncle had quarreled, then, over the murder of John Brown by the Kansas Separatists. They had come to blows, and parted with rancor and finality.

—Nephews. It is hard to be so ill-met after so long a separation.

Jeff's right hand crept across the blanket of the bunk and sought the fingers of his brother's left. They felt rough and cool and dry.

—Well, the rector demanded, have you nothing to say?

Have you? Jeff worked the words with his fingers against Frank's. *Not to a Tory bastard like him.*

—Well? said the rector again.

Jeff looked up into the bony florid face of his mother's brother. The eyes were grave and held pity and fatigue. The lower lip of the mouth was like their mother's, full and sorrowing. The sight of it, the memory of her, of his failure to kiss her that night in the coach, filled Jeff with an obscure anger.

—God save the Ohio Rebellion! he cried.

The boys of C Ward whistled and hooted and crowed. There was the whiz of a hornet at Jeff's ear and then its sting. Jeff pitched forward and the hand he slapped to his temple came away shining with blood.

—Good heavens, the rector said.

The uncle caught hold of Jeff with his left hand, by the shoulder, and set him back upright on the bed, keeping a tight grip on him. He held out his big right hand, closed in a fist. The pale eyes were pink-rimmed, their whites stained yellow as if from exposure to some poisonous reagent or fumes.

—God save you, my boy, he said.

He opened the great white anemone of his hand, palm upward, revealing a smooth red stone.

—I assure you, Sir Thomas, the boy who threw that shall be punished, the rector said. None of them will eat today until he comes forward or is named.

There was a groan from the boys, and then silence. The rector worked at the silence with his glare and the twitching of his jaw. It would not give.

A damp cloth and a wad of bandage were found and applied to the jutting bone behind Jeff's ear, and then the uncle applied a plaster. His ministrations were brusque but patient and in the care he took Jeff sensed or perhaps even remembered a vein of tenderness.

—On your feet, the uncle said, both of you.

They went out of C Ward for the last time, followed by the rector, and stood in the great echoing central stair. It seemed dark for this hour. Jeff looked up to the ceiling of the stairwell, where an iron-ribbed skylight generally let in a portion of the fair sky that mocked, or the foul one that suited, the unvarying gray weather of an orphan boy's day. It was filled with something that Jeff took at first to be the shadow of the bell tower but which then moved—floated—to one side and seemed, ever so slightly somehow, to ripple.

The uncle's hand lay heavy on Jeff's shoulder.

—Let those boys not, he said to the rector, be punished for a display of patriotism, Father. I do not desire punishment.

The rector nodded. Then the uncle pushed Frank and Jeff toward the stairs.

—Up, boys, he said. We must hurry.

—Up? said Jeff.

He dug in his heels, gazing in uneasiness at the rippling shadow that filled the skylight. In spite of the gentle attention his cut had received, he felt a violent spasm of mistrust for the uncle now. Perhaps they were to be pushed from the roof, or thrown to a crowd of ruffians, or consigned to some unknown oubliette in the bell tower, like the poor little princes he remembered from his *Lamb's Shakespeare.*

—We go up?

—Quite a considerable way, the uncle said. As a matter of fact.

8.

Though he was to observe and ship out in dozens of them during the course of his life and career—from the world-spanning, titanic *Admiral Tobakoff,* with its concert hall and natatorium, to the worlds-spanning *Lancet,* hardly bigger than a racing scull, from the trim transpacific racer *Gulf of Sinkiang* to the sturdy, homely freight blimps of the Red Star line—Frank would never entirely lose the sense of melancholy majesty that stirred his heart when he first saw an airship, moored in the troubled sky a hundred feet above the St. Ignatius Boys' Home. He was moved by her delicacy, by her massive silence, by the rich Britannic red of her silk gasbag. She was like a divot, bright as clay, cut into in the dull gray turf of the clouds. There was a wind in the southeast and she strained at the guy that moored her to the campanile, and once tossed her nose like a mare sniffing fire. An oblong car of silver and dark wood dangled from her underbelly, part Pullman sleeper, part clarinet, its windows haunted by dark mustached faces.

—The *Tir-Na-Nog,* Uncle Thomas said, as if she were a present he had brought along for his nephews. My own design.

He watched them watching his airship, pale eyes crinkling, face flushed. In the presence of the *Tir-Na-Nog* he seemed fonder of them; he draped his arms across their shoulders.

—There isn't another like her in the world.

A hatch opened in the forebelly of the black gleaming gondola.

Two of the mustached lascars peered out. One raised an inquiring hand and the uncle nodded, and taking his arm from Frank's shoulders signaled, palm downward, twice. The blue-capped dark heads disappeared from the hatch and after a moment a large wicker basket dropped into sight and dangled, slowly falling.

Frank held his breath and pressed his lips together so hard they turned white. He suffered, with erotic intensity, from the signal passion of his age: engineering. He reverenced the men on whom was shed the peculiar glory of the second half of the century, when adventure went forth with gearbox, calipers, level, and chain. Thus he was mad to know the organization and capacity of the *Tir-Na-Nog's* engines. He would gladly have indentured himself, for long years, to studying the system of cable, flap, and rudder that guided her, the science and finesse that regulation of her buoyancy and altitude required. He longed to subject his uncle to a close and niggling interrogation, as they had used to do on long July afternoons at Tir-Na-Nog, to draw fabulous facts and anecdotes out of Sir Thomas Mordden, pioneering aeronaut, penetrator of the trackless bush of the sky, deliverer, as the *Illustrated London News* had once phrased it, "of the key to making Britain the queen not merely of the land and sea but of all the vast empyrean girdle of the earth." But gazing up at the wondrous contraption in the sky in which, most wondrous of all, he was now evidently to take ship, Frank maintained a silence as absolute as that of the *Tir-Na-Nog* herself. Their uncle invited them to marvel; Frank refused. He wanted, if momentarily, then with all his heart, to see their uncle punished. Frank knew that this was unjust of him, that his uncle could not be held responsible for things that had transpired and decisions taken while he was sequestered with his assistants in the famous Mordden Laboratories. Frank knew that in holding his tongue he was only punishing himself.

—Is that the one you flew in to Africa? Jeff said.

—No, I fear the *Livingston* was destroyed upon my arrival there, Uncle Thomas said. He smiled. Hacked to bits by the Mtabebe.

—Can we fly all the way to England in that? Without even stopping? How high will we go?

Frank applied a furtive knee to his brother's bottom, hard. Jeff crumpled and then turned his traitor's gaze to Frank. For an instant he looked angry, but the reproach in Frank's eyes banked his fire and he rubbed at his backside with a sheepish air.

—We ain't going anywhere, Frank said.

The basket scraped the tiled cornice, bounced against the galvanized tin of the roof, and settled. Uncle Thomas took hold of Jeff under the arms, and hoisted him over the side of the basket. Frank stood, fighting against the longing to fly. He would not abandon his mother. He would ensure that there remained at least one man in New Orleans, in the Louisiana Territory, in all the vast Crown Colony of Columbia, to mourn the death of Cuyahoga Drake.

—We shall make London easily, my boy, Uncle Thomas said, as if to Jeff. We could make it as far as Istanbul. The Mordden Mark III is a dreadfully efficient engine.

He looked at Frank, fixedly, his womanly mouth curled at one corner, as if reading the hunger to know that underlay his nephew's stoical demeanor. He scattered specifications like crumbs to a reticent deer.

—There are a pair of them, he said. Four-cylinder compound engines. Vertical coil, parallel-flow flash boiler. Firebox above the boiler coils. Honeycomb condenser with vacuum pumps and complete automatic firing. One hundred and twenty horsepower apiece.

There was a burst of drum clatter from the yard of the old Presbytère, a workman's ragged laugh. Jeff reached for Frank's hand, but Frank would not take it. He did not want his brother distracting him with useless tappings at his palm.

—You won't be abandoning her, Franklin, their uncle said. There is no way that you could.

Frank caught his breath. The laughter of the workmen in the jail-yard became general and merry. Down in the workshops of St. Ignatius he could hear the chiming hammers of a coffin being nailed.

—My poor boy, Sir Thomas said. You must accept that I am all the family you have left.

—That's a lie!

—Come aboard the *Tir-Na-Nog,* Frank. And one day we shall sail her straight to the moon. To Venus or Mars.

Frank craned his head to try to catch a glimpse of the pale Presbytère; he envisioned his father waving from one of its stone window ledges, putting on a jaunty smile, saluting him. But all he could see was the high bell tower of St. Ignatius, part of a spike-topped stone wall, a rounded stucco corner of the prison, a dusty brown patch of tamped earth in the prison yard, a pair of colored workmen leaning on the handles of two pickaxes.

—Stay if you will, then, his uncle said curtly. He gave a signal, and with a jerk the basket rose off the pitted zinc of the roof.

—Frank!

Jeff threw himself against the side of the basket and tried to climb out, wild, in tears for the first time since the night of Custer's surrender. He managed to get one leg over the side. Sir Thomas caught him by the collar and hauled him back in.

—Frank!

Frank remembered the promise he had made to his father; surely to have broken it would be the greater abandonment.

The basket dragged, skipping, along the roof, and snagged against the cornice. In the instant before it would have freed itself and started upward, Frank crossed the roof and threw himself headlong into it, landing in a heap at his uncle's feet. He stood up, steadying himself. He wiped his hands against the knees of his patched cadet's uniform, and looked levelly at his uncle.

—You're a liar, he said. There is no atmosphere in interplanetary space.

Then he could see the bare tree, the scaffold, the platform with its neat square trapdoor. Sir Thomas gathered Jeff into his arms, and covered his face, hooding his eyes with his great hands.

—We're all liars, Franklin, he said. We lie, and then we wait and hope for time and hard work and the will of God to make us honest men.

They bumped up through the hatch of the *Tir-Na-Nog,* into the dark innards of her gondola. Strong arms hauled them from the basket. They were set on their feet in a bright room, trimmed in brass, paneled all around with windows and the glass faces of gauges.

Sir Thomas Mordden took a yachtsman's cap and settled it onto his head.

—London, sah? said the helmsman.

The captain of the *Tir-Na-Nog* nodded, his smile wistful and aimed curiously at his nephews. He might have been picturing them alighting, one day, on the dark red sand of Mars.

—At present, he said. Yes, London will do for now.

LOOK FOR THE SECOND INSTALLMENT OF THE MARTIAN AGENT, "THE INDISTINGUISHABLE OPERATIONS OF EMPIRE AND FATE," IN *MCSWEENEY'S SECOND MAMMOTH TREASURY OF THRILLING TALES*.

SHERMAN ALEXIE lives in Seattle with his wife and two sons. He writes poetry, short stories, novels, and movies.

AIMEE BENDER lives in L.A. and is the author of two books: *The Girl in the Flammable Skirt* and *An Invisible Sign of My Own.* She read her first Agatha Christie mystery in eighth grade and practically dropped the book on the floor when the twist got revealed, it was so amazing.

MICHAEL CHABON is the author of two story collections and four novels, most recently *Summerland,* a novel for children.

DAN CHAON's story collection *Among the Missing* was a finalist for the National Book Award. He lives in Cleveland, with his wife and children, and waits.

MICHAEL CRICHTON was born in Chicago in 1942. He lives in Los Angeles.

DAVE EGGERS has written two books and four songs.

HARLAN ELLISON has written and edited more than seventy-five books and approximately 1,700 short stories, scripts, essays, and reviews. He is the winner of eight World Science Fiction Hugo Awards, three Nebula Awards, and five Bram Stoker Awards.

CAROL EMSHWILLER has two books just out from Small Bear Press: *The Mount* and *Report to the Men's Club and Other Stories.* She lives in New York and California, and teaches an adult education fiction class at NYU.

KAREN JOY FOWLER is the author of three novels and two short story collections. Her most recent novel, *Sister Noon,* was a finalist for the Pen/Faulkner award. She lives in Davis, California.

NEIL GAIMAN has written approximately twenty graphic novels, three nonfiction books, four adult prose-only books, and two children's books. He has won the Hugo Award, the Bram Stoker Award, the Locus Award, the World Fantasy Award, the Mythopoeic Award, and several Eisners.

GLEN DAVID GOLD is the author of the novel *Carter Beats the Devil.* A strapping man with a square jaw and windswept teeth, he stands in splendid proportion: five foot nine inches in height, some of it churning with muscle.

NICK HORNBY is the author of five books. The most recent, *Songbook,* was published by McSweeney's in December.

LAURIE R. KING has lived a life of crime since the publication of *A Grave Talent* in 1993, having come from a life of academic theology. Her thirteenth novel, *Keeping Watch,* is out in March.

STEPHEN KING's most recent book is *From a Buick 8.* He divides his time between Maine and Florida.

ELMORE LEONARD is the author of many books, including *Rum Punch* and *Cuba Libre.* He lives outside Detroit.

KELLY LINK's short stories have won the World Fantasy Award, the Tiptree, and a Nebula. Her collection, *Stranger Things Happen* (Small Beer Press), was a *Salon* Book of the Year and a *Village Voice* Favorite. She currently lives in Brooklyn with her husband, Gavin J. Grant, coedits the zine *Lady Churchill's Rosebud Wristlet,* and is working on *Trampoline,* a forthcoming anthology of fantastic fiction. She once won a trip around the world.

RICK MOODY is the author, most recently, of *Demonology* and *The Black Veil.*

MICHAEL MOORCOCK is the author of the science fiction series *Elric,* as well as other cycles of books. He has won the British Fantasy Award multiple times, as well as the World Fantasy Award for his novel *Gloriana.*

CHRIS OFFUTT is the author of *No Heroes, Kentucky Straight, Out of the Woods, The Same River Twice,* and *The Good Brother.* He lives in Iowa City, Iowa.

JIM SHEPARD is the author of six novels, including, most recently, *Nosferatu* and the forthcoming *Project X,* and two collections of short stories, including the forthcoming *Love and Hydrogen.* He teaches at Williams College and in the Warren Wilson MFA program.

This Book Benefits 826 Valencia

Open since April of 2002, 826 Valencia helps Bay Area students, 8 to 18, with their writing skills, on a one-on-one basis. The idea when 826 opened was simple, and is still simple: It was our belief that students could benefit greatly from having experienced tutors give their full attention and expertise to their writing work. In an era when classes of thirty-two or more students are not unusual, overburdened teachers cannot possibly get all their students—particularly those with special needs—caught up with their writing skills. So the tutors at 826 Valencia step in to help teachers and students bridge the gap.

Because we have a paid staff of just one—our director Ninive Clements Calegari—we rely heavily on volunteers to make what we do possible. Thankfully, the Bay Area is home to a generous group of writing and editing professionals; at press time, we had a volunteer corps of 267 tutors. Our numbers enable us not only to host students at our Mission District location, but also to send tutors, in almost whatever numbers are requested, into public schools, to work with teachers on projects of their design, and for whatever duration needed.

There's a lot more to say, and already we're running out of room. Briefly: we also offer free workshops, at least one a day, covering everything from SAT prep to playwriting to digital filmmaking to broadcast journalism; we offer scholarships, three a year, $10,000 each, to matriculating seniors from public schools; we help young authors design, edit, print, bind, and self-publish their own books; and we just started something we're calling—and we do need to make the title a little catchier—the 826 Valencia Teacher of the Month Award, a $1500 award going every four weeks to an exceptional local teacher, nominated by their fellow educators and students. Lastly, our building is home to a store that sells supplies to working pirates. You really have to visit sometime.

This collection is a benefit project for 826 Valencia. Though *McSweeney's* takes care of most of the costs of running 826, we can always use more help, and *McSweeney's* issue 10, copublished with Vintage Books, is providing us a needed boost. For more information, please visit www.826Valencia.com, or come see us in San Francisco, on Valencia Street, between 19th and 20th Streets.   —*D.E. & N.C.*

THIS HAS BEEN ISSUE 10 OF MCSWEENEY'S.
THERE HAVE BEEN NINE BEFORE.
THERE ARE FORTY-SIX TO COME.

McSweeney's Quarterly Concern continues to publish on a roughly quarterly schedule, and each issue is markedly different from its predecessors in terms of design and editorial focus. Some are in boxes, others come with a CD, still others are bound with a giant rubber band, and perhaps someday an issue will be made of glass.

Past issues have included writers such as Doug Dorst, Courtney Eldridge, A.G. Pasquella, Sheila Heti, Ben Greenman, Sean Wilsey, David Foster Wallace, Zadie Smith, Michael Chabon, Lawrence Weschler, Denis Johnson, Jonathan Lethem, Chris Ware, William T. Vollmann, Lydia Davis, Arthur Bradford, J.T. LeRoy, A.M. Homes, Gabe Hudson, and Kevin Brockmeier. To subscribe, please visit www.mcsweeneys.net/subscribe.

WE ALSO PUBLISH BOOKS. SOME RECENT TITLES:

NICK HORNBY — SONGBOOK
A collection of essays about the songs Mr. Hornby loves, accompanied by a compact disc containing some of those very same songs. From the author of *High Fidelity*.

SHEILA HETI — THE MIDDLE STORIES
Wildly acclaimed in Canada, *The Middle Stories* is a striking collection of stories, fables, and short brutalities that are alternately heartwarming, cruel, and hilarious.

STEPHEN DIXON — I.
The long-awaited novel from the two-time National Book Award finalist, *I.* is a searingly powerful and deeply personal novel that explores the realities of a couple aging together and the limitations of memory.

MARCEL DZAMA — THE BERLIN YEARS
Marcel Dzama is a young Canadian artist who might very well change everything we know about art that involves alligators and men in bear costumes holding guns.

www.mcsweeneys.net